REBECCA TINNELLY

Don't Say A Word

D0168160

HODDER

First published in Great Britain in 2019 by Hodder & Stoughton
An Hachette UK company

I

Copyright © Rebecca Tinnelly 2019

The right of Rebecca Tinnelly to be identified as the Author
of the Work has been asserted by her in accordance with
the Copyright, Designs and Patents Act 1988.

A CIP catalogue record for this title is available from the British Library

Paperback ISBN 9781473664524
eBook ISBN 9781473664517

Typeset in Plantin Light by Palimpsest Book Production Limited,
Falkirk, Stirlingshire

Printed and bound in Great Britain by Clays Ltd, Elcograf S.p.A.

Hodder & Stoughton policy is to use papers that are natural, renewable
and recyclable products and made from wood grown in sustainable forests.
The logging and manufacturing processes are expected to conform to the
environmental regulations of the country of origin.

Hodder & Stoughton Ltd
Carmelite House
50 Victoria Embankment
London EC4Y 0DZ

www.hodder.co.uk

For my parents, all three of them.
Martin, Sarah and Hildy

Prologue

There are dozens of pages of paper. She has been writing for what seems hours and through the cottage window the sky is darkening. Once she started she couldn't stop and though it is getting late, she needs to finish.

It all needs to finish.

The page in front of her is the last she will write.

But after all she has written she finds she cannot find the necessary words.

Her confessions are fresh in her mind.

There is only one thing left to say.

To ask.

God forgive me for the things I have done.

Praise for *Never Go There*

'Twisty, DARK, fast-paced, shocking. EXCELLENT'
Will Dean, author of *Dark Pines*

'Mesmerising, shocking, I just couldn't look away. I loved it'
Sarah J. Naughton, author of *Tattletale*

'This book sucked me in and wouldn't let go, even after I finished it! Dark and suspenseful. Brilliant characters. Stunning revelations'
Patricia Gibney, bestselling author of the Detective Lottie Parker novels

'A beautifully written, riveting read. Perfectly crafted. Absorbing from start to finish'
Amanda Robson, bestselling author of *Obsession*

'Rebecca Tinnelly created a village so real, so secretive and scary, I know I never will go there! This was edge of the seat reading showing that powerlessness is sometimes the only weapon you have to fight back'
Liz Lawler, bestselling author of *Don't Wake Up*

'A thoroughly excellent debut. Dark and brutal in places with a shocker of an ending!'
Katerina Diamond, bestselling author of *The Angel*

'So tightly plotted [and] totally absorbing . . . the dark, claustrophobic atmosphere kept me reading late into the night'
Elisabeth Carpenter, bestselling author of *99 Red Balloons*

'Creepy, claustrophobic and extremely dark and twisted. This is a very clever debut'
Susi Holliday, author of *The Deaths of December*

Also by Rebecca Tinnelly

Never Go There

Chapter One

Selina

Friday Evening

Selina removed her wig, the stark white, polyester fibres slipping against her fingers as she replaced it into the monogrammed box, and the box into her locker. Were she to leave it out, uncovered, she would run the risk of it catching a stray horsehair from a rival's wig, which would leave her sneezing in court all next day. Fastidious, she did not run this risk. In it went, to the depths of her locker, with her barrister's gown and air-freshened shoes.

Her phone buzzed inside her handbag, thrumming against the leather. She could tell from the rhythm that it was Esther, the ringtone uniquely set for the old friend she found it so hard to talk to.

There was a second where she paused – the urge to hear her friend's voice filling her with such a loneliness that she almost reached into the bag and answered the call. Almost.

'Any plans?'

The plummy drawl startled her: she thought she was the last barrister left in the building. Turning, she saw Dick Chapel standing close by. Too close. His lilac shirt still tucked into his pressed, navy trousers, sterling-silver stiffeners keeping the collar sharp. Only the undone top button and the stray lock of black hair brushing his forehead indicated that he'd stopped working for the day.

She stepped back. 'None,' she said.

'Not going to celebrate? Raise a glass to a job well done, another criminal back out on the street?' He placed one arm on the wall of mahogany-fronted lockers beside her, leaning backwards in a way that should have been nonchalant, were it not for the leer in his eye.

'He was found not guilty, Chapel. Therefore, he is not a criminal.' She opened her mouth to launch into her usual spiel about the right to a legal defence, to be tried fairly, the necessity to ensure as few people are locked up in the over-crowded, criminal-making prisons as possible. She stilled her tongue, took a breath and reminded herself that she didn't have to defend herself to this man, one of the fiercest criminal barristers to share her chambers.

'What's it to you, anyway?' she said instead, turning her back and securing her locker. 'It's not as though you were working for the prosecution.'

'You're gaining on my record, Alverez. It's *unsettling.*'

'You're scared I'm going to win the most cases? Come off it, it's not a competition.'

'Of course it's a bloody competition. Everything's a competition.' He shrugged his shoulders back, a practised gesture that briefly pulled his shirtsleeve far enough up his wrist to show off his Rolex. She'd seen junior barristers, those still slaving away on a paltry wage, stare with hunger at that watch. Only, Selina hadn't been a junior for some time, and such badges of wealth didn't impress her. Besides, she knew that Dick didn't buy the watch himself; it was a present two Christmases ago from his mother.

'I'll take you out to celebrate,' he said, turning his body half away from her, as though he didn't care if she took him up on his offer or not.

A faint trace of whisky lingered on his breath, a sign he had been in with one of the judges toasting the end of the week. A common practice. Frowned upon in some courts, perhaps, but certainly not illegal, and if barristers know anything about anything, it's how to bend the law to suit a purpose.

A sad smile tugged on her lips, nostalgic for a time when Friday nights were spent eating good food and drinking the finest single malt she could get her hands on. And before that, when she was newly qualified, she would have phoned her boyfriend after a win and they would have celebrated together with deli cheese and sparkling wine.

'Early night for me,' she said instead, cloaking her down-filled coat around her shoulders and zipping it up to her chin. Droplets of rain misted the windows, the weather outside as miserable as a January night could possibly be.

'Tomorrow, then. I've got a case to prep this weekend, you could help me. We'd be all alone in the office.'

'Chapel,' she said, sounding out his name like a warning.

He purred hers in return. 'Selina.' He leaned towards her and stooped slightly, so their faces were close. 'Use my first name. Go on. I love to hear you say Dick.'

'God, you're revolting.' She stepped out of his line of reach, about as attracted to this man as she was intimidated by him. She saw him less as a threat and more as an irritating man-child.

'You can't *not* celebrate,' he said, his bottom lip pouting slightly. 'Nobody wins them all; you've got to appreciate victory when it comes your way. I'll buy you dinner at the Ivy. The one in Clifton's just as good as the London.'

'What part of *no* do you not understand?' Facing him full on, she stood as tall as her five-four frame would allow and stared straight into his large slate-grey eyes. She allowed her voice to resume the crisp-edged upper-class accent she usually reserved for the courtroom. She thought she'd been able to shrug it off for the weekend but it slipped back into her mouth like a favourite sweet, warming her tone with a smooth, honeyed confidence. 'Perhaps you could invite someone else if you're lonely. Your secretary, perhaps. One of the female appointing solicitors. I hear they're just as forward as the men. Right up your street. Or, if all else fails and you really do find yourself at a loss, may I suggest you take out your girlfriend?'

He paused, blinked the look of hurt from his eyes. 'Your luck's in,' he said, leaning closer. 'Broke up with the last one a few weeks ago.'

'"*The last one*"? I'm sure she had a name, Chapel, or are all women interchangeable to you?'

But if she had hoped to make him ashamed of himself she was to be disappointed. He smiled broadly and ran a hand through his dark hair.

'You're such a tease. I only offered because I knew you'd turn me down. All the fun of the chase with no real risk of attachment.'

With a roll of her eyes she picked up her bag and walked out of the robing room. In the corridor, her trainers squeaked on the polished wood. She missed the extra inches stilettos gave her, feeling tiny and insecure in the now mostly empty corridors of Bristol Crown Court. Hers had been the last case of the day, a ruling she'd known from the outset would go in her favour. Another man free.

'So, what will you do, then?' Chapel followed at her heel.

'Go home and watch crap TV? Drink a bottle of red alone and fall asleep on the sofa with your tongue hanging out? Call your mother?'

Selina gave an involuntary scoff; the idea of calling her mother was ridiculous. Staying in on a Friday night would receive even more criticism from her than it had from Chapel.

'It's none of your business.' She waved to the security guard as she passed the metal detectors, smiled when he waved in return. 'Night, Martin.'

Chapel quickened his pace so he was next to her. 'Oh, for fuck's sake, Selina, you're too good to be true! You even talk to the proles!'

'Go home, Chapel. You're wearing my patience thin.'

'Are you going to talk to him too?' Chapel stopped by the court entrance door laughing, arms folded across his chest, nodding towards the homeless person on the pavement outside, wrapped up in so many layers it was almost impossible to see the man beneath.

It was tempting to tell Chapel to fuck off and mind his own damn business. But she held her tongue. She was so used to him now, his rakish bad behaviour, his audacity in court, his obnoxious sense of entitlement. The best way to punish him was a complete unwillingness to engage, the same way she navigated her young niece's tantrums.

Outside, the bitter wind and driving rain made her pull her hood over her sleek, dark hair and slip her thumbs through the holes in the sleeves. As she neared the man huddled against the furthest pillar, she opened her wallet and removed one of the many Starbucks vouchers that were tucked behind the photo of her late father. She dropped it into the paper cup in his gloved hands.

Chapel gave a hoot of incredulous laughter from the crown court lobby.

'Cheers,' the man muttered through layers of scarf wrapped around his mouth and neck. 'God bless.'

Too late for that, Selina thought, and turned towards home. Her phone vibrated in her bag again. Esther.

Over the last three years, her friendship with Esther, her best friend since they were both eight years old, had deteriorated to such a point that Selina wasn't sure it would ever recover. It was all her doing. Visits to Taunton had been reduced to once a month, popping in to see her friend for a coffee, each visit a few minutes shorter than the last, all topics of why Selina was distant swatted away as soon as they arose.

Even now, with Esther's father dying slowly and painfully in his tiny Somerset hamlet, Selina found it impossible to offer the level of support she knew she should.

The buzzing went on and Selina didn't answer.

The pavements were quiet, considering it was early evening on a Friday. Even the roads were devoid of traffic. The university students hadn't returned from the Christmas break and the rest of Bristol was hiding indoors, either huddled into the nooks and crannies of the Victorian pubs or nursing their January-empty wallets at home.

A steady drizzle of rain was falling, invisible unless caught beneath a street lamp, yet saturating all the same.

Two more homeless men on Selina's route benefitted from a coffee-shop voucher. Each offered some gratitude or blessing and Selina shrank away from their thanks.

She followed the pavement, head down, and gradually Bristol became Kingsdown and Kingsdown became Clifton. She caught snippets of laughter and the smells of food from restaurants as she passed, and had to fight the urge to return the call and talk to her friend.

To say, *'I did something, Esther. Something I shouldn't have done.'*

But she could never say this.

'You're the only one I want to talk to about it, but I can't. I can't tell you a thing.

'It would tear you apart.

'It would land me in prison.'

Selina fiddled with the key in the sticky lock of her door, gaining entrance to the long corridor of the Georgian block on the outskirts of the Durdham Downs. Her flat was down a flight of stairs and the view of the Downs, the zoo, the Clifton rooftops and the suspension bridge was impossible to appreciate from its solitary barred window. The place was saved from the label 'bedsit' by a thin partition concealing the kitchen from view of the bed, and the aeroplane-style bathroom squeezed into what had once been, Selina presumed, a broom cupboard. The flat was intended to be somewhere to stay when court cases ran late and the thought of commuting back to her apartment in Taunton was too much, but over the last three years, she had slept in this prisonesque flat far more than anywhere else. There had been a fleeting idea to sell the Taunton pad and buy a more comfortable Bristol home, but the questions it would raise would be unwelcome. More than that, the comfort was wholly undeserved.

Selina's floor was littered with post: a letter from the bank, a reminder to renew her car tax, three statements from charities she donated to every month. Holding the post in one hand, she pulled out her phone with the other.

Seven missed calls.

All from Esther.

Something was wrong.

Friday night. Before her father's illness Esther would have been out all night, drinks in some hidden, exclusive bar, a date with her partner or a dinner party with friends. She was thirty-four and guiltlessly childless with a *joie de vivre* that bordered on hedonism. Friday night was a night to enjoy life, not sit and phone an old friend who refused to answer her calls.

Something is wrong.

Selina pressed the button to return the call, holding the phone tight to her ear.

Chapter Two
Selina
Friday Evening

The words took a moment to sink in. Esther's voice was clear, if a little weary, yet what she was saying made no sense.

'Hang on, I just can't . . . say that again?' Selina massaged the bridge of her nose and closed her eyes.

She had been sure that the problem was going to be Esther's father, that the stage four cancer he had been diagnosed with a month before Christmas had spread or the chemotherapy was causing anxiety.

'Mum's in hospital,' Esther said again, 'in Musgrove Park. They brought her in this morning, she—' Esther's voice caught, but Selina knew better than to interrupt. Esther had always been a stoic. Selina heard her sniff back any traces of tears and continue, composed. 'Madeleine found her this morning, by Dad's bedside at home. She'd injected herself with his morphine; there were a dozen or so vials of the stuff emptied out on the floor, the needle was still in her vein when Madeleine found her.'

'Who's Madeleine?' Selina felt guilty even asking the question. If she had been there more she would know this.

'She's the St Moira's nurse. She moved in a few weeks ago to help look after Dad.'

'Jesus, I thought they only stepped in for palliative care?'

'They do.'

Selina winced. She hadn't spoken to Esther for over a month. She had been telling herself her friend needed time and space to be with her family over Christmas, but really Selina had been hiding.

'He stopped the chemo when they discovered the cancer had spread, he just wanted to be at home, with us. Look,' Esther sniffed back again. Her voice when she continued was harder and straight to the point, concealing her grief with solid facts. 'That's not the issue right now, that's not why I called.'

'I know, I'm sorry, it's just a shock. Are you OK? Is there someone with you? Where are you?'

'Well, there's Madeleine; she wanted to stay with Mum, so she's arranged for another nurse to take over Dad's care for a day or two. I've gone back to mine whilst they're running tests. I needed to collect some things, I'll be sleeping in the hospital tonight.'

Esther's flat in Taunton was next door to Selina's, the apartment she had intended to use as her home. Selina felt a pang for that old life and the friendship she had sacrificed. *I'll come straight away if you need me,* Selina thought. *I'll hold my shit together, bite my tongue, and I'll be there.* But she didn't say this, the words were too tangled with fear. 'What's happening with Connie?' she asked instead. 'Have they given her anything to counteract the morphine? Do they know about her problems—'

'Her problems?' Esther coughed out, exasperated. 'Of course they bloody know! Of course. For Christ's sake, Sel, the first

damn thing I tell anyone is that Mum has special needs, that she doesn't speak, doesn't like to be touched, doesn't like to make eye contact. Have I told them about her *problems*? Honestly?' Esther paused and the phone line filled with the sound of her slow, deep breathing as she tried to regain her composure. Selina pictured Esther in her large, airy flat that looked out over the cricket ground, saw the granite kitchen counter they used to share brunch over, the espresso machine, the wine rack that had slowly been filled with better quality booze the older they got.

Selina had the urge to pull her in for a hug, rub her shoulders and tell her it was going to be OK, that she'd get through this. The same thing Esther had done for her when Selina's father had died.

'They gave her naloxone to counteract the morphine,' Esther said, 'and it's working so far. They think they've got it under control but they won't know for sure until the results of the blood test come back, which will be in another couple of hours, possibly the morning. More critical is that she's been suffering from minor pulmonary embolisms ever since the paramedics found her, small heart attacks which they think are being caused by a large clot somewhere in her circulatory system that was disrupted by the shock of the overdose and has started breaking down.' The details came through in a monotonous drawl, the simple act of passing on information from one source to the next without pausing to consider its meaning. It would be too much, Selina guessed, to contemplate the significance of the words. 'The debris from the larger clot is causing minor blockages in her pulmonary system. She's suffered two small attacks already. They're taking her for an MRI scan to see if they can locate it and then, depending on the size, they'll either operate or inject a dissolvent into the clot to break it down safely.'

'Shit, Esther, I'm so—'

'Don't. Just don't.'

Selina imagined Esther tensing her jaw, mustering her strength. She had something else to say. It occurred to Selina for the first time that Esther may not be calling her for support, that maybe her distance in the last few weeks was the final straw on the already strained spine of their friendship. What if Connie had left a note? One that pointed towards Selina?

'She asked for you,' Esther said.

'What? *Connie* asked for me?' Selina reached out a hand to lean against the wall, a swell of relief that Esther didn't know more mixing with dread that Connie had uttered her name. 'She *spoke*?'

'Yes. She came around, briefly, and asked for *you*.'

And there it was, the real reason for the anger hidden behind a three-letter word. Selina's barriers swiftly came up. Connie had asked for her. *Shit*.

'Did she say anything else?' The need to know was so urgent that the question spilt out in the same brisk manner she used to cross-examine a witness.

'She said, "I need Selina." Nothing else.'

Curtailing a sigh of relief, Selina imagined Connie waking from sedation; the fear in her face, the words sounding out in that strange, hoarse voice. 'OK. OK, I'm on my way. I'll be there as soon as I can.' She had to make sure Connie didn't say anything more, didn't write anything down.

'That's pointless: HDU is closed to visitors overnight unless you're immediate family. Come tomorrow.'

'OK, I'll be there first thing.'

'Selina?'

'Yes?'

'Aren't you wondering *why*?' Esther said, and Selina realised it hadn't been anger her friend was trying to conceal. It was hurt. 'Why my mother asked for you and not me?'

An answer that wasn't the truth seemed unfathomable, but it was already too late to speak. The line had gone dead.

Chapter Three

Connie

Friday Evening

Where am I? I can't tell. My eyes are taped closed, a tube snakes across my upper lip and into my nose, my head is being held in place by straps and blocks and I can't move. My mind is whirring, thinking, speaking, but my body is dead to me, my muscles and bones stock-still.

Someone has done this to me.

I'm not safe.

The thought is even clearer than the deafening sounds of clunking machinery or the voices of strangers that surround me. Something about an MRI. Something about sedation. I make out the words 'blood clot'. It makes no sense; my head is too full of other thoughts to understand.

What's happened?

I remember a very small something, it falls like a grain of sugar in black tea.

It could have been five minutes ago, could have been five days, but I remember opening my eyes and seeing my daughter. Her eyes widened when mine opened, she leapt up and hovered her hand above mine, knowing better than to touch me straight away. My sweet girl.

I spoke. I asked for *her* and when I did, Esther's face clouded with hurt for just a second. But I saw it. I felt it, the look on her face making my ribcage ache. Poor Esther.

She will come, I know.

When did I call for her? Why can't I remember? The machines are so loud in my ears, other voices coming in and out of my hearing. I know I'm not awake, not really. I can hear and I can think, but nothing makes any sense.

Where am I?

The notion of home rises like bile, it's acid burning through all other thoughts. I've never been away on my own. I've never been away from my husband. Is he here? He can't be, I know I left him in his bed, dying, dying, dying so slowly I could not bear to watch for one minute longer. Where is he? Who is caring for him? Is he alone?

My mind begins to fight these thoughts, I can't focus. Memories pour through me instead, I am flooded with them. So real I can touch them, smell them, hear them.

And just like that I am not in a loud, grinding machine, there are no strangers talking around me, no tube snakes its way beneath my nose. I am not a middle-aged woman strapped to a bed.

I am inside my memories, reliving them in the same way I relived them years ago. Back then I wrote them all down and shut them away at the bottom of a rusted tin box. They were the only way I could bring myself to explain why I have lived the life I have, the reasons I am what I am.

For all the good that it did me.

June 1960

I was six years old, standing in Grandmother's parlour with Grandmother herself and three other women. It was 1960 but to look around the room you would think it was still 1940.

Grandmother was sitting in her regal wingback, the scuffs on the arms hidden by chair covers brought out for special occasions. Today was the monthly 'ladies' tea' that the four women ensconced in this tiny hamlet took it in turns to host. On the coffee table was an over-baked Madeira cake, eight thin portions ready sliced; the butt end left thick and uncut. No one had taken a piece, each choosing a garibaldi from the patterned plate instead. I wasn't offered either. I stood by Grandmother's chair as instructed, watching the plate with my mouth open and watering, silent.

The heavy-set labourer's wife with thick hair on her forearms, Maud from two doors down, dunked the tiny biscuit in her tea. The other women nibbled daintily. I could tell they wanted to scoff the lot and let crumbs fall all over them. That's what I wanted to do.

'She looks awfully like them,' said Bethany to Rose, the two women interchangeable in their high-necked, shapeless brown dresses, white aprons at their waists to hide the stains that wouldn't wash out, curled grey hair. 'Like both of your dear girls.'

One woman, I can't remember which, was a teacher who'd retired from the schoolroom on her wedding day. The other did nothing but breed; six children she complained of incessantly. Even the women's legs were the same; swollen and fat, mottled flesh showing through patched-up stockings. Mummy never wore patched-up stockings.

Bethany and Rose glanced at the mantelpiece in unison. A framed photograph sat there, above the fireplace. Two little girls in pinafores and plaits stared out of the picture. My mother and her identical twin. I've never been sure which was which.

Fat Maud swallowed and looked straight at me, one hand over her mouth. 'How hard it must be for you,' she said when the biscuit had disappeared down her throat. I thought that someone was finally talking to me – Maud had two adult daughters, Maria and Rosemary, so maybe she had the mothering instinct Grandmother lacked. But she said, 'She really is the spit of Caroline.' And her hand squeezed Grandmother's arm, not mine.

I couldn't see it, this likeness. My mother, Caroline, had been a beauty. Pale, blonde hair in a backcombed bob that smelt of hairspray and scent, the curls smoothed out with an iron, dark-blue eyes the colour of the late-afternoon sky rimmed with kohl, her eyelashes thick with block mascara. I was a child, wearing uncomfortable clothes I had been forced into, nothing like she would have worn. I do have pale hair, and my eyes are blue, but I'm not the same, not at all.

'She really is the spit,' Maud repeated, though she shook her head as if she didn't agree with what she had said.

The grown-ups all looked again at the photo and I grasped the opportunity. My hand reached towards the biscuits. Lightning fast, my grandmother slapped it away.

'Devil!' she snarled.

Thin gold rings decorated her fingers; one dusted my knuckle but I didn't make a sound. I never did.

She looked at me as though I was dirty. A dirty little girl in polite company, although they were only a labourer's wife, a

charwoman and a failed teacher. I never spoke a word, the cat
that was my parents' death still having a firm hold of my tongue.

'She saw it,' Grandmother said, her tongue stained dark
purple from last night's sherry. 'All of it.' There was disgust in
her voice. But I couldn't quite tell if it was I who was disgusting,
or what I had seen: the crash; my parents' car rolling down the
steep hill to our cottage; my mother and father like balls rattling
inside a tombola; the car hitting the oil tank; my parents turning
into ash and dust and bright flames.

Looking back, I remind myself that it was her daughter's death
she spoke about then. That, when she saw me, she must have
seen my mother or her twin sister, Charlotte, as a six-year-old
in my place. Because, as the fat woman said, I was their spit.

That's what Michael always said, too. That's what he liked
about me most, I think. It's what she hated about me, my
likeness to her daughter. Daught*ers*. Perhaps she thought I was
destined to have the same fate as my mother, who married
above her station and denied her modest roots as soon as she
moved away. Or even Charlotte, though no one ever talked
about her.

But then, in this particular memory, I was six and my mother
was dead, my father was dead, and my knuckles burned from
the hit of her ring; my cheeks too, from the disgust in her voice
and from the fact I had to live in that pitiful house that didn't
even have its own phone line, let alone a television set.

I ran out of the room, through the kitchen and into the garden,
overgrown because Michael was still too young to use the push-
mower. Just eleven years old. It would be three years before he
had a handle on it and showed his worth. Before he became
known as a man who could fix things.

I ran past the small shed that housed the outside toilet. The only toilet. I kicked the door and it swung on its hinges, a flake of paint peeling away as it slammed. *Ha*, I thought, *take* that.

I ran past the bunker that held the coal for the hot-water boiler. I spat at the coal, made it wet. *Double ha.*

The sun was low. I looked behind me, expecting to be followed, but no one came and I carried on.

Over the fence at the back of the straight, narrow garden. I landed in the ditch with soft mud right up to my ankles, the mud slipping into my socks and squelching grit and wetness beneath the arch of my foot. My shoes were ruined.

As I ran I thought of how much I hated Grandmother, and how much I suspected she hated me. Why else would she have said such cruel things? *'If you weren't such hard work your mother would have never wanted to leave you with a nanny and drive off.'* Michael used to tell me to ignore her. He said she was so sad about Mummy's death that she couldn't feel anything other than grief. I knew she meant it, though, for as well as the pain in her voice there was a conviction impossible to ignore, even for a mute six-year-old like me.

The ditch was a shallow one. I made it to the other side and there they loomed ahead of me, those dark, green-skinned grain silos in the farmer's field behind our garden. They were larger than anything I had ever seen, their scale making them appear as majestic as they were terrifying. They were twin structures – sixty or seventy feet high, a ladder scaling each. I stood beside the nearest one, craned my head and looked up. They were almost brand new, still shiny and smelling of plastic, so tall that they blotted the sun.

I was alone with them and I was not supposed to be.

I shouldn't have been there and I think, looking back, it's exactly why I headed that way. Because to do something I shouldn't, be it stealing biscuits or scaling silos, reminded Grandmother I was alive and needed looking after.

Looking to the sky, another thought occurred to me. Perhaps I'd be able to see right the way to my Gloucestershire home over fifty miles away and even catch sight of my glamorous mother on a cloud up in heaven.

I noticed mud on the prim white sleeve of my blouse, the blouse that smelt of camphor and was, I was certain, intended for my mother when she was my age. I bet she hated it too – the frills and the lace and the stiff starched edges – and I suddenly felt closer to her. I felt sure that were I to climb up I would see her after all and she could tell me herself how she had hated this blouse, this house, Grandmother, and that it was all right because one day I would escape, just as she had done. I'd be free.

No one watched from the house.

I was six. My shoes were white plimsoles soaked brown with mud, my skirt lined with cheap, itchy tulle. I wasn't dressed for running through the garden, let alone scaling a sixty-foot silo, but I had made up my mind. I was going up.

'You're not to go there, understand?' had been Grandmother's warning, when she had brought us out here on our first day, our eyes still red, raw from crying.

Let her worry, I thought.

I could see the kitchen window and wondered if anyone could see me from inside. I was standing in stark white skirts in front of the dark, backlit silo. I must have been visible.

But no one came.

I shivered a little.

My teeth chattered.

My foot touched the first rung of the ladder and my hands

gripped the holds either side. My head was full of that determination six-year-olds are so good at showing when they've made up their minds to be naughty, spurred on by that need for attention.

Adrenaline took over then and I stopped thinking of Grandmother. My heart thumped fiercely in my little-girl chest and I pushed myself up and up higher, my scrawny thighs burning with effort and my arms aching before I was even a quarter of the way up.

'You'll fall to your death,' Grandmother had said in her vicious way, knowing full well that I knew what death looked like.

I didn't want to see it any more, death. Those flames that had stolen my parents and my voice, made me too scared to utter a sound. I wanted to see *them*, Mummy and Daddy, playing harps in a cloud full of angels with their own set of velvet-soft wings. I wanted my mummy to hug me and to smell the apricot scent of her skin. I wanted Daddy to hold me high in the air and swing me around with the speed of an aeroplane.

I climbed and climbed, not looking down, looking only up, waiting for my head to reach the clouds, to reach them.

Up and up.

And then there came a sound from below.

'Connie!'

Someone had seen me, after all.

Chapter Four

Connie

1960

And there he was below me, calling and waving his arms; my cousin Michael.

His hair was dark, almost black, and his eyes were deep brown, his skin olive. So different from his mother that Daddy had presumed the boy looked just like his father. That man had lured Aunt Charlotte away to a world of drugs, sex and no rules, where children were a hassle best left to be raised by someone else. For Michael, that someone else was my mother. When I was three he appeared on our doorstep, sewn into his underwear, with two paper bags of dirty clothes and a note scrawled out to my mother from her twin. They raised him alongside me, an older brother. A best friend.

Grandmother had never met Aunt Charlotte's tempter, so Michael reminded the old woman of no one. A beautiful clean slate for her to start again on.

Looking down at him, I realised how very high up I was. I felt small. I felt, very suddenly, like a child too young to be alone.

'Come down!' he called, his head spinning back over his shoulder, eyes wide with fear in case Grandmother should come out and see us. 'Connie, come down!'

I felt dizzy, the world below me pulsing in and out of focus. I looked back up. I still had a long way to go but looking upward was easier, not nearly as scary as contemplating the bare distance below.

My hands moved upwards, I stepped my left foot onto the next ladder rung.

There came a gasp from below, carried up in the wind, and a scuffle and brush at the base of the silo. I looked down again, but he'd gone, he wasn't at the bottom any more. He was standing at the foot of the second silo; climbing up the ladder of that beast, lithe as a monkey, his eyes never leaving my face.

I realised then that I was crying.

I couldn't move.

I wanted to get down, but I was scared to.

I wanted to get to the top, that vain childish hope that Mummy lived in the heavens egging me on.

I wanted to fly across the gap that bridged our silos and have Michael carry me inside because back then, when I was six, I still wanted to be carried.

'Connie,' he said, even though he knew I wouldn't answer, 'please climb down.'

I shook my head, felt my eyes widen in terror and another tear slid down my cheek.

'I know you're scared,' he said, and I knew that he was too, even though he was using the voice of a grown-up, trying to be strong in the way Daddy always was. He couldn't hide the fact that he was eleven, just a boy in short trousers and knee-high socks.

The wind ruffled his hair, carrying with it the smell of the land; moulding straw and a rotten vegetable sweetness.

I pictured the biscuits on the table inside. I pictured them all waiting until I was gone before Grandmother called Michael downstairs and offered him the flowered plate full of garibaldis. I pictured him tasting the treacly tang of the baked raisins, chewing the biscuits that I was not allowed. Knowing Michael, he would have saved me one, hiding it in his pocket, but it never took away the pain. He tried his best, but he never fully understood what it was like.

I stepped upwards again and heard him call, 'No!' and I took my hand off the ladder to wipe my eyes dry.

I wanted my mother.

The desire to be naughty had dissolved, so too the idea that I would see angels. Part of me knew Mummy wouldn't be there at the top, in the same way that part of me knew that when my next tooth fell out the fairy wouldn't leave me a halfpenny. They had died in the same car crash.

Michael called out again. I heard his feet on the ladder of his silo.

I faltered.

My hand was slimy, my feet still wet with mud.

My fingers slipped on the steel hold and my legs buckled, my right knee jarring on the rung.

I looked down and wished I hadn't. I remembered Grandmother, she would be so cross if she saw me, and my determination withered.

I was hanging by my hands now, my knees touching the rung, but my legs were so short that my feet didn't reach the next one.

I tried to hold on but I was shaking and my hand slipped a little further.

Even then I didn't make a sound.

I looked down again, but my skirt, all that tulle, blocked my view.

He called out my name, I heard his feet clatter on steel as he fought his way down to the ground.

And suddenly there he was, below me. He had scaled my ladder and the relief of having him close was so overwhelming I almost let go completely.

'It's OK,' he said, as his hands guided my feet. 'You're going to be OK.'

The same words he had used the night my parents died. Our nanny had screamed and cried, but I couldn't. Michael held me on his lap, his arms around me, whispering, 'You're going to be all right.' He looked after me.

On the ladder, his body shielded mine, his feet on the rung below my feet, his hands on the holds above mine. I could feel his heart beating against my back.

'I'm going to take a step down, and then I want you to take a step down afterwards, OK?' His voice trembled and I nodded, knowing he could feel me acquiesce through the movement of my head.

He stepped down and I felt the shift of his body against mine, unbalancing me. I gripped the holds, certain I was going to fall.

'I'm right here,' he said, 'you're OK.'

I took a step down and he was right, I was OK, he had looked after me. Again. We continued this dance for nineteen rungs; I counted them all in my head and thought of Grandmother as I did it.

'Nearly there,' he said, and I glanced down to the ground. It was close. He'd kept me safe.

'Michael!' The name was screamed through the field. Grandmother ran towards us, trying to catch up with her shout.

I felt him catch his breath, our bodies still pressed together.

Jumping and landing like a cat, he reached up and helped me down.

Too old for climbing fences, Grandmother waited at the perimeter of the garden.

The late morning sun gleamed from her nails and her rings as she wrung her hands together.

She stared at Michael with a fearful gaze.

My name wasn't mentioned.

When we reached her she grabbed him.

Held his head to her chest, kissing his crown.

'Don't ever do that.' There was a softness in her voice that she never used with me. 'You could kill yourself on that thing.'

No 'Naughty boy!' for my cousin, no slap on his thighs with a ringed hand. Back through the garden they went, Grandmother dragging Michael, still with his head held to her chest so they moved with an awkward, staggering gait.

I followed.

'No point sulking, now.' Fat Maud was standing by the kitchen door, her hands on her hips and a smile on her fat, stupid face and I hated her. I hated Grandmother. I hated everyone.

I wanted my mummy.

Maud put a hand on my small shoulder, ushered me towards the open door.

'Your grandmother's ever so cross with you, you know, leading your cousin astray like that.' She talked with a gentle laugh in her voice, as if it was all ever so quaint that I was to live with an old woman who resented me. Who thought me stupid because I was too traumatised to speak. 'I'll get you a glass of water, you can drink it in the kitchen with me.'

I didn't want water. I wanted Madeira cake and garibaldis and milk.

I wanted her to take her fat, stupid hand off my shoulder.

'She's just simple.' The voice came from the living room – Bethany repeating the diagnosis of Dr Rowe, the man who had prodded my neck and lifted my chin and asked me why I refused to talk. 'She doesn't mean any harm,' the woman went on, 'she's just not quite right in the head.'

'Here you are, dear heart.' Maud put a glass on the dining table. It was filled with milk, after all.

I sat and drank and thought of what was being said in the living room, of the labels that were being piled onto me, of the unfairness of the situation.

And beneath it all was a bruise I poked at with the words 'dear heart', Daddy's pet name for me.

Grandmother was cruel and neglectful, the doctor unforgiving, the women in brown dresses too eager to judge, but it was Maud I hated most of all then; for her kindness in bringing me milk, in her jolly voice saying, 'dear heart'.

She walked towards me, a plate in her hand, which she planted beside my milk glass. Thickly cut new white bread, thick butter, thick jam. 'Much better than stale cake,' she whispered, and winked, her fat hand patting my shoulder.

Her kindness was too much and I hated her for it.

Chapter Five

Connie

Friday evening

I remembered that day often, copied it word for word in the letters I wrote. I replayed it as I watched my husband waste away, decaying from cancer at home. It is the same home I lived in with Grandmother. He is lying in the same room where she hosted her tea mornings, the sofa removed to make room for the borrowed hospital bed.

It was Maud I usually thought of. Her hand on my shoulder, the gelatinous jam glistening on the doorstop-thick bread, the smell of cow dung on her clothes. But now, alone in this grinding, monstrous MRI machine, my body and head strapped in place, it is my cousin I miss most of all.

He arrived on our doorstep at eight years old, malnourished and uncared for. He would watch my mother with wonder as she wrote at the kitchen table, lifestyle articles that were published in women's magazines. She was the identical twin to his own, but dressed in chic clothes, face made up, no needle marks on her arms. It didn't matter that she rarely had a spare moment for the children. She loved us.

Michael was eleven when it happened. He would nod to people with a trembling chin when they asked if he was all right and he welcomed the embraces of anyone who offered a slither of comfort in the wake of our parents' death. Because they were *our* parents by then: he had started calling them Mummy and Daddy within a year of living with us. When they were gone, despite not knowing if his real mother was alive or dead, we were *both* orphans.

I wouldn't leave his side in the early days, I wouldn't speak and he never asked me to. And, when it got too much and I did cry, he would stroke my hair and tell me it was all going to be all right. We had each other, he'd never leave me, I was safe with him.

With a patience Grandmother lacked, he taught me to read. He taught me numbers with the same dedication, he and Maud, together in front of the fire counting matchsticks. How I miss him, my caring cousin.

Everyone thought it was Michael who brought the measly fragments of my voice back. They thought it was his patience and kindness and love.

But that's not true.

He didn't teach me to speak.

Grandmother had it right all along.

It was the devil inside me that did it.

When I think back to that day on the silo, I think how much easier it would have been for everyone if Michael had just let me fall.

Chapter Six

Selina

Friday Evening

She couldn't stay in Bristol, not after that conversation. Selina grabbed her car keys, shoved a phone charger into her bag and double-locked the front door behind her. She would head back to Taunton, stay in her apartment overlooking the cricket ground, and visit Connie first thing. She had a half-baked conviction that, were she closer to Connie, she'd feel better.

Her car, a decade-old sky-blue Audi, dented in every panel, greeted her with a flash of the headlights as she pressed the key-fob's unlock button.

'I need Selina.'

The words repeated in her head as she headed towards the suspension bridge. The pastures of the Downs were grey with night and so quiet that you would never guess that a city hummed mere footsteps away. But the scenery was no distraction and Selina couldn't shake the memories of other times Connie had asked for her help.

'I need you.'

'You have to come.'

The first was over five years ago and then again two years after that. She had regretted it every day since. Not being able to tell anyone what she'd done had cost her her friendship with Esther, her relationship with her boyfriend, even forcing her to distance herself from her mother and sisters.

The sky was overcast but the lights from the city and the bridge made up for the lack of moonlight, reflecting off the black snake of the river below like stars.

Before hitting the motorway Selina pulled into a service station, her bladder reminding her she hadn't used the loo since court. In the high, wide mirrors her olive skin looked pale, her eyes puffy, her once glossy hair dull. Her forehead showed a faint spray of pimples, stress-spots her mother called them. It occurred to Selina to WhatsApp her mother saying she'd be in town this weekend, but another glance at her reflection changed her mind. She would be sure to comment.

And, if she had poured herself a glass of gin and spent the afternoon staring at photos of Selina's dead father, she might add, 'I was married by your age. I had two daughters already, was pregnant with my third.' Her eyes would well up and she would turn her back on her youngest daughter, advising Selina to get her eggs frozen before it was too late.

Selina zipped her phone away in her bag.

In the service station she ordered a flat white and restocked her purse with gift cards, adding a bag of smoked almonds to her order. She watched a woman on the sofa stroke the hair of her pyjamaed daughter. The child, small and blonde and no more than six years old, yawned widely and scrunched up her eyes. When she opened them again, she looked at Selina and poked out her tongue like a lizard.

'Lisbeth, that's *rude*,' the mother hissed, looking up apologetically from her seat.

Selina smiled a reassurance, thought of her oldest sister's struggles with her tempestuous daughter. She knew it was heartless to think ill of a young child but she regarded her niece as unbearably difficult.

Selina stuck her own tongue all the way out, stretching its tip so it touched her nose.

The child gaped. Looked first at her mother, and then back at Selina before breaking into a gap-toothed grin.

'Have a good evening,' Selina said as she collected her coffee, laughing as she passed them. It was so easy, she thought, pretending to strangers that she was a light-hearted, upstanding woman. A woman with nothing to hide.

Selina had found it impossible to pretend to Esther. Or to Austin, her now-ex-boyfriend, who had been dropped from her life with a callousness she was unaware she was capable of. All it would have taken was one more morning waking up in sheets made hot by his warmth, and she would have told him everything.

A Friday night in early January and the motorway was almost clear. Had it been August, the M5 southbound would've been a throng of caravans and holidaymakers with bikes strapped to their roof racks.

She didn't think about Connie as she drove along the M5, nor Esther. Selina had another person lingering in her thoughts: a man called Peter Flemming. He was a security guard for a bank next door to the court. Selina had noticed him regularly over the last two years, lurking at the doors of the lobby with eyes so shadowed by his overhanging brow that it was hard to determine their colour.

She had just secured his not-guilty verdict. He had been accused of rape.

She contemplated the outcome. She wasn't thinking about the evidence or the witnesses or the judge, not even what she knew and what she merely suspected. Instead, she brought to the forefront a thought she had never allowed herself to address during the trial. A question she had ignored during the preparation of arguments, during the interviews and testimonials, and whilst she'd made her closing speech.

How do I feel about this?

He was a free man now, this suspected rapist. Her job had been done. What she felt could finally be addressed because it was irrelevant. Her bias couldn't change a thing once the trial was over.

Did I do the right thing, defending him?

She doubted he would get his job back. His marriage was over, as a result of the trial. His life was in tatters, his finances too, after having to shell out for Selina's private fee.

Do I think him guilty or not guilty?

The question slipped from her mind as she left the motorway and followed the signs for Taunton.

Had she arrived a different way, she would have passed through the village where she went to school with Esther and Austin and the terraced-cottage pub where she had bumped into Austin years on. She had been twenty-seven, their eyes meeting over half pints of cider as they watched the test match cricket from different ends of the bar. She knew she wouldn't have been able to handle those memories today.

The only drawback with this route was that she had to pass that hotel. Its billboard was brightly lit, the green, white and gold garish against the late-night sky. It was the place she had stayed at one night with Connie, three years ago, after she had received the second of the two phone calls.

'*Need your help.*'

Selina's life had been a shipwreck ever since. She averted her eyes as she drove past, keeping her gaze firmly on the lorry in front. But bile still burned in her throat as she thought of how she'd behaved, the memory far more nauseous than any cheap, chain hotel.

While she had left Bristol with silent streets, most people huddled safely inside a pub, by the time she reached Taunton the town centre was showing signs of the first drinkers heading home. The final patrons of the evening were leaving their tables and the restaurants shutting their kitchens.

Esther had assured her that the cuisine in Taunton had improved vastly in the last few years. Esther still relished food. She had told Selina more than once that her trial for any new date was to test their squeamishness with new dishes. The more open-minded they were, the more likely it would be that Esther would agree to see them again. It had been over two years, Selina realised, since she had last eaten in a decent restaurant. Esther still dined out a few times a month, or at least had done before her father had fallen ill. Selina lived off Pret salads and chunks of cheese bought from Chandos Deli.

Whereas the tiny hideout in Bristol had been paid for with her own hard work, Selina's Taunton home had been bought by her father, a man who had earned a fortune through his Peruvian mines. A show of pride towards the only one of his four daughters who was pursuing a career. It had included a season ticket for the cricket club, a match to his own, and a promise from them both to attend every T-20 game they could together. He had died six months after Selina had moved in. For years afterwards she couldn't bear living there and rented it out to tenants. They had made it to three games by then.

The property was a pale-stone warehouse converted into six apartments. Esther's flat was next door, bought with glee by Esther as soon as it had come on the market. Would Selina have gone there if Esther hadn't confirmed that she was staying at the hospital overnight? No. She wouldn't have run the risk of her friend popping in, a bottle of Malbec in one hand and a bar of dark chocolate in the other. She could imagine the wry smile on Esther's face, the way her eyes would light up as she said, 'For old time's sake.'

As she lifted her hand to the door, she gave a glance over her shoulder, as though checking to make sure Esther hadn't silently, unexpectedly, come out of her flat at the other end of the corridor. All was clear. It wasn't only the fear of Esther's sudden arrival that was making her nervous. It was what was hiding on the other side of her own door.

Inside, the flat was sparkling thanks to the company she paid to clean it every other week, but it still had that faint musty odour of an uninhabited space. Her post was stacked neatly on the mantelpiece by the door, a few stray envelopes on the mat, the usual junk mail and an occasional charity letter. She thought of Esther's father's live-in nurse Madeleine and vowed to add St Moira's Hospice to the long list of charities she already donated to via monthly standing order. Her accountant, she thought in a moment of rare sarcasm, would be *thrilled*.

She moved towards the stairs, which led to the two bedrooms. Each step felt heavier, the quiver in her hands constant.

The flat reminded her of happier times, but these memories weren't the reason her hand shook as she opened her bedroom door.

She was greeted with a lungful of stale dust and trapped air. Her bedroom was strictly off limits to the cleaning company and the floor hadn't been swept in months. The bed sheets were clean and barely slept in, but hadn't been changed in almost a year. It had been so long since she had stayed in this flat.

The last time, she had fled in the middle of the night, unable to bear it any longer. She had woken covered in cold sweat, thrown her coat on over her pyjamas and grabbed the keys to her car.

'I need Selina.'

The words filled her head, Connie's slow, thick speech playing on and on. She couldn't turn back, not now. She had to see Connie.

Her eyes drifted down to the floor. Beneath her bed was all shadow, but still she could just make it out, that thing beneath her bed she had promised to hide. The thing that still filled her with gut-twisting horror and woke her in the night like Poe's *Tell-Tale Heart*.

How much easier it had been to ignore when it beat out the rhythm *this-is-what-you've-done, this-is-what-you've-done, this-is-what-you've-done*.

But the beat had changed, the game too. For the last three years it had called to her in a sing-song chorus of voices that first needled and now stabbed out their lyrics.

'*I need your help,*' Connie had said, five years ago, and Selina had helped her.

'*I need you,*' she'd said again, two years later, and Selina had come.

This-is-what-you've-become beat the rhythm of that thing beneath her bed. *This-is-what-you-are* and it was impossible, impossible, to ignore.

Chapter Seven

Selina

Saturday morning

Sleep had brought dreams of Esther. Waking had been a thump of reality stamping her chest like a boot. She knew where she was and what lay beneath her bed. She could barely look at the thing, let alone touch it, and it was possibly this disgust that had kept it there for so long.

There were safer places: a security safe, a bank vault, a deep hole at the end of her mother's garden. But moving it would mean confronting it, and while forcing herself to sleep in the same room as it was one thing, lifting it out of its hiding place was quite another. What if she were to drop it, spilling the contents? She breathed deeply, stopping the thought's downward spiral. She could have burned it, but there was an awareness, even at this late stage of the game, that she may need it one day. Slim, but still.

She checked the time on her phone: a little after 6 a.m. and still pitch-black outside.

Dressing in yesterday's clothes, she fled her bedroom in the hope that the guilt would be left behind, but of course it followed. She flicked on the kettle to make coffee, but even that small wait was unbearable. The desire to leave her apartment, get to the hospital and face Connie, was too strong.

King's Hall School in 1992. It had been Selina who had made the first move and spoken to Esther, offering her a *'Hello, how do you do?'* as she had been taught, but it was Esther's response that had sealed the deal.

Esther had been a stocky child with curly blonde hair and blue-grey eyes, freckles on the bridge of her nose and across the tops of her pale arms. *'You sound just like one of the Famous Five,'* she'd said, her own accent still the broad Somerset drawl that made the other girls poke fun. She'd trained herself out of it by the end of that first term.

Selina had been struck with pure joy. *'That's the nicest thing anyone's ever said to me! My sisters, all three of them, rib me chronic but I don't care a fig because I can read better than any of them and the oldest one is eighteen, so there.'*

She had looped her right thumb into the gap between her shirt buttons and tapped her stomach with the flat of her hand, the way she always imagined George's father to do in the novels. If this girl liked Enid Blyton, Selina had thought at the time, then maybe there was finally someone she could take on adventures, teach to climb trees, eat boiled eggs with by the half dozen.

Selina had shared with Esther her collection of Blyton books; Esther had taught Selina to make bracelets from strips of willow and how to make whistles from hazel. Esther started staying with Selina for parts of the summer holidays, Selina once or twice going with her back to Kilstock where they shared her bed in the small room. They were inseparable.

It was still dark when she reached Musgrove Park Hospital; a low, brick labyrinth. Plots of grass and small ornamental gardens separated the different car parks, tree-lined walkways desperately trying to ward off the aura of death with natural growth, only it wasn't yet spring and so nothing grew.

Selina's father had died here, eight years ago. It was another place she tried to avoid.

It had been one of the first questions she'd asked Austin whilst they sipped cider and watched the cricket in that small Taunton pub, when he'd revealed he was a doctor.

'Please tell me you don't work at Musgrove?' she'd said. She had visions of meeting him for lunch at the hospital, of not being able to concentrate due to thoughts of how she'd let her father down in his final moments.

'Minehead,' he'd said, with that half-drawn smile of his. 'Department of metabolic biology.' And she'd been so relieved that she'd audibly sighed, smiled, said *thank god*. He'd looked at her then with quiet patience. Hadn't pushed her to explain, though later she would anyway. He had simply waited, and it was that patience, that calm assurance that they had all the time in the world for revelations, that had done it for her.

'For Christ's sake,' she said to herself, pulling her red parka tightly across her body, 'don't think about him now or you will fall apart.'

A middle-aged couple nearby, in his-n-hers brown Barbour coats and wellington boots, looked at her with suspicion as they wandered off towards A&E and she felt foolish for having spoken out loud.

She thought of how it had been Madeleine, the palliative care nurse, who had found Connie mid-overdose. Maybe it would just be a few more days, a few more weeks, and then it would be over and she wouldn't have to hold on any more.

Guilt slapped her in the face in the shape of the wind, a cold icy blast hitting her as she rounded the bend to the main reception building. How could she think such a thing, really?

At the receptionist's desk Selina filled an air ambulance collection tin with loose change while she asked whether she would be allowed in so early. She hadn't thought about visiting hours when she'd left the flat.

'I'll call ahead, let them know that you're here,' the receptionist said, a round-faced older woman with a steel-grey bob. 'Visiting for non-family doesn't start till eight, but they sometimes let people in sooner. Her daughter stayed overnight so I don't imagine it'll be a problem.' She pointed out where to go while waiting for her call to be answered.

Selina could smell fresh coffee nearby and wished she had made herself that cup at home after all. Following the signs for the High Dependency Unit she passed a scant handful of other people: nurses, orderlies, doctors, admin staff, but few other visitors at this time of day. The corridors stretched out, lined with seats no one was yet sitting in, the quiet stuttered with distant footsteps and the occasional bleep-bleep of unseen hospital machinery. It didn't smell as she remembered and she was glad. There was no hospital-food aroma of over-boiled vegetables, nor the specific fetid odour of the ill.

The hospital felt separate from reality, the bright strip lights making you forget it was still black outside. Occasionally she passed a window that looked out to the parked cars and the trickle of people beginning to make their way towards the building, and thought how strange a place a hospital was. A little bubble of its own.

The sign for the HDU approached. Her nerves crept in as she stared at the double doors separating the corridor from the ward.

Shit.

This *was* reality and in a moment Esther, alerted by the receptionist's call, would walk through those doors and face her.

Would Esther still be feeling the hurt that had radiated from her voice last night? Would she resent Selina's presence? Would she be hostile? Or, worse, would she be brutally civil?

Selina sat on a plastic chair bolted to the wall, stood, sat again. She stared at the pictures lining the corridor, designed to take away from the sterility of the place and lighten the mood. Difficult to do when a framed child's drawing of a smoking patient wearing an evil grin hung, somewhat inappropriately, next to a sign pointing towards oncology. Esther must have followed that sign when she took her father for his chemo. They would have walked past that gruesome drawing. They may have paused, right here by these chairs, so her dad could catch his breath.

The image made her feel uneasy and she got to her feet, a noise from the double doors making her turn her head.

There she was.

Esther.

She looked exhausted, her hair cut even shorter than the last time Selina had seen her so it lay almost flat against her round scalp, not a curl to be seen. Her blue-grey eyes were ringed with shadows, wrinkles showing at the corners of her mouth. Her cheeks lacked the natural pink that used to colour them.

'You came,' Esther said with a warmth to her voice Selina hadn't expected.

'Of course, I came right away.'

'For my mum.' Esther smiled with her lips pressed together and her eyebrows raised as if every crease and furrow on her skin was screaming at Selina, *but not for me.*

'How are you?' Selina said, hanging back by the chairs, not ready yet to go through. Esther was thirty-four, the same age as Selina, yet the signs of stress on her face made her look closer to forty. In easier times Selina would have plainly told Esther she looked like shit, knowing she would snort laughter and that, by laughing, she would feel better for a moment.

'You look well.'

Esther raised an eyebrow. 'I look like shit,' she said, in good enough humour.

There were a few feet between them.

'You look like shit, too,' Esther said, but she smiled. 'Thank you, for driving down. I appreciate it.'

'Has she said anything more?'

Esther shook her head. 'She's been on a low-level sedation overnight, combined with some drugs to reduce anxiety, so she's pretty out of it. She's been sleeping mostly and there haven't been any further embolisms, so that's something.'

Selina stepped forward, breached the gap. 'Did the MRI scan locate the clot?'

Again, Esther shook her head. 'Inconclusive. They'll repeat it later this morning but they'll inject her with a dye that illuminates clotted blood, so hopefully that'll show it up. It's just a waiting game until then.'

'And the overdose?'

'Well, Madeleine found her just in time and the paramedics

administered the naloxone immediately, so they had it pretty much sorted from the outset. They've run a panel of her blood to assess exactly what she took and how much, that should come through pretty soon.'

'Well, that's . . .' Selina struggled for the right word. *Good* hardly seemed appropriate. The silence lingered in the air, both women looking at each other, not knowing what to say.

Selina remembered sitting at the wake after her father's funeral and all the people who had said, 'I'm so sorry,' and 'You're holding up well,' and 'At least he's at peace.' The comforting bullshit that had made her wince. And she remembered Esther at the very end of the day, holding her hand and saying, 'This is so shit. It's so painful and hard and just fucking shit.' They had held hands, removed their brave faces and cried. Esther hadn't pretended it was anything other than what it was.

'This is so fucked up,' Selina said now, stepping closer to Esther so she was in arm's reach.

'Madeleine told me she thought Mum was already dead,' Esther said, 'that she was too late to save her. The paramedics said that if they'd arrived just a minute later it may well have been.'

Selina saw her friend's chin buckle and reached out for her. 'What the hell was Connie thinking?'

'She wasn't, she's just . . .' Esther wiped at her eyes with the edge of her thumb, Selina taking her elbow and guiding her to a chair. If Connie wasn't yet awake then there was no rush to see her, she had time to console her friend.

'Dad's the one who looks after Mum, he does everything, he's always done everything. What's she going to do when he dies? What's she got left, without him? He sorts all the bills out, he buys the food, he talks to all the people that need talking to. Even the odd jobs she's had looking after old folk, so they can stay in their own homes, have been sorted by Dad. He's her whole world.'

'She's got you.'

Esther shook her head. 'But she doesn't want me, Sel.'

Selina moved to argue but Esther held up a hand for quiet. 'Her and Dad have always had this close-knit thing going on. I remember when I was a kid, asking how they had met, and all they ever told me was that Daddy rescued Mum from a life she was unhappy in. Even before they sent me away I rarely got a look-in.' Esther hadn't missed a beat when she'd said it, the sentence that used to make her cry as a child, and lash out with rage as a teen. Now it just tripped off her tongue. *They sent me away.*

'If they hadn't fought for your bursary and scholarship you'd have never got to King's, would possibly never have made it to Bristol Uni, wouldn't have a law degree, wouldn't have turned your back on the higher calling of criminal law to spend your days charging a fortune for writing wills and completing property contracts,' Selina said with a wry smile.

'You don't have to go to boarding school to become a solicitor, Selina.'

'You'd never have met me,' Selina said, nudging her friend with her elbow. How natural this felt; no distance between them, their ease with each other fitting back into place like a finally found jigsaw piece. Maybe their friendship could survive after all.

'I'd have been all right,' Esther said, and the magic vanished. She used to agree with Selina on that last point. As students they would drunkenly fall into each other's arms and thank the stars Esther's parents had sent her to King's. Because how could they have got through life without each other?

I'd have been all right. How true that was. She was doing just fine without Selina.

'Is Rosa coming?' Selina asked then, only a hint of jealousy in her voice. *This is what I wanted,* she thought. *Why am I getting tetchy?*

If we'd stayed close, I'd have told her everything and everything would be lost.

'We broke up.' Esther looked at her hands, hanging between her knees. She picked at the last remnants of silver nail polish that clung to the cuticles of her left hand. 'About a month ago, just after Dad refused any further treatment. She was too full on. I needed space to look after Dad, not pressure to organise dinner dates and sodding mini breaks.'

'I'm sorry.' Even though she was secretly glad. She'd met Esther's latest girlfriend only once, but the brash, buxom redhead with her affected London accent had done little to win her over.

'You hated her,' Esther said, nudging Selina back.

'I didn't hate her.'

'You didn't like her.'

'She watches *Love Island.*' They stared at each other, quite solemn, until Esther broke first and smiled.

'Fair point. I was hardly heartbroken to end it. Relieved, if I'm honest.'

A nurse and a white-haired man made slow progress towards them along the corridor, the man's drip stand held in the nurse's spare hand. The rubber soles of his slippers squeaked on the lino and the nurse smiled encouragingly at him.

'I thought Connie would have demanded to care for your dad herself. She's plenty of experience, hasn't she?' Selina said, watching the nurse and the elderly chap walk away.

'She wanted to, she was a complete pain if I'm honest, but we needed Madeleine. Mum couldn't watch him twenty-four hours and though my work has been fantastically supportive, I can't afford to jack my job in and help care for him full-time. I've still got a mortgage to pay.'

'He wouldn't have wanted you to, would he? He's always been so proud of you, raves about your career to anyone who'll listen.'

A flash of remembrance then, captured in black and white. The police station, three years ago. Connie silent and Selina playing the role of solicitor so that Esther would be left blithely ignorant.

'What's wrong?' Esther said.

One of the strip lights above their heads began to flicker.

'Nothing, I—' She stopped. The memory had shot through her like a migraine, she was instinctively rubbing her temples.

'You can tell me. You don't have to protect me just because my world has turned upside down. You can still talk to me, you know.'

The flickering light emitted a low hum, the brightness of the corridor changing ever so slightly with each subtle flash.

Selina closed her eyes. Had an urge to say out loud, *'What the hell have I done?'* and *'Why? Why did I do it? Why?'*

Esther opened her mouth and Selina braced herself for a narky comment about why Selina wouldn't talk to her, but Esther just said, 'It's OK. Whenever you're ready, I'm here, you know that.' That made it worse, the understanding. The support from a friend who surely had enough to deal with right now.

'It's just that damn light,' Selina said. 'It's giving me a headache.' But the conviction was lacking and Esther didn't push her for more.

The double doors opened, giving them a glimpse into the ward beyond. A nurse beckoned Esther and said, 'Could you come through? The blood results are back.'

Chapter Eight

Connie

Saturday Morning

The first thing I see when I open my eyes is the woman who once promised to help no matter what and I know it will all be OK. My head is still groggy from sleep and sedative, my body aches, my arm sore, but I spot her through the door of my room and I know it will be OK. She has tried her best, Selina. Even when she has got it wrong, terribly wrong. She has tried her best and more importantly she has protected Esther.

That's all I ever wanted, for my daughter to be protected from the truth.

Selina looks suddenly pale, looking towards my room but not at me.

She grabs Esther's arm, her expression one of panic, sheer panic. She pulls Esther back and then I can't see them because the doctor has walked in and my view is blocked.

I can't see my Esther.

I can't see Selina. I can't see what it is that upset her so much.

I want to call out for her but I can't find the words. I scan the room, see the expectant faces of strangers staring at me. The grey-haired doctor in the doorway is holding an iPad in his hands and smiling at me. Another doctor stands by my side, a short, plump woman with hair as short as my daughter's. Her face looks harassed, one foot tapping on the floor as she swoops her eyes over my chart.

I want Esther.

I want Selina.

My eyes are adjusting to the room.

I see Madeleine in the corner.

The female doctor lifts my arm, takes my pulse, her fingers touch me on the underside of my wrist.

She is touching me, her skin on my skin and no, no, I don't like that, no, I want her to stop.

I scream.

I scream and scream and scream until a nurse puts a needle into my dripline and everything goes black.

Chapter Nine

Connie

1964

I was ten.

Michael was fifteen and at school most of the time, but not that day. This all happened near the end of August, hot and unbearably dry, the dark-green silos in the farmer's field baked to a near-black in the sun and covered with a fine layer of wheat dust.

The cramped house was like a kiln, drying us out and bringing our true colours to light. There was no air, no breeze. It was so hot.

Our brand-new telephone, the number shared by two neighbours on a party line, was stuck to the door by the kitchen. We even had a television. Grandmother rarely let me watch it, claiming I was ungrateful because I never said thank you, please, beg pardon. She would send me to bed at six o'clock and let Michael sit beside her and watch *Coronation Street*. He used to tell me he hated it, but I knew he didn't. I heard him laughing more than once but I was glad. I had that time to myself. I would read in bed and escape to other worlds far, far away.

I remember Grandmother sitting in the wingback as usual, thin and running a fever. Her cough was clogged with phlegm, the phlegm dappled with red. Her legs were covered with a blanket of crochet squares made by Fat Maud, a shawl round her cardigan-covered shoulders. Still, she shivered.

'You don't heat the soup enough, you feed me cold soup,' she said to me and I looked down at the floor, I didn't answer.

Michael sat next to me on the other side of the two-seater settee. His hair had grown in the holidays, no time to have it cut with Grandmother ill. It will be me who cuts it eventually. My hands will slip, nick his ear lobe and send a droplet of blood onto the clean towel draped around his neck. But that came later. Now, in this memory, he was intact and beside me, his hand on the cushion between us. When I was little, six say, I would have moved my hand over his, but I was older now and had stopped that. I hadn't done it since I regained a bleat of a voice the previous year.

'You let the milk go sour on purpose,' she said to me, her black eyes beady and small. 'You put sour milk in my tea just to spite me!'

She coughed again, hawking into a handkerchief.

'Grandmother,' Michael said, his voice pacifying, 'let me get you a drink, something to ease your sore chest.'

Tears of gratitude sprang to her eyes when she looked at him. She raised her hands, pressed her palms together. 'Thank you, Michael,' she said.

I knew his tactic: he hoped that by being nice to her, as he always was, he would make her forget her anger and bitterness towards me. But it didn't work, it never worked, and as soon as he was in the kitchen she turned to me again, said, 'It should be you getting me a drink, lazy child! What's the use of you, if you can't even do that?'

'I'm ten.' I said this to answer her question, to remind myself as well as her that it was 1964 and not Dickensian England

(I had read some of him by then, the volumes they carried in the travelling library). I should really have been at school but I was still thought of as limited, as *not all there*, because no one could see inside my head. They judged me on what I could say and the blankness of my stare, not my brain. Traditional schooling, they decided, would have been wasted on me, so I was schooled at home instead. Or I was supposed to be.

'You should be able to get me a drink. Get me soup that's hot, milk that's not sour.' She leaned forward until her collar-bones jutted from her chest and her neck was craned to its limit. 'You're a spiteful little wench. You do it on purpose, I know you do it on purpose.'

'Sticks stones,' I said, my voice monotone, my gaze still down at my feet as I completed the rhyme in my head. Michael taught me that rhyme. 'Sticks stones,' I said again, and Grandmother threw her handkerchief at me, grunting at the effort it took.

The mucus-soiled cloth landed beside her foot, her arms too weak to throw effectively. She grunted in annoyance and tried to reach it but it was just too far.

I could've got it for her.

But I didn't.

'There's a devil inside you,' she said to me, keeping her voice low so that Michael didn't hear her. She looked to the door, ears pricked for the sound of his feet coming back, then said it again. 'There's a devil inside you. You turn people into terrible things.'

I stayed silent but my eyes stung with tears at the truth of it. I was a ten-year-old girl with a devil inside her, I made bad things happen to good people, I *turned* good people into terrible things. After all, look at Mummy and Daddy. They're dead and I had watched it all happen. I kept my face blank so

Grandmother couldn't see the effect her words had. I tried to keep my feelings locked like a kernel within a hard shell. It was this blankness, I learned much later in life, that added to my air of stupidity. My face, when blank, looks like a nondescript face. A void that's impossible to fill with anything: knowledge, love, anything at all. My face when I smiled, laughed, got cross, had started to look even more like mother's. Even I couldn't deny it by then.

I couldn't bear the look of my face when I smiled. It made Grandmother hate me even more.

Michael loved it, though. It's why he tickled me: so I laughed and looked more like my mother. Our mother.

That day, though, my blank face annoyed Grandmother, as it always did. My silence annoyed her, my speaking annoyed her, my smile annoyed her, my stare annoyed her.

'Here you are, Grandmother.' Michael walked around the corner and into the room, a fresh glass of warmed milk in his hand. He filled the room with his developing brawn: wide shoulders, strong stomach, arms that were lean and tough with muscle. Grandmother looked at him and formed a weak smile of pride. 'Thank you, my son.'

'Not your son,' I said, too loudly for the small room.

Oh, the look I got from her then.

'What did you—' but she started to cough, pointing to her handkerchief and Michael was so very good that he stooped to pick it up for her. She hacked and hacked and hacked up her lungs, the noise echoing around the limited space. Michael could never do any wrong in her eyes. Even if he had thrown the dirty rag at her face, rubbed the mucus into her cheeks and her mouth, she would have said, *oh thank you, thank you, thank you.*

I waited until the coughing stopped. 'Not your son,' I said again.

Were she not ill she would have beaten me for that. But I knew she was too sick to and I relished every second of her weakness.

Michael hopped from bare foot to bare foot, unaware of where he should look or what he should say, his fingers gripping the hem of his shorts. He wasn't worried about her getting angry at him, she never got angry with him. But he knew that, were *he* to say something unacceptable she would blame *me* for it. His manliness melted, replaced by childish uncertainty.

I salivated with the desire to say more, and I wondered where it came from, this self-destructive impulse to speak things that are better left unspoken. It had started when I regained my words, but my physical capability was far too limited to keep up with the spiteful language that filled my head. *'Your children are both dead to you,'* I wanted to say to her. *'One died in a car crash four years ago, the other good-as-dead living in a commune, spaced out on drugs and unable to look after her own son.'* I wanted to say to her, *'You're horrible to me but you don't have to be. You could have been understanding, you could have been kind. You could help me. You could help me. Please help me understand, I'm only ten.'*

I was only ten.

It would have been foolish, damning, to say those things, yet I felt my hot tongue lick my lips.

From the mantelpiece my mother and her twin looked down on us all, forever in their school uniforms. I still couldn't tell which was which, nor could Michael.

Then came a knock on the front door.

'Is it Maud?' Grandmother said, looking at Michael as though he could see through solid wood.

I got up off my seat, walked towards it, swallowing those words I wanted to yell out.

I knew it wasn't Maud, it was too early.

She came later in the afternoon, sat and read with me, taught me to sew a buttonhole properly. She put her arm around me and then removed it again as soon as she felt me stiffen. She asked me if I was all right. She brought me a biscuit wrapped in brown paper and a small bag of orange sherbet pips. I wanted to slap her face, claw her eyes, for such kindness. I wanted to lay my head on her breast and sob to her. I wanted to fall asleep in her arms whilst she sang to me. I wanted to beg her to look after me, always look after me. Of course, I did none of these things.

When I pulled open the door, Dr Rowe, the local GP, stood there dressed in short shirtsleeves dappled with sweat spots and grey linen trousers crumpled from the heat. His forehead was creased, beads of sweat gathered in each fold. His thin grey hair had dramatically receded since last I saw him. Small, round, wire-rimmed spectacles balanced on the bridge of his nose.

'Well, if it isn't little Connie!' He stooped down to my height, smiled at me, reached out to ruffle my hair.

I stepped back, out of his reach.

'Who is it?' Grandmother called. Her wingback chair was in the corner of the room, the open front door blocking her view of the doorstep.

She started coughing again.

The doctor walked into the room just as Michael said, 'Don't be cross, Grandmother. I called Dr Rowe because of your coughing, and your fever.'

'Well, Mrs Lithgow. Michael here tells me you've been quite unwell and yet won't come to see me, so I thought I had better come to see you. Now, tell me about all this coughing.'

Grandmother didn't have to: she began in earnest, retching up bloody globules, spitting them into her handkerchief, which the doctor took to examine. He listened to her chest, to her breathing, to her heart. He took her pulse, her temperature, her blood pressure. He removed the blanket from her legs, the cardigan from her shoulders. 'All these layers will increase your temperature further.' He wrote out a prescription. Penicillin, for the infection in her chest, Mogadon to help her sleep.

'To bed with you,' he said to her, then turned to Michael and added, 'She needs lots of fluids, lots of rest and make sure she takes the pills. At present, it's a bad chest infection but hasn't developed into pneumonia yet and we certainly don't want it to.'

Michael looked at me, making sure that I heard it all, because he knew it would be me looking after her. He was due to go back to school the following week. I nodded my head, showing him I knew what to do.

Grandmother, meek as a kitten in front of the doctor, let Michael lead her up the stairs. I heard her whisper to him, 'She does it on purpose, the sour milk, she does it on purpose.'

'And how are you, little Connie?' Dr Rowe hunkered down beside me, his hands on his knees, and looked into my expressionless face. 'Are you well?' His voice was a little too loud.

I nodded my head slowly, up and then down. My mouth was slightly open. Michael told me this made me look slow, that people in the village called me an idiot, but I'd never heard anyone say that. Most people didn't talk to me at all.

'And how is your speech these days?' he said, raising his eyebrows expectantly.

'Good,' I said. It was Dr Rowe who had taken my notepad away from me, told Grandmother not to give me any pencils to write with. *'Don't let her get dependant on writing things down or she'll never speak, you need to make it difficult for her to communicate in any other way. Give her no other options and the speech will come, wait and see.'*

Wait and see.

If I'd had a pencil then, I'd have stabbed him in the eyeball.

He rubbed the side of his mouth with his finger. 'You've got a bit of—' he said, and I wiped my own mouth with the back of my hand, found that drool had leaked onto my chin.

My body was an alien to me.

I couldn't feel it, I lived outside of it. Even as the doctor reached for my arm I saw myself from the outside. I didn't feel the drool leak from my mouth, just as I didn't feel the doctor's hands on my wrist, checking my own pulse. I saw it, instead of felt it, as though I was floating above my own body.

'Have you been keeping well? No illnesses?'

'Fine,' I said, and rubbed my chin to make sure no more drool had leaked out.

'And you're still reading, I believe? That's excellent, it'll improve your vocabulary no end.'

I could read far better than I could speak. I could connect my brain to words on a page but had trouble saying them aloud. I still do.

'And what of your nightmares? Do you still suffer from those terrors, or have they gone?' he said, and I froze.

My bones became stiff, I couldn't move. My mind hurtled back towards my body. I was suddenly inside myself again, I could see the things in my head that I didn't want to see, I could hear the noises I didn't want to hear.

The crunch and smash of a car rolling down the road.

The screams I imagined Mummy and Daddy made inside it.

My nanny gripping my arms, pulling me away from the door.

I closed my eyes, screwed them up tight, said 'No,' three or four times.

'Good, good,' said the doctor, misunderstanding me completely.

'No, no,' I said again, and opened my eyes, and I must have said it ever so loudly because I heard Michael's feet on the stairs.

'It's OK,' the doctor said, and pulled me towards him, tried to comfort me, his hands on the curve of my waist.

I felt his hands, his skin hot on my skin. The sensation rippled through me, unwelcome, disgusting, turned my stomach inside out as I tried to wrench myself free.

'No!' I shouted. 'No, no!' and I wanted to be out of my body again, I wanted to be free of those nightmarish daydreams.

I screamed, I convulsed, threw my body to the side, anything to free myself from that touch.

But the doctor was firm, believing he knew what was best, that I was a moron and should be treated as such (he was the one, after all, who had labelled me).

I closed my eyes, but that was worse, as all I saw behind my lids were images I'd been trying to block out. The car rolling, Mummy dead, hands holding me down, Daddy dead, fingers across my mouth trying to stop me from screaming, the flames burning the car. Everything I'd been trying to block out over the last four years came back to me in a flood.

Still, the doctor held onto me, his voice growing firmer as his patience expired.

'Now, now,' he said, trying to stay calm, trying to keep hold of my waist whilst I thrashed in his arms.

I heard Michael's voice, 'Let go of her!', his feet carrying him downstairs like a race horse.

'What's she done?' Grandmother squawked from her bed, her voice hoarse from coughing. 'What's that idiot child done now?' I could hear her desire to grab hold of the brush, or the broom, to lash me until her fingers tingled.

'She just started shouting,' the doctor said, defensive. 'I was just talking to her and she started shouting.'

'She doesn't like to be touched!' Michael yelled at him, his boyish face red with anger. 'She doesn't like anybody touching her!'

But he was touching me as he said this and I saw the doctor look down at his hands, resting on my shoulders.

I was back outside of myself again, Michael's hands had worked their black magic. I was watching myself from above. I could see my own blank, stupid face, my mouth ever so slightly open. I could see the doctor looking on in alarm, nodding to himself, confident again in his assessment that I was an idiot, a moron, destined for nothing more than basic tasks: floor cleaning, arse wiping, soup stirring.

'At least you can calm her down,' Dr Rowe said, wiping the sweat from his forehead. Michael smiled, proud of himself, squeezed my small shoulders between his hands.

Grandmother coughed again upstairs.

She called, feebly, for a drink and I walked towards the kitchen, walked away without saying goodbye to the doctor. I had learned by then that no one expected manners from me.

Michael saw the doctor to the door and I went to get Grandmother a drink of milk to help her sore throat. I didn't go to the small fridge that hummed in the corner, but to the cupboard under the sink. There, sweating in the heat, was the bottle of milk I kept just for her.

I poured an inch into a glass, topped it up with fresh milk from the fridge, stirred the lumps away with a spoon. I smiled inside my head as I watched her nose wrinkle in disgust as she drank it.

Chapter Ten

Selina

Saturday morning

It started as a twitching in the vein above her temple, then her nose began to smart and her mouth became very, very dry. The muscles in Selina's legs spasmed with an urgent need to run. Her heart began to thud so heavily it was painful.

The doctor, standing in the doorway of Connie's room, was Austin Gill. Of course it bloody was. She would recognise him anywhere, even from a scant side profile. Even from the back of his neck, or an inch of his wrist or the scent of his cologne, musk and bergamot, hanging in the air behind him.

A partition wall separated the main ward from a small waiting area and Selina shuffled behind it so at least her face couldn't be seen.

Esther followed Selina's gaze and looked confused.

'I thought *you* broke up with *him*? You said he was holding you back from pushing yourself at work,' Esther said. 'It was, what, three *years* ago?'

'I did.' Selina tried to smile, willing herself to put on the same front she had used for the little girl in the service station café. 'I just didn't expect to see him here. He was a locum in Minehead last time I saw him.'

And even the word *him* was painful, catching in her throat.

She remembered the look in his eyes the day she left him. How those mahogany pools had betrayed a desperate sorrow.

'If a case comes up I've got to take it, unencumbered, I can't be distracted by a relationship at this point in my career,' she'd said, forcing herself to look him right in the eye without flinching. *'I can't focus on winning if I'm feeling guilty about cancelling our dinner plans, and I can't turn any cases down. I need every one I can get to help build my reputation.'* She could tell he had seen through her lies, but he didn't call her out on them.

'Don't do this,' he'd said instead, cupping her face in his hands, trying to draw her towards him.

She had held his hands in hers, removed them from her cheeks and pushed them away. Stepping back, she had hardened.

'I've packed the things you'd left at mine, I've arranged for them to be delivered to your place tomorrow.' She'd felt goose-bumps rise on her skin as his expression turned from one of heartache to disbelief, felt her own internal world crumble invisibly as she repeated the script she'd rehearsed the night before. *'If there's anything I've missed, you can email me to let me know.'*

'Email you? For Christ's sake, Selina.' He'd pulled his fingers through his hair, disrupting the slicked back strands and revealing the curls he tried so hard to hide. She loved his curls, loved his hands, his eyes. She'd loved him.

'I know you, Selina, I know there's more to this. Tell me, just tell me what it is, what's happened, please.' His plea had strengthened her resolve. If she stayed with him she would tell him. She wouldn't do that.

'Minehead Hospital is nurse-led now,' Esther said. 'The

A&E closed after the NHS cuts. All of the specialist services transferred to Musgrove, he must have transferred with them.'

Selina had closed down her social media accounts after the split, telling herself as well as anyone who asked that it isn't sensible to have an online presence when you spend your days defending people who are accused of heinous acts. Really, it was so she couldn't keep tabs on him. She didn't want to wake up one day with the notification that Austin Gill had updated his relationship status.

Esther smiled with pity at Selina and it was the pity that did it. She drew her shoulders back and said, 'I'm fine. Honestly, it was just the shock. I wasn't expecting to see him. I'll be fine.'

'I know it's going to be awkward, it always is bumping into an ex, but stay strong. You're successful, independent . . .' Esther went on, somehow able to put aside her own grief and despair to help her friend. *How does she do that?* Selina thought. *Why can't I do that?*

'He's probably forgotten all about it,' Esther said. 'He'll be composed. Professional. Just like you.'

Selina opened her eyes, looked at her friend, willed herself to show some of the backbone that she'd displayed to Chapel in the robing room yesterday, but her vision was blurred with tears. No matter how hard she swallowed them back they wouldn't clear.

Esther held her by the shoulders, looked soberly into her eyes. 'You've known him since school,' she said, and Selina prepared herself for some cliché about time healing, or a flowery mantra about leaving one's past to the wind, as favoured by her yoga-teaching middle sister.

But no, not Esther.

'He used to sniff his own farts,' she said, deadpan, and Selina cracked a smile, couldn't help it. 'Do you remember? At school, he used to sniff them and waft them around the room until everyone had sniffed them. Don't cry for a man who wafts his farts, Selina. Just don't.'

Selina laughed, but the tears came anyway and she reached out and pulled Esther towards her, felt her soft, short hair brush her cheek, felt the swell of her chest press against her own.

'I'm sorry,' Selina said, speaking into Esther's shoulder. 'I should have come sooner. I've been shit, really shit, and I'm sorry.'

'You're here now,' Esther said, hugging her so hard Selina felt her spine bend. 'So pull your bloody socks up and let's get moving.' The phrase, stolen from their old PE mistress at school, was the final push Selina needed.

She straightened up, inhaled sharply, and readied herself to go into the room.

And then, just like that, the screaming began.

Esther jolted and ran the few steps to the doorway of her mother's room, Selina following.

A nurse gently urged them back, his arm across the entrance. 'Just give us a minute,' he said. 'She's all right, just anxious, we're giving her a top-up of sedative.'

Just as quickly as it had begun, the screaming stopped.

'I should have been *in there*,' Esther said, full of guilt. The unsaid phrase, *instead of out here with you*, hung between them. 'If I had been with her she would have been calmer, she would have been all right.'

Selina touched Esther's arm, tried to rub it gently in comfort but Esther shrugged her off. 'I should have stayed with her.'

'It probably wouldn't have made any difference,' the nurse said, and Selina wondered how much of that was true, whether he had his own professional mask he slipped on in times such as these where he had to reassure distressed relatives. 'It's very common for patients to display a range of emotions and reactions in these cases, particularly when they are coming in and out of consciousness as your mother is. It could even have made her more anxious, seeing you here, rather than less. You never know what the response will be, so don't beat yourself up.'

'What's happening now?' Selina said to the nurse, wanting to say something, horribly aware that she was the reason Esther hadn't been in the room with her mother. Aware, too, of Austin in the periphery of her vision. He hadn't turned yet, was updating the iPad in his hands with readings another doctor was calling out to him. She didn't even know if he was aware of her presence, mentally kicked herself for caring at all.

There was someone else with Connie. A tall woman with broad shoulders and poorly coloured hair that should have been blonde but looked yellow. It wasn't helped by her jumper, also yellow, which clashed against both her hair and the navy and green pinstripe trousers she was wearing. They were pyjama trousers, Selina realised.

'I was with her,' the woman said in a strong German accent, and Selina realised that this must be the charity's nurse, Madeleine. 'She woke up and started screaming instantly, she didn't seem to register anything at all, as though waking from a nightmare. I think it would have made no difference if you'd been there.'

Where Selina and the male nurse had failed in their

reassurances, Madeleine succeeded. Esther nodded solemnly and stepped back so all three women were standing outside Connie's room. Madeleine signalled to the waiting area behind the partition, where six chairs faced each other in two rows of three. 'We'll wait here for the doctor,' she said as she sat down. 'They will be out in a moment.'

Esther introduced the women and they sat together in silence. Madeleine looked as exhausted as Esther, if not more so, but possessed a resigned calmness that Esther did not. Selina supposed that the nurse was well used to waiting, palliative care requiring patience above all else.

An awkward tension settled. Esther kept her eyes firmly on the door to her mother's room, her knees nervously bobbing up and down.

Selina felt she lived two separate lives. In Bristol, she was the confident barrister, forthright in her desire to speak up for the wrongfully accused. Here, in her home town, she felt constantly on the back foot, her feelings more difficult to conceal, terrified that at any moment she would be found out and exposed.

Madeleine looked straight ahead, at a row of posters extolling the virtues of good hygiene. She didn't make small talk. Around her neck hung a thin gold chain, a delicate crucifix hanging at her clavicle. Her hands rested on her knees, so stiff as to look unnatural. Selina wondered if she were fighting the urge to bite her nails or pick at her cuticles. Madeleine looked up and caught Selina's eye and, though Selina offered a smile, Madeleine didn't return it. She looked quickly at Esther and then back at the wall, her hand briefly patting her crucifix before coming back to rest on her knee.

'They will re-administer the sedative,' the nurse said calmly,

still looking at the wall but directing her voice towards Esther.
'Provided the machines are free, they will most likely take
advantage of her sedate state to carry out another MRI scan,
this time with the dye injected to highlight the clot. From my
experience, that's what I imagine they will do.'

Esther breathed out a long, heavy sigh and nodded, looked
at Madeleine and said, 'Yes, yes, you're right. Thank you.'

'Once they find the clot they can deal with it, either removing
it surgically or dissolving it in situ. She will probably have to
take a blood thinner to prevent a new clot forming but should
be fine. *I* think she will be fine,' Madeleine said, but Selina
noticed that her jaw was tight, her hands still stiff in her lap
and she wondered if this were a kind lie.

Esther nodded again. 'Have you called St Moira's this
morning?' She added to Selina, 'Madeleine's arranged for
another nurse to look after Dad, just whilst we're here, though
I'll go home later this afternoon and check on him.'

'There's no need to rush,' Madeleine said. 'He is being well
looked after and your mother needs you, don't you think?'

'I can't leave him. It's not his fault Mum did this.' A quickly
suppressed flash of anger crossed Esther's face. Anger for the
mother who tried to kill herself when Esther's father was
already dying. The façade was beginning to crack and Selina
appreciated fully how much effort it must have taken her
friend to appear calm.

'Do you want to go for a cup of coffee? Take a break for
a few minutes?' Selina asked.

Esther bristled and replied in a tight voice, 'I can't. Look
what happened last time I left her, for Christ's sake.'

'The nurse said that wasn't your fault,' Selina said. 'You
need a break, you need to look after yourself as well as Connie.'

'What part of *no* do you not understand?' Esther didn't look at her. Her eyes were fixed on her mother's door, stress rippling out of her.

Selina stood and moved into the seat beside Esther. She didn't say anything, just put her arm around her friend's shoulder. This time, Esther didn't push her away.

When Dr Austin Gill walked out of Connie's room, Selina smiled with the self-assurance of a successful woman happy with her life. She would keep it together, for Esther. And when the halogen strip light glinted off the platinum band on Austin's ring finger, she kept her smile frozen in place.

Were it not for Esther holding her hand and squeezing with her little finger, so that no one looking on could see how hard she was holding her, the smile may have faltered.

'Long time no see,' he said as he approached, his voice the same calm, public-school drawl. He held the iPad to his chest, folding his arms across it. He included Esther in the statement, as though their relationship had never happened and he was instead talking about their old school days.

'Well, it's certainly reassuring to have a familiar face looking after Mum,' Esther said, bringing Connie to the forefront of their minds. Selina squeezed her hand back with her own little finger in thanks, before letting it go.

'And Madeleine, it's good to see you again.'

Esther looked from Austin to the nurse. 'I used to work in Minehead A&E, before I retrained with St Moira's,' Madeleine explained, with a warmth in her voice that had been lacking before. Selina remembered the gold cross around her neck and wondered if it was Esther's frequent blaspheming that made Madeleine's voice cooler with her. Or, worse, that it was because Esther was gay.

She felt her colour rise at the prospect of it, the same way it had at school when anyone dared make fun of Esther's bursary. When anyone dared make fun of Esther, full stop.

'How's Mum doing?' Esther asked as Austin sat down.

'Well, she's stable and sedated.' He looked down at his iPad, pressing the screen to bring up Connie's information.

'I don't understand, how come you're working in the High Dependency Unit? Did you retrain, become a cardiologist or something?' Selina looked back at Connie's room, saw the doctor with the short hair talking to the nurse by the door.

'No, still a chemical pathologist. I ran the tests on Connie's blood panel. That's why I came down to the ward, I need to talk to you about them. You too, actually, Madeleine.'

Esther leaned forward, elbows on her knees. 'What have you found?'

Madeleine gave Austin her full attention.

'We took samples from Connie as soon as she arrived. Although the paramedics gave her naloxone immediately and it proved very effective in combating any opiates in her system, we needed to be sure there was nothing else she may have taken that needed treating. The only problem is, the results don't fit with the overdose. Now,' he looked back at his screen and then at Madeleine, narrowing his eyes in concentration as he spoke, 'you said you found her with the needle in her arm, vials of morphine on the floor around her?'

'Yes, that's right. The paramedics brought the syringe to the hospital.'

'Along with a couple of the vials that hadn't been emptied. I'm glad they did, as I ran tests on both of those to make sure. There wasn't any morphine in Connie's system. None.'

Esther shook her head. 'But that's a good thing, right? That shows the naloxone did its job and neutralised the morphine?'

'No, the naloxone would have stopped the morphine having an effect on Connie's system, but the morphine would still be there until it had been metabolised. The naloxone showed up, but the morphine didn't. I ran the same tests on the last few drops of liquid in the syringe and on the contents of the medicinal vials the paramedics brought in. They contained sterile water.'

'No.' Madeleine's hands flew to her cross. 'That's impossible.'

'I'm afraid not. That's why it's important you need to know this as well, as I understand the morphine came from your patient's stock?'

'Yes, that's right. Or at least, I believe so. He has stage four terminal cancer; he's on a strong dose of morphine, to help with the pain.'

Austin closed his eyes for a moment, Madeleine's words clearly confirming what he had feared to be true. 'The vials were intact, they didn't show any signs of tampering as far as the glass casing shows, but the labels could well have been switched.'

'You mean I've been giving him water?'

'I'm afraid so. The vials could have been mislabelled at the lab before being sent out to you; it's a very rare mistake, of course, but it has happened in the past. I've sent the serial numbers from the vials I was given to the lab already, so they can recall any stock from the same batch.'

'You're telling me that his pain relief has been nothing but sterile water?' Madeleine stood up, the colour draining from her face, the yellow of her jumper reflecting so she looked jaundiced. 'No, that's not possible, it can't be possible.' She hugged the gold cross tightly in her fist.

Esther was silent. She had turned completely grey, looking twenty years older than she was, the news sapping her last remaining strength. 'He's been in so much pain,' she said finally, looking up at Selina. 'So much fucking pain. I never understood why it was so bad: no matter how much Mum or Madeleine gave him, it never let up. He bit through his tongue, for Christ's sake, because of the pain. He bit through his own tongue.' She looked horrified, her cheeks sunken and eyes dark with shadow.

'I can't . . .' Madeleine said, swaying gently from side to side as she tried to fathom the information. Her cheeks had reddened, her accent becoming stronger as her upset deepened. 'All this time I was controlling his pain relief, it was my job, my *duty* to treat him . . . and it was sterile water? Sterile water? How could this happen? I don't understand how this could possibly . . .' She turned on her heel and ran out of the ward.

'I'll go after her,' Selina said, looking at Esther first to make sure she didn't need her to stay.

'Please do,' she said, her voice quiet and childlike. The information that her father, the one man she loved more than anything, had been in needless pain for weeks was settling in. 'She'll be terribly upset, she takes it very seriously and I think . . . I think I need some time to register this. I don't understand it. Austin, why would this happen? How could someone do this?'

Selina walked away, leaving Esther safe in the company of Austin. He would look after her.

As she walked through the double doors, letting them swing

closed behind her, the last sentence of Esther's played on in her head, settling down with all the other information she had taken in in the last twelve hours.

My God, she thought, had so little time really passed?

How could someone do this?

The sickening realisation that the morphine had been tampered with, that human error, however inadvertent, had caused her friend further heartache, brought another question to the forefront of her mind. A small voice that had been niggling at the back of her head ever since she'd heard of Connie's attempted suicide now became a shout, loud and clear.

Why would Connie try to kill herself *now*?

She knew Connie well enough to know that she would never leave Esther like that.

She would pick up the phone and dial Selina's number.

So why didn't she ask for help *before* she did anything rash, rather than waiting until she had woken in a strange hospital room?

Chapter Eleven

Connie

Saturday Morning

As the sedative takes effect and my mind sinks into the abyss of memory I hear a male voice.

'No morphine in her bloodstream.'

They know.

But do they know what really happened?

Will they try and link it to me? Will they dig up the records of the other old people I've looked after, nursed in an auxiliary manner to the point of their long-awaited deaths? I doubt they would find anything, even if they did. There is no law in England to say you must be medically trained to care for someone at home. Anyone can do it, if that's what the patient wants.

No rigorous training need be taken.

No oath to do no harm.

Why would a local family pay for an expensive private nurse when the village simpleton can wash and dress and pop pills from a blister packet?

The hospital sent the woman from the hospice to us, I would never have asked for anyone to come. Why would I request a nurse to provide round-the-clock care when I can do so much of it myself? When I can have hours and hours a day, to look after my husband in the very best manner?

The very first person I looked after was long, long ago.

It was Grandmother.

Dear Grandmother.

Chapter Twelve

Connie

1968

I remember standing in the living room of our house.

Michael was at work: a gardener for the school nearby. He was nineteen and strong-limbed, solid.

I was fourteen, my hair curly and blonde, though not as bright as Mother's had been. My eyes were blue-grey, but not the same. My skin was pale and unadorned with freckles because I rarely went outside, especially in the sun. I couldn't bear it; the disparity between the warmth of my sun-toasted skin and the coldness in my bones.

It was late morning. The postman had delivered a few letters. Fat Maud had been and gone, sitting beside Grandmother for half an hour and reading passages aloud from Luke and Matthew. She hugged me tightly as she left, said I was an angel, that if it weren't for me Grandmother would be dying in hospital instead of at home where she belonged. She said it again, before closing the door. 'You're an angel, Connie.'

I thought you had to be dead to be an angel.

I closed the front door. Grandmother made a growling sound from deep in her throat. She was thirsty. I knew her odd sounds, her requirements, her wishes. I had been looking after her, for as long as she had been bed-ridden.

I kept the room dark. The front windows looked out onto the road and got little sun. The standard lamp worked perfectly well but I preferred the room in the gloom. When Michael asked me why I didn't turn the lights on I told him it was because the electric light hurt Grandmother's eyes.

Maybe she would have liked to have had the light on, to spend her last miserable weeks in light rather than shadow. I never asked her.

Grandmother was lying in the bed that Michael had helped me carry down to the living room when she was no longer able to cope with the stairs. She smelt of vegetables rotting in their own juices. She smelt of poo and wee and bad breath.

'Going upstairs,' I said to the old woman. 'Need clean sheets for your bed. Pot of water to wash you. Will brush your teeth. Will comb your hair.' In my head, I remembered how Grandmother used to comb my hair, how she would pull the thing from root to tip until I winced. I used to bite my lip so as not to cry. She slapped me if I cried.

I rarely spoke to her when Michael was at home. I still rarely spoke at all. No one seemed to hear to me when I did and Dr Rowe was still advising against notepaper and pencil. Michael never questioned it, raised to respect his elders and superiors rather than challenge them.

When I was alone, however, my voice would break out in the loudest form I could manage; a rough, painful whisper. I spoke more at this point in my life than at any other, the power I held over Grandmother releasing my tongue a fraction. I talked not because she would listen but because she couldn't answer back. She couldn't raise her hand to me, call me a dirty little liar, a fusspot, a naughty, naughty, naughty little devil whilst the smooth backside of the hairbrush spanked my thighs.

The uneven, wooden stairs creaked beneath my feet as I made my way up to her bedroom. I collected the clean sheets. I filled a basin with water, letting the taps run for a long time first to make sure the temperature was just right for her sponge bath.

Michael wouldn't be back until teatime, five o'clock. It had only just gone eleven. The day stretched before me like a cornfield. Michael was working. Normal children were at school, but I was neither normal nor at school. I was at home. I was a carer and an idiot and a simpleton.

The water gushed from the tap, hitting the side of the iron basin with a splash. I didn't need much. Just enough to clean her up, to remove most of the stink from her skin and the shit that had gathered in the creases of her buttocks and thighs.

I stayed with Grandmother whilst Michael went to school and later to work. She taught me to clean floors, he taught me to read. She taught me cooking, he taught me to write, only for Grandmother to steal away my pencil. She taught me to iron his school uniform while he taught me numbers. He went to school, made some friends. I stayed behind, in this house, in this village, in this life it seemed impossible to escape.

Sometimes I read aloud to Grandmother from books I had taken out from the travelling library that drove through the village once a month. *Lady Chatterley. The Monk. Madame Bovary.* I couldn't manage whole chapters, so instead I carefully chose specific sentences. Lots of smut and bodies. Michael never knew I did this. I hid the books very well. Only Grandmother knew and she was beyond talking. I read to her of filth.

'Clean you first, then change bed sheets,' I said as I reached the bottom step, the sheets folded beneath my arm, the basin of water held out in front of me.

I pulled off the top sheet that covered her body. She was

skeletally thin, her body ravaged by cancer. Her nightgown stuck to her thighs with the lightest smear of stale urine; dark yellow in colour. With the top sheet covering her and tucked in at the sides I couldn't smell it. Maud wouldn't have been able to either, not through the fug of cigarette smoke that followed that woman around, but with the sheet pulled back there was little I could do to stop myself gagging.

The smell really was awful.

She groaned again, that same rough growl. She was thirsty. I hadn't given her a drop to drink since the morning before.

'What a treat,' I said to her, as I soaked her body in the water from the basin. I felt her skin tighten as I washed, the ice-cold water bristling her naked, wrinkled skin with goosebumps. She looked like an underfed, plucked chicken. The smell from her body was grim. A stale, rancid stench that briefly strengthened every time I wiped the wet cloth over her groin. The faeces that leaked out of her were very light brown and stank to high heaven of putrefied flesh, as though her very innards had dissolved and were leaking.

Maybe they were.

The skin on my fingers had puckered from the water. My hands looked old and it was at times like this that I remembered I was only fourteen. That surely I should be doing other things, things that felt so far out of my reach they may as well have occurred on the moon.

'All clean,' I said as I dropped the shit-stained cloth in the water. I wrung it out, but some of the stringier pieces remained.

I wrung the cloth again, lifted it out of the fetid water and dabbed at her face, washed away the dried saliva from the edge of her mouth, wiped her nose of its crusted snot.

Grandmother groaned again and, up close, her breath was quite vile.

I picked up the hairbrush and dragged it through the remnants of Grandmother's long, scraggly grey hair.

'You're naughty.' I heard the words in Grandmother's voice, though I knew she wasn't really saying them. Those words had been screamed at me the year before, whilst she beat me around the thighs, bottom, back with the smooth plane of the brush.

'Disgusting child!'

I could hear them so clearly that I winced, the skin on my thighs tingling with the memory of the hit, my face burning with inexpressible fury.

'Disgraceful girl!'

Grandmother's breath began to rattle in her throat, dry and painful sounding. She opened her mouth and her lips cracked at the edges, her eyes rolling back in her head and then forward again. She couldn't focus. I wondered if she could see at all.

The GP had last stopped by a few days before. He had said she didn't have long left. 'You're doing a grand job,' he'd said to me, hovering his hand an inch from my arm, knowing from experience that I don't like to be touched. I had felt the warmth of Dr Rowe's meaty palm as it hung in the air.

'It can't be easy, but you're doing the right thing by her. I know that's what you want; to do right by your dear old grandmother.' His lips were thick and red, his cheeks peachy, skin clear. He never looked at Grandmother, just at me.

'Yes,' I had said, without conviction.

'Yes!' He had jumped on the word, music to his ears. 'It's what she wanted after all, and you've proved to be a fine helper, Constance, a fine helper. You're easing her through the final stages of her life; there's no one she would rather have helping her, than her own granddaughter, I'm sure of it.' He had sat back and smiled, proud of me and maybe himself, his fat stomach hanging over the band of his trousers.

He had rubbed his hands together, looked at his watch. 'You'll be needing another prescription,' he said, and delved into his leather bag for his pad and his pen. 'This for pain relief.' He held up the first sheet for me to take. 'And this to help clear her airways and dry out the mucus from her lungs.'

He left and I had added the sheets to the others in the bottom kitchen drawer. I had stopped giving her the pain medication a month before, when she finally stopped being able to talk. I noticed, very quickly, that without the pain medication she could do very little at all.

But the rattle from her breath was a horrible sound. It sounded as though sharp pebbles were being forced up and down a steel tube. Rattle up, rattle down. Rattle up, rattle down. I should have had the other prescription filled. I should have saved myself from that noise.

I brushed her hair, pulling through the knots as hard as I could.

'*Disgusting, filthy, disobedient child.*' Slap, smack, slap on the back of my body, her anger had been so acute that her aim was way off.

I pulled the brush again and strands of her hair yanked free from her scalp.

Her eyes rolled to the back of her head, to the front again.

She rattled on, rattled on.

I couldn't bear it.

'*Horrible, horrible, horrible girl!*' Smack, slap, smack.

'You did not like it when I started talking.' I said this to her and smiled. I remembered the vomit pooled on the floor. I remembered the fire that consumed the skin on my stomach, my sides, my back, underneath my arms. I remembered the day I found my voice.

'You liked me silent. Quiet. Good.' I put the brush down on the table. To look at her she was clean; fresh bed sheets, brushed hair, no dirt visible on her body or face. Her breathing was shallower, once I stopped brushing.

'Didn't like me crying. You never came in to make sure I was all right.' The words were hard to speak, feeling thick and foreign in my throat. I wasn't used to speaking such long sentences. 'No matter how old I was, whether I was six or ten or thirteen: I was always too old for tears. Too old for a fuss.'

I walked into the kitchen, through the back door and threw the basin of dirty water into the garden. The sun was bright, illuminating the silos in the farmer's field, making them look a brighter green than I knew them to be. Trick of the light.

I breathed in the air: the dung from those fields, the grassy dew from the lawn. I had done everything that I needed to do to give the impression she had been well looked after. Later, I would take the old prescriptions from the kitchen drawer and burn them. I would ring the GP. I would call Michael at work, tell him to come home early, everything I needed to do to keep up appearances.

I sank to the cool grass and lay back, the sun hidden from view by the silos. The shadows they cast made them seem more batholithic than man-made and I found I was not afraid of them. I was not afraid, I realised, of anything.

Swifts darted and swirled above me, their forked tails and sharp wings cutting the hazy sky. I thought of the wind in their feathers, how that same wind would have felt in my hair if I were up there, escaping.

'You can do anything.'

The memory of my mother's voice. At least, I thought it her voice; I couldn't remember it clearly even then.

I closed my eyes, felt a shiver run the length of my body as the dew from the grass crept beneath my thin dress. My mother rarely wore dresses and then, aged fourteen with the experience of living in this small place, I appreciated how different that must have made her in the late '50s. She had worn trousers and shirts, always smart, brightly coloured and chic. Her hair was styled, her bright eyes made up with so much makeup that Daddy would call her Black-Eyed Caroline and she would laugh and pull him towards her by his tie and kiss his earlobe.

She escaped, my mother. So did her sister, Charlotte, but I knew so little of her except for the son she cuckooed into my mother's nest. Two identical girls who lived in this same house, played in the garden I was lying in. Had they endured similar wrath and bitterness from Grandmother? How did they do it? How did my mother become who she was?

'You, my bonny little Connie, are a genius,' she once said to me when she had taken the time to pay me attention, lifting me onto her knee and teaching me the alphabet at our orange, melamine kitchen table. 'You can be anything at all if you set your mind to it. A doctor, even.' My father laughed at this, reached down and tickled her waist until she wriggled in her seat. She had hit him, playfully so, on his chest with the back of her hand.

'Look at her work; she's forming letters correctly and she's barely five years old! And she has the memory of an elephant and the aptitude of—'

'I don't doubt it!' Daddy had interrupted, gently patting mother's hairsprayed do. If he'd messed it up she'd have given his hand a sharp slap, I'd seen her do it before. He had been dressed for work in suit and tie, a silver badge with the emblem of the airline pinned to his lapel.

Mummy and Daddy carried on talking, but I'd stopped listening. I was watching Michael. He had heard the commotion and run into the room, his face ruddy red with happiness. He stood at the doorway, laughing along with the joke, raising his hands to his face as though holding an imaginary camera. 'Click-click,' he said. 'Click-click.'

Daddy had looked at him quizzically, eyebrows drawn down.

'I'm taking memory snaps,' he said. 'Of our family.' Daddy lightly punched him on the arm, smiled.

'Come and help me teach Connie,' Mummy said, inviting Michael to the table, fishing him out a pencil. 'You're good with letters too, I've noticed.' We sat with her and wrote out our letters, listening as she told us again that we could do anything in life, be anyone. At five years old, sitting on her lap in our kitchen, a bowl of tinned peaches and condensed milk waiting for me to gobble up, my body warm from her body, I knew I could be anything.

I never thought I would turn into *this*. My mother, I thought then, would have been disappointed in me. Worse, she would have been ashamed. I had grown into a nobody. A nothing.

The sun had shifted in the sky and peaked from behind the two silos, a shard of light slicing my face. I squeezed my eyelids together to stem the tears.

The change of light returned the silos to their man-made ugly horror but still I wasn't afraid of them. All my energy, my emotion, was wrapped up in the old woman dying inside.

I walked back into the kitchen on legs that were stiff from lying too long on damp grass. I looked at the clock; a quarter to twelve.

It was time.

I lifted the cushion from the wingback by the living room door, the same that the GP had sat in earlier that week. The same that Grandmother used to sit Michael in to eat sweets, cakes and biscuits for his after-school treat.

Despite everything she had done to me, he loved her, just as she had always loved him.

I lifted the cushion and, as I placed it over her face and pushed my weight into it to block her airways, I thought of what Michael would say when I told him that she'd died in her sleep.

She stiffened beneath me. Her neck tautened as she gasped for breath, her arms twitching uselessly by her sides. Even as I held the cushion I knew that I didn't have to. She was dying anyway. Another few days and she would have been gone.

But there would have been no triumph in that.

I wanted her to die knowing, full well, what this moron was capable of.

Chapter Thirteen

Selina

Saturday morning

Unless it was a manufacturing error, the morphine had been tampered with. And Connie, unaware, had used the doctored drug to try and kill herself.

It felt wrong; messy and unconvincing.

By the time she found Madeleine, Selina had already made up her mind that the nurse must, *must*, have something to do with it. Though what the *it* was, she still couldn't pinpoint.

As a lawyer, she knew that the simplest, fact-based explanation was usually the right one. As a barrister, she knew how easy it was for those facts to be spun.

With each step through the pale linoleumed corridors, Selina formed a case against Madeleine in her head that proved beyond reasonable doubt that the reason she had run from the HDU ward was not because she was horrified that the morphine had been tampered with, or upset that her patient had been needlessly left in pain, but because *she* had done the tampering, an angel-of-death in reverse. People only ran away when they felt guilty, after all.

And if this was true, it meant Selina's other fears were unfounded. The possibility that Madeleine somehow knew about Connie and Selina's shared secret, that she had confronted

Connie and it was this that had driven her to suicide. This skewed angel-of-death scenario, however, was so rare as to be almost impossible.

Images rose in her mind of the tin box hidden beneath her bed. Could Madeleine really know what was inside it? Was that why Connie had acted so rashly?

And if Madeleine had somehow discovered the truth, if she'd already confronted Connie, how long would it be before—

'Selina?' The German accent, harsh and echoey in the austere coffee shop, startled her.

Madeleine looked awful. Sitting upright on the edge of her seat, her hair hanging in lank curtains either side of her face, the gaudy yellow ends reaching the tabletop. She had visible grey roots. Dark and greasy, rather than shiny. Her hands, though, were immaculately clean.

As well as the pyjamas and gaudy jumper, the nurse wore pale-grey sheepskin slippers tinged on the seams with mud. The clothes she must have been wearing when they brought Connie into Musgrove Park.

'I came to make sure you're all right,' Selina said, relying on the half-truth to give her an edge of sincerity.

Madeleine smiled back through a face lined with exhaustion.

'Can I get you a coffee?' Selina asked, seeing that Madeleine was shaking slightly. 'Or something to eat?'

'No, no. I was going to go, but I wanted also to speak to you before I leave. I was about to come and find you.'

'You're going home?'

'Esther slept last night in Connie's room, but I can't sleep in hospitals, which is stupid for a nurse but there you have it. I've been awake since I started my shift on Thursday night.

The news from Dr Gill was the last straw. I can't think of it.'
She touched her crucifix again, a flighty gesture, over almost
as soon as it had begun. 'I wanted to make sure before I go
that you're staying here with Connie and Esther? Connie will
want to get home as quickly as possible, to see her husband,
but she really needs to get better and Esther falls over herself
to please her mum. It wouldn't surprise me if she agreed to
take her home early. I'd feel a lot better if there was someone
here to talk sense into them.'

'You really think Connie would try to leave? She's in a
fairly serious state.'

'As soon as she comes round she'll want to get back to
her husband. I know she will.'

'Is he going to be—'

'I wouldn't be staying with them if he was going to be OK.
I'm a palliative nurse at St Moira's, I only offer end-of-life
care. I *would* say he hasn't much longer, but I've been saying
that for two weeks. He's very weak, though, and the pain is
such that, that . . .' She shook her head and looked down.
The idea of the unnecessary pain hung in the air like a
guillotine's blade, swiping momentum from their conversation. *Did you cause that pain?* Selina thought, retesting the
idea to herself.

Madeleine tried and failed to supress another yawn,
rubbing her eyes with her fists like a child.

'You didn't know? That he is dying, I mean,' Madeleine
asked after a few moments. 'You looked shocked.'

'I didn't know it had gone so far,' Selina said. 'I've just been
so busy that I haven't had a chance to come and see him.'

Selina noticed the glistening sheen on the nurse's brow.
How exhausting it must be, she thought, to care for the

dying. Or how exhausting to continually try and cover your tracks.

'He told me about you,' Madeleine said, 'mentioned you, just the once. The best friend of his incredible, brainy daughter. His solicitor daughter.'

'He's always been very proud of Esther,' Selina said, thinking of how close he and Esther had been. Then another thought, more threatening.

'Did he talk about anything else?' Selina slipped into the toffee tones of her courtroom voice, covering any hint of nerves. 'You must be a confessor of sorts, staying at his bedside through the night.'

She was aware that the barista was glancing in their direction, no doubt wondering when they were going to order drinks.

The nurse's eyes seemed to narrow and Selina was sure then that he had told her exactly what Selina had done to protect the Lithgow family. But she said, instead, 'He only ever spoke about Connie.'

The din from the barista seemed to heighten, the clanks of the coffee machine, the rustle of cardboard cups being stacked. 'In what way?' Selina's vision began to blur in and out. She felt light-headed, imagining late-night vigils where secrets were spilt and promises broken.

Even the smells became stronger, to the point of being nauseating. The rich, buttery scent from the baked goods, the bitter headiness of the coffee.

Madeleine shook her head, looked at Selina as though she were indecent asking such a question. 'How much he loves her, of course. How worried he is about her and what will happen once he's gone.'

The urge to breathe out a sigh of relief was overwhelming, but Selina held back, one more question niggling at her, but she couldn't rush for fear of raising the nurse's suspicions, wanted to appear conversational and not interrogative. 'He never spoke of anyone else? Old friends, colleagues, his parents?'

Madeleine shook her head, but said, 'Once or twice, but recently it's only been Connie.'

'And Connie,' Selina asked, building up to it, 'has she spoken to you at all about . . .' She let the sentence hang, hoping Madeleine would pick up the trail, begin speaking of her own free will but instead she just raised one eyebrow.

'Connie doesn't say anything at all. She occasionally writes things down, but they are just general things: would I like tea, would I like her to light the fire, do I need anything to eat? She doesn't chat or make small talk in the way a . . . more normal person might.'

'Nothing about Connie is normal.' Selina felt the sting of betrayal as soon as the words left her mouth.

'She is not normal, no, but none of us are.' The nurse touched her crucifix again, tucking it beneath the neck of her jumper.

'Has it made it more difficult to do your job? Navigating Connie's silence, I mean?'

Madeleine offered a small smile, shook her head. 'Of course not, it doesn't interfere with my calling.'

'And your calling is what, exactly?'

'To ease their journey from their physical body to their spiritual one.'

Three doctors walked in, dressed in pale-blue scrubs. One had a spray of dark brown liquid across his left sleeve. Dried blood, Selina presumed, though it could just as easily have been spilt coffee.

'Changing of the guard.' Selina watched the doctors at the counter, relieved to have a distraction from the unsettling gaze of the nurse. 'One shift finishing, the other one just about to start.'

'I really must go,' Madeleine said, still perched half on and half off her chair. 'I just wanted to make sure you would keep Connie here until she's been treated.'

'You must be familiar with long shifts,' Selina said, still watching the coffee-shop counter. The three men were chatting quietly, each with an iPad in their spare hands and Selina imagined they were handing over patient notes. It was hard enough to do when you were a barrister, giving up a case mid-trial because some emergency had arisen, let alone walking away from a life-or-death situation. How did they do it? 'I don't imagine you would leave a patient who needed you just because your time was up?'

Madeleine made a guttural gasp that reeked of hurt and Selina snapped her head around, looked at her again, realised with a guilty horror that Madeleine had taken her comments as a slight.

'I'm sorry,' she said, 'I wasn't criticising your need to go home, I was just thinking of those doctors changing shifts, that's all, and how difficult it must be to leave—'

'I *am* used to plans changing,' Madeleine said, staring at her unflinchingly. 'To patients' needs changing, to their health changing. What I'm *not* used to is going to bed after caring for a patient for twelve hours through the night, changing his catheter and his drip and his medication line, listening to him moan in pain for hours on end, watching him slowly die before my eyes and to then come down for a glass of water to find his wife comatose by his bedside, a needle in her arm. I wasn't a nurse when I found Connie. I was just a woman getting ready for bed. I've done my best, I brought her here, I called Esther, I've waited and waited for her to wake up, to talk, to say something but she hasn't. And I am *so tired.*'

She dropped her head into her hands, elbows resting on the coffee table. Selina put a hand to her forearm and gently rubbed the soft wool of her jumper.

'I'm sorry, I spoke out of turn,' Selina said. 'Of course you should go home.' And then something Madeleine had said jumped back at her, coiled around the unease Selina had felt ever since Esther's phone call the day before.

'Why did you want to wait for Connie to speak?' Selina asked, wariness pullulating, Madeleine's frazzled appearance, the sheen of sweat on her brow, her trembling limbs all combining to scream one word in Selina's head. *Guilt.* 'Connie never speaks, you said so yourself. What were you hoping she would say?'

Or were you worried she'd point the finger at you, Selina thought.

Madeleine stood up, her face losing its sheen and becoming, instead, deathly white.

'What do you think?' she spat. 'I want her to tell me *why.*' Behind the venom in her voice there was anguish, a crack in her nurse's veneer. *I was just a woman when I found her*, she had said, and Selina felt it then, how these masks are just masks, that they conceal but don't protect.

'I'm sorry,' she said again, and felt her own barrister's mask slip out of place, exposing the truths and the fears that she couldn't bear to let out in the open. The idea of Madeleine being involved melted away, boiled with the heat of a much more frightening truth, that Connie really did try to end her own life and Selina held the key as to why. It hid beneath her bed.

Chapter Fourteen

Selina

Five years ago

She was down from London for a long weekend and staying at her mother's house, alone, which was odd in itself. Normally at least one of her three elder sisters were there, barging in with a squalling child on their hip or a yoga mat rolled under their arm or a bill for car repairs they couldn't pay.

'How long will you stay?' Lauren Alverez said, placing a china teacup in front of Selina, an amoretti biscuit on the side.

'A few days,' Selina said. 'But I'll be staying with Esther tonight and Austin tomorrow, so I'll not be in the way.'

'You're never in the way,' Lauren said, too quickly Selina felt, and sat opposite her at the round table in the kitchen.

'You could invite Austin over for dinner?' Lauren smiled encouragingly. Selina smiled back but didn't concede. She loved Austin far too much to make him sit through an entire evening of her mother.

Selina sipped her tea.

Lauren nibbled the edge of her biscuit, unpicked the crumbs from her slick, red lipstick. She was still beautiful, tall and willowy-thin, the lines that age and grief had tried to draw on her skin smoothed by Botox. Her eyes were heavy-lidded and turquoise-blue, her face a perfect oval framed by a dark-blonde bob she had never allowed to turn white. Selina looked nothing like her, had always taken after her father. Her strong, square jaw, olive skin and heavy eyebrows all feminine mimics of his.

'The table's nice,' Selina tried, running her palm over the smooth surface. Her mother's face brightened, looking at the table with affection.

'It took a while to refurbish, but I think it was worth it, don't you? Of course, I had to order in the chalk paint, it's almost impossible to find the right brand anywhere on the high street.'

Selina tried her hardest to look interested. Her mother carried on, describing her process in choosing the right colour for the painted table legs, the right varnish for the top, how many of her friends so far had complimented her on it and how many had stayed green-eyed silent. In her mind's eye, Selina saw her father with them. Colbert Alverez would have been sitting to the right of his wife, his black hair badger-striped with grey, his cheeks grooved with smile lines and crow's feet. Somehow, he would bring Selina into the conversation, weave a story that miraculously included furniture refurbishment and cricket. In doing so he would unite the two women; they would find themselves talking easily after all. Without him, Selina didn't know how to speak to her mother. Lauren clearly didn't know how to speak to Selina, either.

'You could help me if you like?' Lauren said, and Selina, mortified, realised that her mother had offered her an olive branch and she didn't have a clue what it was.

'Which part could I help with?' Selina said, carefully.

'Well, you can sand down the dresser-top whilst I do the drawers. How about that?' Selina couldn't tell if Lauren's offer was genuine or just an effort to appear affectionate. She was smiling, but the artificially smooth skin on her forehead and around her eyes made it difficult to assess how heartfelt that smile really was.

'That would be great.' Selina couldn't think of anything she'd like to do less, but saw that her mother looked tired. More than that, Lauren looked lonely and Selina desperately wanted to comfort her. 'We can listen to the test match whilst we work,' Selina said, adding silently, *Dad would have liked that.*

'The cricket?' Lauren looked as though Selina had suggested painting the furniture with baby's blood. 'No, no. I'll put on some classical, or we could just talk?'

'I always think of Dad when I listen to the test match.'

Lauren stood from the table and took the teacups to the Belfast sink, keeping her back turned to her daughter. Selina could see her shoulders were tense. The kitchen seemed to swallow her mother up, its scale shrinking Lauren to the size of a Borrower. She seemed impossibly lost, impossibly alone, in this plexus of a six-bedroom house.

'So do I,' Lauren said, her voice close to breaking, 'I can't bear it.' She put the cups in the sink and held on to its rim, the gold rings on her fingers hitting the porcelain with a clink.

It had been meant to be a home for Lauren and Colbert, with a bedroom for each of their girls and a guest suite for visitors. She was never meant to live in it without him.

Lauren stood very still, and Selina knew that her mother was holding her breath. Composing herself. Part of her wanted to go to her, to put her hand on her mother's shoulder and say, *I miss him too. Please talk to me about him. Please remember him with me.*

But part of her, the part that always won, wanted to run far away and hide.

Selina opened her mouth as if to speak honestly and, by some divine providence that she would later curse, her mobile rang.

She paused, knowing she should ignore the call and offer her mother the comfort they both needed.

Selina picked up her phone; saw *Esther – Kilstock* on the screen and the number for her parents' landline. Esther, Selina knew, was working at her office in Taunton and would be for another four hours.

'Mum, I need to—'

'Take the call,' Lauren said and, without looking at her daughter, walked out of the kitchen.

Selina watched her go, the familiar cloud of filial disappointment colouring her world quite black.

'Hello?' she said, watching the space by the sink where her mother had stood.

There was no greeting from the caller.

'Hello?' she said again, louder this time.

Silence.

'Is anyone there?' She drew a deep breath of frustration, annoyed that she had let a moment of potential connection slip away for *this*.

A sound, then.

A low, guttural moan, as if someone were trying to speak through a cloth.

She knew who it must be. It wasn't Esther at all.

'Connie? Is everything all right?' Patience was the key; if Connie was trying to communicate she would find a way.

'I'm in Taunton but not with Esther, I'm at Mum's. Is it Esther that you wanted? You can tap the phone if you like, if that makes it easier. One tap for yes and two for no. Is it Esther you need?'

Two taps.

'OK. Is it me you wanted to talk to?'

One tap.

'Right.' She was at a loss as to what Connie could want. She hadn't seen her in years and even then, had rarely been alone with her. What help could she possibly be to a mute who lived out in the farmland by the mudflats?

And then Connie spoke.

It was a muffled, slurred sound that, she could tell, took great concentration and effort. Just one, single, frightful word.

'Help.'

Total quiet. Connie had hung up.

Selina called straight back but the phone rang on and on without an answer and no answerphone.

She could call Esther. But what would Esther do? She was at work, *busy* at work. There must have been a reason for Connie to call Selina and not Esther.

The word *help* throbbed in her ear.

'I'm just popping out,' she called to her mother and drove straight over the top of the hills to Kilstock.

'This is like bloody vinegar!' Esther laughed, holding the half-empty bottle up to the light. 'It's not even a variety; it just says *red wine*! Who the hell buys wine that's just labelled red wine?'

'It was all they had,' Selina said, knocking her glass back

with a grimace. 'I thought the red would be a safer bet than the white. You need to move to somewhere that has a better corner shop.'

'You need to learn what to buy in a corner shop.' Esther leaned back on her sofa, her legs stretched out and her feet on the coffee table. 'They sell Gordon's, you know, and Schweppes. We could have had low-rent G&Ts.'

'I'll know better next time.' Selina leaned back herself, letting her head rest on the soft butter-brown leather of Esther's armchair. She curled her legs up and sat with her feet beneath her, like a child. 'We've probably had enough, anyway.'

'You've had enough,' Esther said, nudging her own wine glass with her toe. 'I could do with one last decent glass of red. Amarone; now that would do the trick.'

Selina glanced at the coffee table; three empty bottles of Rioja, a crumpled-up wrapper of dark Green & Black's and another of salted caramel Lindt. There was a second empty bottle of red in the kitchen, along with the abandoned bottle of cheap plonk. They didn't normally drink this much, but they hadn't seen each other in three months and Esther had had, by her account, a shit of a week at work.

'But you've no excuse,' Esther said. 'You're on holiday. You should be lovely and relaxed, not pent up.'

Selina looked at her friend. She had known Esther since they were children. They had dormed together at King's, kept close throughout their university years despite Esther going to Bristol and Selina abandoning Somerset for Durham. Even now, with Selina working from her grandfather's chambers in London (nepotism having its advantages) and Esther working as a property solicitor in Taunton, they had remained close.

Esther's support when Selina's father had died had cemented their adult relationship.

'You look like you're going to cry,' Esther said, and threw a cushion at Selina, hitting her square on the head. She laughed and Selina did too, trying to hide the fact that Esther had been right, she did feel close to tears. Esther was Selina's rock.

'Fuck off.' She threw the cushion back, watched as it sailed across the living room and landed on the coffee table, knocking Esther's foot into the wine glass and sending a splash of the cheap red across the cream carpet.

'No no no no no!' Esther jumped up, held her hair in her fists and threw her head back in a play of pure histrionics. 'My deposit! I'll lose my security deposit!'

Selina laughed, feeling tears of a better kind fill her eyes as she looked at the stain. It was small, thankfully. The smallest, by far, of the six or seven other red wine stains on Esther's living-room carpet. She was nothing if not clumsy.

'I'll get the salt,' Selina said, standing up and feeling the full force of the wine hit her. 'Salt is *great* for red wine stains.'

'Yes,' Esther slurred, 'it has worked so very well in the past.' She waved her hand at the other stains and both women fell back into their chairs laughing, tears streaming down their faces.

'I've missed you, Sel,' Esther said when the laughter finally stopped. 'When are you going to move back to Taunton?'

'Soon.'

'You always say that.' Esther looked at her friend and Selina could see the first faint lines across her forehead. They were only just twenty-nine, but for the first time, Selina realised that they weren't *that* young any more. They were living their lives now, rather than planning what their lives would be like.

'I think you're avoiding your mother,' Esther said, pointing one wobbly finger at her friend. 'You're hiding in London so you don't have to see her.'

'I'm here now.'

'Only for three days. Anyone can cope with three days, especially when they spend most of that time shagging their boyfriend. You hate London; you're always complaining about how cut-throat the other barristers are, how sleazy the appointing solicitors can be. Come back to Taunton permanently, kick out your tenants and take over the flat your dad bought you. Or move to Bristol, at least. You can help me look after my mother if you don't want to look after yours.'

Selina felt herself blush. She had meant to tell Esther about her visit to Connie earlier that day, the help Connie had asked for, the box she had pushed into Selina's hand. *'Help,'* she had said in that odd slur of frustration. *'Help.'* After Selina had lifted the lid on the small metal box, leafed through the contents with gut-wrenching horror, Connie had slipped her a note, reading, *Don't let Esther know.*

'Your mother?' Selina said now, trying to sound nonchalant but paranoid that Esther could see straight through her.

'I wish I had yours.' Esther's eyes were glazed over, her mouth downturned.

'You don't want my mother, she's impossible.'

'No, she's not.'

'She is; everything's awkward with her, everything I do is wrong.'

'At least she can look after herself,' Esther said and held Selina's eye, her face hard and angry and embittered. She really was drunk, Selina thought, if she was saying that. 'At least she's a capable adult,' Esther said.

'I think we've had too much wine.' Selina smiled at her friend, tried to bring warmth back to her face.

As Esther had grown older her love for her mother had grown more complex, maturing from an adolescent need for affection into a dutiful love fringed with resentment. Selina suspected that the lengths Esther had gone to to make her mother's life easier (online grocery deliveries, offering to pay for a cleaner and a companion from a charity set up to give assistance to those cases the government deemed it not necessary to help) had been rejected by Connie. Selina imagined it wasn't because she didn't want Esther's attention but because the older woman didn't want her daughter to spend her hard-earned salary on her. But when one woman is too scared to speak the truth for fear of rejection and the other mentally, possibly even physically, incapable of speaking, communication is almost impossible.

'I mean it,' Esther said. 'What would happen if Dad died? I'd be stuck with her; I'd have to spend the rest of my life caring for her. Have you any idea how scary that is?'

Selina thought again of the box Connie had given her, now stored underneath the passenger seat of her car.

Don't let Esther know, Connie had written down on the back of a Spar receipt. Not 'Don't tell anybody', not even 'Don't tell the police'. Just *Don't let Esther know.* Connie had looked terrified as she passed the note to Selina, the effort it must have taken her to ask for help evident in every shake of her hand, in every nervous glance. She was a woman who knew not what to do, only that she could no longer go on harbouring such a secret.

'*Leave it with me,*' Selina had said at the time, not knowing herself what she would do. '*I'll sort something out.*' She had intended on telling Esther everything. But, with every new sip of wine it somehow got more difficult. Now it seemed impossible.

There were other options, other routes Selina could take. They weren't the right routes, as such. They weren't the paths she wanted to follow, that an upstanding member of society would take. Then again, this wouldn't be the first time that Selina had defended someone she knew, for a fact, to be guilty. She'd only been working as a junior barrister for two years and had already crossed more lines than she felt comfortable with.

'I want to do what's best for her, but I always get it wrong. I don't know where to start.'

'You needn't worry about it.' Selina said this to herself as much as Esther. She would go back tomorrow, she decided, talk to Esther's parents. Make it clear that she wouldn't tell Esther what had happened so long as it never, never happened again.

She would keep tabs; come back to Somerset once a month and methodically search the cottage. There were other checks she could make, she was sure of it. She could manage this, handle this, stop it from escalating further.

Prevent anyone else from getting hurt.

Esther smiled sadly. 'I'll have to worry about it one day,' she said. 'At some point, I'm going to have to take responsibility, unless Dad outlives her.'

'That's a bit morbid.'

'Spending all that time with your mum, after your dad passed away, made me realise how fragile it all is. Lauren's strong, despite all her faults. She'll cope. My mother wouldn't know where to begin.'

'At least you still have your dad,' Selina said.

Esther, shocked, put her hands to her mouth. 'Sel, I didn't mean it like that. You know I didn't.'

'I know,' Selina said. 'But it's true.'

She would keep the tin box as evidence, an insurance policy to make *sure* it never happened again.

She would do this, for Esther.

Chapter Fifteen

Selina

Saturday morning

The sun had risen whilst she had been sitting with the nurse, the time on the wall clock by the counter saying it was now mid-morning. Without the distraction of conversation Selina could hear the bustle of the hospital picking up. More footsteps in the corridor, muffled voices, closing doors. The three doctors had collected their hot drinks and gone; the barista was refilling the pastry display.

'I'll take two flat whites, please,' Selina said at the counter, mind on Esther, resting her eyes on the flaky pastries and thinking that they really should have breakfast, even if it wasn't a healthy one. 'Make that three, and three croissants.' Austin would want one too, surely. He'd always loved a bakery breakfast. She doubted he'd had time to eat and even if he had, he wouldn't turn down fresh coffee.

She paid in cash, poured her change into the tip jar, and slotted the three cups into a cardboard tray, hooking the burgundy and white paper bag around her index finger.

Her stomach churned as she walked through the corridor, the gentle weight of the food tugging on her hunger.

She'd made a mess of it with Madeleine. She regretted talking to her in such a way, letting her spiky nature obstruct her humanity. What was she thinking, questioning her like that? Who was she to judge?

As she rounded the last corner before the HDU she paused. Austin was outside, looking at his iPad, deep frown lines betraying his concentration. She looked down at the cups, the bag. What *was* she thinking? She was losing it.

Why had she ordered a coffee, unsolicited, for a man she had broken up with so long ago? A man who was now married to someone else?

She was going to turn back, give the third cup to the first overworked nurse or medic she saw, but he looked up. He must have smelt the coffee, the freshly baked dough of the croissants, because he looked at those with his eyebrows raised before he even looked at Selina's face.

'Coffee run?' he asked her as she approached. There was no point in turning back now.

'Well, of sorts,' she said, forcing herself to take a bright tone, a light step. 'I'd bought one for Esther, one for me and one for Madeleine but, well, I upset her, I think. She stormed off before I could offer her a cup. I can't blame her.' A semi-truth, but far, far better than the whole.

'Were you too honest or were you too brash?' His understanding of her made her feel uncomfortable. She'd forgotten how thoroughly he knew her.

'I thought she was in some way connected with all this . . . stuff. The overdose, the mislabelling of the morphine, the lot of it.'

'Madeleine? Seriously?'

'She said she'd been waiting for Connie to speak, and it just hit a nerve because Connie never speaks. She would know that, wouldn't she, having lived with them these last few weeks? It made me suspicious.'

'What did you say?'

'I didn't, I mean, I may have been a bit off, but I didn't say anything, not really.'

He folded his arms across his chest, looking at her with one eyebrow raised.

'I may have pushed her a bit to tell me why she was waiting for Connie to talk. She said she wanted to know why Connie would take her own life.'

Austin sighed, looked down at his feet. 'She's a palliative care nurse, she spends her time helping people who *don't* want to die—'

'So being faced with someone who seemingly does must be difficult.'

'Even more so for her. Her daughter died. Liver failure. Madeleine nursed her through the final stages, it's what made her switch from being a trauma nurse to a St Moira's nurse. It might help put into perspective why she found Connie's actions difficult to deal with.'

'Shit.' Selina closed her eyes momentarily, opened them to see Austin smiling with pity and wished the ground would swallow her, coffee and croissants and all.

'Do you want this?' She proffered the third coffee cup towards him. 'It's still hot and going spare.'

'It smells great, but I can't. Off caffeine.'

'Oh Jesus! Really? Why the hell would anyone give up caffeine?'

He slipped his left hand into the pocket of his white coat and Selina thought, for a moment, that he was trying to hide his ring, maybe even his regrets—

'We're trying,' he said, and Selina forced a smile so wide that she thought her face may crack, 'for a baby.' He added, is if he needed to clarify, 'Caffeine is strictly off limits until we've, well, you know.'

'Right, well. Super. Gosh, that's . . . super.' She winced at her own ridiculousness, stopped herself just shy of punching him lightly on the arm. He was married and they were trying for a baby. Of course they were. She didn't even know his wife's name, didn't want to know it and was suddenly so, so pleased she had closed her Facebook account.

'I better go and give this to Esther,' she said, making a move for the door. 'Is there any news on Connie?'

'No, not in the last half hour.'

'OK, well, if I don't see you again, good luck.'

'It was good seeing you, Selina. I'm glad you're well.'

You know nothing about me, she thought.

Esther was still sitting in the plastic chair when Selina walked through. Her hair was dishevelled, unbrushed following her night on the camp bed in her mother's room. Selina had an urge to neaten it. She held out the Costa cups instead.

'I bought you a drink. And something to eat.'

'Oh, right.' Esther reached for the bag, opened it. 'There are three in here?'

'Madeleine's gone home,' Selina said.

'And three coffees. You bought one for Austin, didn't you?'

'Do you want a coffee or not?'

'I don't do caffeine, haven't for three months.'

'Oh, come on, not you too?' She put the cup down on one chair, sat in the adjoining seat and began drinking her own damn coffee. She'd drink all three of them. Eat all three croissants, too.

'I was getting migraines and the GP advised I give it up. Why do you think I've only been drinking peppermint tea?'

Selina nearly said she hadn't seen Esther for so long that maybe she'd missed it but thought better, said instead, 'I thought it was just a new preference.'

Esther shrugged. 'You've been distracted, caught up in the wonders of Bristol, centre of the criminal universe.' Her words may have been sarcastic but her manner wasn't. It was the calm, friendly tone of a woman making gentle fun of her friend.

'How's Connie?' Selina held out the paper bag, offering Esther a pastry after all, her own way of patching up singed bridges. 'Have they taken her up for the MRI yet?'

'The machine isn't free. They've only the one, can you believe that? Or only one that works, anyway. They're fund-raising for a second. Mum's being checked over and then we can go back in. Why's Austin not drinking caffeine?'

'He and his wife are trying, apparently.'

'Good for them,' Esther said with both eyebrows raised, testing the phrase.

Selina smiled, said, 'Yes, quite,' and kept her smile in place even whilst she chewed, surprising herself with how forcefully she tore at the pastry with her teeth.

She didn't want children of her own, had never wanted them. Knew, in her core, that if Austin craved fatherhood then it was better that he was with someone else, married to someone else. Knew also that, as a successful criminal barrister with a first-class degree from Durham and two properties in her portfolio, she would be a catch by anyone's standards, should she choose to dip her toe back in the murky pool of dating. Which she didn't. So there.

Still, she couldn't help thinking how different things may have been, had she not broken up with Austin, had she not answered the first phone call from Connie, had she not sold her soul to the devil.

'*Help me.*'

Chapter Sixteen

Connie

Saturday morning

A lone, my head fogs. I know I am in a hospital and my more lucid thoughts focus on this, ask: who is with me; who has touched me; why am I still alive?

Why?

I should be dead. There are plenty of people who, if they knew of the things I have done, would wish me dead. One in particular has tried.

Will they hunt me down? Wait until I am alone and push a pillow to my face or inject me with enough insulin to still my heart?

My eyes are closed, I am aware of fleeting shadows and sudden bursts of light but no more. I hear footsteps, trolleys, muttered voices but the sounds are so far away. I can't tell if they are near me or far. I've been sedated, but the dose was minimal and I am trapped in the space between waking and sleep.

The thought strikes again: am I alone? Panic distorts my senses; the shadows change to shadows of her. Is she coming?

The sedative is a mind-messer, thoughts appear like rabbits from a warren, pop-pop-pop, slipping away just as quickly into long grass.

I hear a noise and the rational part of my brain tells me it is a door, hinges creaking. The less rational part tells me it is the hinge of a rusted tin box.

And there I am. Not in a hospital, but at home, five years ago. I have folded my letters and hold the paper in my hands. They are dry, the paper crackles and I look down; I've been holding them so tightly they've creased. Selina is coming. I called her, told her to help me. I need her help. I know that I cannot do this alone, that I need her help so desperately that I can almost taste it, but for her to help she must first understand.

And so, this mute wrote it all down.

I hear a car arrive on the road outside.

I close my eyes, let my fingers feel the way because I cannot bear to look and confront what I am about to do. I lift the lid of the box, the hinges creak, I put my letters in the bottom.

And then it's too late to take them out again, hide them or burn them to ash.

Selina is here. She takes the box, full of those unspeakable acts, full of my explanations. She promises to help me.

I wait for the help to come and I wonder if they will lock me up.

Let them try, comes a voice from the depths of my soul, a devil mixed with a feral child. *Let them try*.

Chapter Seventeen

Connie

1971

I was seventeen. Michael was twenty-two, with a full-time job as a caretaker at a school four miles away. The very school he had gone to, the same that our mothers attended when they were snapped by the photographer in their uniforms. Their picture had never left the mantelpiece.

I was sitting on the bed upstairs, hands in my lap. From the window, I could see the distant shape of the silos. They were looking at me, peering through the glass like a gaoler. I wondered if Grandfather had complained when they built those towers. Did he ever resent them as much as I did? They saw all that happened in that house, but never told a soul of the devilish girl inside it.

Downstairs, Fat Maud sat with Michael, side by side, on the small sofa by the fireplace. Dr Rowe was in the wingback Grandmother used to favour. She had been dead for three years.

'It's your future you have to think of,' Dr Rowe said, and Michael stayed silent. I could picture him nodding slowly, looking at the doctor in the distrustful way he had done ever since catching Dr Rowe with his hands on my waist.

'Do you really want to be chained to this village for the rest of your life? And what happens when you want to get married, start a family? What will you do then? It would have to be a very understanding woman who would take her on along with you.'

'You make it sound as though he has no choice, Doctor,' Maud cut in, and I wanted to squeeze her large, soft hands, whisper *thank you*. I had the urge to kiss her plump cheek, now dotted with age spots and smile lines. It was an urge I had often had since childhood and those years of spoon-ladled jam and new bread, but I never did it.

She was defending me, looking after us just as she had promised Grandmother she would.

'You don't have to do anything you don't want to do,' she said, and I knew she was talking directly to Michael, maybe even turning her body away from Dr Rowe.

'She's no burden,' Michael said. 'I want to stay with her, I want to look after her.'

'You say that now, but what about when she's thirty or forty or fifty? There's no cure for retardation. She'll never lead a full life, never get married, never have children. It's well known that, in cases such as Connie's where the brain stops developing after a sudden trauma, the body stops developing with it. To look at her now you wouldn't think she was more than twelve or thirteen. She's never going to get better, Michael, and as you have the longstanding power of attorney, it's your decision what happens to her.'

'I want to look after her.'

'Michael, *Michael,* there are places—'

'I've heard of those places, Doctor,' Maud said with a strained voice, the topic upsetting her. 'You get thrown in and you never get out again. They prod you and poke you and pump you full of drugs, lock you away . . . she doesn't belong somewhere like that. She belongs here, at home.'

'These hospitals are very different to how they used to be.' I could hear, from his voice, that Dr Rowe was smiling his most patronising smile. The same one he had used when he told us that Grandmother had a bad cough, that's all. Then a chest infection, that's all. And then, three years later, after constant coughs, infections and spitting blood, that she had stage four cancer. 'They're more like homes now rather than hospitals or prisons.'

It was these words that I remembered when, the following day, we stepped off a train in South Wales. We walked a mile along a country path to one of those homes, convinced by the good doctor to go and take a little visit.

Pyntanworth Home for the Mentally Ill. Dr Rowe had assured us that, should *Michael* like it, he could find me a place.

It looked like a seventeenth-century mansion; a Thornfield Hall or a Mansfield Park. It looked beautiful and grand. I could, indeed, have spent hours walking those grounds, reading beneath those rowan trees or on the bench in the damson orchard.

I wouldn't have had to worry about this devil lurking within me.

Or what he might make happen next.

'We're just visiting, Con,' Michael said, a phrase he had repeated all morning. 'I'm not really going to send you away.' Michael looked at the house too, eyes wide with awe.

The windows were dark; staring out from the house to the empty gardens.

We got closer and my thoughts shifted. I felt a sudden panic rise like a bubble in my gullet. I felt clammy and Michael dropped my hand, wiped his own on his thigh to get rid of my sweat.

The windows were barred.

And despite the day being bright, warm, not a patient was outside.

The front door had a small brass sign with the name of the home, a brass bell and a brass knocker. Michael knocked and, from the sound, I knew that the door was thick and heavy, a perfect seal.

'We've been expecting you!' The woman smiled at Michael. She grinned at me and raised her eyebrows. Michael nudged me gently in the ribs; the way he did when I'd been drooling. I lifted my hand to my chin and felt the wet slick of saliva. I didn't do this on purpose. I spent so much time out of my body, pretending I was far away, or watching myself from above, that my flesh felt alien to me.

I knew, before even stepping over the threshold, that I did not belong there.

'My name is Elizabeth, I'm the matron here, but please do call me Lizzy.' She held out her hand for Michael to shake and I noticed that she wasn't wearing a uniform. She was dressed instead in pale-blue flares and an orange pullover. She was in her forties, slim, brown hair cut short and a feline face framed with blue glasses. Her teeth were small, a gap between each, and her thin lips set in a smile that never faltered.

'I'll give you a tour. We're a much more modern facility than you might expect; huge steps forward have been made in mental health in the last ten years and we're putting all of that new knowledge into practice.' She held a door open and beckoned us through, before locking it behind us.

We had stepped into a corridor lined with doors, a window in each.

'This is the dormitory,' Lizzy said. 'Each patient has their very own room and each dorm (we have five in total in this wing) has a bathroom with shared access.' She strode ahead, following the sign on the wall that read *Day Ward*.

Michael walked on, looking all around him silently.

I did the same.

Through the windows in the doors I spied the bedrooms. Each room had a bed. Nothing else.

Each room also had a window, secured with thick, iron bars.

I tried a handle, but it was locked.

The floor was solid wood, showing signs of wear and the occasional black skid mark. Wheelchair tyres could have caused them, I reasoned internally. Food trolleys, maybe.

At the end, Lizzy paused, waiting for us to catch up. She had a ring of keys in her hands and looked through the glass in the door, her smile wavering for the briefest of moments, and then she turned the handle and let us through.

'This,' she announced with aplomb, 'is our day ward.'

The room would have been beautiful, once. The walls were papered with pale-blue wallpaper dotted with flowers and birds. The floor was solid wood, too. On one side were two long, solid oak dining tables; one holding packs of playing cards, chess boards, backgammon sets, paper, crayons, chalks and an incongruous green pull-along train. The second table was empty, save for a plastic jug of water and a column of melamine cups.

'This room has the best view,' Lizzy said, pointing to the window.

Chairs lined three of the walls, most pointing to face the windows that looked out to the garden through the same iron bars.

On the chairs sat the patients.

And I wanted to go home.

'We have a number of activities, as you can see,' Lizzy said, pointing to the first oak table, 'and the patients are encouraged to use any of these at all. And, Connie,' she turned to me with a grin, her small teeth on show, 'I hear from Dr Rowe that you like to read. Would you like to see our bookshelf?'

I opened my mouth to say no, to say that I wanted to go home, but words wouldn't form and I looked like a carp with its mouth hanging open. I stared at the patient nearest me; a woman in a beige smock and purple clogs staring out of the window. She was rubbing her hands together in her lap and then patting her palms on her cheeks, as though warming herself up. Rub-rub-pat she went, rub-rub-pat and then Lizzy took me by the arm and I froze.

She wanted to pull me to the bookshelf but she was touching me and I couldn't move a muscle.

I saw Michael stare at her hand, worry on his face as though he knew what was coming, but before he could warn her she had slid her other hand around my back, her fingers pressing the side of my waist, and my body came back with a jolt.

My back arched.

My elbows jabbed.

But it was OK, it was all right; I didn't hurt her. Not half as much as I wanted to. Michael pulled her away just in time, so I only imagined the satisfaction of elbow-jabbing her square in the ovary.

Michael gave her the vital warning: 'She doesn't like being touched.'

'Oh, that's all right!' Lizzy said, as though he had told her I didn't like strawberry jam, not that I'd just tried to physically render her infertile. Her voice was chipper, her eyes wide open and head nodding so vigorously that I felt the urge to shove the melamine cups deep down her patronising, cheerful throat.

'I understand,' she said, so brightly I internally winced. 'You just follow me, then.'

She walked on ahead, looking over her shoulder to make sure I was following. The bookcase was on the other side of the room and it was very small. Three shelves of books. I'd probably read them all.

'We would be very understanding,' Lizzy said to Michael. 'We would put measures in place so that minimal contact occurred, if that's what she liked. But there may be therapies that can help her overcome that. We have a fully functioning ECT machine; it's very useful for all sorts of behavioural problems.'

'ECT?' Michael asked, hopeful. Desperate.

'Electroconvulsive therapy,' Lizzy said. 'We run a slight electric charge through specific points in the brain. It's ever so effective at controlling . . . odd behaviour.'

I looked again to the woman rubbing her hands. Rub-rub-pat. I looked at her shaved head. Unconsciously my own hands, as though sensing my doubt, rose up to touch my blonde curls.

'Here we are,' Lizzy said, and pointed to the bookcase, made of the same grand oak as the dining tables.

I hadn't read any of those books. The spines were brightly coloured and thin as whips. The writing was large, clear. Lizzy took one out and held it for me to see.

Topsy and Tim Meet the Baby.

'Lovely pictures in this one,' she said.

There was no Dickens, Collins, Brontë, Austen, Waugh. Not a single book that I'd borrowed from the travelling library. But plenty of Topsy and Tim.

In the corner of the room someone laughed. A single noise quickly strangled. A man stood and looked at me with large, bright eyes. He was as plump and as pale as a plucked chicken thigh. His hands worried at the hem of his cream shirt, which was dappled with oil stains and crumbs. His trousers were tan corduroy, his feet slippered in white.

'Why are these people here?' Michael asked Lizzy, his eyes set on the three androgynous, shaven-headed patients sitting nearest the windows, scanning from one silent, rocking form to the next.

'We look after all sorts of patients on the long-term ward. All sorts of manias, chronic insomnia, anorexia nervosa, Down Syndrome, depression. We used to specialise in women with *unhealthy appetites,* shall we say, but we've broadened our reach now.'

'What do you mean by that? Unhealthy appetites?'

'Women who have difficulty controlling themselves, sexually.' She whispered the last word as though it was a delicacy she couldn't wait to try. She was still holding the Topsy and Tim book, her thumb rubbing across the word *Baby*. 'Times have moved on a great deal; we no longer section women for having children out of wedlock, or being intimate before marriage, but many more deep-rooted problems are still dealt with here. Women who have an unhealthy interest in children or old men. Women who commit incest or those who attempt to seduce other women, for example.'

The man in the cream shirt walked across the room. He kept looking at me as he moved, his walk a hippo's lumbering gait. He scratched his chin. He made another short, loud belly laugh.

'What about Connie?' Michael asked her, and he was watching me, just like the man in the cream shirt watched me. 'How would you help Connie?' He was nervous, swallowing between phrases. He stared at my shoulders but not my face, he couldn't look me in the eye.

Michael wanted to send me here, I suddenly worried. He wanted to send me here.

I looked away, to the windows and the patients rocking in front of them, to the woman rubbing her hands and patting her cheeks, to the flaking wallpaper, the iron bars behind the glass, to the man in cream as he lumbered along.

He stopped beside the first of the three rocking patients.

He was fumbling with himself.

Lizzy called out for a nurse and a heavy-set man dressed in white ran in, made a beeline for the cream-shirted patient.

But it was just a second too late.

The patient held his penis in his hand, soft and fleshy as a slug. A stream of dark yellow spurted out, the urine hitting the person rocking in the chair. I saw that the patient was another man, five o'clock shadow showing on his fine-boned profile. The liquid hit his cheek, splashed onto his collar.

The nurse pulled the offender away, held his arms stiffly behind his back, dragged him off whilst the patient guffawed. His penis still hung out of his trousers, an ochre dribble staining the corduroy. His feet skidded against the polished wood floor, dark skid marks left in their wake.

'I'm so sorry you had to see that.' Lizzy stood in front of us, mortified. She was still smiling, trying to cheer us along, trying to pretend nothing had happened, that it was all normal.

Pretend that that place was normal.

'Let me please assure you, that is not a regular occurrence; and as you can see, it was dealt with very swiftly and that man shall be dealt with also. Let me take you somewhere else; the dining room! I'll show you the dining room, it really is lovely . . .'

She prattled on and led us away. I noticed, as we left, that no one had checked on the fine-boned man at the window.

No one had cleaned him up. The urine glistened on his face, catching the light from the sun as it broke through the bars on the windows.

On the train home I thought of the dining room with its austere white tables and chairs, the blunt plastic cutlery, the smell of over-boiled vegetables hanging in the air.

I thought of Grandmother; her old claim that a devil lived inside me, that everything I did and everything that happened to me was spurred on by that badness that lurks in my bones. I thought of her face beneath the pillow.

How tempted was Michael to send me there? I wondered. It struck me, as the train rolled away, that the freedom I presumed I would get when I turned twenty-one, the ability to walk away from Kilstock and the memories it housed, as my mother had done, wasn't so simple as packing a bag and waving goodbye. Freedom was a changeable thing, controlled by whoever took charge of me. Grandmother, when she was alive. Michael, directed by the misguided Dr Rowe. Michael for ever, unless I one day married. But who would want me? I understood then, as the tracks clattered beneath me and the valleys of Wales disappeared along with my hopes of independence, why Aunt Charlotte had run away. But she had never been labelled a moron. If she'd been caught, the worse that would have happened was a return ticket to her mother. If they caught me running away, there was a good chance I'd be locked in a hospital *for my own good*. Nobody would ask me why I wanted to leave. My opinion was never asked, for anything.

On the back of my ticket I wrote, *I promise I won't be a burden.*
I had to keep myself out of that place.

'I know you won't,' Michael said and smiled a resigned smile. 'It's best that you stay with me.'

I thought of the treatment room. The cold, metal bed, its leather straps. The machine snaking wires and electrodes across its prim mahogany stand, the hair clippers. *I promise not to be any trouble,* I wrote next.

'You're not any trouble to me, Con.'

I thought of the bathrooms smiling Lizzy showed us, showed Michael; the row of three white tubs in the middle of the white-tiled room, the toilet cubicles with the doors removed.

I could carry on cleaning in the village, help anyone who needed looking after. I'd be good, really, just don't send me there, please don't send me there. These were the words that I wanted to say, but they came out differently, a staccato list of pleas. 'Not there, not there.' My throat closed, my words were slurred and hardly audible.

I tried to speak again. I felt the tufty wool of the train seat sticking against my bare thighs, the bump and thud as the carriage hurtled us back towards home, towards Dr Rowe. Michael squeezed my hand in his.

'I'll look after you, Connie. Stay with me and I'll keep you out of that place. I'll look after you until the day I die.'

What will happen then? I wanted to ask.

I'll be a good girl, ever so good. Just keep me away from that place.

Chapter Eighteen

Selina

Saturday Morning

'You're away with the fairies,' Esther said. 'It doesn't matter anyway, what's done is done.'

Guilt was a cold hand on Selina's neck, forcing her head up and demanding her attention. The HDU waiting area was quiet, the only interruptions the gentle murmuring from patients further along the ward and the soft tide of footfall from hospital staff.

'God, sorry, Es. I was trying to make sense of this all, my mind ran away with me.' She put the last of the three coffee cups down on the chair beside her, still half full of lukewarm flat white. She hadn't the stomach for any more coffee, or any more memories of the mistakes she had made. As Esther said, what was done was done. Still, she felt there was something she was missing, a key piece of information lost in the myriad. 'You were talking about your dad.'

'Madeleine always said that the quiet Hollywood death scene can be elusive.' Esther picked at the last of her silver nail polish, the flakes falling and settling on her shoe. 'The most common reason patients are returned to hospital isn't because they've changed their mind about dying at home, it's because the relatives can't cope. They see their loved one in pain, or struggling to breathe, and they panic, call an ambulance, readmit the patient into hospital and then that's that. Often they won't come out again. Madeleine prepared us, told us to be strong, but I tell you now, if she hadn't been there we wouldn't have been able to do it. I'd have called 999 after his first seizure. Madeleine was calm, eased him through it. She thinks the cancer may have spread to his brain or spinal column.'

No wonder she was so tired, Selina thought, if that was what she had been dealing with. 'Shouldn't a doctor have been called in to check? I mean, if it's spread further, shouldn't he have some more tests?'

'What would be the point? He'd already refused any further treatment – that's why they sent Madeleine to us, so she could give him the care he needs outside of hospital. We knew it would spread, it's the nature of the disease.

'But I'm not so sure it was the spread of the cancer causing the seizures, not after Austin's news this morning. I think it was the pain,' Esther said. 'I've read of patients who had refused all medical care, not just life-prolonging care as Dad's done but all pain relief, anti-anxiety, the lot. The pain gets so bad that they have physical seizures. What if all he needed was decent pain relief to stop them and some fucking lab cock-up robbed him of that? What if all he needed was some decent fucking morphine?'

Selina rubbed the small of Esther's back. 'It's OK.'

'It's not fucking OK. It's not.' Her face was red, her eyes puffy from the stubbornly held-back tears. 'He is in *so* much pain. Constantly. I used to hope he would just fall asleep, because I thought at least then he's not hurting. I used to pray—' She paused and leaned forward, elbows to knees, fingers steepled over her nose and mouth. 'I used to pray that he would die, for fuck's sake. My own father. Can you even imagine how that feels, knowing I wanted him to die so it would all just end?'

'You wanted him to be out of pain, I understand.' Selina pictured him, prostrate on his rented hospital bed, his wasting body rigid from agony.

Esther shook her head, hid her face in her hands. 'I just didn't want to see it any more. I wanted it to be over because I just can't. Fucking. Take it.'

It began, then, the torrent Selina had been expecting.

Esther sobbed, shoulders heaving, and Selina pulled her towards her, smoothed her short blonde hair with the flat of her hand in heavy, rhythmic strokes, suspected that this was the first time Esther had cried since her mother had been admitted.

She wanted to say, *'Who did you call? Who was there for you? Who helped you through this?'* But couldn't. The answer should have been that Esther had called *her* and Selina had been her rock.

But Selina wasn't there for her. She didn't know who was, especially as she'd broken up with Rosa. Who were her confidants now? She had always been close with colleagues from her office, but was she close enough with them to garner their support? Esther had never been bad at making friends but Selina couldn't imagine her picking up the phone and saying, *'I need you,'* to anyone other than her.

'Connie will be OK.' Selina watched her friend swallow hard, her chin trembling like a child and Selina had to remind herself that Esther was a fully qualified solicitor with a home of her own, a career, a wide circle of her own friends.

'But Daddy won't be,' Esther said, her words small and quiet, and Selina remembered her at school. It had always been her father Esther had looked forward to seeing. They would go on trips together, he would travel on the bus to watch her play hockey, would take time off work to see the school plays. It was her father who attended her graduation from Bristol; he had sat with Selina in the stalls cheering, whilst Connie had stayed at home.

Selina's own father had died so suddenly she hadn't had time to process his impending absence. One day he had been with her, the next he was gone. What would it have been like, knowing in advance that his death was approaching? Would it be harder stretching a goodbye across six long months, rather than missing the goodbye altogether?

'Your mum will help you through it, she loves you,' Selina tried again, picturing the hand written note Connie had pressed towards her five years ago, *Don't let Esther know.* The lengths Connie was prepared to go to, to keep her daughter from pain, even if her efforts were misguided. 'She just can't express it in the way other mothers can, you know that.'

'I should be *there*, looking after him, spending my Saturday at his bedside. Not here. But I have to stay, she can't be left on her own. You heard her screaming earlier; what if she's like that when she wakes up again, scared, worried about strangers touching her? Even Madeleine got a smack in the mouth when she first met Mum.'

'What?' Selina leaned back with an incredulous laugh. 'Seriously?'

'Madeleine tried to convince Mum that she should stay and help with the night shift, which she did do in the end, thank God. She touched Mum's arm and her hand brushed her waist. Mum screamed and hit out. Luckily I was there, as Dad was far too weak to deal. I calmed Mum down. Madeleine wasn't hurt but she was pretty shaken.'

'Understandably so. I'm surprised she agreed to stay after that.'

'She was very understanding, actually. I think knowing how difficult Mum can be spurred her on to help more.'

Esther wiped the half-moons of shadow beneath her eyes, drying the last of her tears. 'Oh God, what if he wakes up now, whilst I'm stuck here, and he's lucid? The weekends are the only chance I have to be with him for any length of time. It's been happening less and less, but what if he wakes up and wants to speak to me, properly, and I'm not there? What if I miss it?' The last words eked out from between clenched teeth, the distress wiped away by her bitterness for what her mother had done.

Or what she *thought* Connie had done to herself, reasoned Selina.

She followed Esther's gaze to Connie's door. Madeleine had been waiting for Connie to say something. The suspicion rose again.

'You said Madeleine spoke to your dad a lot.' Selina chose her words carefully.

Esther nodded.

'Do you know what they spoke about?'

'No, of course not. It's confidential; Madeleine says she treats it as seriously as a priest treats confession. Why do you ask?'

Selina's breath was still in her lungs. 'Did Connie ever worry about it? What he might be saying?' She felt Esther stiffen.

'Why, what are you thinking? Stop pussyfooting and just say it, for God's sake.' The ward was quiet, the only sounds their hushed voices and the occasional beeping of heart monitors.

'Why do you think Connie did it?' Selina said.

'Because Dad was her saviour, her whole world, and he's dying. I don't think she can bear to watch.'

Her voice was defeated, and Selina appreciated how the past few months had taken their toll. The constant heightened emotions, the lack of sleep, the worry, the fear, the anticipation that at any moment something else would happen to make everything even worse.

'All that matters is that she gets better,' Esther said, pinching the bridge of her nose, 'that she gets home in time to see Dad before he—'

'Esther, I'm sorry, I'm not trying to upset you, it's just that—'

'She doesn't want to be left with me.' The words were spilt quickly. 'She knows that, once Dad passes, I'll become her legal guardian and I'll have power of attorney. She doesn't want that. She doesn't want to be left with me. She never has.'

'That's not true.'

'She asked for *you*. As soon as she woke up, as soon as she saw *me*, she asked for *you*.'

Selina flinched.

'Why?' Esther asked, spinning in her seat so her back was to her mother's room, her face towards Selina. 'Why did she ask for you?'

Selina couldn't avoid answering, she knew that no nurse or Saturday work call was going to save them with an interruption.

And maybe it was time to start speaking the truth.

Half a decade of keeping this godforsaken secret had cost Selina so much. What was the harm, at this stage, of telling Esther part of the truth?

'Because she knows I wouldn't take this at face value,' Selina said. This was it, she realised. She was telling her.

'Stop talking in bloody riddles.' Esther's eyes were as cold as her voice. Selina scanned them with her own, flitting from left to right, left to right, her heart a hummingbird beneath her ribcage.

'I don't think Connie tried to kill herself.' Saying the words aloud cemented the idea, transforming it from a persistent niggle to an implacable truth.

'Neither do I, not really. It was more likely a cry for help—'

'No, I don't think she did this to herself *at all*.'

Esther shook her head, her face confused. 'You think someone else did it to her?'

Telling her friend felt suddenly foolish but the words were already out. Selina nodded her head.

Esther stood, squared her shoulders. 'You think someone tried to *kill* her? My mum? Who would want to? For Christ's sake, she lives in a hamlet in rural Somerset. She has contact with a handful of people, her whole life can be drawn on the back of a postage stamp.' Esther's arms were folded tight across her body and her expression made clear that not only did she not believe her, but she thought Selina insane. 'Who the hell would want to kill her?'

Selina reached out but Esther shrugged her away, her disbelief turning to anger. 'This isn't a courtroom, Selina. The world is not solely made up of rapists and murderers. Most people are good. I don't know what's been going on in your head, you haven't spoken properly to me in years. But you are wrong. And you're making this whole thing ten times bloody worse.'

Then, two minutes too late to undo the damage, the blessed interruption arrived. A nurse, strawberry blonde and freckle-faced, hurried out of Connie's room and towards them. 'She's just coming round, far calmer than last time,' she said as she approached, not smiling but looking reassuring all the same.

Esther ran her hand through her short hair. 'Right, OK, that's good, what do we—'

'She's asking for Selina?' the woman said.

It must have been the look on Esther's face that stopped the nurse in her tracks. Selina could see the vein that ran behind Esther's ear begin to pulse.

'She's still very foggy from the sedative,' the nurse stammered, 'she's not fully awake yet, but she's said the name Selina twice so far. It might be worth both of you coming on through.'

'No, I . . . I'll let you go in.' Esther swallowed before speaking again and in that brief pause Selina wanted to take back all those texts she had never answered, phone calls she had never returned and hold her friend as Esther had held her five years ago when her own father had died.

'We can go in together, surely?'

Her friend turned, her profile sharp against the bright hospital lights. 'Don't you dare upset her, not whilst she's in this state. I'm going to go and get something I can *actually* drink, I'll give you ten minutes,' Esther said, voice as tight as the tendons on her neck.

The nurse smiled mutely and stepped back, clearing the way for Esther to leave.

The double doors swung shut behind her and Selina was left winded, not just from the hurt of her friend, but the terrifying realisation that, had Esther pushed her then, she would have told her everything.

This was why she had distanced herself.

Because, beneath the preservative need to keep this soul-rotting secret, was the urge to offload her guilt, tell all and beg forgiveness. The childlike need to whisper, *'I've done something I shouldn't have done. Something bad,'* and have her shame soothed with that most comforting of platitudes, *'Everything's going to be all right.'*

She knew it wouldn't be all right. If she told anyone, then everything was over. Her career, the last thin strands of her oldest friendship. Even her freedom. The only person she could talk to was the one person she knew wouldn't tell anyone, because their secrets were interwoven.

Connie.

She followed the nurse to the room, the curtains pulled closed and the light far dimmer than in the ward proper.

'She's awake, but only just. It'll take a while for the sedative to work its way out of her system, and until it does she's likely to be a tad disorientated.'

Connie was still beneath her white bed sheet, her arms pale and freckled, the skin on them thin and slack. Her skin was the only sign, really, of how old she was. Everything else was so childlike. Her frame was that of a thin twelve-year-old. Her hair was long and, though not as thick as it had once been, the sheer volume created by the curls hid this. Her blue-grey eyes were as large and round as a frightened child's and the image was too much.

Selina looked away.

'Thank you,' she said to the nurse, eager to be alone.

'Someone will come and collect her as soon as the MRI is free,' she said and Selina repeated her thanks, waited until the nurse had gone and then pulled her chair close to Connie. The door was open and she longed to close it, but was worried about the attention that would draw. It was best just to keep her own voice low, she decided. It's not as if Connie would say much, after all.

When she looked back Connie had turned her head, her face illuminated in an eerie glow from the second-hand light of the hallway, a green tinge added by the screen on the heart monitor and the small lights on the oxygen pump.

'You're in Musgrove Park Hospital, do you remember what happened?' Selina whispered, needing to speak to Connie before they were interrupted. Ten minutes, Esther had said. 'Do you know why you're here?'

For a second Connie was still, but her body began to go rigid with what Selina recognised to be fear. Her face became panicked. It was not the reaction Selina expected of a woman coming out of sedation after trying to kill herself. It was the reaction of a woman who had nearly been killed. Her hands scrabbled at the wires; the drip needle; the oxygen tube. Her breathing was ragged, the beeping of the heart monitor speeding up as her pulse increased. Last time Connie came round, Selina remembered, she screamed so fiercely the doctors put her back under.

'Connie, stop, you have to stop.' Selina held her firmly, feeling Connie's panicked body fight even more against the touch, but she couldn't let Connie pull these wires out or medics would come rushing in. 'Breath, Connie, take a deep breath. You're scared, you're panicking, but I'm here, Connie, it's going to be all right. You have to calm down, or the doctors will come and we won't be able to talk.'

Connie's eyes focused on Selina's face, her body still writhing, but she nodded her head and Selina risked letting her go, sinking into the chair beside her.

'You asked for me,' she said again, holding Connie's gaze. It was like staring into an iced-over lake. 'You spoke, Connie. You said the words, "I need Selina,"' so I came. I said I would come whenever you needed me, didn't I, the last time we spoke?' She didn't use the melodic voice social workers had used on Connie in the past that Selina suspected drove Connie mad, but the calm, authoritative tone of an equal.

Connie nodded.

Footsteps sounded in the corridor, approaching Connie's small room, then went quiet.

'Do you need my help, Connie?' Selina's whispers became urgent.

Again, Connie nodded and those frozen-water eyes softened, before she blinked hard and they became vacant once more.

'You need to tell me,' Selina said. 'Did someone do this to you?' She held Connie's gaze.

Connie flinched.

Her eyes darted away to the door and back again, fear etched into the wrinkles.

'You need to tell me,' Selina said, trying her best to keep calm but needing to know, now. Not just whether Connie was in danger, but whether their secret was too. 'Did someone hurt you? Does someone *know*?'

And there it was. The briefest movement of her head. Connie nodded.

Selina sank lower into her seat.

'Is it her? The girl in the, the—' Selina couldn't bear to complete the sentence. 'Did *she* do this to you? My God, what were we thinking? What was I thinking?' She scrubbed at her eyes with the heels of her palms, could feel her empty stomach churning.

Leaving her chair, she walked to the other side of the room, the window letting in the bright, mid-morning sun. She saw a tree-lined car park and the maternity wing opposite.

'I should never have done it. I don't know what possessed me. I was so damn cocky, thought I was so clever.' She stared out at a young, ginger-haired man pacing outside the front entrance, sucking on a cigarette and blowing clouds of smoke behind him. Even from this distance Selina could feel his apprehension. He's young, shabbily dressed and clearly anxious, but despite all this Selina envied him, the fact he was surely here to support another person, that he was worried about someone outside of himself.

'I hid that damn box in my flat. I can hardly bear to go in there now, knowing it's waiting, reminding me of my own sodding hubris.' The glass misted with her breath but she didn't take her eyes off the man, trying to fathom if he was waiting for his partner to give birth, or hear news of a pregnancy scan or waiting to discover if his wife's having IVF twins. Why did she even care?

A flash of pain seared through her and she closed her eyes against the picture her imagination was trying to force her to see. Not a ginger man smoking and pacing, but Austin. Waiting for his wife to give birth to the child they'd raise together.

Selina's inability to focus annoyed her. The immediate

problem so insurmountable, her mind was desperate to think of anything else.

'I lost him because of this,' she said, but she couldn't look any more and turned her back to the window. 'I can hardly be in the same room as Esther, for fear she can see right through me. My whole life, for these past few years, has been built around no one finding out what I did for you.' She walked back to the bed, aware that she didn't have long before Esther returned.

'And now *she's* here? Mia?' She forced herself to say the name as a form of penance, the same way she forced herself to drink in the Three Bells pub, *their* pub, immediately after breaking up with Austin, as she forced herself to sleep in her flat during the first few years of taking custody of the tin box. 'The worst thing is, I'm not surprised. I've always known she would come back, you can't keep a thing like this hidden forever. It *was* her, wasn't it? It was Mia?' Selina was so sure of it that she could feel her fingertips tingle in the same way they did in a courtroom, waiting for a not-guilty verdict.

But Connie didn't nod her head, didn't move. She stared at Selina with that unreadable, unflinching gaze.

'What are we going to do?' Selina said, though she was asking herself, not Connie. Arrogance had got her into this mess, the belief that she knew better than the system, that she could control what could not, should not, be controlled. A cocky junior barrister who'd thought they knew the law inside out, could act as judge, jury and jailer.

'What are we going to do?' Selina needed to think, to get a plan set in her head but she stopped, looked down at her arm. Connie had grabbed Selina's sleeve, she was shaking her head.

'What?' Selina said, alarmed by the look of pain on Connie's face, her cheeks red and eyes bloodshot. Still, Connie shook her head, back and forth on her pillow.

'It's *not* her?' Selina sank back into the chair beside the bed. 'Is that what you're telling me?' Connie stopped still, raised her eyebrows as if to say, *yes, yes, that's it.*

'But it must—' Selina said. 'Who else could it be? Who else would have reason? It *must* be Mia—'

Connie pulled Selina towards her, grasping her coat and pinching the skin on her arm in the process.

Selina's ear was inches from Connie's mouth.

'She's already dead.'

Chapter Nineteen

Connie

Saturday morning

The three words freeze Selina in place. She stutters, her olive skin washing pale and eyes blinking hurriedly, her face telling me, *no, that can't be right*.

Had I a different body, I could tell her so much more, but whereas my thoughts are rapid-fire, my words are slow and painful to form and before I have a chance to collect another sentence, the room is invaded by porters and medics who usher Selina outside.

The MRI is free. I've been injected with a dye that will cling to the clot in my veins. It will help them locate the coagulated blood that threatens to kill me and, by doing so, they will save my life.

Does my life really warrant saving? The fire that once roared in the pit of me, that Maud used to call my inner pluck, has reduced to a candle flame and even that is beginning to flicker.

The porter wheels my trolley out of my hospital side room, the nurse trills, 'Off we go for your scan.'

Sweat beads on my spine. The thought of the MRI isn't making me feverish, but the fact I'm alone with strangers.

I could tell them who did this, I realise. I didn't have time to tell Selina, but I could tell them.

So why don't I?

The usual hospital smells are overshadowed by an incongruous scent of peppermint tea. My daughter's choice, but I can't see her anywhere. What would happen to her if I tell someone now? There would be upheaval, more so than there is already and I can tell she's already stretched to her limit.

When she was a girl I dreamed of her future; she deserved more than the meagre offerings of her parents. The world was hers. Yet she shackled herself to Taunton to look after us. If the police are called in and the truth uncovered I know she will stay, and she will fight.

Can I really do that to her?

I keep my lips closed, give myself time to think, but the sedative makes my head dull.

The porter pushing my trolley is a fat woman with firm round cheeks and calloused hands. She reminds me of Maud, so I don't look at her. I can hear the wheels on the lino, footsteps tapping the floor with various speeds and weights.

I'm pushed into a lift, feel my stomach drop as the lift moves me upwards.

The nurse talks to me in lulling whispers, telling me what they will do to me, asking me to stay very still, saying it'll be noisy but that's all normal. She is speaking as though I'm a child and I have an impulse to dig my nails into her wrist.

I'm not a child, I want to shout, I'm not a moron. Everyone thought it a miracle that Esther was so bright, when her mother was clearly an idiot and her father average at best. I wanted to shout at them, *It's me, she gets it from me, I've read Faust, for Christ's sake!* But I could never say it, or I would open my mouth to speak and drool would leak out and everyone would look away, embarrassed on my behalf.

I'm pushed into a room; a tubular scanner centre stage.

I look around, head foggy, body aching, the patch of skin on my inner elbow sore from where the pointless syringe broke its surface.

A nervousness takes over. The scanner looks monstrous, like a silo laid on its side.

Does Esther know that I'm here? Is she coming? I want to feel her hand in my hand, the soft palm, narrow fingers. She's one of the few whose touch I tolerate.

The machine burrs to life and is so, so loud and they are sliding me in and I don't want to be here but I can't say that. I want to move, to run, but I find that my head has been strapped down to the bed. When did they do that? Why can't I remember?

The remnants of the sedative dulls my senses.

I close my eyes.

I picture the fat porter who pushed me here, away from Selina and without my daughter. Only, she changes, in my mind. Her face melts away and is replaced by another. She becomes taller, broader, smelling of cigarettes and beef dripping. I remember Fat Maud.

I wrote about Maud in those letters.

And the things I did to her.

Chapter Twenty

Connie

1972

We knew we would lose Maud eventually, but we didn't think it would happen as soon as it did.

She'd had a fall whilst walking up the hill to St Nicholas' church.

In hospital they discovered that her leg, thanks to her obesity, her diabetes and her struggling smoker's heart, had turned gangrenous.

The doctors all said it needed to be amputated.

Maud, who was as stubborn as she was portly, had flat-out refused.

'Not yet,' she'd kept saying. 'Not yet. Give me a week at home, to recover. I've some things I need to set straight before I have any surgery. Just in case.' The hospital had agreed and booked her operation for a week later.

I had seen this attitude before. I was just nineteen and had looked after three people by then as a hired carer, the children of the elderly in question not wanting to give up their lives to look after their parents themselves. Not when they could pay me to sit with them, turn the radio on and off, clean their kitchens and cook food for them, dress, bathe, medicate them. Michael found the work for me, and Maud acted as a character reference, my care for Grandmother laid down as proof of my experience. I may have been an idiot, but even an idiot can change a bedpan.

It was a modern age, apparently, though this modern age passed me by. All these women who had received educations, who were expanding their horizons beyond the arbitrary border of Somerset, seemed as alien to me as those shaven-headed patients in the asylum.

Michael took me to see Maud the day after she was sent home. Our breath hung in the air; dragon steam we used to call it. The moss on the flagstone path was brittle with frost, the silos looming behind us a muted, sage green in the winter light.

I had a key to Maud's house. It had been Grandmother's, but Maud let me keep it when Grandmother . . . died.

We had expected her to be in her bed, convalescing. She wasn't. She was in her armchair by the fire. 'I lit it myself,' she said as we walked in, the smoke hitting us and making our noses run. Her house, like many in those rural parts, didn't have central heating yet. She hadn't even got around to installing an indoor lav, still relying on a bedpan at night and an outdoor loo in the day.

'Shouldn't you be resting?' Michael asked and she shrugged.

'Resting would kill me,' Maud said. She wouldn't take her eyes off me.

I sat on the floral sofa. Her house had the same layout as Grandmother's (I have never got used to saying 'as mine'. Even though, by rights, it *is* mine).

I had not seen Maud since the blood.

It was she who found me.

She who called the doctor and stood by my bedside with

her hands on her hips, pressing Dr Rowe for a better diagnosis than the archaic 'delayed menstrual flow'.

'She was lying in a pool of it! Shouldn't you run some tests, examine her, for pity's sake?'

'It's a common factor in girls such as Constance,' Dr Rowe had said as he put a bottle of paracetamol at my bedside.

'Her mind is forever stuck as the mind of a child. Her body, as a result, has delayed its progression into puberty and her menstrual cycle has been duly affected. It was a very heavy first period; the tummy cramps are more evidence of this. A hot-water bottle and the appropriate sanitary wear will sort her out.'

I could tell Maud didn't believe him. She asked me to tell her what happened.

I couldn't.

I thought of the asylum hidden in the valleys of Wales. Thought of the man fumbling with himself, the toilets with no doors on, the shelves full of Topsy and Tim. I clutched my stomach and groaned, rolled onto my side.

Maud fetched me a hot-water bottle.

When Michael came home from work he sat by my bedside and cried for me, for the pain I was in. He poured me a hot bath of salt water and watched as I submerged myself into it. He dissolved penicillin in bowls of soup as though I were a child who could not swallow tablets.

Maud came by every day for three days whilst Michael was at work.

'Just tell me,' she'd say. 'Tell me the truth of what happened.'

On and on and on she went.

I got out of bed in the end just to shut her up, to stop her calling Dr Rowe back again.

The blood left a small stain in the kitchen, dark brown by the time I discovered it. It had dripped from the gap in the boards above, dripped from between my thighs and through the floorboards onto the kitchen floor. I would never manage to scrub that stain out. Esther, at three years old, would point to it and ask what it was. I would stay silent.

Maud's house was warmer than our own. It had no chilly memories of Grandmother beating me with her hairbrush. None of Dr Rowe urging Michael to send me away. None of the blood that pooled beneath me as I lay, unconscious, on the bedroom floor.

Maud's house smelt of cloves and cigarette smoke. Whenever I smell cloves, I think of her still. She was wearing a dress that looked more like a sack; shapeless and tight where it clung to her thighs and her bust. Her face was paler than usual but her cheeks were still gloriously pink. Her hair was unkempt and a smudge of jam marked her chin.

You would never have known that she was so ill that doctors were gunning to take off her leg.

You would never have thought, to look at her, that by the end of that week she'd be dead.

'You really should be resting,' Michael said again and she looked at him queerly, I thought.

'Why don't you make us some tea?' she asked.

I stood up to go, but she held up her hand to stop me.

'You need to rest, too,' she said, looking at me. 'Michael will make the tea; won't you, Michael?'

He left us and went into the kitchen. I could hear him fill the kettle and place it on the Aga.

'I'm glad you came,' Maud whispered. Her words were for me only, just like her slabs of new bread and jam were just for me as a child. 'I've told Dr Rowe that you'll come and look after me this week, before I go back into hospital to have my leg sorted.' She patted her thigh and I could see that the lower half of her leg was bandaged thickly in cream linen. 'Will you?'

I nodded.

'Good, because I want to talk to you.' She glanced sidelong at the kitchen door to make sure Michael wasn't coming.

I spent the rest of the visit staring at my toes, counting out the seconds in my head. I thought of Carl Friedrich Gauss's biography, remembered his method of using clocks as calculators. I thought of H. G. Wells' *Time Machine*. I thought of winding back in time, erasing and subtracting the damage I had done, the pain I had caused, the lives I had taken, until I was a baby again in my mother's arms.

I would go back further.

I imagined myself inside her.

I pictured her finding a wire coat-hanger, uncoiling the twisted neck, crouching on the floor and forcing it inside, purging me from her womb. I wanted her saved from the torment I would cause.

'Come by tomorrow then, Connie.'

I snapped my head up, looked straight at her, though my vision was still clouded by the daydream of my mother. I saw myself in the glass on the picture above Maud's head and for the first time in a long time I realised I looked nothing like my mother. How could anyone have ever thought I did?

My mother had been beautiful: pale, freckled skin; thick curls of blonde hair she would straighten with the iron; those deep, blue-grey eyes full of ambition, kindness, spirit. I was a void.

I was nothing.

'Connie?' Maud cocked her head to one side, narrowed her eyes, looked at me as if trying to read my mind and I thought, *Don't do that. Please, don't do that.*

I nodded, indicating that I'd see her the next day.

I followed Michael out of the house. I felt a jolt run up the length of my spine. I glanced behind, as the door to Maud's house swung closed. I caught her gaze as she watched us walk away.

That night, through the gauzy film of the thin bedroom curtain, I saw the tops of the silos in the field behind the cottage, peeping in. They saw everything, on the day of all the blood. The day my child oozed out of me like melted ice cream. They saw me cry and beg for forgiveness. Watched as I clawed my face with my hands, crying out a thousand apologies. They saw me hide the coat-hanger beneath the bed so that no one would know what really happened, so I could lie and people would believe me. They saw it all.

Maud saw the aftermath.

She thought she knew but she didn't. She asked questions and probed and thought she was doing the right thing but she wasn't, she had it all wrong; and I saw that hospital again, that asylum, the urine on the neck and the shaven heads and I knew she would speak and talk and probe and send me there.

It happened on the second day I looked after her, when she'd mustered up the courage to confront me. I say I looked after her, but really she was so stubborn as to be impossible to care for. When I arrived that morning her bad leg was up high on a stool in front of her. Despite asking me to come and help, she had already done most of the housework herself. The fire had been cleaned and relit, the old ash saved in a bucket to smother the flames later. Even the tea was brewing in a pot in the kitchen; I smelt the tannin mix with wood smoke as I walked through the door.

'I need the company more than the help,' she said, watching me eye the swept floor. 'You can sit with me today, we can talk.'

On the coffee table were several pieces of paper. They looked somehow official, similar to those reams of paper that were brought out after Grandmother died. That was when it became apparent that I was to inherit the house in place of my mother, that Michael had better act as power of attorney to stop anyone taking advantage of me. It was nothing to do with Grandmother's kindness. It was an oversight; she had never changed her will. She had left everything to my mother and, as my mother was already gone, it reverted to me. She left nothing for Aunt Charlotte.

'Sit next to me,' Maud said, and patted the space beside her.

'Sheets,' I said and looked upward, towards her bedroom. My voice was quiet and sounded strange, even to my own ear. That single word was difficult to say, the connection from my brain to my vocal cords hard to manipulate. But I said the word because I knew it would make her happy. Michael liked me silent, just as Grandmother had preferred me silent; he said he was just used to me better that way. Maud always liked me to speak.

'You did all that yesterday. Sit down next to me. I need to talk to you.'

I looked at the papers on the table, remembered the look in her eyes when she watched Michael and me walk away from her house. I remembered her with Michael and Dr Rowe, talking through the options of a hospital placement; her voice then was challenging, disgusted at the very notion of sending me away. But what if she had changed her mind?

'Connie, I go back to hospital tomorrow. The doctors are adamant that I go in as soon as possible, they think it's dangerous me coming back home at all; risk of infection and so on.' She lifted her leg off the stool an inch, signalling to the foot that was to be amputated. The smell leaked from beneath the bandages, vague and quick to pass but unmistakable; putrid flesh. She looked pained but I knew it wasn't the leg that was hurting her, it was her words. 'I'm going to be away for a good few weeks, recovering, and surgery always carries its risks. Now my girls are all grown up, I've no need to worry about them, but I do worry about you, Connie.'

She put her hand on my knee and I flinched. I wanted to smack it away and my fingers itched to hit out.

She saw my discomfort but held on, her fingers curling around the cap of my knee. 'Connie, I know that something's not right. I know that it wasn't menstrual problems, a delayed cycle or whatever tosh Dr Rowe thought up. I asked some of the nurses at the hospital about it.'

I jumped then. I knocked her hand away and looked at the papers on the table, read the words. I had thought, at first, it had been her will. That she wanted to sort out her finances in case she died on the operating table, leave instructions for her adult daughters, Maria and Rosemary. But these papers had nothing to do with her legacy.

'Please don't get upset, Connie. Please.' Tears were in her eyes. She lowered her leg from the stool, readying herself to stand up but I didn't want her anywhere near me. 'I didn't mention any names, just said that I was worried and told them what had happened. The nurse I spoke to confirmed what I already thought; that it was possibly a miscarriage. That you were pregnant. That's right, isn't it?'

I shook my head so fast I felt sick, the world blurring in front of me.

'No,' I said, again and again. 'No, no, no, no, no.'

She hushed me softly, said she was sorry, that she wouldn't tell anyone and if circumstances had been different she would have taken it into her own hands, confronted whichever of the local men it had been that had taken advantage, but she couldn't.

I knew it was too late. She'd told the nurses at the hospital. The county was small, population-wise, everyone was connected. They'd know it was me. They'd come for me. How many mute simpletons were there who lived out here on the mudflats?

They'd lock me away.

Call me retarded, even though I wasn't.

Call me dumb and deficient, even though it wasn't my fault I couldn't speak.

Accuse me of having *unhealthy appetites* for opening my legs, when morons should keep their knees pressed together.

I stopped shaking my head but my whole body still trembled. I saw the papers on the coffee table more clearly. I saw the symbol for the hospital in Wales, the words *care, respite, treatment*. They would shave my head and leave me to rock, back and forth, by a barred window. My books, I thought, my books. I'd never read a decent one again.

'It's not right for such a young girl to be in this position, Connie,' she said. I was so angry I swear I felt my liver begin to boil, my insides hot with rage. 'I want to look after you, to make sure you're properly cared for and I can't do that when

I'm in hospital. I thought Michael was looking after you, but he can't be, can he, if you got pregnant?'

I opened my mouth, closed it, opened it, closed it. My jaw was tight, my tongue like a calcified bone in my mouth, my throat narrow. I couldn't speak, couldn't find the words, any words. Michael was at work at the school. I was all alone with Maud and she wanted to send me away.

She wanted to send me *there*.

She hadn't even seen it, had no idea of the place she was trying to trap me. For her, hospital meant a bed and nurses fussing over her for a week. For me, it meant lopping my hair off and running electricity through my brain, the only sacred part of my body that worked the way I wanted it to.

She had no idea. My hands coiled, nails dug into my palms.

'I'm not trying to scare you, child,' Maud said and she was beside me, I felt her hands on my shoulders. 'I just want to look after you. I want to help you. Please let me.' She squeezed me and my skin burned.

I lashed out.

I pushed her away and she fell, hit her bad leg on the coffee table and landed with a grunt on the floor.

She was quiet, for a moment.

The space was too small for her to have landed flat-out, so instead she was on her large bottom, legs splayed and her back resting against the sofa.

A smell leaked from her bad leg. Blood spotted the cream linen bandages and Maud looked at it, moaned softly. Her wiry hair was in disarray, her hands shaking.

'Sorry.' I stammered out the word, to please her. I was sorry.

'I just want you to be safe. I just want to look after you.'

She put her hands on the floor, ready to push herself up, and I rushed forward to help her; I didn't want to hurt her. I could feel my heart thudding wildly in my chest, could still see the hospital paperwork on the coffee table. One sheet read *Voluntary Admission*.

I didn't know what to do.

She grabbed for my arm and I helped her up, guided her back to her chair, sat her down. Her leg was bleeding, but not so heavily as I had feared.

She had always looked after me. She had always done what she thought was best. This was no different.

I heard a buzzer in the kitchen, whipped my head around as though someone would be there.

'It's the alarm reminder,' Maud said, low and sad. There was no blame in her voice, no anger at me for pushing her. Grandmother would have struck me for what I had done, but Maud had never been like Grandmother. 'For my insulin. Be a pet, won't you?'

She wanted me to give her her injection. I had done it before, I knew what to do.

I nodded and went into the next room where the insulin kit was waiting on the table. I pulled back the zip and there were the needles. Five were in the bag, all made up, but she would only need one at a time. Any more than that could be fatal, in the delicate condition she was in.

I took the bag with me to the living room, where Maud was twisted in her seat with her back facing me. She never liked watching the needle go in.

I knew I was going to do it, but still my mind closed, my thoughts stopped.

'I'm sorry to have frightened you,' she said.

I lifted her cardigan, her blouse, her vest. Her skin was pale and thick on her waistline, pockmarked with bruises from other doses.

'I just need to know you're being looked after whilst I'm away.'

I wiped the skin with an iodine wipe and watched it turn orangey-brown.

'And I know it's scary, but it's only for a short while, I promise. If you agree to it, if you sign yourself in, then I can collect you again when I'm out of hospital.'

I knew she believed this. I also knew of the countless other people who had gone into an asylum never to come out again. I had read about them, every account I could get my hands on, everything from *The Woman in White* to *The Bell Jar*. It wasn't as simple as saying, *'I want to go home.'*

She breathed in sharply, as she always did when the needle broke through. She didn't notice that it wasn't just one. I squeezed the tops on three of the syringes, forcing their fluid into her flesh all at once.

My hands shook. I pulled them out of her skin, threw them into the medicine bag, zipped it closed.

She moved her hand to her back, rubbed the injection site. 'Thank you, my love,' she said.

Maud turned to look at me and held my hands between hers.

'Get us a cup of tea. Let me talk to you properly, tell you my plan.' She smiled at me, her kind face full of worry.

I nodded and stood up, took the medicine bag with me and returned it to the dining table. I stood and stared at the empty syringes for what felt like hours, though it must have only been a few minutes.

What had I done?

Maybe it wasn't too late, I thought. Maybe three syringes weren't enough to kill her. Maybe she would be OK. She was hugely overweight, after all. She had been taking insulin for the past four years. Surely her body would have been able to cope with three at once?

I went to the sink, washed out the cups and made fresh tea and, as I turned, I saw the food that Maud had laid out on the counter. A fresh loaf of crusty, white bread. A pat of butter. A jar of new jam.

The kettle boiled slowly and I spent the time slicing the bread, spreading the toppings, thinking how I would find a way to solve this problem, to sort this mess out. There had to be another way, something else I could do.

I heard a noise from the living room. Not a scream or shout, not a gasp or call for help.

I heard a dull, heavy thud.

When Michael found me later that evening, after he came home from work, I was sitting on the floor of Maud's living room. Her body was largely in the same position it had been in when she slumped to the floor from her chair. Her soft, cold face was between my hands, her head on my lap, a few wiry strands of her hair clinging to my cardigan. My eyes had dried, but my face was still tear stained.

It was Michael who called the hospital and they sent a coroner's ambulance. Michael talked to the police officer, explained what he thought had happened. I was ushered away, given tea, asked if I was all right in too-loud voices. Everyone looked at me with big smiles and sad eyes, poor girl etched into the lines of their faces.

I don't know what they thought she died of, whether they put it down to a heart attack, something to do with her diabetes or her leg. Her daughter Maria came down and dealt with the arrangements, I never found out. But no one checked the bin for the bag of syringes. They didn't see the hospital paperwork burning in the grate. They never knew that, by the time they arrived, I had covered my tracks as best I could.

I have never been as stupid as people think.

Chapter Twenty-One

Selina

Saturday

When the first seeds of doubt began to take root, after Esther's phone call on Friday, there was only one person Selina could think of who would want to hurt Connie.

Mia.

It had seemed such a certainty, even the half-baked idea that it could have been Madeleine came to crumbs.

And yet . . .

'She's already dead.'

The memory of Connie's words broke through Selina's thoughts with the rush and pull of a tide, never making sense but breaking, again and again, across any other logical option.

It couldn't be possible.

She couldn't be dead. Selina would have known if she was. Yet she was certain it was true.

She didn't know how long she'd been sitting in the far corner of the HDU ward, trying to piece together her thoughts. Connie had been wheeled back into her room, but the nurse had told Selina not to go in whilst the doctors were with her. There was no sign of Esther yet, either.

It was Austin who came out of Connie's room first. He strode towards her, the way he used to do when they arranged to meet in a bar in the early days of their relationship. He would spot her in the Friday-night crowd and carve his way through the throng, not smiling until he had reached her.

As he walked towards her now, she knew that he hadn't changed. It was she who was different. Her carefree temper had been replaced with watchfulness. Her sense of humour negated by shame. Even her arrogance was gone, and what was a barrister without arrogance?

Cold.

Hard.

Impenetrable.

'Have you seen Esther?' she asked when he was within earshot.

'No, but someone's going to track her down, Connie's asking for her.'

'How is she?'

Austin frowned, his iPad held to his chest. 'Stable, but we're keeping her on a low-level sedative for now. Bit of an odd result, to be honest. What's stranger is that she doesn't want Esther to know, just yet. Connie asked that I speak to you first.' He raised his eyebrows and Selina was struck by another memory, that of him teaching her chess in the Three Bells. He would lull her into a false sense of security and then wipe the win from beneath her.

Selina didn't respond to his eyebrow raise, so he sighed and asked her to follow him to a consulting room.

Two pairs of black, upholstered chairs sat facing each other across a low coffee table, a water machine in the corner, as though they had suddenly stepped out of a hospital and into the waiting room for Esther's solicitors' firm.

Austin took the chair opposite and placed the iPad screen-up on the table with Connie's handwriting clearly on show. *Tell Selina first.*

He nodded towards it. 'She wrote that after I talked her through the location of the blood clot. She was adamant that Esther wasn't to know. She said you're her lawyer, of all things.' He gave an awkward laugh, expecting her no doubt to deny it, explain it away as one of Connie's oddities.

Selina didn't say anything. The puzzle deepened. If Connie wanted Selina to know and not Esther, that meant that the injuries Connie sustained *were* connected to that damn box of secrets. But if Mia was dead, then who else could be involved? What was she missing?

'I thought she must have made a mistake, the sedative confusing her, but she was adamant.' Austin's look changed; it was as though he was seeing her for the first time, as if he didn't know her at all.

He doesn't, she thought, unable to keep the poignancy at bay.

'Are you not going to explain?' Austin snapped. 'Why the hell does Connie need a lawyer? And why you? You're a criminal barrister, not a solicitor.'

'I can't go into it.' She gave a tight-lipped smile, paused long enough for her refute to sink in. 'She wanted me to know the results of the scan and I'm happy to comply. Do you have them?'

Austin mirrored her smile. 'Of course.' He sat up straight and laid his hands on his knees. His wedding ring glinted on the finger of the same hand that had once cupped her face as he asked her not to leave him.

He had never begged. He had accepted her decision and left her alone. It had been his willingness to respect her wishes that had driven home what she had lost.

His manner was all at once the professional bedside manner one would expect from a good doctor. 'The results of the scan are, to say the least, confounding. The biggest clot is located beneath her right armpit, deep in the axillary artery—'

'Her armpit?' A new feeling began to worm through her. She felt the ground tilt and if she hadn't already been sitting she would have stumbled.

'Yes, at the point where the subscapular branches from the axillary, about here, look.' He removed his white coat, the short sleeves of his shirt revealing tanned skin despite it being January. He held his right arm up and pressed his index finger into the point where the crevice of his armpit gave way to the first gentle slope of his pectorals.

Selina stared where he pointed, her breath becoming shallow. 'You said the largest of the clots. You mean there's more than one?' She tried her best to keep the tremor from her voice and to pretend it was a client he were briefing her on rather than her best friend's mother.

Even as he gave her his answer, the answer she already knew he was going to give her, she tried to distract herself. She looked at the hair on his toned forearm and tried to picture that arm around another woman during a winter holiday. Wondered that, if she could perhaps fathom how Austin could go from being in love with her to married to someone else in the space of three years, then maybe she could make sense of this. Perhaps he was going to say something different, that the second clot was behind her knee, or in her pelvis or anywhere, anywhere other than—

'The second clot is beneath her left armpit, smaller, but it's still vital that we remove that too. From the scan, that one looks intact, so it's less likely to break down as the right-hand clot is . . . Selina, are you OK?'

'No, I need a bathroom, or a sink—' She stood up but the movement was too quick, too unsettling to her stomach, which felt as if it were turning waltzer-like inside her. The room began to spin. Austin must have seen the sudden green shade that enveloped her cheeks because he reached for the wastepaper basket and thrust it to her.

'I'll walk with you to the bathroom,' he said, but too late. Doubled over the small bin, she emptied her stomach in cramping heaves, filling the room with an odour of coffee and bile.

'Here, have some water,' Austin said when the heaving had died down. He placed a transparent plastic cup beside her. 'Sip it, don't gulp or you'll be sick again.'

'I'm sorry,' she said, looking up but not able to meet his eyes, her cheeks red with embarrassment now. 'Where should I . . .' She nodded to the bin in her hands. She felt both mortification and gratitude when he took it from her and disappeared, returning moments later empty-handed.

'Feeling better?' he asked, resuming his seat, eyebrows raised in concern.

'Yes, a bit.' It was a lie. Her body was wracked with nausea. She had been desperately searching for another piece of this puzzle, but she didn't want this to be it.

'Selina, perhaps you should tell me what's going on. Why

Connie wanted you to know and not Esther, why the news of Connie's thrombosis made you ill?'

She sipped the water, pressed a tissue from the packet on the coffee table to the corners of her mouth.

She wanted to delay it, to have a few more hours, a few more minutes even, of no one else knowing what she'd done.

'What happens next?'

'Our cardiothoracic surgeon isn't in until Monday; she'll operate first thing and remove the right-hand clot. The one on the left is small enough to be dissolved by injecting the clot directly, which will be done at the same time as her operation. It's a sensitive place for such a big needle, so it's best we do it in one go when she's out for the count.'

'Why not operate today?'

'If she suffers another embolism we'll conduct an emergency operation, but that would be done by a trauma surgeon, not a specialist, so we'd rather wait if we can. We've sedated her mildly to keep her calm and stop her moving too much, which will limit the chance of another embolism occurring.'

'And you'll keep her sedated until Monday?' That would give her nearly two days to find out what she could. No need to panic, no need to tell Esther anything yet, either.

'Yes, at the lowest level we can get away with. She'll not be intubated or anything so severe, just kept calm and sleepy for another day and a half.'

There may be an opportunity to talk to her then, Selina thought, get some more facts before jumping to conclusions in the dark.

'Can I see her?' she said, tentatively, lifting her gaze to meet Austin's.

He looked incredulous. 'Are you not going to tell me

anything?' As if it were that simple. The look on his face reminded Selina of how different their working lives were, he curing the vulnerable, she defending the indefensible.

'I can't, or at least not yet.'

'Look, if you know something that could help us treat her, you need to tell us.'

He had her there, almost. Her saving grace was that she didn't know, not irrefutably, and she wouldn't until she had a chance to investigate.

'If I find something out for certain I'll tell you, but I need to speak to her first.'

'Esther should be in with her by now.' He was sulking. He always hated being kept out of the loop. Believe me, Selina thought to herself, this is one enigma you want to keep well away from. 'I can take you through to them, but as I said, Connie was sedated after I spoke with her; I'm not sure how much you'll get out of her now.'

'No, leave Esther and Connie together.' Selina changed tack. She had time. The moment to tell Esther the truth was approaching, but not until she had confirmed her suspicions.

'Do you have a copy of her scan I could take?' Selina asked before leaving the room.

'Afraid not. You may be her lawyer, but that doesn't give you rights to take her medical files off-site.' Good, she thought, be grumpy and moody and throw your toys out of the pram. Be someone I can dislike. But, of course, his face softened and he said, 'I'm not being awkward. Rules are rules and I'd get bollocked if I gave you them. If there's anything else I can do to help—'

Damn him for his sodding niceness.

'It's OK, I understand.' She forced a smile for his benefit.

'I need to head home for a bit but I'll be back.' She pulled out her phone, sent a quick text to Esther telling her she had to go but to call if she needed her, and left the HDU.

In her Bristol chambers was a file, pieced together after Connie's second plea for help three years ago. Selina would go through it, try and make sense of this sickening situation. She prayed to God her suspicions were wrong.

Chapter Twenty-Two

Connie

Saturday afternoon

Esther's here, but my head is so heavy that I can't make out what is happening and what is not, what is real and what is simply a nightmare.

My eyes open a crack but the lids are heavy and they fall again. I flit from dull light to total dark and back again, a dullness overtaking my senses.

I smell peppermint or is that a memory? I see the doors swinging shut from the HDU ward but that can't be, because my eyes are closed. It takes a moment for me to realise what that means, and even before the thoughts have formed a clear stream in my head, my daughter speaks and her words shatter my senses.

'I heard you, talking to Selina,' she is saying to me, and I think no, oh no, don't say that. She can't have heard that and again I see the double doors swinging. She had been there, outside my room. How much had she listened to?

I try to open my eyes, but my lids slide back down almost instantly and all I get is the shape of my daughter in the chair beside me, her shoulders rounded and hands clasped on the side of my mattress.

The doctors have been and gone, they have found her and

told her a white lie because I asked them not to tell her the truth. My results will be with us shortly, the doctor said, and an operation has been scheduled for Monday morning. They left us alone after that but I don't know how long ago, my mind slips and slides, concentration wavers between the past and present.

Please tell me this is a nightmare. Please tell me my daughter doesn't know what I've done.

'Or rather, Selina talking to you. She hid something for you, Mum. What was it? Tell me, please.' I feel my chest deflate in a relieved exhalation. She didn't hear my words then, only Selina's.

'What did she hide? Why did you need her to hide anything, for Christ's sake?' Her voice is tinged with frustration and I would give anything to touch her, stroke her short hair and tell her not to worry.

My thoughts float. I remember her father telling me about a school play she was in, ten years old or so. I didn't go. I remember word for word her school reports, all glowing. I didn't attend a single parents' evening. I wanted her to grow up to be independent, confident that she could steer herself through life without the need for anyone else's help. I wanted her strong so I cut those apron strings. Hearing her voice now, I wish I hadn't done it quite so well.

I hear her pain at being rejected, it flavours every word and uneasy movement. With her father she has always been easy, assured of his affection and pride. He told her at every opportunity how he loved her more than anyone else could ever love her. With him she is confident and happy. With me she is nervous and unsure and, now, resentful. Bitter.

I open my eyes and she's not by my bed any more but at the window, chewing her nails. She sees me and darts over.

'What needed hiding?' she asks and I can't tell her that.

'Just tell me, let *me* help you for once.' She is angry, but still I can't tell her. Her head is in her hands. I want to hold her, but I can't.

My eyes close.

'I'm so tired, so fucking tired,' Esther says, and I don't dare flinch at her language.

'I've been on high alert for months, caring for Dad, shipping him to and from chemo because you can't drive and you won't talk to doctors, to anyone. So I would take an afternoon off work every week and take Dad to his appointment and that was fine, it was fine, because I was helping him get better, only it didn't fucking work and it didn't make him better and the next thing I know he's refusing all treatment, all of it, and saying he wants to die at home, wants us to look after him, stay with him and I begged him, Mum, I begged him to give it one more try, I begged the doctors not to listen to him, to make him get treatment but he wouldn't listen, he'd given up. So, I took him home, I arranged for a hospital bed to be set up in the living room, did everything I could to make him comfortable and sat by his bedside every evening, whilst holding down a full-time job in the day, watching him get worse, writhe in pain so bad that he bit the tip off his own tongue.'

She inhales sharply, and I know she is thinking of the day she came home to that red slug of flesh on the floor, to her father mid-seizure with his jaws shut tight, blood dripping down his neck and chest.

She screamed, frantic, the noise waking Madeleine who,

when it was all over, cleaned and stitched the wound. I stood in the doorway and watched, not helping, just standing. *I couldn't help*, I want to tell her. *I couldn't do anything but watch him and pray to God that it was finally over, that the ordeal was finished and he was dead.* Even if I could talk, how could I say those words to my child?

'I expected it to last a few weeks,' Esther says, 'a month perhaps, but he hung on through Christmas, through New Year, and now into January and I've had to watch his agonising, slow decline, knowing there isn't a fucking thing I can do to make it better, and then it turns out that his pain relief, the one thing that was meant to make this easier, had been cocked up and he'd got nothing. Nothing. And whilst I'm doing all this, watching my own father *dying*, you go and try to fucking kill yourself, because that will help, won't it, Mum? That'll make it all better. Only it doesn't work, and you develop embolisms, scream when doctors try to examine you and you don't need to talk to anyone because I'm here, as always, to navigate. Only you don't want me. You want Selina.'

Esther sinks her head into her hands and I know she is in pain.

'I want to be with my dad,' she says in a broken voice. 'I just want to be at home with him.'

I can't keep my eyes open, can't move my hand to hold hers. I float.

I remember my home. I remember writing the letters, my explanations. They are among the things Selina hid. What would have happened if Esther had been given that box of hell and not her friend?

They were written in good faith; I thought Selina would read them and understand.

She did neither.

How can I blame her, really? She looked, glanced, was suitably horrified by what she saw and must have been too sickened to look in greater detail, to read the explanations I had so carefully written. I wanted her to understand how I had come to be in this position, why it had taken so long to ask for the help I needed.

The barest facts were there to see, why would anyone want to delve any deeper if they thought they didn't have to? It had taken every ounce of my resilience to go to her, I hadn't the strength to ask for more, I was wiped out.

I finally manage to open my eyes again and it is dark outside. It could be late afternoon, evening, early morning, I can't tell. The room is quiet, cool.

Esther has gone. Did she go home for the night or just to the café for a drink and some food? Will she be back?

What is Selina doing? Has she spoken to Esther, to anyone, about the situation she thinks she has a handle on?

What happens when we presume to understand what we see? Take me. I have starved and mistreated the sick, withheld comfort from the dying. I have killed people. I am a monster.

Selina opened the box and saw monstrous things.

I don't think she could bear to see any more. No, I don't blame her.

I blame myself. I have always blamed myself, for everything evil that has happened.

Chapter Twenty-Three

Selina

Saturday afternoon

Thrombosis in the axillary artery. Selina had come across it only once before in court but had read several more accounts from previous trials during her case research. In each instance the thrombosis had been slow to develop, the result of the artery in question being compressed for relatively short but regular bursts of time over several years. By compressing an artery, the flow of blood would slow, leading to a minuscule clot. Over time these would clump together to form a larger clot; the thrombosis. They could stay in situ indefinitely, or they could become dislodged, either through accident or design, and result in pulmonary or cardiac embolisms which could, in turn, be fatal.

Each arterial compression would have been painful and debilitating, rendering the victim immobile for the duration of each.

As she manoeuvred her Audi out of the hospital car park and made her way back onto the M5 towards Bristol, Selina tried to fathom how Connie could have received her injuries in any way other than the one Selina was familiar with. Her surroundings seemed to conspire against her, the gloaming sky keeping her thoughts dark, the slow traffic forcing her to stop and take stock.

Those prior cases had all involved rape. One victim's injuries weren't discovered until her post-mortem. Each had centred around long-standing abuse, most commonly from a partner, though occasionally from another close relative. The bruises beneath the armpits were caused by the assailant's hands or elbows as they pinned the victim down, the ensuing marks easy to conceal and impossible to detect unless you were looking specifically for them.

That couldn't be the case with Connie, surely? Esther would have known if her mother was being abused and would have done something to stop it, Selina was certain. How could anyone put up with *that* for so long and not tell anyone?

Yet Selina had come across it so frequently. Victims were reluctant to come forward, paralysed by fear or adequately conditioned not to. Conditioned to think it was normal and they deserved no better, the abusers homing in on women who had had cripplingly low self-esteem.

If Connie had indeed been the victim of abuse, and longstanding abuse at that, then it would also be possible that the person who was abusing her may well have been the same one who tried to end her life yesterday? Did he try to prevent her speaking out or was it possibly an escalation of the abuse itself?

The only person Selina could think of that would have been able to treat Connie this way for so long was her husband and, besides the fact that Connie was utterly devoted to him, the logistics of it made no sense. He was dying from cancer. By Esther's own admission he could hardly speak, let alone get up out of bed, attack Connie and stage a suicide, particularly as the morphine that was meant to be dulling his pain was rendered otiose.

And what of Mia? The woman Selina first suspected, whose image was shut inside that box of revolting things. She had reason to be vengeful, to seek her retribution. Yet Connie claimed Mia was dead.

By the time Selina had driven past the statue of the Willow Man, his long thin arms slicing the sky, her frustration was reaching its peak. If everything was connected – the possible abuse, the apparent suicide, Mia – Selina couldn't yet see how. Some piece of this puzzle was still missing.

What angered her most was that Connie didn't fit the role of victim.

There had always been a fire in her eyes and coming to Selina had required great strength. Selina remembered her determination that Esther shouldn't know anything of the box, or of what Selina had had to cover up. She didn't have an ounce of the frailty Selina would have expected. But then, Selina's main exposure to those poor wretches was in court, a place so far from reality to warrant it fictitious. Victims were asked by their barristers to portray particular kinds of behaviour the jury would sympathise with, the defendants asked by theirs to show themselves as the epitome of hard-done-by innocence. In court you're not a victim unless you look like one. In reality, you must try your best not to look like one in order to survive.

The traits that would mark Connie as being a potential victim to, for instance, social services – her silence, her unwillingness to be touched, her disassociation from the world – were a result of witnessing her parents' death and had been present since she was a young child. It would make her abuse more plausible, as it was unlikely she'd be able to effectively communicate what was happening to her. But at the same time those same symptoms reduced her contact with potential abusers. She saw so few people and other than her immediate family she had no relatives that Selina knew about.

But what *did* Selina know, really?

Connie saw her husband and her daughter, who else? Selina remembered finding letters from a mother-in-law tucked away in a drawer during one of her frenzied searches of the cottage. The wording had been odd, saccharine in its sentimentality, unsettling, but certainly not abusive.

Connie's education had mostly been self-taught. She could read well but Selina was clueless as to her other abilities. Was there a teacher, a social worker, a doctor she was in regular contact with who could have been doing this? Experience told her the abuser was usually someone close, yet Connie had no one other than her husband and, again, how could it be him? Was there a family member Selina didn't know about, someone that Esther hadn't mentioned?

A lorry approached and flashed its lights, sounded its horn. She had been sitting in the middle lane going at fifty. What was wrong with her? Why couldn't she focus?

Her Audi, though old, was well insulated and the noise of the motorway was reduced to a bland hum. The solitude of her car was usually conducive to calculating reason and motives, formulating arguments, planning the win. The problem with this, though, was that each new piece of information brought with it a web of unanswerable questions.

What had happened to Mia?

Was her death in any way related to what had happened to Connie?

Who has been abusing Connie and why?

And why now? Why this weekend?

Selina passed the exits for Highbridge, Weston-super-Mare, Nailsea. The traffic thinned and bulged, the sky grew ever darker and still nothing made sense. What was she missing?

Her sharp mind, her greatest asset, was letting her down and the frustration was unbearable, her knuckles pale from gripping the wheel. She pulled off the motorway, past the sign for the services and on towards the toll bridge to Clifton. She'd been here less than a day ago, sticking out her tongue at a little girl in the café, smiling at the child's mother.

Selina felt it then, the missing element her mind wasn't allowing her to slot into place.

Her limbs became heavy as she navigated the roundabout, her feet dull weights on the foot pedals. She stopped the car at a bus stop, ignoring a woman's look of disapproval from the shelter.

The air in the Audi became stifling, impossible to breathe, and she wound down her window. The January wind blew in the cold air and the smell of exhaust fumes. Her teeth began to chatter.

Ordinarily she would shut the victim out, concentrate on the bare facts of a case and not the emotion. This was no ordinary case. It wasn't a case at all; she had hidden everything to make sure it would never get that far and she had done it very well.

She had made a mistake.

'Help me.'

Connie had asked her, twice.

Selina had acted, defended, presumed she knew best but hadn't *listened*. What if Connie had given her that box not because she wanted it hidden away, but because she needed to talk about what was inside it? She needed to have her story heard? What if there was something else in that box she had only skimmed through and slammed shut?

If she had taken the time to ask Connie the right questions, would Connie have told her more? Written down what had happened, communicated the kind of help she needed?

Would she have told Selina then who had been doing this to her and for how long?

Chapter Twenty-Four

Connie

1963

I remember back to a time when Maud was still alive.

The asylum in the Welsh valleys was still unknown to me.

Grandmother was not yet dead.

I was nine years old.

Three years an orphan, three years in the care of Grandmother, three years since I had last spoken.

'No.' My chin trembled as I said the word.

Maud covered her mouth, but I could see her eyes smiling, filled with happy tears of shock and relief.

'I don't understand it,' Grandmother said, and even she looked pleased, her thin wrinkled cheeks puffing out in a smile. A smile! 'You really are a miracle worker, Michael.' She patted him on the shoulder. Her smile wasn't for me. 'It shows such testament to your character, really it does. Well done, my boy, well done.' She pulled him in for a hug and his face pressed to her wrinkled cheek. He looked at me; I could see his face grimacing in my periphery but I didn't meet his eye and turned my face towards Maud.

'Can you say anything else, child?' Maud lowered herself to my level, sitting her huge bottom back on her heels. She smelt of her kitchen: of Yorkshire puddings and gravy. Her meaty hands rubbed my shoulders, her face was expectant and I wanted to make her happy, I wanted her to be happy, but the word still choked me, my body hurt, my sides and stomach still ached from all the vomiting.

I could taste the sick in my mouth, under my tongue, could feel strings of semi-digested apple flesh caught between my teeth.

'Stop,' I said to her, so quietly she had to bend her head forward to catch it. She realised what I said, her forehead furrowed.

'What did she say?' Grandmother shouted. 'What else did Michael teach her to say?'

'I think she's a little overwhelmed, Agnes,' Maud said, giving me a worried half-smile. 'I think she might need a bit of a rest. I'll take her upstairs.'

She took my hand and neither Grandmother or Michael objected. I still let people touch me, then; the fear of skin on my skin was yet to develop.

Maud walked me up the narrow, winding staircase at the edge of the kitchen, through Grandmother's bedroom with its cast-iron double bed, the tin bath by the window in the centre of the room, the small wardrobe. She led me through to our bedroom, the bedroom I shared with Michael right next to Grandmother's. It was only when I was with an outsider that I appreciated how very small our house was, how very tiny a space for three people to live in.

A heady scent of fruity bile hung in the air, a pool of thrown-up apples on the rug. I began to cry.

'What on earth happened?' Maud asked.

I rubbed my hands over my face, tugged my fingers through my hair. I didn't know how to tell her. I didn't know how to describe it.

She put her hand on my shoulder. I shuddered.

Her instinct being to comfort anyone in distress, Maud hunkered down and her hand slipped onto my waist.

Instant fire.

My skin, beneath her hand, burned and itched in a way I had never felt before. I pushed her away and she fell back onto the rug. Still, my own hands stayed on my waist, trying to rub myself free of the feeling, the sensation of fingers on my skin. Up until that day it had never bothered me, but from that day on I couldn't bear it. It was as though the memory had embedded itself physically into my skin; one touch brought it all back with violent clarity.

'Connie? Connie, stop it!' Maud tried to stop me but I had the fight in me of a tiger, the fight that had abandoned me that morning. I clawed at her, at myself, rubbed the skin on my waist to raw sores. I couldn't bear the feeling of anything there, touching me there, tickling me.

It was horrible. Intolerable.

I heard feet running upstairs and it was then that I realised I was screaming. No words, just noise, bursting from my throat, accompanied by the scratching sound of my nails on my clothes and my skin.

'What the hell are you doing?' Grandmother yelled, pulling me towards her and pinning my hands to my sides.

The tender underside of my arms pressed against my waist and the sensation became worse, even worse.

'Look at your clothes!' Grandmother shouted, spittle landing on my cheeks, mixing with my tears. 'You've torn your clothes!'

'Agnes, she's upset!' Maud tried to interject but Grandmother shot her a look.

'You stupid girl,' she said, looking back at me. 'You stupid, wicked girl. Everyone out, everyone!'

Dumbfounded, everyone obeyed her. Michael backed out of the room, so too Maud despite the uncertainty written on her face. She had never seen Grandmother so het up; so shocked was she by her friend's outburst that she didn't know what else to do but obey.

Grandmother looked at me as though I was a wild dog, unpredictable and frightening. She, too, backed out of the room, closed the door. Bolted it. Left me with my vomit and my wretched, tingling skin.

'I'll call the doctor,' she said, and they all walked away. 'Michael, tell me again what happened.'

My skin was still sensitive at my waist and my chest and my groin.

My throat still burned, not from being sick but from fighting for breath, from the effort of speaking after so long in silence.

It was a game, a harmless tomfoolery. Michael ran up behind me that morning. Chased me up the stairs after I had splashed him with sudsy water from the sink.

'Hey, you cheeky monkey!' he'd shouted, him chasing, me laughing, Michael laughing. 'Come back here!' Through Grandmother's bedroom and into our own.

I had tried to close the door, booting it with my foot before diving on my bed and trying to hide beneath the covers. Michael was fourteen, his legs strong and fast and his arms bulging with developing muscle. The flimsy door was no match for him.

I hid, stifling a giggle as best I could, beneath the blankets.

He grabbed my foot.

Pulled me out.

His fingers found me, as they had done so many times, and began to dance across my skin.

'I'll teach you to soak me!' he said, as his fingers slipped beneath my cotton top and tickled the skin on my waist.

I writhed and twisted on the bed, his leg pinning me down. I was only nine, still thin as a whip and small for my age, my skin stretched taught against my ribcage.

His hands kept going, I kept twisting, eyes squeezed shut, kept writhing and then I felt something. Something brushed against my arm as I squirmed and he . . . he groaned.

I opened my eyes and saw his trousers, a bulge at the crotch.

His hands were still all over me, touching my skin and I suddenly felt this was wrong. I didn't understand it, the same way that I didn't understand why, a year ago, he started sleeping in his own bed on the other side of our tiny twin room. The same way I didn't understand the noises he made in the quiet of the night when the moon shone through our thin curtains and hit on his silhouette, shaking and rocking beneath the bed sheet. Even if I had been able to speak, I knew that I wouldn't have asked him about it. The best thing was to turn my back, face the window and the dark outlines of the silos.

But this wasn't the middle of the night.

This was a bright, cool morning and I didn't like that look in his eye or the way he was pinning me down with his legs whilst he tickled me, or how he had moved my legs so that they were between his and my thigh rubbed against that bulge in his trousers.

'No,' I said.

I spoke aloud, I know I did. I felt the air move over my vocal cords, my throat strangely open.

A pause, a beat.

He didn't stop. He smiled, mouth wide and teeth on display. He tickled me harder, his hands moved further up and down my body and the feeling was suddenly dreadful; a torture rather than a tickle, an unbearable itch I couldn't scratch.

'No,' I said again. I said it. I did.

I couldn't breathe.

His teenage body loomed above my childish one, trapping me.

'I'm making you speak,' he said. 'I've made you speak again!'

I couldn't move my legs. My arms, birdlike and weak, flapped uselessly against his heavier frame.

The look on his face was the most frightening thing of all.

'Stop,' I said, and he smiled wider. I didn't recognise him. He was so suddenly changed from the boy who had protected me and hugged me, wiped my tears and saved me biscuits. He was my confidant, my friend, my cousin. He wasn't this thing.

'Stop!' I said, over and over and over.

He laughed; manic and excited, so horrible to hear.

Did he think I was laughing?

Did he think I enjoyed it?

Is that why he moved his hand down, down below the waist band of my skirt?

Just tickling me, that's all.

It was too much.

My body fought back.

I was sick.

He stopped, just like that, and jumped off me. His face looked shocked, not horrified.

He dragged me downstairs, breathless and excited, to tell Grandmother and Maud what had happened.

Numb with shock, I repeated these exciting new words I could suddenly say and thought how useless they really were coming from a mouth such as mine.

I never said them again. I knew no one would listen to me. Not even when he returned to my bed, a few weeks later.

I haven't been able to bear the touch of another person since. The slightest brush of a hand on my arm sends me wild and makes me lash out. Should a person hold my waist, or touch that sensitive spot at the base of my spine, then it's all I can do not to hit them, bite them, scream.

Michael's touch was always different. He always knew this, too. His touch seemed to calm me almost instantly and what a miracle worker he was. Everyone always said so. It was Michael who made me speak again, it was Michael who would bring me down from one of my moments of unacceptable high passion. He was always so proud of that, believing it was this connection that kept us together.

If he had accepted the truth he would never have been so proud. I feared his touch so much that it detached my mind from my body and made me breathless with dreadful anticipation to the point where I couldn't bear it. I was never calm, I was afraid.

I was afraid of the way his face would change in the night. Of how his body would slide up to mine, one of his strong hands holding my arms above my head, pinning me down to the bed. How his elbow would press into my armpit, the pain of it immobilising, the bruises perfectly hidden from view. The pain that would follow, searing between my legs, the dry, grating pulses of him inside me. The hot, wet mess he left behind.

I was afraid of Grandmother, who heard these night-time horrors from her room just next door and would beat me the following morning when Michael had gone to school or, later, to work. I had turned him, she said. I had infected him, made him do things he shouldn't be doing.

I had to stop it, she said. *I* had to stop.

I was afraid, most of all, of myself. At first this fear was one born from self-loathing, an understanding that I did, indeed, turn good people bad. It wasn't until I was older, fourteen, and my hands lifted the pillow from Grandmother's dead face, that I began to fear myself. What I could drive people to do. What I could be capable of.

Chapter Twenty-Five

Selina

I f what Selina suspected was true, which she was almost certain it was, then she couldn't waste any time. She had to get back to Taunton, explain everything to Esther and start giving Connie the support she had needed all along.

But first she wanted more information, some clue as to who could have been behind this. When it had happened and if it was still happening. The thromboses could be years old, decades even, or they could be recent; there was no way to tell. Connie would be out for the count until morning, a window of time Selina could use to go through the papers in her locker.

The car park nearest the crown court was a drab tarmac pitch with no security cameras and a graffiti problem. It wasn't a place sensible people went after dark, and certainly not one you'd leave a nice car in. Selina's, however, had been bought when Labour were still in power and had at least one dent for every year since. As for being sensible, her sense had been overwhelmed by the guilt of what she had done.

Or hadn't done.

She made her way towards her chambers with a Starbucks voucher for the homeless man already in her hand, but he wasn't there. She felt, absurdly, as though she had let him down, as if it were her fault she couldn't give him something. Her conscience missed the salve of donation.

The office was usually quiet on a Saturday. Perfect for what she needed to do. The file she kept there, secured at the back of her locker, was all the paperwork she had on Connie and her family. It held the details of the arrest three years ago, the release papers from the police station, the witness transcripts. All the things that kept Selina from having a peaceful night's sleep. Among them were scant papers relating to the family's past.

Inside, she paused. Electric light bled from beneath the reading-room door.

Dammit.

Another barrister must be working the weekend, preparing for a case. She wouldn't be alone after all, but it wasn't the end of the world. The locker room would be impossible to work in; it was too cramped and would raise suspicion should someone come in. No, she would take a desk at the far corner of the reading room (no one had offices of their own any more). She wouldn't be disturbed, it wasn't a done thing to interrupt a fellow lawyer beyond the usual pleasantries.

Five minutes later and with the file secured under her arm, Selina walked into the reading room and took back every presumption she had just made.

Most barristers would respect each other's space and privacy. Most would be too consumed with their own case, and their income, to stick their nose in. Most.

'Fucking hell, Alvcrcz, not Saturday night too?' Dick Chapel sat at the only desk in the centre of the room, as if basking in a spotlight. His workaday suit had been replaced with weekend attire: tailored jeans and a close-fitting Welsh rugby top, his hair carefully styled to look tousled, as though a lover had just run their fingers through it. The attention-loving, forty-something Peter Pan was far from a regular lawyer.

"Fraid so.' Selina marched towards the corner desk, determined to stick to her plan. It wouldn't take her long to rifle through her file, it wasn't thick, and if needs be she could always abandon the chambers and take the paperwork home. She didn't like to do that, preferred the security of the chambers where a file of abandoned criminal proceedings didn't look at all out of place and the name Lithgow rang no bells. Besides, her Clifton flat was her last remaining sanctuary from what she'd done, she couldn't bear to taint it.

'Wotcha working on?' he asked in his upper-class drawl, lolling one arm over the back of his solid oak chair. His desk featured two neat piles of what Selina recognised to be transcripts, though she wasn't close enough to be sure.

The reading room, normally loaded with the scent of old leather and the mustiness of legal tomes, smelt strongly of Eau Savage, the cologne masking an underlying aroma of hair-of-the-dog. Chapel went out last night after all.

'Case research.' She hoped her clipped answers would ward him off.

Sitting at a desk of her own she rifled through the file, slipping to the back anything she certainly didn't want to be seen – the police paperwork, the witness statements, the evidence log – and secured them firmly with a bulldog clip. That left her with the more generic paperwork she had lifted from the Lithgow house.

Mia obviously couldn't be involved, so Selina had to look elsewhere. She had no idea what she was looking for, but somewhere, in this humble pile of birth certificates, pension statements and similar must be *something* about Connie's past that would help Selina fathom who could have done this to her. Ten minutes sifting through Google on her phone in the car had confirmed Selina's worst fears. The chances that Connie could have developed two clots in her armpits in any way other than violent abuse were so remote as to be implausible.

Would Esther do the same search, when she found out where her mother's thrombosis was located? Almost certainly. Selina only hoped that the doctors hadn't told her the specifics yet. How much time did Selina have?

'You didn't pop by to see me, then?' Chapel was still looking at her, his mouth raised in a half-smile.

'No, Chapel, I did not.'

The pension statements were just that, statements offering nothing more than numbers and dates. She didn't even know why she had picked them up, only remembered that when she had first searched the cottage in a mad hound-dog frenzy, she had been struck by how little there was and, in the end, had taken whatever she could find. The weight of the bounty was more important than the bounty itself at the time, it made her feel as if she were *doing* something. Now, it seemed quite pointless.

'So, what's the case?' Chapel asked. He really was like a child, she thought, with an incessant need for attention.

'Nothing of great interest.' And then, in the hope of distracting him, she said, 'How about you?'

He sighed and leaned back in his chair, his elbows splayed behind his head. 'Transcripts,' he said. 'From seventeen hours' worth of sex tapes.'

Even in her stressed state, Selina couldn't hide the smile from her voice. 'Sounds right up your street. No wonder you were prepared to work a Saturday.'

'You'd think they'd at least let us watch the damn things. There's nothing arousing about reading script from a home-made movie, believe you me. Lots of ohs and ahs and only the most mundane of descriptions. I'm more likely to get a hard-on reading the shipping forecast.'

'Better boring than traumatising.' She put down the pension statements and picked up what was next; Esther's acceptance letter to King's. Why the hell did Selina take this?

'You think I should be grateful I'm not listening to some dreadful child abuse case? Dream on, Alverez, at least that would get me gunning for the conviction.' And then he added with juvenile triumph, 'Bloody puritan.'

'A puritan that's gaining on your record.' She couldn't help it, he'd provoked her into gloating. There was something unique about being in the presence of another courtroom junkie such as Chapel. It ignited the fire in her, the need to win. She started reading more quickly, abandoning the school forms and flicking through old house insurance papers.

'I have to admit, winning suits you,' Chapel said, affecting a huskiness in his voice that, Selina hated to admit, really did suit him. But she wouldn't let him distract her.

Christ, there wasn't anything in this file she didn't already know. It was starting to feel useless.

Looking back, it seemed odd there was so little paperwork in the Lithgow house. In Selina's flat there was more of everything: photos, tax returns, parking tickets. The only thing that had really struck her had been the strange letters from

Connie's mother-in-law, the paper yellowed with age but the writing still crisp.

'It gives you a glow,' Chapel said, standing up and walking towards her. His jeans were tight and clung to the muscles on his thighs as he moved. He looked like a peacock, ready to swish out his tail. 'I bet, if you were to learn how to relax a bit, have some fun, you'd look bloody stunning.'

Selina looked him in the eye. He was goading her, she knew that, and she also knew how much he loved a reaction. She said, simply, 'No,' and looked back at her papers.

Connie's birth certificate was next. It gave the details of her mother, her father, her place of birth. Gloucester. Interesting, Selina had always presumed she had been born and bred in Kilstock. Esther had never mentioned that her mum was from Gloucester, but then why would she?

'Can't blame a chap for trying.' Chapel leaned one arm on her desk, the smell of both his cologne and his alcohol-tainted sweat getting stronger.

'I believe I can, Chapel. It's called harassment.'

'Oh fuck off, I'm only pulling your leg.' He didn't look at all phased.

Perhaps there was someone from Connie's past that she didn't know about, someone from her childhood in Gloucester. Perhaps her husband did know about the abuse and protected her from this person whilst he could but now he was ill it was impossible. Or perhaps the abuse had stopped long ago and was all a distant nightmare. Esther had said Connie thinks of her dad as her saviour, her whole world. Maybe that's why.

Perhaps she could go to Kilstock whilst Connie and Esther were both at the hospital, talk to him if he was at all lucid.

'Oh Jesus.' Dick Chapel hooted with laughter and slapped the desk with his palm. 'Very bloody Somerset!'

Selina snapped her head up, saw with horror that he had lifted a piece of paper from her pile. She made a grab for it but, of course, Chapel held it just out of reach.

'I need that.' And then, realising what Chapel had just said, asked, 'What's that supposed to mean? *Very Somerset?*'

He rolled his eyes and let the paper float back down to the desk. 'I forgot you were born in Taunton, probably all seems terribly normal to you.'

'Oh, piss off back to your sex tapes.' She really didn't have time for his stupid games. Still . . . 'What seems normal?' She hated having to ask him, hated the self-satisfied grin on his face.

With one tanned finger he pointed to the marriage certificate he had been holding, his nail directing her gaze to the names.

'Most of us copulate outside of our own gene pool,' he said.

She read the certificate where it lay, the details of the bride, the groom and both of their parents clear.

The room was all at once colder.

Constance Lithgow and Michael Lithgow. She had married her cousin.

Chapter Twenty-Six

Selina

Saturday early evening

The theory she had been working on since discovering Mia's death, that Connie's abuser and attacker had been one and the same, fell apart as she stared at the certificate.

Michael was Connie's cousin. Had he groomed her from childhood and married her, trapping her in an impossible, hellish existence?

'You look pale,' Chapel said, a hint of warmth in his voice that Selina hadn't heard before. 'You all right?'

Words wouldn't come, and she nodded mutely, thinking of Connie.

'Help me.'

Good God, what had Selina done?

'Let me help,' Chapel said and pulled a chair up to the other side of the desk. All at once his rakishness was dropped, his manner becoming sombre. He lifted the stack of papers on her desk and formed a neat pile. 'What are we looking for?'

'You're not looking for anything,' she said. His cologne was too much this close and beneath its spicy scent and the smell of last night's whisky, was the bitter stale note of espresso. 'I have to sort it out myself.' She would take the file home after all, she would . . .

What the hell would she do?

Thoughts wouldn't order; she felt weak and empty, the dark wood-panelled walls and the vast shelves of books oppressive. What was wrong with her? She did this day in, day out, had read far more harrowing witness accounts, seen more graphic images than the ones now filling her head and she had never failed to get on top of them and think clearly. Why couldn't she now?

Because this case is personal.

And because she'd made it worse.

'You didn't know they were related, this Constance and Michael Lithgow.' Chapel wasn't posing a question, rather stating his conclusions aloud. 'So I'm presuming it's to do with them. They live in . . . Kilstock. Ah, look at this.' He had flicked to Esther's school acceptance. 'Their daughter went to King's, same school as you and the same school year. Esther. I know that name. Is that the same Esther you used to hang about with? The one you haven't mentioned in a while?'

She reached for the papers and took them back, slotting them into the file with the bulldog-clipped police paperwork. There was a reason Chapel was so successful, she reminded herself. That rascal persona hid a very intelligent, astute mind. All those flippant comments she had said over the years, he must have actually listened.

'The files you've clipped back, there's a police emblem. So . . . what? You helped them out in court or with a police charge? Got them off? If that's the case, then why would you be so horrified to find out they were related?' He rubbed his chin with one hand, assessing her. His forehead furrowed in concentration, his grey eyes serious and without a hint of their previous lasciviousness.

She had to get back to Taunton, talk to Esther. Did she know her parents were related? How easy would it have been for them to hide?

Very, she realised. With so few living relatives to testify, all they would have had to have done was spin a white lie about how they met and not show Esther their wedding certificate. Or, rather, all Michael had to have done. Why didn't Connie try and tell Esther what Michael was doing? Was she worried Esther wouldn't believe her?

She thought of her friend's face when she spoke of her father; adoration. He had been her champion growing up, the only one who ever attended school plays or parents' evenings. Esther had assumed all this time that her mother was indifferent.

Selina stood up, tucked the file beneath her arm, forced herself to stand strong and not tremble. 'Private case,' she said, 'it really doesn't concern you.'

'It does when it upsets a friend.' He mirrored her, standing when she stood, walking when she walked.

'Bugger off, Chapel, I'm hardly your friend.' She tried to laugh it off, using their banter to cover her grief.

'You are actually,' he said. 'You're the only one who tells me to fuck off when I'm being a cock.' He gave a genuine enough smile but his eyes remained concerned.

'Someone has to.' Again she tried to laugh it off; again she failed, her words sounding harsher than they were meant to. 'I'm sorry,' she said, 'I've just got a lot on. Look, it's nothing you need to worry about. I'm going to take it home with me, sort it out.' But she couldn't keep the catch from her voice and she felt it, the weight of her mistakes.

'You did something,' he said.

She couldn't look him in the eye; his expression was making her lose her nerve. She wanted him to stop this, to make an inappropriate comment so she could tell him to leave her alone and escape. She couldn't take this side of him that apparently wanted to help and listened to her. Kindness.

She was going to keep it together. She could sort this, there was still time. She could go and talk to Esther and tell her what happened. But then she stared down at the file. She saw the logo from Taunton police station. She remembered the name Mia.

She could make some atonement towards Connie, but Mia?

'I know a guilty look when I see one.' Chapel's hand was on her shoulder. 'Stop being so sodding proud and tell me what happened. It might help.'

If she told him, he would help her. She knew, by some providence, he would. Her load would feel lighter, she may even be able to think more clearly and yet—

'Thank you,' she said, 'but I can't.' She needed to tell someone, but that someone wasn't Chapel.

She left the room, the strength she needed to move forward innate.

It was Esther.

'If you change your mind, Alverez—' She turned back to see Dick standing in the doorway of the reading room, face still worried. She nodded and walked outside.

The wind had picked up in the short time she had been inside, curling itself beneath the collar of her coat. With each cold blast she felt her brain waking up, her focus returning. The chill air cleared her mind, the simple act of one foot in front of another restoring her sense of control.

What did she know?

Connie was married to her abuser, but it was impossible it had been he who'd attacked her. So who?

Someone who knew what happened years ago? If Mia really was dead, could it be someone acting in her memory? A relative, a friend? Christ, even a policeman gone rogue?

The homeless man had returned to his perch, face hidden by a scarf and hands tucked beneath his armpits. The white cup at his feet showed a few copper coins and Selina pulled out the Starbucks vouchers, gave him three.

The picture of her father was in her purse, Colbert Alverez. He had left Peru for England when he was in his forties and fell for Selina's mother, Lauren, despite her being twenty years his junior. As she looked at the photo, it wasn't her father she thought of, but her mother.

The pavement was lit by streetlamps and shop lights, the road full of cars. She tucked her wallet away and walked with her coat pulled tightly round her, the file secreted between the layers of her clothes and the red lining of her down-filled jacket.

Lauren's devotion to Colbert had been unshakable, and had bled into her love for her daughters, however difficult she may be to handle. When Selina was at her first year in prep, her elder sister had nearly been expelled for possessing cannabis. Lauren's wrath had been indomitable, but it wasn't for her daughter. She had aimed it solely at the Headmaster because how very dare he threaten expulsion. She won, of course. Mothers could be terrifying when they needed to be. Where was Mia's mother now? But more pressing, considering what else Selina knew about the Lithgows, where was Michael's?

The saccharine sweet words from a letter written long ago

echoed as she walked to her car. A letter for Michael from his mother, Charlotte. The syntax was so flowery it had bordered on the unhinged. How far would that woman go, Selina wondered, to avenge her son if she suspected someone of doing him wrong?

Was she aware that Connie had taken that rusted tin box, given it to Selina, putting Michael at risk?

And did she know what her darling son had done?

Chapter Twenty-Seven

Selina

Five years ago

A throbbing head and an ache behind her eyes greeted her when she awoke, the cheap wine she had got drunk on with Esther casting its evil morning-after spell. Movements sounded from somewhere in the flat; Esther clanking about in the kitchen.

Selina rolled over on the lumpy mattress and hid her head beneath the duvet.

'Morning, sunshine.' Esther hovered in the doorway, steam rising from the coffee she held in each hand. The smell of bacon drifted in with her, tempting Selina's head back out from beneath the covers.

'I feel like shit.'

'Me too.' Esther placed one cup on the bedside table and sat at the foot of the bed. 'I never sleep well when I'm that pissed. I've been up since six. It's nearly ten now.'

'Jesus!' Selina bolted upright, her head screaming at her for daring to sit up at all. 'We've missed the park run.'

'I don't think either of us are in a decent state for a 5K run, do you?'

'It would have done us good; flushed out the toxins.' As the stab of pain in her head receded, Selina became aware of the other pains in her body: a sore back, stiff limbs. 'You need to buy a better spare bed. This one's about as comfortable as a bag of spanners.'

'You're welcome,' Esther said wryly, raising one eyebrow. 'I'm a junior solicitor; you're lucky I have a spare room at all. We don't all get paid by the devil, you know.'

Selina threw her pillow at Esther's head, laughing as her friend ducked and the pillow landed with a soft thud on the carpet.

'I'm going out, I need a few bits from the shop.' Esther's voice was sweet with laughter. 'It's good to have you back.'

Selina felt a stab of something else then. Not the pain in her head from too much wine, but one born of betrayal. The events of the previous day spearheaded to the front of her mind, the phone call from Connie, the mad dash to Kilstock, Connie's struggle to tell Selina what had happened.

The front door had been on the latch when she'd arrived. Connie was standing in her kitchen, stock-still with bare feet. Her loose hair hung in blonde curls down her back, her flat chest and narrow frame adding to her childlike appearance. She never met Selina's gaze, never made eye contact with anyone, but there was something more wretched about her that day. She had chewed her lip until it cracked, her brow furrowed and wrinkled.

'I'm here,' Selina had said, walking towards her and leaning against the end of the ancient oak table. 'I'll help however I can.'

Connie's eyes showed fear. Selina smiled reassuringly, and was surprised to see tears clinging to Connie's lashes. She was such a strange-looking creature; her eyes vacant, as though her mind was constantly elsewhere. Her thin body and long, curly hair were so incongruous with the aged, troubled face and the dry, bony hands. A middle-aged woman trying to escape a child's body.

'I've known you and Esther most of my life, I'll help you in whatever way I can. What do you need me to do?'

And she had looked so grateful then, so relieved, that Selina thought she'd misread the situation all along. Maybe Connie just needed help moving furniture around or filling out a government form. She didn't expect Connie to reach behind her and pull out a metal box with a rusted, hinged lid, the width and length of a paperback novel and about six inches deep.

'What's this?' she asked as she took the box from Connie's hands. 'Do you want to write it down; shall I get your pad?'

Connie shook her head, violently, her hair fanning out, strands catching her lip and tongue.

'OK, it's OK,' Selina said, palms outstretched. 'Can you tell me, instead?'

'Michael's.' Connie's voice shook as she said his name.

Selina's stomach dropped. The air in the small kitchen-diner felt thicker, difficult to breathe. She knew, before she opened it, that she wasn't going to like what was inside.

The first few photographs were nothing unusual. Esther as a child running through the garden in her knickers. There was even one of Selina, about nine years old, playing with Esther with the two silos looming in the background. A photograph of Connie as an adult in a shapeless brown dress, her arms wrapped around her waist and her head bowed.

Then there was a face Selina didn't recognise.

A little girl who looked so much like Connie and Esther

that she could easily have been related, only her wider jaw and forehead and her larger, rounder cheekbones marking her as different. She stared at the camera with wide, frightened-rabbit eyes. She looked nine, maybe ten, years old, dressed in a generic blue and grey school uniform. Her hair reached to her shoulders in wavy lengths; a spattering of freckles decorated her nose and cheeks, positioned so perfectly that they could have been painted on. She was not a strikingly beautiful child, but instead looked very, very sweet. And very afraid.

The second photograph showed her in the same uniform but without her cardigan. Her face more frightened still.

The third showed her without her socks.

There was a fourth, a fifth, a sixth and then Selina found she could not look any more. There were a pile of photos and a stack of papers at the bottom, but she'd seen enough to know what she was dealing with. She closed the lid, her back still to Connie, and shut her eyes. The little girl was there, behind her lids, looking as frightened as ever.

She thought of Michael. His jokes, his friendliness, his overall amiability. He didn't look like a paedophile. He didn't behave like one. He had his eccentricities, his biases, but he had always seemed so very normal. They often do, Selina thought.

'Has anyone else seen these?' Selina asked over her shoulder, still not ready to turn and face Connie. Did she understand the gravity of these photographs? Was she aware of how serious this was?

'This is Michael,' Connie said, and Selina could hear her opening and closing her mouth, struggling to find the rest of the words she needed to say. 'Help,' she managed, at last.

She wanted Selina to help her . . . with what? Help to cover it up, help to stop it happening again, help to stop the girl from pressing charges?

'Does Esther know?'

Connie grunted, began to shake her head and slammed her hands onto the table with such a force that Selina jumped. Connie was trembling, the effort of having shown these to Selina seemingly taking all her strength from her.

Connie reached for her small pad of paper, for a pencil she kept in her top pocket, and scrawled, *Don't let her know.*

Selina knew that she *should* go straight to the police.

But something held her back.

Connie had clearly come to her for her help as a criminal barrister, wanting someone to defend her husband should this case go to court. Why else would she want Selina's help? But what, she thought, if it need never get that far?

'Police?' Connie said, her face wretched with fear. Connie must be terrified, she thought. Who would look after her if Michael was sent to prison? Esther, of course.

'Leave it with me.'

Now, hungover and achy in Esther's spare room, Selina's mind went back to the box, and to the reason why she hadn't gone to the police yesterday, as she should have done.

It was the same reason that stopped her telling Esther whilst they talked last night.

The metal box was in the boot of her car, wedged between the spare tyre and the jack. She had taken it on impulse, knowing only that she didn't want to leave it in Michael's possession. Connie hadn't told her anything else; not where she found it, who the girl was, whether Michael knew she had it. She had seized up, the stress of finding the thing and presumably the relief she'd felt when Selina said she would handle it robbing her of her voice. She had stared dumbly with watery eyes, fretting at her skirt with her small, childlike fingers.

'*Help me,*' was all Connie could manage.

'*Of course,*' was the natural reply.

Downstairs, Selina heard the front door close as Esther left the flat. A packet of paracetamol sat beside her coffee cup on the table, and Selina swallowed two, sank the remnants of her coffee and dressed. She was sitting in the driver's seat less than ten minutes later, a hurried and apologetic text sent to Esther letting her know she had to leave.

She took the back roads over the hills to get to Kilstock. It was quicker, by far, and less populated by police. She wasn't entirely sure that the wine from last night had left her system, but the desire to confront Michael overruled her better judgement. And heaven forbid she was caught in possession of these photographs.

He was in the back garden when Selina arrived, dark-green overalls smeared with mud and a mustard shirt buttoned to the collar. A short man, five-seven at a push, but still taller than Selina by half a head. His eyes, when he realised who it was that had come calling, brightened.

'Well, if it isn't our favourite Peruvian!' he called, standing with his hands on his hips. His face was leathery from a lifetime of working outdoors, the deep-set lines around his eyes and mouth creating a look of friendliness rather than anything else. 'Are you here alone or did you bring my Esther with you?'

Selina didn't say anything at first. She had the small metal box in her bag, the weight dragging on her shoulder. She didn't want him to admit to what he had done and confirm himself as a monster. She wanted to freeze him as he was, smiling in the garden of Esther's childhood home, the farm and the silos behind him. She wanted to keep him just so, her best friend's father.

'It's only me,' she said as she approached, unsmiling. 'Is Connie around?'

Michael brushed mud from his hands onto the thighs of his overalls. 'She's cleaning at the B&B. Does it every Saturday morning, for her pocket money.'

She nodded, looking at the ground. The phrasing made her uncomfortable – not just the condescension of Connie's hard work, but the infantilism of it. 'We need to go indoors, Michael. I need to talk to you.'

'Righty-o,' he said, a slight confusion washing over his face, but no panic, no guilt. 'Nothing serious, I hope?'

Selina couldn't bring herself to respond; how would she quantify the seriousness of what she needed to say? She felt the metal box shift in her bag, images of the young schoolgirl flashing through her mind.

She walked back towards the cottage, letting herself in through the kitchen door. She could hear him following, padding through the dewy grass. She didn't move towards the kettle, no point in niceties.

From her bag she pulled out the metal box, sat in the nearest dining chair with the thing in her lap. 'I need to talk to you about this,' she said.

The friendliness disappeared from his face. His swarthy skin paled, turned muted yellow, and his mouth pulled down at the corners.

'Where did you get that?' he said.

'Do you realise, Michael, that if the police got hold of this you would go to prison? You *should* go to prison.'

'It's not what it seems.' Desperation dripped from every word. He sat opposite her and Selina remembered coming here for Christmas two years before, when she hadn't been able to face Christmas at home without her own father. It was Esther who had made that season bearable.

'And how do you think it seems?' Selina said, careful not to lead him, to let himself dig his own pit.

'You think I'm a paedophile, that I touch little girls, but I don't, really I don't.'

'There are photographs in this box that prove that you do.'

'It was years ago, and I've never done it since. It was just that one time, that one girl, I swear it, and they're just photographs; I never touched her, I never did. I just took her photograph, no harm in that, is there? Not really. I didn't hurt her, I would never hurt a child, I'm not like that.'

'How many other girls have there been, Michael?'

'None, I swear it! None!'

'How many?'

'None! I said already! None, I swear it, Selina, I swear it!' His face had crumpled, the skin on his cheeks washing green.

'Have you any other photographs?'

'No, none. That's the lot.'

'Did you ever touch Esther?'

Michael jumped from his seat. 'Jesus, no! I would never. Never. How could you even think that?'

Selina looked at him, disgusted. 'That little girl looks a lot like Esther. Do you realise that?'

'No, no, it's not Esther she looks like.' His face was still twisted in horror, a mirror of Selina's disgust. 'It's Connie she looks like. Not Esther, not at all.'

'That doesn't make it any better. She's a little girl, for Christ's sake. How old was she? No, don't answer that. The less I know, the better.' She dragged her eyes away from Michael and back onto the box in front of her. The wooden table it was resting on was bare, no tablecloth or runner. She had pulled crackers at this table with Michael, Connie and Esther, drunk too much wine, eaten too much cheese. She had watched Michael kiss Connie's forehead and had wondered, cruelly, how anyone could love a thing like Connie.

Now the feeling was twisted, switched around. How could Connie love Michael? How could she know what he was capable of and stay with him anyway?

She thought of Esther, too, kissing her dad on the cheek, telling him she loved him, watching with joy as he unwrapped the present she'd bought him. It had been that moment that had been hardest to watch. Esther loved her father so much. At the time, it had made Selina realise how much she missed her own dad. Now, it made her fear for her friend, how heartbroken she would be to discover who her father really was.

Could she save her from that devastation? Could this be the way she could silently repay Esther for helping her with her grief, for running interference with her mother, for holding Selina up when her whole world had fallen apart in the months after Colbert Alverez's death?

'What are you going to do?' Michael said. 'Are you going to take these to the police? You can't, please, you can't. Who would look after Connie? I can't leave her, I can't leave my Connie.'

Esther would have to look after Connie if Michael went to prison. Esther would lose her father. A different loss to the one Selina had experienced, but it would be equally painful.

'You're going to stop working for that school.' She spoke slowly, allowing her mind to race ahead with a plan. 'You're going to get a job somewhere away from children. I'm going to check your laptop every month to make sure you've nothing even vaguely dodgy. And I can check to make sure you haven't simply deleted files.' She looked at him, held his eye, willed him to show an ounce of regret, of guilt. He didn't. He looked like a child who had been caught sneaking chocolates; worried about the punishment that would follow but not the original theft. What am I doing? Selina thought. Am I actually going to cover this up?

She didn't let the thought take root.

'That won't be a problem,' Michael said, running his small, dark hands through his hair. 'You can do whatever you need to do. As I said, it was a one-off. I've never done it again, and I won't. It was a difficult time; Esther had gone off to school and Connie was preoccupied. I was a bit lost and this girl comes along who looks the spit of Connie. I just got away with myself. It hasn't happened since. And it won't, it won't!'

Michael smiled, no doubt to appear relieved and grateful, but Selina found it quite revolting.

He willingly showed her his laptop, his phone, even rifled through the various photo albums in the house to prove that they were full of family snaps. Selina watched his hands flick through the pages, thought of those hands pressing the button on a camera, thought of his thick, smiling lips ordering a young girl to undress.

She told herself, again and again, that she was doing this for Esther, and for Connie. That Michael wasn't getting away scot-free, that she would continue these checks for the rest of his life if she had to.

She knew prisons, had visited them too many times to count, thought them barely fit for purpose. She could spare Connie and Esther the pain of visiting rooms, of the judgement and vitriol that would be spewed onto them from the press, would save them from the ordeal of sitting in a public court whilst Michael was sentenced for paedophilia. He didn't have to go to prison to be punished, she reasoned. There were other ways.

'I'm keeping these,' she said at the end, holding up the tin box of photos. 'If I ever find out you've done something like this again, or even looked at any images like this again, I'm going straight to the police.'

He nodded. 'Of course, of course.'

Selina left the house feeling sick.

It wasn't until later, however, when she was driving back to her mother's, that the true horror sank in. It hadn't just been his lack of guilt that bothered Selina, she realised. Not even his overbearing gratitude. It was the way he had spoken about the incident, as though he had been caught having an affair and the infidelity was the issue.

Who was that girl? Selina wondered as the hills gave way to the houses and cars of Taunton. Where is she now?

Chapter Twenty-Eight

Connie

Saturday Evening

Sedation makes me float in and out of consciousness. I don't know what the time is, only that it's dark. Each time I wake up I am alone. Where's Esther?

My heart monitor beeps and I wish it wouldn't; the stab of noise is a cruel reminder that I'm trapped.

What a strange thing it is to be drugged. When I sleep I dream as though I'm reliving my life, when I wake I'm so paralysed that I can barely move.

My daughter's not here, nor is Selina.

Perhaps they're together, I think.

Then my eyes are open, wide. I don't want them to be together, because what if Selina is telling Esther what has happened? How I got the clots under my armpits? How my disgusting body and devil-fuelled soul turned her father, that man she loves, into a monster?

'There's a devil inside you,' Grandmother said. 'You turn people into terrible things.'

Esther would turn away from me if she ever found out. Grandmother beat me for it, Maud tried to send me away, Michael himself has been telling me these fifty years that no one would believe me over him. No one. Even Selina took his side.

Well, didn't she?

I want this to be over. I want Michael dead, I want Esther never to know, I want this rotten box and all its curses to burn in hell and I want to be at peace.

A nurse comes in to check my readings. 'One more check-up after this one,' she says, 'and then I'll try not to disturb you any further, if I can help it. Let you get a good night's rest.'

Her cheery voice is a mimic of Lizzy's, the nurse at the asylum decades ago. It makes me want to do to this nurse all the things I had craved doing to *her*. Would she take Michael's side too, if she knew?

Probably.

Definitely.

Years ago Esther tried to get social services involved, to give her blessed father a break. It would have involved visits and assessments and strangers in the house. Michael said, *'No, I'm happy to look after her myself, we get by perfectly well. The system's strained enough as it is; save the resources for people who really need it.'*

What a good man, what a dote. He must love his wife ever so much.

Esther loves him so much.

The nurse takes my pulse, her fingers brushing my wrist so lightly that most people would hardly notice. Still, my body arches, my jaw tenses.

'Ssssh now, I know you don't like it but it's just for a second.' She speaks as if comforting a baby. 'Ssssh now, there we are, all done. I'll be back for your last check just after midnight.'

That urge again, to see her teeth fall bloodied to the floor, her hands nursing her swollen smacked-in mouth. I'll show you how to shush, I think.

She's only trying to help, I think.

She's a patronising, blind, stupid witch, I think.

She's someone's daughter, I think.

The battle continues, my inner good fighting my devil. Who will win?

Michael. He always does.

The nurse leaves and the darkness is not true darkness at all. It is lit up by the strange glow from the monitors around me. I turn my head away from them.

I turned my head.

I realise I can move; the sedative is wearing thin.

I turn back to look at the machines: the heart monitor, the drip stand, the syringe driver, the catheter. I know these machines. I use them on Michael. A number on the bottom corner of the heart monitor isn't one of my readings; it's the time. Just after 8 p.m.

I feel, all at once, a little less helpless.

This feeling won't last long. The nurse has just replaced the vial of sedative in the driver; in another few minutes I'll be drawn back into floating unreality.

But it will grow thin again, in time.

This moron has had an idea. I cradle it, nursing it in my mind as I feel myself going under.

Chapter Twenty-Nine

Connie

1974

I remember the early summer when I was twenty years old.

The sun was high and hot, but I didn't feel it. I stayed in the shadows, the silos on the farm behind me shielding my white skin from the heat. I sat, cross-legged, by the vegetable patch; Ballard's *Concrete Island* rested in the grass by my side. Between its pages was a piece of thin wood, *Return to Williton* written, in Michael's handwriting, on one side of it. *Homeward to Kilstock* written on the other. It was my bus-pass, of sorts, as well as my bookmark. He made it for me so that I wouldn't have to speak to the bus drivers when I did the bi-weekly shopping at the Spar. He gave me just enough money for the return fare. Michael had the Spar charge the bill to an account, which he paid at the weekend.

He did whatever he could to make sure I was under no pressure, at all, to speak.

To tell.

My fingers worked through the soil, needling little holes into which I slotted bright green, twin-leafed carrot seedlings from a tray in my lap.

I had my back to the silos but I felt them watching me, just as I felt them watching me whenever I walked to the other side of the village and cooked lunch for the old chap I was paid to look after. My pocket money, Michael called it.

My skin remained cool in the shadow. It wouldn't last. Within an hour the sun would shift, the shadow moving, and the bed of carrots would bathe in the full force of the afternoon light.

With the last of the seedlings planted I stood, dusted my shapeless trousers of the dirt, clapped my hands together so the bulk of the mud rained down. I took the tray and left it by the door of Michael's potting shed, the small wooden structure that used to house the outdoor lavatory when Grandmother was alive. The door was always locked.

Michael had the key.

It was his hobby shed. He built models inside it, turned it into a darkroom once a month and developed the pictures he took with his Nikon. They were mostly of me. The record player lived in there, too, and when it was played I could hear the reedy, wood-muffled voices of Eartha Kitt, Billie Holiday, Ella Fitzgerald. All the songs my mother used to listen to. Never any punk or rock. No soul.

I stooped to retrieve my book. It wasn't holding my attention that morning, but I knew I would be able to disappear into it later. I would recount every word and greedily dive into its bleak other world. It was books like that one, novels that bore no resemblance to my life, that had characters like no one I had ever met, that I held in highest regard.

The chance to read someone else's nightmare.

Inside, at the sink, I filled a glass with tap water and my lips prised apart with a pop as I opened my mouth to drink.

I heard the familiar ring-ring from a bicycle bell, the crunch of gravel as the postman rode his bike down the lane. I heard him whistle.

I ran to the door; I didn't want to miss the one daily exchange that didn't leave me wanting.

'Morning,' he said, smiling as he handed me a brown envelope. His hands were tanned and freckled, his nails clean. I always thought he looked kind.

I turned my mouth into a grin, realising with regret that I'd been standing there with my jaw hanging open.

He nodded his head, perfectly polite, ever so normal. 'Have a good day, Miss Lithgow.'

There wasn't an ounce of judgement in his manner, no presumption that I was an idiot. His eyes never wandered to my under-developed chest or my thin childlike hips.

This is what it must be like, I thought as I walked back indoors, to be treated like a person.

Would he have believed me, if I had told him? Would he have helped me? I never had the courage to test it.

My eyes fell to the envelope.

Miss Constance Lithgow, read the first line.

C/O Mr Michael Lithgow, read the second. A reminder that I was not a woman in my own right. Not even vaguely. I had a legally appointed guardian, someone who held power of attorney.

I turned the envelope over in my hand, read the return address.

I froze.

The envelope fell to the floor.

My legs trembled, heart palpitated.

A cramp-like pain gripped my torso and I doubled over. I couldn't breathe.

My mind filled with images I had tried, for the last three years, to forget. Images of shaven heads, of drooling mouths, of hulking guards strapping people onto metal beds, of a woman rocking back and forth by an iron-barred window.

My fear was physical. The pain from my abdomen combined with the pain inside my lungs, added to the panic inside my head, my mind shouting at me, over and over, *there is no escape, there is no escape, there is no escape, there is no escape.*

I am going to die.

It didn't feel like fear. It felt like an inevitability. I was going to die.

I didn't want to die.

I wanted to escape.

But I couldn't.

I couldn't escape.

I couldn't breathe.

'Connie?' Michael shook me awake by the shoulders.

My body was wracked with pain from having fallen asleep on the floor. I don't know how long I had been there. I don't know when it was that my brain finally overcame the panic attack and forced me to sleep.

'It's OK, Connie. I'm here, I'm here.' He helped me sit up, rest my spine against the edge of the sofa.

He followed my wide-eyed gaze to the letter from the Welsh asylum that still lay, address-side down, on the wooden floor. Lifting it up, he read the return address and his expression filled with pity.

'Oh, dear girl,' he said and crouched back down to me, eyes level with mine. 'This scared you? You don't have to worry, it's just a letter. They send them every now and then, just leaflets and things, nothing to worry about.' Condescension tainted the warmth of his voice.

I looked down at the scene as if floating above it, as I always did whenever he touched me. I saw his hands on my arm, but

I didn't feel them. I saw myself nod mutely. I saw him fold the letter and secrete it away in his pocket.

He cooked me dinner, I ate it.

He talked and I stared straight ahead, pretended to listen.

He gave me a bath.

He took me to bed.

'Up you get,' he said when he came home the next day, finding me crouched once again in the garden. I'd planted more seedlings. I'd cleaned the house. I'd read just over half of my book. 'We've visitors coming by in a minute for tea; a couple of ladies from the school.'

I heard paper crumpling against the folds in his pocket as he walked me into the kitchen. It could have been anything – a receipt, a to-do list, a memo from the school – but I knew it was the letter from the asylum. I just knew it.

He sat me down at the table, filled the kettle with water and put it on the Aga to boil. Before the steam even began to rise from the spout there was a knock at the door.

I wasn't ready to meet people. I ached from work, my mind was still fogged from the effects of the panic attack yesterday and the nearness of that letter in Michael's pocket. My dress, when I looked down, was dotted with soil marks and my hands were brown with dirt. My hair was unbrushed and lay in wild, blonde curls about my shoulders. Even without looking in the mirror, I knew that I looked a mess. No, not a mess. I looked mad. I looked like the moron Dr Rowe and Grandmother believed me to be.

'Knock-knock,' came a sing-song voice from the front door that led straight into our living room. Michael must have left it open when he came inside; the visitors had let themselves in.

I wasn't ready for this. I didn't like to meet new people, I didn't know what they would think or expect of me. Their presence was a reminder of everything I was not. Everything I wanted to be, that my parents had wanted me to be, that Grandmother knew I would never become.

I felt my mind close off. I was floating again above everything, disconnected from my body. I didn't even turn as they came in.

'Connie, this is Miss Granger and Miss Park. They've just started working with me at the school.'

Two women sat opposite me at the table. They were young and slim, one with a beakish nose and hair cut into the same fringe and curtains as Lesley Judd's on *Blue Peter*.

'Miss Granger, indeed,' the Lesley Judd lookalike said, sitting down. She wore a shirt the same colour as her blonde hair and brown bell-bottom cords. 'You can call me Alison.' She held out her hand to me, her smile changing to a look of confusion when I didn't take it.

Michael rushed over, a Rover Assorted Biscuits tin in his grip. He placed his hand on top of Alison's, moving it away from me. 'Connie prefers not to be touched, if you don't mind. She doesn't talk much either, but she likes to listen. Don't you, Connie?'

He smiled at the women and they smiled back, embarrassed and unsure of where to look. Neither tried to meet my eye again.

'You said she was your cousin, is that right?' said Miss Park, her pink cheeks framed by frizzy brown hair that flicked out at the sides, a poor attempt to mimic Farrah Fawcett. Her nose was too long and too thin, a mismatch to the rest of her soft features and she gazed at Michael with a wide-eyed simpering stare whilst Miss Granger, Alison, looked on with poorly concealed amusement.

'Yes, that's right.' Michael was making them drag the information out of him, the way I'd seen him do before, a too-obvious attempt at normalising the situation. They fell for it hook, line and sinker.

'And you look after her?' Alison asked.

'I'm her guardian, legally speaking, but you don't really need much looking after, do you, Connie?'

I didn't answer. The tin of biscuits was passed around, both women choosing a pink wafer. Suddenly hungry, I took three chocolate bourbons and one custard cream, then stuck my index finger into the party rings, Michael's favourites, and hooked out four. I wondered how far I could go before one of them confronted me, said *'don't be rude'* or *'leave some for me'.*

No one said anything.

I ate them all, putting each biscuit into my mouth whole and chewing until it was small enough to swallow. I wanted to embarrass Michael.

Miss Park eyed me sidelong. I felt crumbs drop to my hands and realised I'd been chewing with my mouth open. *Good,* I thought.

They talked about the grounds of the school.

The food, which was cheap and easy to make and as bland as food could get.

The teachers, all much older than them, weren't interested in anything like music or parties or fun and I thought that Michael must have more in common with the teachers than with these gregarious girls. I'd never known him to go out to a party. I'd never even seen him drink alcohol, for that matter.

The kettle screamed from the Aga and he went to make four cups of tea.

'You really are making tea?' Alison said, and Miss Park, who still hadn't graced me with her first name, shot her a warning look. 'I thought it was a euphemism,' Alison whispered back, laughing, as though I wasn't there. She was mocking you, I realised. She thought you a bit odd. Miss Park was clearly your defender but why, I couldn't tell.

Alison noticed my copy of *Concrete Island* and before I had a chance to grab it she lifted the book up. 'I was thinking of getting this,' she said. 'Any good?'

I watched her slim fingers leaf through the pages, saw my bus-pass bookmark slide around. I didn't want to lose my page. If the bookmark fell out I'd lose it and I couldn't let that happen. I wanted it to be there, ready for when I needed it.

'You'll have to ask Connie,' Michael said, pouring milk into a small jug and carrying a tea tray over. 'She's reading it; I'm not one for books myself.'

Both women looked at me, incredulous. Ordinarily I would have felt proud to have shocked them and made them realise I wasn't as stupid as I appeared. But Alison was still flicking through the book and I could see my bookmark shifting position.

I reached for another custard cream and ate it whole.

'She can read then?' Miss Park said, not even trying to hide her disbelief. I imagined what it would feel like to lift the boiling kettle and pour it over her head.

'Oh yes, you're a great reader, aren't you, Con? You don't find talking very easy, but you can read and write well, can't you?'

I didn't tell them that I had read every book in the travelling library by the time I was eighteen, both fiction and non-fiction, and that they had to order in books especially for me from the libraries in Taunton.

'Well, that's good.' Miss Park smiled but the smile was thin and unconvincing.

And still Alison held on to *Concrete Island.*

'You're very domesticated,' Miss Park said to Michael, her voice simpering. 'Your mother taught you well.'

He stiffened. 'I was raised by my aunt, Connie's mother, until I was eleven. And then by our grandmother when Connie's parents died.'

'What about your real mother?' A crumb of pink wafer stuck to her lower lip.

'I don't—' he began, but I saved him from having to explain that his junkie mother abandoned him. Not for the first time I wondered what he had seen growing up on that commune, his protector tripped out on LSD and Valium, surrounded by people who thought nothing of letting children wander around as free as the adults, seeing things and doing things they shouldn't have to.

Their photo was still in the living room, the ten-year-old twins in their uniforms. We never were able to work out which was which.

Alison put down my book and I reached for it, eager to jam the bookmark back into place.

The edge of my wrist brushed my cup.

Tea, steaming hot, spilt across the table, slopping into the biscuit tin and onto the digestives that nobody wanted.

Miss Park jumped up with a shriek, tea soaking her white flares and turning the fabric translucent. I could see the outline of her knickers.

I lifted the book up before it could get wet. It was from the library, I didn't want to pay a fine. 'Here,' Michael said, handing her the tea towel from the back of his chair. 'Do you want me to wash the trousers? You can borrow a pair of Connie's.' He stopped mid-sentence, assessing Miss Parks as though she were a plant in the vegetable garden in need of a trestle. She was a womanly woman, with hips and a firm, fleshy behind. 'Or a pair of mine if you think Connie's may be too small.'

Miss Park blushed, dabbing the tea stain with the towel. If she took the comment about her size as a slight she didn't show it. She stood side on, trying to hide the see-through patch of her trousers from view, unaware that the tea had soaked through the gap between her legs and her bottom was as wet as her crotch.

Alison put one arm around Miss Park. 'She'll be fine, won't you? Bleach will get the stain out,' she said, trying to defuse her friend's upset with a jolly tone. 'That's the good thing about white trousers; you can bleach them back to rights.'

'Are you OK?' Michael said. 'Did the tea burn you?'

'I'm fine, really.'

I know I should have apologised but I couldn't. All I could do was stare at them, my head filling with thoughts about what they might be thinking, and I couldn't find any words to tell them I was sorry. When Miss Park sat back down I could see she was trying to fight back tears of embarrassment and I felt awful.

I didn't mean to turn her trousers see-through with hot tea. I sincerely hoped I hadn't burned her.

I just wanted to save my book, because I knew I'd need it later. Maybe, I thought, I could tell these women and they would understand. Maybe they would help me. I could open my mouth, I could try to—

'We better head off soon?' Alison said, posing the statement as a question to her friend. Miss Park shook her head, smiled.

'Not just yet. Let's have a fresh cup of tea, how about that?' She smiled at Michael and I realised she was on his side, in his corner. She didn't know the first thing about me, neither of these young women did. Why would they believe a word I said, if I managed to say anything at all?

'Righty-o.' Michael hopped up and refilled the kettle, saved the dry biscuits from the tin and put them on a fresh plate. 'You didn't mean any harm, did you, Connie? You're just a touch clumsy sometimes, that's all. I know you didn't mean it.' He said this to me, but his eyes were fixed on the two women, who were sitting in silence surveying the room as though this last cup of tea must be endured so Miss Park could leave with her head held high. It would have been impolite, I supposed, to leave suddenly just because mute retarded Connie spilt a drink.

That's what they thought of me.

I could tell.

I thumbed through the pages of my book, keeping the spine tight in my fist so the bookmark remained wedged.

'You were about to tell us about your mother,' Alison said, a nod of encouragement for Michael to carry on where he'd left off.

'How are you feeling, now?' he said to Miss Park, ignoring the question. He wasn't going to be drawn in to talking about his own mother. 'Not too uncomfortable, I hope?'

She shook her head, smiled down at her fresh cup of tea as though touched by his consideration. 'I'm fine, really.'

I looked at Michael and tried to see him as she must have. He was slim, his muscles well defined but not bulky. His hair, thick and dark, reached down to his earlobes in a smooth, shiny mop. Did she think him handsome?

I thought back to the only other relationships I had witnessed. Mummy and Daddy, always warm and affectionate but I couldn't clearly remember their dynamic, not really. Television offered me other clues, the burgeoning relationships in *Grange Hill*, the monochrome flirting occasionally shown on *Coronation Street*. Benny Hill incessantly chasing young women who pretended to be stupid.

Miss Park looked at Michael with a strange mix of adoration and vulnerability. I couldn't ever imagine looking at someone like that. Why would you want someone to think you were thick?

He rose from the table. 'If you don't mind, ladies, I'd best be getting dinner ready.'

'Ladies? Michael, you talk like you're an old man.' Alison laughed, well-naturedly enough, but still Miss Park jabbed her in the side.

'You cook?' Miss Park's eyes lit up even more at this marvel. He could cook, make tea and look after retards. What a catch he must have been, in her eyes. A man of twenty-five with all the domesticity of a middle-aged housewife. He didn't drink, didn't smoke, didn't take drugs or go to the parties I imagined all the other twenty-something men in England must have attended.

She looked at him and saw a husband. Good Lord. If only she knew.

The women left shortly afterwards.

He cooked lamb chops, sliding one onto my plate and spooning over gravy. A dollop of Smash mashed potato. Sliced carrots from a tin, lukewarm.

I chewed and swallowed and stared at the vague stain of tea left on the wooden table.

'Bloody nosy, they were,' he said. 'Jabbering on and on. "Tell me about your mother".' He mimicked a female voice, making it sound far more whiney and high-pitched than Miss Granger's. 'Jabber, jabber, jabber. It's what they're like in the school kitchen, too. They invited themselves around here! Can you imagine that, the cheek? "Oh Michael, you're only around the corner, can't we come by after school?" Like they're bloomin' teenagers still. And you should hear them in the kitchen, nattering on as if they're high-flying businesswomen just because they earn a few pence pocket money slopping out overcooked mush to village kids. The way they talk to each other, you'd think that women are all about wearing trousers and having jobs, but nothing's changed, Connie. Nothing. All they're after is a meal-ticket in the shape of a husband.'

My mother was nothing like that. Nor was Grandmother, not really. Nor Maud. But then I thought of the rest of the world, the world he inhabited and I didn't. The women he worked with at the school, the parents I presumed he brushed shoulders with, the passengers on the bus that he may or may not talk to. I never asked. I didn't know. Is that what women were like? Is that what I would have been like had I gone to school, got a job? Is that what the women in the audience on *Top of the Pops* wanted?

I wanted to be alone. To be left alone. That's all. I imagined escaping, saving up for a bus ticket further away than Williton, living in a small house where no one could touch me.

Michael talked on.

I chewed and swallowed and chewed and swallowed and wiped my chin of gravy.

'Fancy a bit of telly, Con?' he asked me when he'd cleared the plates from the table and put them in the sink for me to wash up in the morning. We never cleaned them at night. There were other chores to be done, at night.

His eyes lingered on me and I knew he didn't want to watch television but still I turned towards the small living room, as though he might. As though I might get another half an hour of peace.

'Actually, let's leave it for tonight. Thursday, isn't it? Nothing's on, on a Thursday,' he said just as I reached the living-room door. *Top of the Pops* is on, on a Thursday, I thought.

He stood at the foot of the stairs. 'Bath night, tonight, isn't it? Come on then, up we go.'

I didn't let it show on my face, the feelings those words inspired. It amazed me, even then, how I still dreaded it, how the numb blank stare I gave the world had not penetrated me fully, even after all those years of him.

'Come on, chop-chop,' he said, following me up.

The bathroom had been carved out of the upstairs space. The two bedrooms, Grandmother's and ours, used to be separated only by a thin wall. When she died we added another, making a narrow bathroom just big enough to fit a sink and a bath.

Michael had stopped talking. His hands played at the taps, filling the bath with hot water. His eyes were on me as I undressed.

Inside my head, I was at home, my proper home, dozing on the sofa. Mummy was running the bath for me. Daddy was putting my pyjamas in front of the fire so they'd be warm for me to wear to bed. I was not twenty years old, I was six and the last fourteen years had never happened. They were a dream, a bad dream, and any minute Mummy was going to wake me from my nap and I would be six again and everything would be—

'In you hop,' he said, breaking into my thoughts with the cruel hammer of here-and-now. The water steamed and pricked my skin as he helped me step into it. I was perfectly capable of doing this myself. I dressed myself in the mornings, I fed myself when he was at work, I went to the shops, cleaned the house, cared for the elderly all by myself, yet he insisted on carrying out this routine.

He washed my hair with a jug and soap. He cleaned my back and made a show of letting me wash my own tiny breasts and the wisps of hair at my groin, as though he had any respect for my personal space.

'You're so perfect,' he whispered to me, and I thought how ridiculous we are. His words were said with such honesty, with such a soft voice, with such love that I could very easily have believed him. How Miss Park would have swooned to hear him say those words, in that soft way, to her. I thought of how he used to stare at my mother and call her perfect in the same way and how she would cup his face in her warm hands.

'You're a little lamb,' she would say, holding his brown-eyed gaze in her blue. *'But really, you shouldn't ever call a woman perfect. It's not true for starters and it puts one under such pressure.'*

I thought of how young we were. How ridiculous it was for two people technically in the prime of their lives to be cooped up in the tiniest of houses in the tiniest of hamlets in one of the least populated counties in England. I thought of how very different our lives should have been.

But my thoughts stopped, dead, as his lips grazed my wet, naked shoulder.

I was aware, in my nakedness, of my nipples stiffening as the cold dread seized me. I was aware, too, of how he would purposefully misinterpret this, pretending to himself that I desired him when he knew I didn't. He knew.

Taking my hand, he told me to stand. The water had turned my skin bright red, the flesh on my scrawny buttocks pink and raw.

His hand moved from my arm to my waist, still as thin as a child's, and my mind abandoned me, my consciousness flew from my body so I was not there, not really. I wasn't there when he discarded the towel, when he kissed my neck and told me to 'Relax, for God's sake, it's just me.'

No, I was inside Ballard's *Concrete Island*, replaying the chapters I'd read so far. Maitland, hemmed in by motorway and trying to keep sane, was trying to find a way home. The cars and vans rushed past, the long grass concealing the Jaguar where it lay in the wasteland, written-off by the crash and fallen from the road. I am Maitland, worrying about my wife, my son, my job.

When it was all over, you'd think he would have left me in peace, but he wasn't so benevolent as all that. He was so convinced that he really did love me, that we were soulmates of the oddest degree, that he could never leave me alone. He was made to care for me and I was made to please him, that's what Michael believed.

It's the lie he'd told himself for eleven years to make this scenario excusable.

'We better clean you up.' He giggled the words like a schoolboy caught mid-lark. 'The water's still warm, luckily. Come on, I'll help you in.'

'I love you so much, Connie,' he said. 'It's like someone took all the best bits of your mother and kept them safe inside you. You're so pure. So perfect.'

He dressed me in a nightgown that stretched down to my ankles. I sat on the small sofa as he flicked through a copy of the *TV Times*, Larry Grayson looking camp on the front cover. He decided that we would watch *The Six Million Dollar Man*.

I read more of *Concrete Island*, holding the book between my hands as though in prayer, giving thanks to J.G. Ballard and his blessed gift of escape.

'There's a devil inside you,' Grandmother used to say to me after discovering your stain on the bed sheets in the spot I had been sleeping. *'A devil that makes people do terrible things. There's something wrong with you, in here.'* She would rap her knuckles hard on my skull, her eyes wide with anger and fear, and beat me with a hairbrush for being so wicked, for being a dirty, dirty, dirty wretch. *'This wouldn't happen to a good little girl.'*

Through the thin curtains covering the window I could just make out the shape of the silos.

Next day he cooked me breakfast of bacon and eggs and I ate it.

He left the house with a kiss to my cheek and I flinched. He ignored it.

I went to the house of the old man over the hill and cleaned his toilet and his bath and changed his bed sheets. I came home and ate lunch of cold bacon and stale brown bread and read the last few chapters of *Concrete Island*.

He came home and cooked dinner and I ate it and I thought, *This is my life. This is the entirety of my world.*

He talked about the work he did at the school, mowing three pitches in a single day. He talked about the two women I met yesterday, accused them of being two-faced bitches because they hardly spoke to him. He talked about how different I was. How I listened to him. How perfect I was, just like my mother.

It dawned on me that it was Friday. He had the next two days off. He would be there, all the time.

My throat burned with that word that never worked.

I remembered the countless nights I wept myself to sleep, first because my parents were dead, then because of Grandmother's vituperative cruelty. Then because of Michael.

I thought back to how it felt to kill Grandmother. I thought of killing Maud and my eyes pricked with tears and I couldn't bear to be in that house a second longer. How often had I thought of doing to him what I had done to them? It seemed impossible. And what would happen to me, if I did?

I pushed my plate away and stood; my hands were shaking, my arms, my shoulders.

I wasn't going to stay. I was going to escape. I would go somewhere else, find help.

There must be help for me, somewhere.

'Connie!' he shouted as gravy slopped onto the table. 'Don't you like the dinner?' His voice was injured and hurt. He was so simple, so stupid, that he lacked even the basic levels of insight required to see that I hated him.

He moved towards me, treading carefully as though I was a rabid dog.

I picked up my dinner knife, gripped it in my fist.

'Connie.' His voice was a warning.

I felt that useless word rise up my gullet, my stomach sick from the sudden rush of adrenaline.

He licked his lips, held out his hands. 'Connie,' he said again.

I said it.

'No!' I tried for a shout, for a scream, but it came out as a whisper. 'No!'

He stopped in his tracks. I thought of his words last night, his words over dinner tonight, the kiss on my cheek from that morning. He wasn't a bad person, I reasoned. He wasn't. He'd let me go. He had to let me go.

But I didn't really believe it.

He put one hand up towards me, palm out and fingers splayed in a show of peace. The other hand went to his pocket. He felt around inside and I heard the crease and rustle of paper.

He pulled out the envelope.

He held it so I could read the return address, see the name of the asylum.

'You don't want to do anything silly, Connie.' His tone wasn't angry, but wary. He was trying to talk me around. 'Remember where you'll go if anything happens to me. Remember this place, Connie? Remember the nurses and the bookshelves of Topsy and Tim? Remember the patients and how they treated each other? That's where all the doctors want to send you.'

My mind filled with the sight of the shaven-headed patient pissing on another man's neck. The guard that dragged him away. The toilets that had no doors. The ECT machine with the wires.

My hand still gripped the knife, a butter knife of all things that would barely puncture his skin.

As he neared me I felt the adrenaline leak out of my system. I felt tears rise in its place.

'Just remember that I'm looking after you, Connie,' he said to me. 'I'm your legal guardian. Without me you'd be lost. Or worse.' He plucked the knife out of my hand. 'You'd be *there*.'

He pulled me towards him and I sobbed, I couldn't help it. I felt his hands work through my hair, keeping my head in place against his chest. My body heaved with each cry, his strong arms keeping me close so my body pressed against his.

'There, there, now,' he said. 'You're just having one of your episodes. There, there, now.' He rubbed my back, stroked my hair, I could hear the saliva growing in his mouth as he shushed and tried to console me. 'You'll be right as rain in a little while, Connie. You always are.' And then, as if it would solve everything, as if it would make it all better, he said to me in the cheeriest of voices, 'Come on, now. Let's clean you up in the bath.'

Chapter Thirty

Selina

Saturday Night

The plan had been so clear when she left Bristol. She used her journey home to piece together what she thought may have happened. She was going to do the last pieces of necessary research online in her flat to confirm her theory and then she'd be able to go to Esther with all the details. It was time to be frank, both in what had happened so far and her unforgivable role in it.

She took the back roads to Taunton, sick of the motorway. The narrow roads were quieter, fewer cars to dazzle her with their oncoming headlights and add to the pain in her temples. She had barely eaten all day, or had anything to drink other than coffee, and the neglect of her body was taking effect.

She stopped to refuel her car and buy a bottle of water and some chocolate. The sugar, she reasoned, would help her keep focused. It would also help keep her awake.

The sky was overcast and Selina could detect the scent of rain in the air. She hoped it would hold off; driving in the dark was bad enough.

Forty minutes later she pulled up in front of her Taunton

flat. The rain had held off and the drive had done some good, cleared her head. She almost had it nailed; it had to be Michael's mother. The rest, or so she hoped, was just logistics.

Charlotte Lithgow, having kept in contact with her son in later years, had perhaps become worried at not having heard from him. She visits, is horrified that he is so ill and sits with him, talks to him, and maybe it is to his mother that Michael confesses and not his nurse. Selina could picture it clearly: the emaciated, bedridden Michael shrouded in white sheets, a small but feisty old lady holding his hand, telling him it is OK, he can speak, she will listen.

And then what? Charlotte, unable to fully face the fact that her son is a criminal of the lowest degree, focuses more on what has been done to him rather than what he has done. Perhaps she has always resented Connie for marrying Michael, a jealous maternal streak, and the news that Connie involved a lawyer in the mess sparked her fury.

Or, perhaps, she is as unstable as her letter to her son would suggest. Perhaps she was angry with Connie for not telling her Michael was so ill, or for calling in a St Moira's nurse when his elderly mother could have helped. Maybe it had nothing to do with Michael's crimes at all.

For every answer Selina came up with, another problem arose. Charlotte would have to be in her late eighties, would she be able to physically restrain another woman? Possibly, if she found Connie asleep in the chair.

Could she plunge a needle into a vein so accurately the hospital would mistake it as a suicide?

And what of the morphine? Charlotte wouldn't rob her son of his only pain relief. Did that mean it was a genuine lab error?

Where did she go, after attacking Connie? Was she still in Kilstock, hiding, waiting?

The chocolate was gone now. She screwed up the empty wrapper and added it to the collection in the pocket of her car door. It was late, gone 10 p.m., and despite the streetlights and CCTV around her block of flats, Selina was wary. A symptom of spending her life in the criminal courts. She slid the file back beneath her jacket before climbing out of the car, her house keys held in the palm of her hand with the keys pointing out through the gaps between her fingers. Just in case.

They were addling her, these unsolved elements. Her trainers crunched on the ground, the noise bouncing from the brick walls and parked cars around her, and the wind bit at her cheeks. It was unsettlingly quiet for a Saturday night, the cold adding to the eeriness.

She made it inside in one piece, of course. Taunton was hardly *The Wire*. Still, she felt nervous climbing the stairs, the hallway only dimly lit. Walking along the passage to her apartment she found herself looking over her shoulder once, twice, three times. Esther's door was shut tight at the other end. Was she home, Selina wondered, or still at the hospital with Connie? Or had she gone to join the reserve hospice nurse at Kilstock and see her dad?

She would see her in the morning, Selina decided. If she was home they would discuss everything there. If not, Selina would find her at the hospital.

By then, she thought, she would have it worked out, or enough to be sure at least.

She was wrong.

Inside her flat she sat on the tan leather sofa with the iPad on her lap and her bare feet tucked beneath her. She needed to find out where Charlotte was now, work out if she could be strong enough to overwhelm Connie, hopefully even find out if she had indeed been to visit Michael.

Esther had never mentioned her, nor had Madeleine, so the visits presumably either were kept secret or took place when only Connie was on duty. With Madeleine taking the night shifts and sleeping during the day, that latter was the most likely.

First Selina needed to know if Charlotte had married; she needed her surname to track her down. She filled in the details of Charlotte's birthname and date, both included on Connie's wedding certificate, on the registry website.

The page loaded in seconds; there were thirteen records mentioning a Charlotte Lithgow from 1874 to present day. Six birth records, three marriage records and four deaths. Only two of the Charlotte Lithgows on the list were still alive.

Selina's theory fell to pieces.

Neither of the two were Michael's mother.

Her death had been recorded in 1988.

The iPad fell from her hands.

Useless.

The question rose up, the first one she always asked herself when preparing any defence. *What do you know?*

She knew she had let Connie down. Connie had come to her for help, years ago, and Selina had misunderstood. By not listening and jumping to conclusions, she had kept Connie trapped in a cycle of abuse that had resulted in her developing blood clots so severe they threatened her life. Selina could have helped her. She didn't.

Selina was empty and raw with regret. She had thought herself so clever.

She abandoned the sofa, climbed the stairs to her bedroom. She was exhausted and she knew she couldn't do anything further tonight. She had nothing left to give.

The idea that Connie hadn't done this to herself had been a lifeline, a way that Selina could make up for her past mistakes. If she could have brought someone, anyone, to justice, then perhaps she could have atoned for covering up Michael's crimes. For not helping Connie properly when she should have done.

But the lifeline was gone and, as Selina collapsed on her bed fully clothed, she thought of Esther's certainty at the hospital that day; Connie had done this to herself.

She had tried to end her own life.

There was no one else responsible; no vengeful mother; no rogue attacker.

Selina had made a mistake.

Chapter Thirty-One

Selina

Three years ago

The crying was subtle. The sound of it was masked by general commotion in the background, but Connie was definitely crying.

'I need you.' Connie said.

Those words again, said in the very same tone as two years before. Selina's heart sank. What was it now? What could he have *possibly* done that Selina had missed? True to her word she had kept tabs on him. Her mother was thrilled when Selina announced that she'd secured a place in a Bristol chambers and was moving back to Taunton.

As for Austin, he had swept Selina into his arms and kissed her so hard her breath caught.

For the two years since then, Selina had been watching Michael; searching his computer, his phone, making sure he really was now working at an old people's home and had nothing to do with schools, children's clubs or sports teams. Once, after a particularly nasty court case involving a suspected paeodophile and seven ten-year-old girls, Selina had arrived unannounced and searched Michael's bedroom, the shed in the garden, every cupboard and chest she could find. She searched until her fingertips were sore from flicking through papers. She searched until her guilt at having success-fully defended the man in court had abated.

'I've kept my word,' Michael had said as he followed her around the small house. 'I have Connie, I don't need anyone else. I swear it.'

She ignored him as she hunted for evidence she prayed she wouldn't find. And she hadn't found anything; he had kept his word. Or so it had seemed.

Why then, two years after the first plea, was Connie back on the phone, saying those same two words?

'Where are you?' Selina moved her phone to her other ear and secured her locker behind her, undoing it again when she realised her robe had caught in the door.

'Taunton,' Connie said, her words slurring out in a burr. 'Police . . . station.'

Selina paused for breath and concentrated on the scent of the air; spray-on deodorant and a hint of shoe polish. 'What's happened?' She swallowed, carefully and slowly, making sure not to panic, to keep her head clear.

'Help me,' Connie said again and Selina knew it was useless to push any further.

'I'll come, but it's going to take me a while. Hold tight and wait for me to arrive. And don't say anything until I get there.'

She hung up, grabbed her bag and her keys and left the crown court behind her. As she reached her car she got another call, from Michael this time.

'I've told them you're my lawyer,' he said.

'I'm a barrister, Michael, not a solicitor.'

'That's why I said lawyer; it covers both, doesn't it?'

Not really, Selina thought, thinking of the lectures her grandfather used to give her, drumming the difference at an early age into the only grandchild he knew would make the bar. And she did. She was successful.

So why was she risking it all for this man who deserved everything he got? It was what she was good at, she reasoned, only this time she knew him to be guilty, for a fact. It wasn't just unethical to defend him, but illegal.

'Esther's a solicitor. She could come and give you counsel,' she said, testing the water with the statement. And there it was: the sharp intake of breath, the desperation in the stuttering response.

'No, no,' Michael said, and she could practically smell his fear down the phone. 'Please don't let her find out, please.'

It was the same desperation she felt.

The initial desire to protect Esther from the reality had given way to a pulse-racing paranoia that she would find out Selina had helped cover it up. The fear of losing her friendship was as bad as the fear she would be disbarred. Worse, even. Her job offered her financial gain, but Esther was the only real friend she had.

It was her acceptance, Selina realised, that was so important. The feeling that she was fine just as she was. With Austin she was always trying to prove that she was good enough, deserving of his time when time was so precious. With Esther she didn't feel the need to worry, she just *was*.

'Of course I won't tell her,' Selina said, resolved to see this through to the end. Convinced that she could make it work. 'Tell me the charges.'

'The girl went to the police,' Michael whispered into the phone and she could picture him at the station, cupping the phone in his hand and peering around him with nervous eyes. 'Made all these claims about me. False claims, I swear it, *false claims*. The police came to the house. They found a photo.'

Selina went cold. She had searched that house and found nothing. 'Where was it?'

'It had slipped out of that box years ago, had fallen into a crack in the floorboards of the shed. It was just one.'

'It must have been a pretty bad one if it gave them cause to arrest you, Michael.'

There was silence for a moment, broken only by the moist sound of Michael opening and closing his mouth, searching for words that would excuse him.

'Look, I'll be there in an hour. Don't say anything in the meantime.'

At the station Selina found Connie first, huddled in the corner of the waiting room with a cold cup of water in her shaking hand. Her curly hair was loose, the blonde darker in her middle age and showing strands of grey. Her freckles stood out against her pale skin, her eyes ringed with shadows. She had lost weight since Selina had last seen her and her face was haggard, as though she were the portrait to Michael's Dorian Gray.

'Are you all right?' Selina whispered. Connie opened her mouth, looking pained, and Selina handed her a small lined notebook and a pen.

They found a picture, Connie wrote, feverishly. *That girl. Older now. Went to the police. They came, took Michael.*

'Yes, I know, he phoned me. That's why I'm here.'

To help me? Connie pushed the pad with the desperate words into Selina's hand and gripped her arm.

'Yes, of course to help you.'

Connie pointed to the words again and with her jaw hanging

open revealing a mouth full of saliva. Selina had to look away. She patted Connie's arm, moved to the desk and asked to be shown through to Michael.

There wasn't much she could do on that very first day. They hadn't formally charged Michael but were keeping him in overnight for questioning while they searched the rest of the property. They were contacting the school he had once worked for and his current employer.

'And what about the girl, is she here?' Selina asked. She was sitting beside Michael in the interview room.

'Of course not!' the detective, DC Ali, said, eying Selina with the familiar contempt that all police officers showed her.

'Can I see her statement?' Selina remained upright in her seat, hands clasped loosely on the table in front of her, never dropping eye contact. 'I'd like a copy.'

DC Ali handed them over, both the written statement and a transcript of the initial conversation. The girl's name, Selina saw, was Mia.

The cottage in Kilstock was out of bounds, so Selina booked herself and Connie into a hotel. Selina was living next door to Esther now, her friend jumping at the chance to buy one of the flats in the converted warehouse where Selina lived, and so couldn't risk going there.

I want to go home, Connie had written on her pad when Selina had ushered her into her hotel room. She was scared, needed familiarity and comfort rather than more upheaval.

'Not yet. Tomorrow, hopefully. I'm in the room right next door, should you need me.'

'Book?' Connie said aloud, looking hopeful, the lines smoothing from her weary face as she said it, as if the very prospect of reading a story could eradicate the stress of the day's events.

'I've a couple of Agatha Christies in my glove box. I'll nip down and get them for you.'

Selina thought something simpler would probably have been better, something by Enid Blyton or even a new David Walliams story. She wasn't sure that Connie would grasp the plot of a murder mystery and worried that the subject matter might upset her, but Connie had looked delighted at the prospect.

Whilst Connie sat in her room alone, presumably reading about Roger Ackroyd, Selina read Mia's transcript.

When she slept, she dreamed about it, combining the photographs she still had in her flat with the words from DC Ali's interview. She awoke several times, bathed in sweat, gasping.

She read things like this nearly every day. Why was it bothering her so much more now? Because this time, she knew it was all true, without a doubt. She couldn't blithely hide behind her client's not-guilty plea, when she had hidden the evidence herself.

She tried to push the words away, focused instead on the defence she already knew she would use, but still the bare facts haunted her sleep.

'Ten years old when it began.'

In the morning Selina was weak with tiredness and with hunger. She knocked on Connie's room, to see if she was coming down for breakfast, but Connie wouldn't come out. 'Book,' she said through the closed door.

Selina went to the restaurant alone, filled her first plate with fruit and a slice of cold, glistening ham. She drank a bitter coffee and watched as a tired-looking father guided his two daughters around the buffet.

'He would tickle . . .'

Selina stood up and went back for more. Croissants and a pain au chocolat, an apricot Danish and a splodge of jam spooned from a bowl. She filled a dish with Weetabix and drizzled syrup on top.

The father had let each girl fill their own plate. One had opted for nothing but meat: ham, bacon, sausages, black pudding. The other had a banana and three strawberries. Selina watched them return to their table, wondering where their mother was and why they were here. She wondered what Mia would have ordered, had she had the opportunity.

After the pastries Selina had scrambled eggs, fried mushrooms and thick, oozing tomatoes. Another bowl of cereal. Then she went upstairs, back to her room, into the bathroom and threw up until her guts were empty.

'. . . undress and sit on his lap . . .'

Connie would not come to the police station and so Selina went alone. She had phoned her chambers that morning to explain that there was an emergency and then turned her phone off.

Michael looked awful. She met him in the interview room and watched as he rubbed his neck, sore from a night lying on the police-cell bed. She imagined those fingers on the button of his camera. Imagined them tickling Mia.

'Don't say a word,' Selina told him as DC Ali walked in.

Ali laid various notes on the table and Selina read them all upside down. There was the original transcript and statement again. Beneath it was a list of evidence and the timeline of custody.

'Have you any other photographs in your possession, Mr Lithgow?' Ali began, no time for pleasantries.

'Are you charging him?' Selina asked, smiling slightly at the detective to unsettle her.

Michael opened his mouth but Selina put a silencing hand on his arm. It was the first time she had touched him since arriving at the police station. It was the first time she had touched him, she realised, in over two years.

She pulled her hand back and looked down again at the evidence log.

'You were the caretaker at that school, Mr Lithgow. That's how you first met the girl, isn't that right?'

Michael looked sidelong at Selina but said nothing.

'You knew she liked science, didn't you, Mr Lithgow? You lured her to your shed with a promise of a new Bunsen burner that the school didn't need any more; you told her she could have it if she came with you. Isn't that right, Mr Lithgow?'

'Can I have a copy of this?' Selina tapped the evidence log with her unpolished fingernail. Ali looked at her with disdain, flipped the paper over and pushed it across the desk towards Selina.

'Which statement are you reading?' Selina asked, scanning the evidence log as she spoke.

'I gave you a copy, yesterday. Now, Mr Lithgow,' Ali went on, 'you then proceeded to take her photograph, isn't that right? And threatened to show everyone those photographs if she were to tell. Then you threatened her mother, isn't that right? You said you would hurt her mother if she told anyone. Threatened to hurt her mother if the girl didn't agree to come back the next day, isn't that right?'

'So this is the mother's statement, not Mia's. Is that correct,

DC Ali?' She hated herself. The more she spoke, the more that self-loathing mingled with the adrenaline that always surged through her system whenever she proved a detective wrong. The drug was so addictive that even while Selina despised herself she also glowed with the thrill of her own audacity.

'Did Mia make a statement herself?'

'No, it was—'

'If Mia won't talk to the police in a quiet, comfortable witness suite, do you really think she'll take the stand?' Michael gave a small groan and Selina had to silence him again. She could feel his arms tense beneath her fingers, as though he were bracing himself. She continued. 'A third-party statement is hardly cast-iron, DC Ali. Do you think it will hold up in court?' She felt disgusting but she couldn't stop. Selina reminded herself that the crime DC Ali was accusing Michael of couldn't be proven with this information alone and therefore she was doing what any decent defence barrister, or solicitor for that matter, would do in her place.

'It's not just the witness statement—'

'The mother didn't see anything, so can't technically be called a witness.' She just had to push the image of that little girl out of her head, concentrate on the facts the police were in possession of.

'It's also the photographic evidence. You can hardly dispute *that*.' Ali sat back, arms folded, and Selina felt that buzz rise through her spine and the beat in her head that went to the tune win-win-win.

'There's a gap,' Selina said, and smiled with fake apology. 'Right here. The photograph was bagged for evidence at the Lithgow property and signed off into the care of one of your

PCs. It was then a further four hours before it was signed into evidence at the station. Four hours. What happened during that gap?'

Ali paled, looked down at the piece of paper. She didn't quibble or argue, as Selina thought she might. Nor did she try and nervously excuse the mistake, possibly knowing that Selina would eat her alive if she tried.

'Kilstock is an hour, maximum, from Taunton. It doesn't take four hours. Was the photograph in the custody of the PC the whole time?' Selina hid her self-disgust and forced herself to look confident. She sat up as straight as she could in her seat, her hands clasped once more on the table. Her heartbeat was through the roof. 'I hope the PC has a good explanation. Surely he knows that, had he let that piece of evidence out of his sight for even a minute before logging it at the station, it would be inadmissible. Do you have any other evidence, DC Ali? Or is the whole case built around a second-hand accusation and one solitary photograph you found in the floorboards of a very old house?' DC Ali stood and walked out of the room, the evidence log held out at arm's length.

Selina knew before they even confirmed it that the charges would be dropped, not because the police thought Michael innocent, but because the CPS wouldn't pursue a case with no other evidence and no corroboration from a single witness other than the parent of a supposed victim. She knew she had them.

And then, as she turned to look at Michael's pale, worried face, another line of the transcript echoed in her mind.

'She said he tickled her until she cried and then he undid his trousers.'

They kept Michael in for one more day before they ran

out of time and had to admit defeat. The PC in charge of the evidence had gone home on the way to the station. He had been so horrified by the case that he had wanted to see his wife and daughter. He had left the photograph, in the evidence bag, in the glove compartment of his car.

Michael was released without charge.

'Help me?' Connie had said again when Selina had collected her from the hotel.

'I've already helped you, Connie. Michael's free to go, no charges will be pressed. He has no criminal record and can keep his job. Esther doesn't need to know.'

Connie cried silent tears all the way home. Selina thought Connie would have said thank you, but knew she was difficult like that.

Chapter Thirty-Two

Connie

Early Hours of Sunday Morning

It is nearly 1 a.m. when the nurse comes to give the final check of the night. I concentrate on each of her movements. I force myself to relax when she touches my arm. When she leaves she says, 'See you in the morning.'

Oh no, you won't, I think.

I have a plan.

As soon as the nurse leaves I test myself, raise my arm and reach for the heart monitor. My limbs are heavy and unwilling, but I can do it. I press the 'silent' button and the incessant beep-beeping stops. The screen is still on, my heart rate shown as a jagged line, but it doesn't make any sound.

I look at the drip stand. The sedative is connected to the syringe driver; the dose I don't know but I do know how the thing works. A set quantity releases at intervals. The nurse has just replaced it with a fresh vial, so I'm presuming another measure will shortly wind its way into the saline and then through the feed tube and into the needle on my hand.

I don't want to be sedated any more. I don't want to be numbly trapped in my body, forced to remember why I am here and all that has happened to me.

In the semi-clear space of light sedation another thought

forms in my head. I think of the reason I am in this hospital bed.

Until now the events have remained cloudy in my mind, but they are starting to form.

The attack came early on Friday without warning, no questions asked, and no mercy shown. The motive, I know, was revenge.

Where is Esther? Has she gone home to her flat or home to Kilstock, to see her father? She won't stay in the hospital for a whole weekend; I know her, she will want to go to him. But what if my assailant returns? What if they hurt her for the things I've done?

I must get to them first.

If they think I'm in hospital they won't see me coming, just as I didn't see them coming. Surprise, I know, is my friend.

My plan develops, adrenaline flushing through me, and I can move with a touch more freedom as each minute passes.

I rip out the needle from the back of my hand to stop more sedative affecting me. Blood blooms from the hole, seeps along the crevices between tendons. The needle leaks clear liquid and the bed sheet is becoming damp.

There will be an alarm attached to the drip, I know. It will alert the nurses if the fluid runs out or if anything interrupts the flow.

There's another problem. I am tethered to the bed by a winding tube that snakes up between my legs. The catheter, too, is linked to an alarm, which will sound if the bag stops filling with urine; an early sign of kidney problems.

The solution is simple, but I don't relish it.

Squeezing my eyes shut I take my left hand and grab the catheter tube.

I breathe in, hold the air in the pit of my lungs, focus on the need to get home.

I wrench.

A burning pain and a dribble of piss, but it's done. The drip needle I insert into the catheter tube. I watch the slow flow as the sedative-spiked saline drips along the tube and into the clear bag by my bed.

I need to put the drip on its slowest setting, to give it as much time as possible before an alarm rings out that it's empty, but my head is foggy again, the exertion too much and I lie back. It will take time for the drug to clear my system enough to stand up, an hour or possibly more. Do I have that long?

The nurse said they'd leave me until the morning, but what time will they come?

I need to go home. I need to finish this.

In a minute I will stand and wrap the hospital dressing gown around me, slide my feet into the slippers by my bed. I'll leave this room. I will sneak out of the hospital. I will get home, even if it kills me to do so.

I will finish this.

I will finish him.

And if the clot in my artery does dislodge, if my heart erupts from the pressure and I die, so be it. Let my daughter think I died at her father's bedside.

Let Selina be free from her burden.

And let Michael burn slowly in hell.

Chapter Thirty-Three

Connie

1984

In the attic Michael found Grandmother's wedding dress. It must have been sixty years old and the white lace had yellowed with age. He said we could clean it, get rid of the mothball smell and raise the hem so it didn't drag as I walked. I didn't bother.

It's difficult to look demure when you're seven months pregnant. The growing bump was easy to hide behind my garden-flower bouquet, but the hiding of it made it all the more obvious. I doubt most brides cling to their flowers over their midriffs throughout the whole service. It was such a long service, too. I felt faint by the end and Michael was quite feverish, glancing to the church door again and again to see if his mother had arrived.

She didn't come, despite her letter.

He had used the same law firm that sorted Grandmother's will to send her the invitation. We didn't know anything about her. The lawyer had searched for her, I don't know how. She'd been informed of the death, though she hadn't attended the funeral, or even sent a card. When he wrote to her the lawyer made it quite clear that her son was alive, but we didn't hear from her. Maybe that's why Michael didn't write to her directly straight away, even though the lawyer passed on her address, but waited until he had some *happy news*. Happy, indeed.

Michael didn't tell me he'd written, I found that out for myself. I'd seen the indentations on the notepad I'd long stopped using and employed the same methods he had done when he wanted to know what I'd been saying to people when he wasn't around. I got a teaspoon of very fine coal dust from the fire grate, sprinkled it on the paper, blew off the excess and I could just make out the words.

> I'm getting married, to the lovleyest girl.
> I would be pleased if you would come.
> Its at St Nicholas church, at 10am, on the first Saturday in May.
> Its not much notice, I know, but we're having a baby and want to do things propley.

The poor grammar and spelling made me wince. Michael wasted his education. What I wouldn't have given to go to that simple village school. Even I never made those sorts of mistakes in my notes, when I still wrote them. That was before I found him with coal dust on his fingers, feverishly reading over the instructions I'd given to the milkman (One bottle, please) and the butcher's boy who had bicycled over from Stowey (A pound of bacon, two pork chops and a small beef brisket, thank you).

It made me feel dirty, that he'd read my notes. Made me wonder what he'd expected to find.

A week or so later he came to me, smiling, held me by the shoulders. 'Guess what, Con? Guess what? You never will guess, never.'

Then why are you asking me to? I thought.

His eyes darted about as if he'd asked the whole garden to guess the news, the flowers and carrot seedlings and the silos.

'She's only coming! She's only bloody coming!' He squeezed my shoulders and kissed me hard on the mouth and I had to press my lips together tightly to keep his filthy tongue out.

He spun me round and round, as if I wanted to be spun around, and said it again, 'She replied to my invitation, said she'd be delighted to see me get married!' He laughed some more and did a funny little jump, kicked his ankles together in the air but couldn't quite land properly and so stumbled. He carried on laughing.

'You're smiling, Connie!' he said and the look on his face was pure awe.

Smiling? So I was, I realised.

He cleaned the whole house in the week before the wedding, not because I was heavily pregnant but because his mother was coming. I sat and read in the shade of the silos, four books in one week. Michael cleaned so hard, every crevice of that house, every cupboard, that on two of the nights he fell asleep without even touching me once and I thought yes, oh yes, thank Christ.

'Do I look well?' he said to me on the Saturday morning, fiddling with the bowtie at his neck. He looked a fool, wearing Grandfather's suit that was too long on the leg and the cuff, his shoulders even broader than Michael's. His face was cleanly shaven, hair cut and slicked back with Brylcreem and a spray of Old Spice.

'What do you think she'll wear?' he asked, and I stared at the table and ate a slice of toast with marmalade. A wedge of citrus pith landed in the skirt of my dress and I didn't bother to wipe it off.

'Do you think she'll have one of those power suits?' He was

holding the picture from the living-room mantelpiece, the one of our mother-twins in their school uniforms, impossible to tell apart. 'You know the ones, with the shoulder pads? Do you think she'll have that blonde, flicky fringe like Princess Diana?'

Do you think . . .

Do you think . . .

Do you think . . .

On and on he went, all morning, and it took my mind clean off what we were about to do; I had to put all my energy into blocking out his voice. *Why would you think she'd wear a power suit?* I thought. *She left home and became a junkie, not a business-woman.* The thought that you could change your life never occurred to me.

Michael thought she'd be waiting at the church, but she wasn't. There were a few from Kilstock, the churchwardens, the daughters of one of the invalid old men I cleaned for. Maud's daughters didn't come. Michael hadn't invited anyone from work, *none of their business*, he said. I couldn't help but think of poor Miss Park and her tea-stained trousers. I would have liked her to come. I would have invited the whole world, had I been asked.

The more people that saw the bump of my child, the less likely it was that Michael would appear in my bedroom with a bottle of chloroform and an unravelled coat hanger, like last time. I wasn't going to take his apparent exuberance for granted. He could change his mind, decide he didn't want our life inter-rupted by crying and feeding and nappies. I'd thought that, considering the damage he caused aborting the last one, I would never get pregnant again.

This baby was going to be mine.

I had read so many books across so many genres that I knew full well what was happening to me. At first, I had faked blood-stained knickers once a month so he wouldn't suspect, biting my cheeks and spitting red into the gusset. I began eating more, putting on weight so he'd think I was just getting plump. I didn't show for a long while, though. By the time my stomach rounded and he realised what had happened, I was nearly six months gone, or so the new doctor reckoned. Dr Rowe was long-since retired. Or dead. I hoped he was dead.

Michael wasn't angry. Perhaps it was his maturity, perhaps it was that everyone who would have objected to such a thing was already several years buried.

Thanks to me.

No, he wasn't happy. He was *elated*. He felt the firm bulk of my womb, the little kick the baby gave turning his face from confusion to joy in an instant. We were going to get married, he said. I would be his wife, an honest woman; it wouldn't matter what anyone thought if we were wed.

And I realised the mistake I had made.

I really was trapped now.

He would control my life in all the ways it was possible to do so, not just my legal guardian but my owner.

I would be his wife.

A few weeks before we were to be married a letter arrived. I opened it over the kettle.

> To Michael,
>   Don't write to me agen. You have your own life now and I have mine and its best we leeve it that way. You are not a child, you don't need a mother.
>   I wish you luck in you're married life.
>   Charlotte

I read the letter and my first thought was, *Ha! He inherited his grammar from her.*

I smiled a rare smile, for myself and my baby. I thought how smug he had looked when he decided we should marry. I thought about smacking that look off his face.

I kept the envelope but tore the original letter to shreds, buried the pieces with the carrot seedlings so the damp earth would turn them to mulch. I tore out a fresh leaf of paper from the pad, leaning it onto the table top so as not to leave those tell-tale pen ridges.

> *My Dearest Michael,*
>
> *I am so honoured you have invited me to your approaching wedding day. I think of you often and have indeed wondered if you have yet settled down, and with whom, and if you have started a family.*
>
> *How I have missed you, how I have regretted ever giving you up. I am sorry, Michael. Please forgive me, my darling son, for letting you down so horribly in your formative years.*
>
> *I shall indeed come to your wedding and, if you can find it in your heart to forgive me, please let me kiss your cheek and let's put the past behind us. I would so love to be a part of your future.*
>
> *Your ever loving, humble and regretful mother,*
> *Charlotte.*

A tad ham-handed perhaps, but I wrote what I knew he wanted to hear and he swallowed every word of it, read it with saliva dripping down his chin as though he were the retard, not me. He memorised every line.

He made big plans, talked about moving his mother in with us, living together as a happy family as if that would be normal – as if every thirty-five-year-old man dreamed of living with his mother and his wife and his baby all in the one tiny, two-bedroomed house.

I thought I was being so clever.

Michael cried, on our wedding day, and the tears in his eyes were twofold. When he saw me nod yes to those sickening vows, to love, honour and obey, obey, obey, his tears fell, it's true. But also when he looked over the small congregation for his mother, who'd promised to be there but was not, his eyes filled too.

I had been so happy, standing in that church and watching his bottom lip tremble like a pathetic child. I had wanted to hurt him, to exact a small slice of revenge and I'd done it. I imagined the other letters I would write: Charlotte's fake apology for not having come, some disaster or illness perhaps. Charlotte could offer to visit, I could watch him madly prepare the house knowing she would never come. I could watch him break, piece by piece, as he was rejected again and again and again by a mother who was so loving in her letters and yet so very absent. Perhaps he may one day go to her house and knock on her door and she would then reject him face to face and maybe, just maybe, he would take me with him and that would be marvellous because then I could watch.

The church service finished at lunchtime. No reception, no cake, no village-hall party. Michael took me home and tried not to cry as he held me tightly to his chest, so hard I couldn't move my head, could hardly breathe, and as my chest ached from his hugging I thought, *Ha! Serves you right!*

'You're all I've got, in the world,' he said to me, tenderly, lovingly, cruelly and I stopped feeling happy, my victory snubbed out.

I read easily enough between the lines.

I'll never let you go, he was saying.

And, now we're married, I won't have to.

He took such full advantage of our wedding night, emptying his frustration, confusion, juvenile heartbreak into me, that I knew that I'd never write any more letters. What a pointless revenge that would be. I'd be lining my live-in coffin with sandpaper.

Chapter Thirty-Four

Selina

Early Sunday Morning

On waking, Selina realised she'd slept well, deep and dreamlessly. Unusual for her Taunton pad, but she'd been so damn tired she must have just passed out.

A noise had woken her but, now she was awake, she couldn't determine what it had been. There were no crows cawing outside, no traffic to be heard. She didn't know exactly what time it yet was but doubted it was past 6 a.m.

Selina was still wearing yesterday's clothes, she realised, her suit trousers, shirt and sweater. The same clothes she had been wearing on Friday, too. Her mother would be horrified.

Her mother.

Connie.

Charlotte.

Selina closed her eyes, longed for that blissful ignorance to return. She felt cold, listless, reality sapping the burst of newly woken energy. She had an urge to crawl beneath the musty bed sheet and stay there, head covered. Why go out, why talk to Esther? What good would it do?

And how could she visit Connie, look her in the eye, after failing her so terribly?

This feeling of inertia wasn't new, but it had been a long

time since she'd last felt it. Then it was her father's death that caused it and Esther had pulled her through. Esther couldn't help her now.

She didn't climb beneath her duvet. Beside her bed was the file of paperwork, dragged upstairs after the grim discovery of Charlotte's death and abandoned as jetsam on the floor. She could make out its shape in the darkness. Maybe it wouldn't make Esther feel any better knowing why Connie had tried to end her own life, but it was information she had a right to. Selina had a duty to give it to her.

She reached for it but, from the opposite side of her bed, came the same sound that had woken her up; it was the thrum of her phone vibrating.

Twisting towards it, she saw a local number flash on the screen. Above the number, in the top left corner, a notification that she had three missed calls and a text.

'Hello?' Her voice quivered as she answered, the scenario an uncanny reminder of Friday evening.

'Selina? It's Austin.'

She sat bolt upright, head light from the speed of her movement. His voice was grave, jumping ahead of any niceties and straight to the point.

'It's Connie,' he said, and Selina thought, it's over, she's dead. And when Austin said, 'She's gone,' Selina felt the prick and sting of tears and the voice in her head screamed, *because I failed her*.

She knew she should speak but her throat had grown thick and constricted.

'Esther's on her way,' Austin said. He sounded harassed. 'But I think you should come too, help her out. We haven't the resources and can't report it for twenty-four hours—'

Selina nodded, aware of how stupid that was because of course he couldn't see her. Then she twigged, her head catching up with her ears. 'What do you mean you can't report it?'

'That she's gone, fled the hospital.'

'She's not dead?'

'Dead? No, no, she's left. Walked out on her own.'

Connie had walked out of the hospital.

'Thank God,' Selina said, 'I thought—'

'There's no thank-bloody-god about it, she's at a huge risk. If she had another embolism outside on her own at five in the goddamn morning—'

'I know, I know, it's just when you called, I thought she had—' She could explain to Austin later if needs be. Right now, she had to help Connie. 'I'm on my way,' she said.

She brought up the text, expecting it to be from Austin or Esther. It was from Chapel, sent at 1 a.m.

Don't be a stubborn mule. If you need anything at all, just call.

She typed out a thank-you and pocketed her phone, not prepared to draw anyone else in. No time to shower and change, she rammed her feet into her trainers and picked up the file from the floor. Esther still needed to know.

Where would Connie have gone? Selina pictured her stumbling to the bridge over the river Tone, jumping off and either drowning in the river or freezing to death in its icy churn. Walking into the road in front of a bus or heading for the railway track.

There was something else Selina needed to get before leaving the flat. Kneeling on the floor she slid one arm beneath her bed, felt through the dust motes and cobwebs for the box.

Perhaps Connie is heading for home, to finish herself off as she intended, intent on slipping into the abyss with an armful of morphine. Maybe the new nurse could stop her in time? Maybe if Selina called ahead to the house, asked the nurse to keep an eye out?

Selina couldn't feel the box.

She stretched further, thinking it must have somehow slipped towards the back, knowing it must be there somewhere, it had to be.

But it wasn't.

She dropped her head to the floor, looked in the shadows beneath her bed. There, on the floor, was a clean, sharp rectangle cut into the dust.

Someone had been in her flat.

The box, and all its secrets, was gone.

Chapter Thirty-Five

Connie

Early Sunday Morning

It's surprisingly easy to escape from a hospital. It's not prison, after all.

A new patient was admitted to the far end of the ward a little before five in the morning; I could hear the bustling it caused outside my room. That was me two days ago, I thought.

I was still shaky, the sedative not yet fully out of my system – it can take up to six hours even on a low dose – but I couldn't let the chance pass me by.

I groped my way to the door, unsteady but strong enough to stand. I wrapped the dressing gown tightly around me, slid slippers onto my feet and snuck out. No one saw me leave my ward and, once I had made my way to the main hospital corridor, no one stopped me.

A janitor looked up from his mop as I stumbled past, my legs Bambi-like. He smiled at me as if it was the most normal thing in the world and I thought, *oh yes, this is what it's like to be a person*. I thought of that nice postman, from years ago. I thought of all those letters from the asylum Michael kept.

I had forgotten, in my need to get home, that it was winter still and outside the cold shocked all other thoughts away. I padded along the pavement, towards the traffic lights and the town centre, without a clue as to how to get home.

There aren't any cars on the road, not even a bus. Maybe that's a good thing, I think. I must look like a madwoman.

The dressing gown is made from flannel; it's thick but not warm, and my teeth chatter inside my head. I remove the cord from the waist and tie it again and again round my neck as a scarf, use my hands to keep the gown wrapped around my body.

An abandoned glove rests on top of a garden wall. A child's glove, and only one, but it's better than nothing and I slip my own small hand in. The outside of it is damp from dew and it's stiff from the cold, but the inside is dry. It's carrot orange, a picture of a fox on one side.

I wish I had socks on. It hits me that I may not make it home. I may get stopped and dragged back. I may die of hypothermia. Or is it hyperthermia? I can't remember. The weather has frozen my brain.

I was going to hail a taxi, ask them to take me home and pay when I got there, but there aren't any around. Esther uses some thingamy on her phone, but I haven't a thingamy and I haven't a phone. What do I do?

I could stick out a thumb for a lift, but who would pick up an old woman in a dressing gown wearing one orange glove and no socks?

What if the stranger talks to me, what would I say? What if they haven't a pencil or paper?

What if someone touches me?

I walk on towards the town, deathly quiet. Kilstock is fifteen miles, at least, from Taunton. I haven't the energy or the time to walk there.

How long until they know that I've gone? When will they start looking for me?

I see the shadow of a person disappear into an alley and I think it's very early for anyone else to be out and I think, *What is the time?* and I think, *I don't want to be out here on my own.*

I know it's morning but the sky is still dark, all the street-lamps are on, and it feels as frightening as the night.

I can't go back, I must get home, but I'm scared.

I want my daughter.

And as if the devil himself were earwigging my thoughts, a car approaches and I know, even before the number plate is near enough for me to see, that it's my Esther.

And I can tell by the look on her face she's not happy.

'Mum!' She pulls up beside me, her window already wound down before she's come to a stop. 'Get in, now!'

No *What are you doing?* No *You'll freeze to death*. I don't blame her, I've made her angry. I'm making her even more so by not getting in. I can't. She'll take me back to the hospital and I can't go, I have to finish this mess. I want to finish it.

I shake my head and she looks at me with tired disappointment.

'Will you get into the car, Mum?' Her teeth are gritted. 'You're not well, you shouldn't be out here.'

Again I shake my head and through my own chattering teeth I say, 'Home.'

She is mustering her patience. I've tested her to the limit, this final stunt the last thing she can take.

'You can't go home, Mum, you've got an arterial thrombosis in your sodding armpit. You need to go back to Musgrove, wait for your surgery. *Then* you can go home.'

I still don't move. The cold has seeped into every part of me, my body is numb with it. But I can't get into the car with her, I can't let her take me back. I need to get to that man.

'Home,' I say again.

'Will you get in the fucking car?' She has shocked herself, with that shouting. Her face is white and I don't know what to do. I want to be warm, I want my daughter, but I must finish this.

'I'm sorry,' she says, 'I'm so sorry, I didn't mean to shout at you, the nurse on the phone said that sedation can sometimes make people paranoid, delusional, scared . . . I'm just . . . Mum, I'm so fucking tired. Won't you just get into the car? Please?'

I see her cursing her luck for having me as a mother. But how much easier is it cursing your luck than the truth?

I don't want her to know what has happened to me, what I have done. I don't want her to know that her dad is not a hero but a monster. Let her think he is a good man. Let her think I am just a simpleton.

'Home . . . to see . . . Mich—' But I can't say his name.

She rubs her eyes, then leans forward so her forehead rests on the steering wheel.

As she moves I see something on the rear passenger seat. My legs nearly buckle; I have my gloved hand on the roof of the car to steady myself. I'm no longer shaking from the cold.

She has the tin box.

It's on the back seat of her car.

How did she get it? Has she looked inside it? I think not, or she wouldn't be talking to me like this. What do I do?

'You don't need to go home, Mum. I'll go back later to sit with him and there's a nurse there to take care of things till then; Madeleine arranged cover until Monday.' She looks at me with tired eyes; the only emotion they show is her exhausted patience. If she had looked inside the box they would show horror.

Why hasn't she looked inside it?

I think of what she said, think of another way I could make this work.

'Take me,' I say, and I point towards home. Take me home, I will her. Take me home and let me sit by Michael's bedside. Go with the nurse to the kitchen, make tea, and by the time you come back he'll be dead, the pillow already removed from his face. You'll think he died in his sleep, it will all be over, and then I can go to your car whilst you're crying over his dead body and hide that box until it's safe to burn it.

Yes, I have a plan.

But Esther shakes her head. 'You need to go back to the hospital, Mum, you've got an operation booked.' I interrupt her, shaking my head, mime with my hands that the operation's not till tomorrow. I point back towards home.

I'm being cruel, I know, but I play her. I begin to walk, my legs creaking and painful from the chill.

I hear her swear, the clunk of her car as she begins reversing back.

'For Christ's sake,' she says. 'Fine, you bloody win. Get in. I'll take you home but only for an hour, then I'm bringing you straight back to the hospital.'

That's fine by me, I think.

I know how long it'll take. After all, I've done it before.

Chapter Thirty-Six

Selina

Early Sunday Morning

Thinking that perhaps Connie had wandered through the backstreets, Selina used those small, residential roads to reach the hospital. She didn't see her anywhere, the streets of pale-brick terraced houses quiet, the lamps lighting nothing but parked cars and dustbins.

Was it Connie who had snuck into her flat, taken the box? Selina prayed that it was, that by some miracle Connie had walked all the way to Selina's flat in the freezing night whilst Selina slept, let herself into the building by the keycode at the entrance, picked her un-pickable lock, crept through to her bedroom and had taken it.

What was more likely, Selina thought, once the gut-wrenching adrenaline had abated, was that Esther had overheard her conversation with Connie the day before. She would have used the spare key that Selina had given her years ago to let herself in whilst Selina was either still at the hospital or in Bristol.

There was only one fact now that kept Selina moving forward; the knowledge that all was not yet lost. Esther couldn't have looked through it in detail. If she had, she would have called the police, possibly unaware that her father had been the one to take the photos. Her integrity, unlike Selina's, was unbendable, probably why she had never made it far in criminal law. The saving grace was that the incriminating pictures were hidden beneath an inch-thick wodge of family snaps. Either Esther hadn't yet opened the box at all or, if she had, she hadn't looked beyond the first few photographs.

There was time for Selina to find her, to explain before she looked any deeper.

The mixture of emotions was painful; the regret making her insides cold, the fear churning her stomach, the guilt burning her cheeks. She remembered as a child being caught stealing chocolates from her mother's cupboard, that swelling dread between the theft being discovered and Selina being scolded. The anticipation had been far greater than any punishment, surpassed only by her father's disappointment.

Emotions don't change, she thought as she pulled up in the hospital car park, we just learn to bury them. Wisdom, however, had taught her that owning up before you were found out gave you the chance to at least explain yourself before blame developed into anger.

She could barely look Austin in the eye when she saw him. It wasn't the fact that she looked like shit, her hair unbrushed and clothes sour, but the sense of urgency and confusion he emitted. *This could all have been avoided,* she thought, *if I'd owned up long ago.*

'Is Esther here?' was her first question and she didn't know whether to feel relieved or panicked when Austin shook his head. Relieved that she didn't have to face her friend just yet, panicked that Esther could at any minute lift the lid and discover the dreadful things Selina had helped cover up.

'She's gone out to look for Connie. CCTV showed her

walking away out of the town centre exit; Esther went to see if she could track her down.'

Dammit, she thought, I've missed them. 'How come you're still here? I'd have thought you'd be finished by now?'

He gave a small laugh. 'I've been home and come back again, silly; I spoke to you at the end of my shift yesterday.' He was looking a damn sight fresher than Selina, his open lab coat revealing a pressed lilac shirt and clean jeans; even his cologne smelt re-applied. The fact that the patients waiting in the A&E reception looked as neatly attired as Selina made him stand out all the more.

'So what now?' Selina said. 'Who else is looking for her?'

The look on his face – eyebrows arched and lips pressed into an apologetic smile – told her the answer.

'No one? She's in delicate health, what happens if she—'

'She's an adult who left the hospital of her own free will; we can't stop people leaving if they want to and we haven't the resources to send people after her. If she hasn't turned up in twenty-four hours then Esther can file a missing-person report but until then, well . . . that's why I called you, so you could give her a hand.'

Selina nodded, but the lack of available help was daunting. Scouring the streets *wasn't* a pointless task, she reassured herself; she was sure they would find Connie somewhere, they had to. But despite her best efforts, she felt defeated.

'Do you want me to come with you?' Austin asked. 'I could take a break for twenty minutes, so you're not on your own?' Behind him, the phone on the reception desk rang and was answered.

Austin stood with his fingers in his pockets, his thumbs tapping his hips, waiting for her to say thank you and accept.

Selina moved closer and smiled at him; she could smell something else as well as his cologne.

'I appreciate it, Austin,' she said. His fingers, tucked into his trouser pockets, hid his wedding ring. 'But I'll be fine on my own.'

He had gelled his hair, styled it more carefully today than yesterday. Selina wondered why he had been the one to phone her himself instead of asking someone less senior. Surely it wasn't normal practice for a metabolic pathologist to run patient liaison. She wondered why he still had her phone number at all; she hadn't given it to anyone at the hospital.

'I want to help you,' he said, and she knew that he was being truthful, he was being kind.

'I don't think there's anything else you can do,' she said. 'But I'm glad you called me to let me know, I appreciate it.' She smiled but all she could think of was *I don't need your help* and she longed for that time when she did.

'I'll let them know, thank you for calling,' the receptionist trilled down the phone. One of the patients rustled a crisp packet. Someone coughed into their hand. Austin stared at Selina.

It was coffee she could smell, she realised. A vague hint of coffee and mint, as though he had necked an espresso and chewed gum to hide it. She thought of his wife.

'Will you come back, when they find her?' he said and in her head the Selina from five years ago shouted *yes*, slipped her hand in his.

'Probably,' she said aloud, and put her own hands into her red coat pockets. He looked disappointed.

I'm not that person any more.

'That was a message for you, Dr Gill,' the receptionist said.

'She said she's found her mother and is taking her home.' The woman, expecting her message was good news, was clearly pleased with herself.

In a unison of incredulity, both Selina and Austin said, 'What?'

The receptionist's pleasure faded and she stumbled over the first words. 'She's taking her mother home, said she'd bring her back in plenty of time for her operation.'

Austin groaned, 'There won't be a sodding operation without her! She's essentially un-admitted herself; the slot will go to someone else. We'll have to readmit her and start the process all over again. Jesus Christ, what is she thinking?' Austin directed the barrage at Selina, saving the nervous-looking receptionist from scrutiny.

Even when she felt defeated she'd be damned if she'd admit it. So instead of *I don't know*, Selina said, 'I'll find out.'

And she would.

'I'll drive to the house.' She was thinking on the hoof. 'If I'm fast I'll not be far behind them and can either convince Esther to drive Connie back or I'll bring her back myself.'

Austin nodded. 'I didn't mean to snap, I'm sorry.'

'It's fine, really. Look, if you want to help, maybe you could phone St Moira's and ask them to give the nurse in Kilstock a heads-up; it would be helpful if there was someone there who knows about Connie's condition before she arrives home.'

Chapter Thirty-Seven

Connie

Sunday morning

I sit so quietly my breathing is silent and more than once Esther looks at me, panicked, as though I may have expired altogether. I want to put my hand on her knee, want to tell her it'll be all right, that she's doing the right thing, but I don't.

Esther's phone rings, the handset buzzing around the pocket in the door. She slides her hand down and glances at the screen.

'It's Selina,' she says, and her arm becomes stiff on the steering wheel. I stare out the window at the shops and then the houses and flats and small parks. I can count, on both hands, the number of times I have been to Taunton and each time something has changed: new buildings going up, new schools, swarms of people of all different colours, foreign languages spoken like songs.

'I thought it might have been the nurse,' Esther says. She sounds so very tired, my daughter, and I wonder what she is expecting will happen when we get home.

She just wants to be with her father, I know that. I'm not jealous, I understand. We hid everything from her to protect her and her memories, to keep her from having to face up to the reality of who we both are.

She thinks that we'll sit beside his bed, give him pain relief that *works*, hold his hand.

But it won't be at all like that.

'I remember coming here as a child, one half term,' she says, as we drive past Corkscrew Lane and the brief stretch of countryside between Taunton and the large village where Esther's boarding school sprawled. 'Dad came on the bus and we walked the river together, in our wellies. We walked all day, stopping for sandwiches at lunchtime and those crisps he liked. You know, the ones that came with a little packet of salt you had to shake on top yourself? I got sunburn on my nose and the back of my neck.'

I look ahead. I do not say a word, make a sound, nod or smile. My heart is in my throat as she speaks. I did not know this. I did not know he had been alone with her, I'd made him promise he never would. My hands, in my lap, look ashen and I hope she doesn't notice.

'You didn't come,' she says and there's an edge to her voice, as brittle as dry, autumn leaves. 'You never came. You stayed at home and read your books and folded your laundry and never once came to see me. Didn't even come to see me collect my GCSEs, or my A-Levels. You didn't come to a single play or sports match or visit me in half term.'

I stare out of the window at this place that claimed my daughter's childhood. I cannot look at her, the pain in her voice is enough; if I were to see it on her face it would be too much. I would tear open and everything else would pour out, all the hurt and the despair and the unfairness of it all.

How I would have loved to walk the river with her.

'Why?'

The road ahead is hazy and blurred and I wipe at my eyes

with my sleeve. I know what she means. It was the same question she asked me at eight years old.

Why did you send me away?

Even if speaking came as easily to me as reading, I wouldn't be able to utter a syllable.

'I was a child! I needed my parents.' The words are a wail and Esther brakes, the car stopping dead in the quiet road.

I read the signpost for King's School, the beautiful old buildings from the brochure hidden from the road by banks of trees and high fences.

'I never had any choices, no one ever talked to me. And now you're looking at me as though you were the fucking victim.'

I sit very still, as though I could close my eyes and disappear. I melt my expression, hiding my pain like a seed in an apple. I need to listen. I need to hear the pain I have caused her, each word needles and knives and bludgeoning, heart-battering hammers.

'I've had nothing from you. *Nothing.* It's Dad who's showed pride, encouragement. It was Dad who came down to Bristol when I graduated, who cheered when I collected my degree, who encouraged me through my training.' Esther looks at me and the grief on her face is unbearable.

I want to hold her. I want to touch my daughter and tell her everything. Not what *happened* to me, but what's inside me. I want her to know how fiercely I love her, how I would do anything, have done everything, for her.

I say nothing.

Her face changes, no longer painful but bewildered, exasperated.

I feel the drool on my chin. My mouth is hanging open again. She is looking at me as if trying to fathom how I can possibly be her mother. How I, who can sit in a room for hours on end with a vacant look on my face and my mouth hanging open like the moron I'm labelled to be, can also be the same woman who kissed her knees when she fell as a child and taught her the intricacies of daisy chains. How I could create a child who secured a scholarship to a private school, who received straight A's at A-Level, who received a 2-1 from Bristol in law. She has seen me at my lowest ebb and at my best, and I don't think she has ever truly grasped what is wrong with me.

A car approaches from behind, touches the horn to give a light beep and Esther looks at it from her rear-view mirror.

'It doesn't matter now,' Esther says, restarting the car and pulling away from her school and onto the road that will lead us over the hills and back home. 'We can talk about it another time. It really doesn't matter.'

It matters, I think.

It was everything to me, that I should tuck her out of harm's way.

Chapter Thirty-Eight

Connie

1992

I folded the clothes: navy-blue tunics, navy pullovers, white long-sleeved shirts and white vests. I let each piece sit in my hands, smoothing it with my palms, my fingertips tracing the seams and edges. My daughter's clothes. It was when I reached the pyjamas, the navy-blue jersey, I had to take a break.

Once, these had been the cotton dresses of a baby, the pastel booties and cardigans I had knitted myself, resting the needles on my growing bump, Esther kicking inside me and jostling with the needles for my attention. I could trace her feet through the skin on my belly, could see the swell of her head move from side to side as she swished and summersaulted. And then, there she was. The pain of birth was nothing compared with the joy of the release. All that loneliness, all that desperate longing for my mother, my father, melting with the first touch of her mucus-slicked head.

I had her.

Esther.

I dressed her in the cardigans I had knitted, dressed her in the cotton dresses and the pale socks and held her to my chest.

These were not knitted cardigans I was folding. These were stiff, white cotton shirts, knee-length tunics, a blazer with a crest sewn onto the pocket. A school uniform, made of the thickest, finest fabric I had ever felt, despite it being second-hand. It looked good as new, to me, and yet I feared for her. I feared the children would see it wasn't new, that they would taunt her for it, discover her background, her parents. I had been assured that her scholarship was secure and the bursary confidential, that no one would be told, but I still worried. Did she have the backbone to withstand taunting? Would she stand out as different from the rich children in her class? Would she find a friend?

I didn't know.

Would she miss me, as she dressed in these jersey pyjamas and tucked herself into bed?

A distance had developed between us. The hugs and sticky kisses of Esther at four, withering into the nonchalance of an eight-year-old girl grown tired of a mother who doesn't speak. The easy relationship where words didn't matter had dissolved into something more complex. She could speak, read and write, but wasn't interested in reading long notes from her mother. It was Michael who read her her bedtime stories, who took part in all those conversations.

I pretended that this was natural, all children grow distant from their mothers. But not all mothers push away their children, as I had been doing. I thought, at the time, it had been for the best.

My body ached for her as I folded those clothes.

I reached out, held onto the headboard of her bed. My bed, once upon a time.

I stiffened every muscle, willed the tears not to spill. Children go to boarding school all over the country, I reminded myself, I'm just being melodramatic.

A sob broke forth, guttural, afflictive, but it wasn't my sob.

It was my child's.

'Oh sweetheart, oh Esther,' Michael went to her, in the living room downstairs and I could picture him holding her to his chest, stroking her hair as she cried into him and my fingers gripped the headboard still tighter.

'I . . . don't . . . want . . . to . . . go.' A sob between each of her words. 'Don't . . . make . . . me.'

'Hush now, hush. It isn't as bad as all that.'

'Please, don't make me go. I'll do anything, please, Daddy, please, Daddy.'

I could see her face in my mind's eye; I knew exactly how her cheekbones would round with each cry, how her eyelids would be swollen and nose running, the set of her trembling chin and her downturned lips.

'It's a wonderful opportunity, Esther. You'll have fun, you'll see. There's a swimming pool and a woodland playground.' Michael's voice was far from convincing and I knew the next thing Esther would say even before she said it.

'Is it because of Mummy? Is Mummy making me go?' Her voice was high-pitched and so desperate.

'Yes,' he said, and I closed my eyes against his betrayal, pushed my fist to my mouth to stop crying out.

'Why does she want me to go?' And I knew my little girl. I knew she wanted her daddy to tell her what I couldn't, that this was the best thing for her future, that she was a lucky girl to be accepted to this school, even luckier to receive a full scholarship.

But he didn't say any of these things.

Nor did he tell her the truth. Of course, he wouldn't do that.

No. He said, 'Mummy finds it too difficult to look after you. She's not like other mummies, she can't cope.'

He thought he was punishing *me* with those words. He thought he was teaching me a lesson, showing me how wrong I had been to fight for that scholarship. He wanted to prove that sending Esther away really wasn't necessary. That he could control himself and I was overreacting.

But it's not only me he was punishing.

Esther said, 'But we've been OK so far, Daddy. I won't be any trouble, I promise I won't.' He didn't tell her not to worry, he blamed me and hoped that she would blame me too, but she didn't. She blamed herself.

'I'm scared,' Esther said, and I knew she didn't understand. I had tried to explain it as best I could, but our easy way of communicating without words had melted. I tried writing her a letter, made my print large and easy to read, said it was best for her, she'd have fun. I showed her the photos in the brochure, the testimonials the schoolchildren had written. None of it had helped.

'No need to be, no need. You'll make lots of friends! Far more than you would in this little hamlet. You're bored at the village school anyway. You're so clever, Esther, that I can't keep up with you and it's not like your mother could teach you at home.' I imagined him smoothing her hair in stilted, awkward strokes. His ease with her had melted along with mine. His touch had become hesitant, wary, his face tattletaling his concern at showing affection when I was in the room.

'And you'll be home every Saturday, to stay the night, as well as all the holidays.'

I could hear Esther breathe in a juddering breath. She was trying to be brave. She was doing a far better job of it than me.

I would not go to the school, that first day. Michael would

do that, it had already been decided. He would show her around the dormitories and take her to the library she would no doubt love. There was a swimming pool, a woodland park, a sports hall; I'd seen them all in the brochure. I'd listened attentively whilst the principal explained to me the benefits of the school and how well Esther would do there. 'It's not every day we come across a child with such natural academic ability,' he had said, talking to me as much as Michael, making sure he met my eye despite my silence. Though a small man, he had filled our little cottage with his personality. He had a booming voice, warm and lacking in the condescension I had braced myself for. 'Her school report is glowing and, as if her test results weren't enough, her teachers all commended her intelligence. Some schools, you know, get frightfully protective of their cleverer candidates, but with one as sharp as Esther, it's clear that she would benefit greatly from the wider breadth of study that King's can offer. We're very excited.'

'Gets that intelligence from her mother,' Michael said and squeezed my shoulder. 'Autodictatorate, both of them.'

Autodidactic, I silently modified, allowing myself the small pleasure of watching the principal bite his pedagogical tongue and smile, clearly desperate to correct.

'Connie had read every book in the travelling library by the time she was eighteen. Had to join the one over in Williton.' Michael was red with pleasure, as though my ability to read a book were testament to his own literacy. The principal looked at me, his eyebrows raised.

'Is that so?' he asked me, directly. I nodded. I didn't look down, but nor was I proud. It had offered me nothing but momentary escape in the more difficult periods of my day-to-day life. It hadn't improved my prospects or helped me escape physically. But Esther was different, her reading would get her far. I would make sure of it.

After that meeting with the principal I was taken over by a sort of fever. I filled out the forms with a fastidiousness I hadn't ever possessed. Everything was double-checked, the figures in the bursary application triple-checked, my sums coming true every time. The warm glow of pride and hope burned out the misgivings; the fear that she would be growing up without me, of all I would miss, her constant, quiet companionship.

She was still crying, downstairs, but with less vigour than before. She was resigned, perhaps.

'Connie?' Michael called up the stairs and I released my grip from the headboard. I touched the pillow, still indented with the shape of her skull, lifted a blonde hair from the fabric and held it.

'Connie, it's time!' he called again. I let the hair fall to the floor and lifted the handle on the suitcase, pulling it out of the room and towards the stairs.

It jolted on each step, heavy and cumbersome, weighted as though it was not just Esther herself leaving but her whole childhood.

I steeled my resolve, gritted my teeth as I entered the room. I wouldn't let her see me cry, I had already decided that; I would show her I could be strong. Looking back, I must have just seemed cold.

She was seated in the wingback in the living room. I could see her, from the bottom step, through the open living-room door. Her face was just as I knew it would be: red, blotchy and swollen. She looked younger than her eight years.

I looked at the floor, not at her.

I handed Michael the suitcase and he lugged it out of the

house to the car he'd borrowed from our neighbour for the journey. I can't drive and, though he could, after the incident he had agreed to sell the car and travel to work on his pushbike. We told our neighbours it was to help pay for the expensive school uniform and the invoice for the meals and laundry service; we told Esther the old car had worn out and we'd get a new one in time. Truth was, with the bursary, the money left us by Grandmother and the fact we lived on such a very small expenditure, we didn't need the extra money. No. It was one of my conditions. I didn't want it to be so easy for us to reach her.

'Mummy?' Her voice was soft and quiet.

Still, I didn't look at her.

As well as encouraging her about the school as much as I was able, I had also been gradually withdrawing my affection. Her night-time hug and kiss had been replaced with a peck to the forehead. I thought it prudent at the time. I hoped that by reducing physical comforts she would learn a new sense of independence, self-reliance. But, when I saw her crying in the wingback chair, I could see that I'd been wrong. I hadn't instilled self-reliance. She was confused, lost and deeply, deeply hurt. She did not understand.

Michael beeped the car horn outside, shouted, 'It's time to go now, Essie, come along.'

She stood up but her eyes were downcast.

I opened my mouth, made a grunting noise, pointed to the door with my thumb and a nod of my head.

She sloped out of the house, her shoulders slouched and head bent.

On the front steps she stopped and looked back at me.

I turned away.

I couldn't hug her goodbye, my baby.

Because if I did, if I had run to her and lifted her from the garden path, wrapped my arms tight around her small body, I would never have let her go.

Michael drove away with my daughter and our neighbour.

The ache of missing her was overshadowed by the doubt. Had I done the right thing, sending her away?

It lingered like a tumour extending a web through my brain. I couldn't concentrate on anything. I started to wash the breakfast things and scalded my hand beneath the hot tap. I burned toast, made a hash of the ironing, couldn't even read a book. I stood at the kitchen sink and stared out at the September sun sinking behind the silos.

The calendar hung on the wall, the first day of term circled with red pen. She had caught me standing before it, one week ago, counting the days till she left. I thought I'd been alone, but she'd seen me. She was a young girl whose only experience of counting down days on a calendar was waiting for Christmas. She misunderstood.

'You want me to go!' she said, and then I confused things because never got the knack of reading other people's feelings. I nodded, I smiled, and she ran off in tears to her room and I tried to tell her that it was because it was good for her future, not because I wouldn't miss her, didn't love her, but my words would not come and every note I wrote her she tore up in her upset.

Have I done the right thing?

I should have hugged her goodbye, I realised then. Why did I not kiss her? Why couldn't I tell her I loved her when she needed to hear it?

Lost in a haze of memory and doubt, I didn't hear Michael come in. The first I knew of his arrival was the hand that slipped around my waist.

'I've missed this,' he said, no mention of how Esther was when he left her.

My mind was filled with Esther. I heard her laugh, saw her face, bright red from giggling. The picture I conjured was of Esther in the exact position she'd been in a few months before.

Lying on the floor of the living room, as her father tickled her.

I didn't have to haul him off. Perhaps that was the worst part. Michael stopped of his own accord, his face red with the look of one who knows he has done wrong, even if only in thought.

'You're overreacting,' he said later, with a consideration that set my teeth on edge because I had not yet overreacted, I hadn't confronted him about it at all. He raised the subject himself and, in doing so, took control of a conversation I didn't have the capabilities to partake in.

What would I have said, had my thoughts connected to my stubborn vocal cords? How could I have possibly put into words my fear and anger?

'You're the one I want, Connie. I've only ever wanted you. There's no one else.' As though I was *jealous* of my eight-year-old daughter. As though he wasn't a pervert and I was just a green-eyed monster.

You turn people into terrible things. Grandmother's old words came flooding back to me, the familiar self-loathing and guilt that it was me that made Michael what he was. The understanding that, should I not act now, my daughter would suffer my fate.

I wanted to fight for her and so I walked away from him. I made to go upstairs, planning to pack a suitcase, rouse my sleeping child and take her to a safe place.

But he read my mind, it seemed. Perhaps he had been stewing on this as I had all afternoon.

'You know you can't leave, Connie,' he said, pulling me back from the bottom of the stairs and putting his arms around my shoulders, forcing me into his chest for what he called a cuddle. I stiffened. 'You're not fit to raise Esther alone; the doctors will contest to that. And without me, you'd be in *that* place. Do you remember it, Connie? That place with the bars on the windows? The place they send backward women who won't talk, who won't let people touch them, who've been known to have violent outbursts when they do? You'd be there, Connie, if I wasn't looking after you. And I'd be at home, with Esther, having to look after her all by myself. And I don't want that. All I want is for us to be together, you and me. Like it used to be.' And his hands slipped from my shoulders to my waist to my buttocks.

Like it used to be.

Since Esther's birth his treatment of me had been different. He came under cover of night, pinning me down, silent so as not to wake the child. Brutal but quick, as if it were a nightmarish blip in an otherwise mundane dream. But the daytime had become my own – the night too, for the most part, my body relaxing with relief once his business was over with.

That night I tried to leave, he reminded me of what it used to be like.

'You're the only one I want, Connie,' he whispered to me. 'I love you. It's only ever been *you*.'

But I knew what I had seen. It had been like going back in time, a little girl being tickled on the floor by a boy who was older and knew better. It hadn't gone further, not yet. I had time to get Esther out and, of all the options I investigated, the school seemed the best at the time.

If I ran away with Esther I was convinced they would track me down, lock me up. That Esther would be left with him.

If I wrote to the doctor, to social services, to the police, then they might take Esther away, put her into care, and I couldn't bear that.

The school was a solution, but one that came at a cost I had to pay with my soul. Esther would be out of his reach for six days a week and when at home I would make sure I was always with her. I would give her an out, a better life, and in return Michael would get the thing he said he wanted. He'd get me, in the way he used to have me. Alone, completely alone.

I wrote down my plan and showed it to him. He begrudgingly agreed and burned the paper so no one would see it.

And now Esther was twenty miles away in a school that would keep her safe.

I was alone with him.

I fought back the familiar tears, the urge to sob, to wash myself clean of his stain.

I had done the right thing for my daughter.

That is what would get me through.

Chapter Thirty-Nine

Selina

Sunday Morning

B ack in the hospital Austin had looked taken aback when she'd asked him to help. 'I . . . could see if I can dig out the number,' he had said, 'I guess, but I don't know . . .'

A nod and a *yeah, sure thing,* was the reaction she'd expected when she asked him to phone ahead to St Moira's.

'Esther said the hospital had sorted it all out last year; I'll get the number from reception, don't worry.' She had smiled to show that she didn't mind.

He shook his head, looked confused. 'It's the family and the patient that contact St Moira's, not us.'

'Esther said the hospital had sorted it all out?'

'Perhaps it was C—'

'It wouldn't have been Connie,' Selina said.

A searing bolt of clarity shot through her previous doubts.

'Don't worry about it,' she said, 'I'll go now and bring Connie back. I'll call ahead to the house from my mobile.'

Her fatigue melted, and momentarily so did her guilt, both overshadowed by a sense of urgency so great that everything else was eclipsed.

Now, in her car, she didn't dare start the engine or drive until she had made this call. But it wasn't to the house in Kilstock.

'Hello, St Moira's hospice and home care,' said the voice on the end of the phone, a woman with a Northumberland accent.

Selina explained what she needed and was transferred to another line for local enquiries.

On her iPad she flicked through the search results; the name at the top of the screen read: Madeleine Becker. Austin had confirmed her last name.

No Facebook page, no Twitter account, no Instagram. She tried Pipl.com next, relying on the dark web to draw something up, but there was nothing.

'Can I help you?' A broad Somerset voice this time, patient and calm despite the early hour.

'Yes, please. I needed to contact Madeleine Becker; she's a nurse with St Moira's based in West Somerset.'

'Can I ask the nature of your inquiry?' Sensitive, but firm. Selina pictured a woman with grey hair, neatly pulled back in a ponytail. Tweed jacket, glasses on her nose, pale blue eyes.

'Of course,' Selina said, lying smoothly, 'she nursed my uncle a few years ago and now his wife is ill. I wanted to talk to her to see if she could also care for my aunt. Is there a way I can get hold of her?'

'I am so sorry to hear that,' the woman said, 'I can understand your aunt's wishes. Unfortunately, I can't put you through to Nurse Becker at present.'

'Is she caring for another family?'

'It's not that – I'm afraid she's taken a sabbatical, as of the beginning of December last year.'

The time she started looking after Michael.

'I can take your details and pass them on if she calls in,'

the woman went on. 'She is planning on returning to us, I just can't tell you exactly when.'

Selina thanked the woman but said no. She had all the information she needed.

Madeleine hadn't been sent by St Moira's at all.

She had come of her own volition.

The question was why had she come to the Lithgows' and where was she now?

And who had she sent to care for Michael in her absence?

Chapter Forty

Connie

Sunday morning

'I heard you,' Esther says, her eyes still swollen from the memories of her school days. 'Or rather, I heard Selina talking to you, yesterday.'

I glance sidelong to the back of the car, see the tin box with its rusted hinged lid.

My daughter stares straight ahead. The road meanders, the bends often tight, and she focuses on the curves of the road and not me. She has struggled, since boarding school, to talk about her feelings. They're linked, I am sure, her absence from home coinciding with her closed-off heart, but I don't know how to break down that wall. I've made so many mistakes, raising her.

I don't interrupt.

Her phone rings in her driver's side door, an incessant vibration against the plastic pocket. She glances down but does not answer and waits for it to finish before continuing. It's probably Selina, or the hospital.

'I heard her tell you that she hid something, in her flat, and hated herself for it and I was so angry with you, so fucking angry.'

The swearing is a shield, I know that. She uses it to mask

her true feelings. It began when she was a teenager, to shock me, I think, but I never chastised her. I was always so relieved to see her home, for that short day once a week, that I could never bring myself to tell her off.

'At first I thought great, thanks, Mum, first you steal my fucking childhood by sending me to boarding school and then you poison my one true friendship by making her keep secrets from me. I thought it would explain it all, the reason Selina's been so distant these last few years, and I hated you for it. I hated you. I went home and dug out the spare key to her flat. I let myself in; can you believe that? I let myself in to her house, without her permission. I snooped in all her cupboards, her drawers and finally found this.' She gestures to the back seat. 'Dad's old keepsake tin, the one he used to keep his spare camera films in in the shed. I'd know it anywhere. It looked so ominous hidden away, I thought it must contain some terrible secret, evidence of some dark deed.'

I keep my hands very still on my lap as she speaks, keep my face forward; I do not look at the box again.

'I couldn't bear to open it. I took it home, sat on my sofa and stared at it for what felt like hours. I convinced myself that not only did the box hold all the answers, but that the answers would somehow . . . I don't know. Change things? By the time I lifted the lid I was feeling sick and then what did I find? Family sodding photos and a wodge of loose paper at the bottom. Some pictures of you, some of me, some of Selina. Why did you want her to hide them?'

She looks back and forth between me and the road, waiting for me to answer.

Her phone rings again from the driver's side door and goes unanswered.

She couldn't have looked through them all. I have no idea what to say. I try to say sorry but can only grunt. Ideas whirl through my head; a surprise photo album for her or maybe the photos were too painful for Michael to look at. Nothing seems right and the message doesn't connect with my throat; my head aches with the effort of trying to speak and before I know it I'm grunting again. Esther sighs.

'It doesn't matter. I realised it didn't at the time; it wasn't going to help me understand what went wrong with Selina and that's all I'd wanted to know. I don't understand why she's changed so much. I just—' She doesn't say anything more but wipes at her eye with the sleeve of her coat and I understand. She misses her friend.

I've ruined that for her, too.

We travel in silence, no radio, no music. The birds and animals that would fill the air with noise in the spring are gone, hiding from the cold January air in burrows or nests.

As we reach the Pines café, the crossroad at the summit of the hills, the road begins to narrow, winding us down towards Kilstock and the mudflats near the coast.

Her phone has stopped ringing.

Another image: Selina hearing the news that I have gone and desperately trying to get hold of Esther. She will not let things lie so easily and it is only now, when I finally have a clear plan in my head of what I will do and how I will end this, that I no longer want her help.

As the roads writhe downhill, I feel a sense of foreboding but also of inevitability. My arm itches where, early on Friday morning, I was held down to a chair and a needle pierced the flesh. They will come back for me, I know, but I hope that the news hasn't reached them that I've left the hospital.

If they don't know I'm coming back I'll be safe, so too Esther, and I can deal with Michael myself.

I think of Esther's assertion earlier, that there is another nurse looking after Michael, and I find comfort in that. It will be someone for Esther to talk to in the kitchen, making tea, or so I envisage, as I quietly, quickly press the pillow to Michael's face. By the time the kettle has boiled, he'll be dead. By the time Esther enters the room with a cup in her hand, the pillow will be returned to the wingback. I don't know how my own body will react, whether the blood clots lurking in my veins will once more erupt with the exertion and I don't care. I just want this to be over. I want to be free.

Esther yawns widely as we approach Kilstock, fighting off tiredness.

I see the silos before I see our house.

Chapter Forty-One

Connie

2005

For most of my life I avoided mirrors. Yet here I was, at my age, staring into a vanity mirror that once belonged to Grandmother. It normally sat on the mantelpiece above the fireplace, near to our mothers' picture.

There were black spots beneath the glass, the silver tarnished, and it was probably not showing my true likeness, but it was enough to see what I had become. Dark, twisted, frightened.

But not broken. Not yet.

The television we owned was larger now, a monstrous black rectangle I never turned on and tried my best to ignore whenever he watched it. His favourite programme, in his middle age, was a juvenile offering called *You've Been Framed*. He'd sit there and laugh in a high-pitched giggle unique to his schadenfreude, the sound piercing my concentration. I'd lose my place on the page I was reading. I could feel my teeth on edge and I'd have to squeeze my eyes shut to stop myself hurling my interrupted book at the TV. Twice over recent years I had taken shears to the lead, gnawing away at the unplugged wires so it looked like mice had chewed their way through. Days of peace whilst we waited for a new lead to be delivered. He'd tried a few times to read but his concentration was as poor as his intellect and he'd given up. I'd smiled to myself, delighted to be superior in something.

Once, however, it wasn't *You've Been Framed* he was watching, nor was it *Last of the Summer Wine*. He'd changed the channel and there were four women talking in American accents, sipping cosmopolitan cocktails in a dimly lit bar, all with perfect make-up and tailored clothes. One of them, I realised, was supposed to be my age, a few years younger, maybe. She was blonde, mid-forties or thereabouts, with sharp features and a sly smile and spoke in such a plain way about sex you would almost be fooled into thinking she enjoyed it. Michael turned the channel almost immediately, called it trash, disgraceful, disgusting, immoral. She'd stayed with me, that woman. It wasn't how she spoke or what she spoke about, but rather what she looked like.

Not since a teenager had I felt so remote from the other women in the world. I always ignored the magazines in favour of books, kept my head down on the bus, hated that television with a passion. I had long ago stopped noticing how other women behaved and dressed, what they ate and what products they used in their hair. They were so far removed as to be on another planet. Still, when I saw this woman on the screen of our TV, I thought how very different she was to me.

That day I sat in the wingback chair and for the first time saw a female face I could wholly connect with.

Grandmother had once sat in that same place and coughed up blood; Dr Rowe sat there when he gave me the diagnosis of trauma-induced retardation that would blight the rest of my life. It was the same chair Maud sat in when she counselled Grandmother on her deathbed, where Michael sat and opened letter after letter from the asylum and reminded me, in a worried, maudlin voice, of what should happen to *me* if anything happened to *him*. The thought always placated my murderous impulses. I sat in the chair where my daughter had sat and cried on the day she left for school.

In the mirror I saw a face that showed every ounce of fear I had felt in my life, every sorrow and difficult decision. I saw the lines on my brow, echoes of the lines that crossed my forehead on the day I killed Grandmother, on the day I killed Maud. I saw the vacant, lifeless eyes, the mouth that didn't smile.

I never wanted my daughter to look like this. That was my primary goal. My only goal.

I never wanted anyone else's daughter to look like this, either.

Beside me, on the floor, was a small tin box, holding some of the photographs Michael had taken throughout his life and developed in the garden shed that used to be the outside lavatory. I'd found it that day, whilst he was at work at the school. He had left the shed unlocked for the first time in years and I went in to listen to the old record player.

I found this tin, instead.

He was still a caretaker at the school. My God. Why did I never worry about that? How had I not seen this coming?

The first photographs were of me, dog-eared and well thumbed, but nothing strange. Certainly nothing risqué.

The next were of Esther, some of Selina too, on the rare occasions I let her come here in the holidays to play.

I looked through the photos of Esther's early years, hoping for something I had never seen of my daughter I could soak up and bathe in.

Instead, I found *her*.

A young girl, thin and sweet with curly blonde hair, freckles.

The look on her face in that very first photograph warned me well enough what the remaining photos would contain.

She looked like me. Not only in the set of her features, her colouring, but in the blankness of her face and the fear in her eyes.

There was a crash as I lost my grip on the mirror and it splintered on the wooden floorboards, sending shards across the room.

I thought I was keeping Esther safe. I got her away, I gave Michael myself in return. But really all I'd done was keep him at liberty.

I didn't know what to do.

I didn't know who I could turn to.

I needed someone to help me.

I needed help.

I forced myself to look at the photograph again. Something caught my eye; a newspaper in the bottom corner of the photograph, discarded on the floor of the room this young child stood in. It had a date. 2003. Two years ago.

Had he been doing this for two years?

Were there others? More girls he had messed with, ruined?

Esther was at university, her final year studying law at Bristol. She would know what to do. But how could I go to her with this? How could I look her in the eye and convey all that had happened to me?

She was such a daddy's girl.

She would have tried to defend him, solve the problem, as if it could be solved, as if anything should be done but locking him away.

My God. What would happen to me if he was locked away?

I saw, again, the 1970s asylum.

There had to be another way. I couldn't go there, I couldn't.

I was cruel, a terrible person, but I couldn't do it. I had sacrificed every ounce of myself for my daughter, but I couldn't do it again. Even Michael's control, his force, his daily desire, was a better alternative to that place I had seen.

I couldn't tell anyone.

I just couldn't.

2014

I sat, for days on end, in blank silence. I forgot to eat and didn't sleep.

I saw her everywhere I looked. That little girl with the frightened eyes.

I told nobody.

The tin was back in the shed.

The door was locked.

Michael didn't know that I had seen it.

In bed I saw her young face and I cried soft, silent tears. He wiped the tears from my cheeks and said, 'I love you, too, Connie. My God, I love you too.'

He was so very twisted.

Esther. She had long grown out of trying to vie for attention; she had grown into a strong woman, independent.

Michael was nothing like Esther or like me.

He had no strength, no control. He had desire and compulsion and he was weak.

But I had been weak, too.

I saw the girl every time he touched me and she spoke to me, too, reminded me that I had told no one, done nothing.

I couldn't bear to be around other people, even more so than usual. Their words were pregnant with the blame that they would surely feel should they know. Their tone heavy with a sense of *you've done something, haven't you? Something bad.*

I had done nothing. Perhaps that was even worse.

Who would look after me if Michael was in prison? I had no education, no friends, no family other than Esther and I couldn't be a burden to her. I wrestled it to the back of my mind, tried to drown myself in books, but nothing worked. I still knew.

One night I sat on the bed, dressed in an off-white nightdress that stretched down to my ankles. I thought of the terrible things I had done. The people I had killed. The people I pushed away.

My silence was the worst of them all.

I heard Michael's heavy tread on the stair.

My heart dropped right into my stomach.

His head appeared first, above the top step, then his shoulders, arms, groin.

'I like you in that one, my flower,' he said and I knew, without even raising my eyeline, that he was licking his lips.

'It's my favourite on you, all white and lacy.'

I felt so sick. Even now, after fifty years of this, I still felt so very sick. He sat beside me on the bed, his hands on his thighs. I stared ahead. I thought, *just get it over with. Just let me be.*

'You look just like a little girl again.' He moved closer; I felt his breath on my shoulder. 'Just like you did as a little girl.'

His hand was on my arm.

At this point my mind normally performed its magic trick of total disassociation. I flew up, high up into the corner of the room, and watched him play me like a puppet, as if I were watching a film on the grotesque black TV downstairs.

Not that night.

Something shifted, flickered inside me.

The words *little girl* jarred.

I saw her.

And I saw Michael too.

I saw him as a coward, a man who did what he did simply because he could, because he had never been questioned, never been stopped.

I could stop him.

I would stop him.

The next morning I picked up my pen, began writing everything down. I couldn't trust myself to say it aloud, and I knew I had to be clear. I wrote the letters.

I would put them at the bottom of that dreadful tin box.

I would find someone who would speak for me, get me away from this man without sending me *there*, and without burdening my daughter with my care.

I didn't know what the answer was, but I couldn't carry this alone any more.

Chapter Forty-Two

Selina

Sunday morning

S elina started the engine on her beaten-up Audi.

Before pulling away from the hospital car park she made one final gut-instinct-inspired Google search and the puzzle was finally, grotesquely complete. As the results came up, her stomach dropped into the heels of her boots. She released the handbrake and accelerated out of the car park. She could make it there in under half an hour, if she was flexible with traffic laws.

It wasn't until she reached the back road that swirled uphill, Taunton town centre behind her, that she thought to call the police. By this stage she was so panicked for Connie and Esther that she was far less concerned about the repercussions on her own liberty. Sod prison and sod her career. She would rather the Lithgow women were alive.

Because Selina knew exactly who was waiting for them, and what they would be prepared to do to Connie and Esther.

The darkness and the camber of the road conspired against her. She reached for her mobile but knocked it and it slid first to the far end of the passenger seat and then down the side, between seat and door. She risked leaning over, tried to reach her fingers to gain purchase on the phone, but in her effort to reach she pulled the steering wheel with her. One ear-splitting shriek of briar scratching paintwork was enough to know it wasn't a sensible move.

She could pull over and contact the police from the side of the road.

But that would mean stopping. She would have to explain to them what had happened, waste time pulled up in a passing place whilst anything could be happening to her friend.

She would call from Kilstock.

She would be there in less than twenty minutes.

Chapter Forty-Three

Connie

Sunday Morning

The road sinks into Kilstock.

I don't see the other car at first. It's not until Esther has parked and I open my door that I catch sight of it, tucked away behind the decommissioned phone box and a hawthorn.

I already have one foot on the frosted ground.

The air is freezing, smelling of damp and manure and the woodsmoke blowing from the farmhouse across the field.

I can't move, petrified by the sight of that car, by the knowledge that the woman who attacked me is here.

Everything happens then, lightning fast.

I lurch back to the car. I will tell Esther I've changed my mind, I think, tell her I need to go back to the hospital.

But the sound that comes out of my mouth is a strangled cry and Esther is already out, rushing to my side, calling my name, saying *Jesus* and *Christ* and *oh shit*.

I realise then that with my body twisted, my face too and this cry coming from my throat, she's misread my fear as another embolism.

If she thinks that, maybe she will drive me back to Taunton.

As she reaches me I see something in her hand. It's the tin

box; she must have lifted it off the backseat before getting out, before she realised I was in trouble.

With no time to ponder any further I play up to it, cry a bit louder, go stiff.

Shit, shit, shit, she says and leaves my side and I think *yes, she's getting back round to her side, she'll drive us away.*

But she doesn't.

'Help!' she calls out and too late I realise where she's going.

'Help!' she shouts again, as I lift myself up from my seat and chase after her.

I see her running towards the house. She's calling for Michael's nurse.

I need to reach her and drag her back. All I've ever wanted to do is keep her safe.

The ground crunches beneath my slippered feet as I follow her. I'm panting by the time I even reach the garden gate, my breath fogging the air in white clouds, throat smarting from the cold.

The front door swings open; dull yellow light floods the path and Esther is swallowed into the cottage.

I'm at the entrance just as the first scream leaves my daughter's throat.

Chapter Forty-Four

Connie

The tin box drops to the floor, the photographs spewing out across the wooden boards.

I see my daughter's reflection in the black TV screen. Esther's hands are at her mouth but her eyes are wide open in horror.

Michael is on the bed. The covers have been ripped clean away. He's naked, skeletally thin, yellow from jaundice.

The oxygen tube, normally taped to his top lip, hangs impotent, the tape still stuck to his face. The drip has been ripped from the back of his hand, the saline leaking onto the wooden floor.

The catheter has been wrenched so forcefully that blood blooms from the tip of his flaccid penis.

It is too much for Esther, to see her daddy like this.

I turn her away, so she faces the door and can't see his humiliation. Nor can she see my face because, God help me, my lips have curled and my smile must look wicked. Lurking between the pain and sympathy I feel for Esther, for all the terror of knowing we're in potential danger, is a satisfaction that Michael is as helpless as he once made me.

Esther fights against me and turns, mouth open to call out

in outrage. But the smell hits her and stops her from screaming again; decay, urine and stale, unwashed skin. He smells like Grandmother did. How apt.

Putting her sleeve across her mouth, Esther battles her way towards him, stepping on and over the confetti of photographs as she goes.

'Find a blanket,' she calls to me. She is watching me scanning the room, thinking I am trying to help.

I'm not looking for blankets.

I'm looking for the nurse.

She is standing behind the front door, watching our reaction to Michael's degradation. Blue eyes turned cold with cruelty. Esther, consumed with horror on her daddy's behalf, hasn't noticed her yet.

'For God's sake, Mum, there, look.' Esther points to the sheet on the floor. She has the oxygen tube in her hand, is trying to place it over Michael's face but she isn't trained and can't do it correctly.

Goosebumps have risen across Michael's yellowing skin. He moves his head from side to side, no doubt in pain, dehydrated and cold.

'For Christ's sake, Mum!' Esther yanks the sheet, all thoughts of my embolism, of getting help for her mother, outranked by paternal adoration. Then she sees her.

Madeleine steps out from the door, her yellow hair in disarray.

Michael thrashes his head from side to side, loosening the oxygen tube Esther has tried to tape back into place. Tendons stand out in his scrawny neck, his toothless gums gnashing. A harsh rasping sound comes from his throat and, despite myself, I remember Grandmother.

'Madeleine! What's going on?' Esther's confusion is absolute.

This is not the Madeleine Esther recognises. Her eyes have lost their tiredness and are instead grotesquely alert. Only I have seen this Madeleine before.

My daughter clumsily drapes the sheet over her father's waist, the shock of the scene and of Madeleine's demeanour making her tremble. 'Why have these been taken out?' Esther fumbles with the drip. Madeleine is sprightly in comparison as she darts to the bed to pull it from Esther's hands.

The needle falls from the tube and saline spurts out.

'You're meant to be looking after him!' Esther yells, but her eyes are on Michael as she feverishly strokes his brow. His thrashing subsides at her touch and his eyes open to hold Esther's gaze.

'It's OK,' she whispers, bringing her face close to his.

'Esther.' The word is barely recognisable, difficult to pronounce with a damaged tongue and no teeth, but she knows her father's saying her name.

'Daddy,' she whispers back, holding his face in both of her hands, a tear sliding the length of her cheek. 'It'll be OK.' And I want to pause her, right here, let her save this memory of Michael as the father she thinks he is. Not for him, never for him, but for her.

But I can't pause anything, I can't even move; paralysed by uncertainty and fear.

'What are you doing here? Where's the other nurse? Did they do this, have you come back to help?' My daughter sounds like a child, desperate for everything to be OK. Her eyes are so earnest it makes Madeleine's reaction all the crueller.

The nurse scoffs.

Esther looks up. 'Well? Where's the other nurse? The colleague you called on Friday?'

Two days ago, I think. Has it really been two whole days? I know what Madeleine will say before the words have left her mouth, but it doesn't make them any easier to hear because I know how they will upset my daughter.

My eyes scan Michael's body. His ribcage and hip bones are ridges beneath the white sheet, which is off-coloured with dirt from the floor and the decay of my husband's condition. The shadows cast by the wall lamps pick out the hollows in his cheeks, his eyes unhealthily bulging from his skull.

'There was no other nurse,' Madeleine says.

'But on Friday you said you had called someone,' Esther says, her gaze set in disbelief on her father. 'You were with me at the hospital until yesterday . . . who was looking after him?'

'He was in God's hands.' Madeleine has gone mad, I think. At the word God she touches her crucifix, closes her eyes.

'You left him alone?' The pain in Esther's voice revives me. I move towards her, pull the sheet over the rest of Michael's legs, hope that she'll see I'm helping her and take comfort in having someone on her side.

'You're meant to be looking after him. You're a nurse, for God's sake!'

'Don't you dare!' Madeleine pushes Michael's bed with her foot and it moves on its wheels, knocking into Esther and making her stumble. She clings onto the drip stand with one hand, the other firmly holding onto the bed.

I move my mouth, I think I say, 'Don't!' But nobody looks my way.

'Why are you doing this?' Esther says. 'I don't understand.'

'Esther,' Michael says again, and she drops her eyes down to meet his. 'Don't listen. Please, don't listen.'

It is the longest sentence he has said in some time; his voice sounds as strained and strange as mine.

'Don't listen?' Madeleine spits, her face contorting in rage and her voice rising to a fearful height. 'As if she doesn't already know!'

Chapter Forty-Five

Selina

Her car arched over the hill crest, past the low, wood-slatted Pines café and down the steep road on the other side. Not far now.

She glided across the tarmac, slid around the bends, going faster than was legal or safe.

At the top of the hill she could almost sense the sunrise, the sky paling from deep black to dark blue, but as she sank towards the flats the atmosphere darkened; trees and tall hedges penned the night in.

Then she slammed on her brakes, hands gripping the wheel, desperately keeping it steady. The wide back of a tractor filled the road; her car skidded towards it and stopped with inches to spare.

Shit.

Her heart thundered in her chest, pulse beating in her temples and neck.

It was a second before she realised that her car had stalled. The tractor rolled on, taking the lane at a lethargic twenty miles per hour.

An infuriating delay.

Or an opportunity.

She could call the police, she realised. Or even Dick Chapel. She could accept his offer, have someone on her side that could help without having to draw the police in.

She leaned over and grabbed her phone from the side of the passenger seat. No reception. A spiderweb of small cracks marred the left corner of the screen.

Her iPad was still on the passenger seat; the movement of leaning over knocking the tablet back to life. The image that filled it was the same as when she had driven away from the hospital.

A young woman of about seventeen, with blonde, curly hair and blue-grey eyes. She could have been Esther's sister, if Connie had had another daughter, or a cousin. But this young woman wasn't related to the Lithgows. Her name was Mia.

Selina had found the photo using Google. It had been on Mia's Facebook page, which had been closed a few months after Mia had died.

In the image her arms were flung around another woman, their cheeks pressed together. They didn't look identical, barely related, in fact; only the colour of their hair and the shape of their eyes similar. The caption read: *wishing the best mum in the world a happy birthday xxx*

Mia's mother was Madeleine Becker.

It was Madeleine who came to the police after Mia confided in her what Michael had done. Madeleine who gave the witness statement, who urged her daughter to do the right thing and prosecute. Mia overdosed less than a year after Michael was released without charge. Her suicide prompted Madeleine to retrain as a St Moira's nurse, so Austin had said.

The tractor turned off the lane and into a farm, the road empty again.

The iPad timed out and went black.

How much courage had it taken for Madeleine to go to the police? Selina couldn't begin to fathom. She restarted the car, still shaken by the emergency stop. Her speed increased steadily; she kept her hands firmly on the wheel, eyes ahead, but she couldn't stop her thoughts from spiralling.

She pictured Madeleine, devout and upstanding, using her nursing experience and recent bereavement to act as a force of good. The quiet, steady woman would have been an excellent comfort to families in need, of that Selina was sure. But she could also see how it would have been too much for anyone to take, to see the name of the man who defiled her daughter on the patient roster for chemo-therapy. She pictured the nurse finding the patient file, confirming it was the same Michael Lithgow, taking the opportunity to offer her services directly to the family who had ruined her daughter's life so she could exact some kind of revenge. She imagined how Madeleine would have reacted when, even on his deathbed, Michael showed no remorse, only offering gratitude to the family who'd stuck by him through everything; the wife who apparently loved him despite all the things he had done and the daughter he was so, so proud of, who had grown up to be a bright, successful solicitor.

Selina sped up through the small villages and farms, across the A39 and out to the flats. There wasn't that far to go, she could still make it before anything happened; she had to.

Because she was sure now that Madeleine blamed Connie

for supporting Michael, had attacked her on Friday as revenge.

And she also knew that she blamed Esther for getting him off.

Chapter Forty-Six
Connie

Madeleine's muscles are so tense she's shaking. She hasn't yet seen the photographs strewn on the floor.

And I suddenly realise, then. I know why she is here, why she is looking at Esther as though Esther is as vile as Michael, as wretched as me.

Esther is dumbfounded, her hand still stroking Michael's head.

'Not. Her.' I say it without thinking, the sounds thick and barely comprehensible as though my throat is full of syrup. Madeleine turns her head towards me, eyes full of fury. Beneath the anger I see the tiredness, shadows stark against her pallid skin. She hasn't slept for days.

There is so much I want to say, the words bottle-necking in my head, trying to worm themselves free. All I can make sense of is thoughts, not words, as though the two are so different they could never combine. All I manage to say is 'Wasn't. Her.'

I don't know if this tired woman, who has lost everything because of the things I have done, believes me and I feel the frustration build in my pressure-cooker of a head.

There is a groan from the bed. Michael holds our daughter's hand in the eagle-claw of his own.

'What the hell are you talking about?' Esther shouts and then I look at her properly.

All this time I thought I was keeping her safe from this, I failed to see what she had grown into. I didn't stop to realise she was so fierce.

My mouth gasps like a fish, the words refusing to make themselves heard, and her face falls. She must see the complex myriad of emotions in my eyes. She has always been such a good girl, she has always tried to save me from worry and stress, always desperately sought my approval. How I've failed her, I think.

Esther's gaze switches to Madeleine and I see something shift in the nurse's expression. 'Why are you doing this to my dad?' Esther says, and Madeleine reaches behind her, feeling for something I can't yet see.

'Why?' A childlike desperation edges my daughter's voice. I've hidden so much from her, all her life.

Madeleine flinches and that small, gold crucifix glistens. 'You know!' she shouts, shifting from foot to foot and I see something catch the light, a scalpel gripped in her right hand. There is an expression on her face besides loss and rage, a fear so familiar that I can feel it worm itself under my skin.

'Not. Her,' I say again, keeping my eyes on her eyes, making her look at me.

She thinks it was Esther who freed Michael from custody, found the loophole in the evidence log that kept him at liberty. 'Didn't. Do. It.'

'Do *what*?' Esther cries.

'No, no, no,' Michael murmurs from the bed, but it is too late.

There's more I want to say to Madeleine. I want to tell her

that it wasn't her fault this happened to her daughter, that she wasn't to blame. I want to tell her I'm sorry I didn't speak out and that I should have done more.

'No, no.' Michael's head moves side to side on his bed, his words slurred from his bitten tongue. He raises a hand, tries to push Esther away but he doesn't have the strength. 'Don't let her hear.'

'I'm sorry.' I force the words out and each face in the room turns to look at me and I think yes, yes, I'm sorry to you all. I'm sorry for the pain I have caused and the devil that I am and the things I have made you all do.

Madeleine's face crumples at the word. But she doesn't let go of the scalpel.

Chapter Forty-Seven
Connie

'I'm sorry,' I say, and I mean it, I do.

'Will someone tell me what the fuck is going on?'

Madeleine flinches at my daughter's language. Esther hasn't seen the scalpel.

I have, though. I see the curve of the short, sharp blade. It stirs something inside me, seeing this woman hold a weapon so close to my daughter.

I inch towards the door, closing it with the heel of my foot. The room, lit only by the dim wall lights, seems even smaller in the gloom. Esther looks confused.

Madeleine looks wild.

This game, I know, is finally up.

'Mum, what happened?' Esther says.

Michael moans from the bed, clutching at Esther's hand with his thin, brittle nails. She puts one hand on top of his, strokes his wrist and hand softly and shushes him. 'It's OK, Dad. Whatever it is, it'll be OK.'

Madeleine sways on her tired legs. 'You took her from me,' she says, eyes on our daughter, spinning the handle of the scalpel in her fist.

'I don't know what you're talking about.' Esther's teeth

are gritted, and I know her, I know her patience won't last much longer.

The wall lights give a flicker, shadows briefly dance, and I step forward, lips open to speak.

'I. Killed. Her.' It's true, it is, and my heart breaks in my chest, each splinter a sting to my eyes.

No one stirs. Even Michael seems unable to draw a rattling gasp.

Esther stares, incredulous, her lips parted and eyebrows drawn, trying to make sense of my words.

'Don't be ridiculous, you haven't killed anyone.' But no one refutes it and Madeleine's eyes fill with tears that she doesn't rub away.

'Who?' Esther asks, when no one rebuts. 'Who did you kill? My God, I can't believe I'm saying that out loud, this is ridiculous, absolutely—'

'My daughter.' Madeleine's whisper is hoarse, her accent less clipped, as if grief has been filing its edges. 'They both did. She's dead because of them, because of what they did to her.'

Esther's hand pauses mid-stroke on her father's wrist. 'Don't be absurd,' she says. 'My parents have done nothing of the sort. How . . . how absurd.' She laughs, a high-pitched nervous giggle. She can't make sense of this. This is not who we are, to her. 'I mean, look at them, for God's sake. Just look at them. As if they could hurt anyone.'

She sees the good in us. Even in me. This thought surprises me. I gasp, I don't mean to but I do, and Esther looks at me and she sees it. She sees she has been wrong to presume my innocence.

Michael tries to push her away, but he is weak. He slurs through toothless gums, 'Don't listen, I can't bear it.'

'You defended him!' Madeleine snarled, stepping closer to Esther. 'You got him off scot-free and Mia knew he was out there, that he could do it again, that everyone thought she was a liar! You knew and that makes you as bad as *him*, so don't play the innocent with me!' She brings up her fist, presses it to her mouth and Esther sees the scalpel, gleaming. 'It took her *years* to muster the courage to tell me what happened. It took me another three months to try and convince her to let me go to the police, to protect other little girls by having him locked away. I stood up for my daughter and did what was right. I told the police *everything*.'

Tears stain Madeleine's cheeks, flushed with anger. Every element of her nurse's persona is gone; the softness, the understanding, even the meticulous efficiency. Instead she is desperate. Her long yellow hair hangs in unruly locks, the finger she points at Esther gnarled at the joint and shaking with fury.

'And you got him off. You discredited Mia or bribed the police or . . . or . . . something. Whatever you did, you got him off and he was free and Mia was in agony and she, she—'

'Mia.' Michael slurs the name and I see his eyes roll in their sockets, his hand still trying in vain to push Esther away.

'Don't you say her name!' Madeleine darts forward, the blade now inches from his throat.

'Don't you pretend not to know anything,' Madeleine shouts, swinging the knife back towards Esther. 'You know what he did and you protected him! You condoned what he did!'

'No,' I say. 'No.'

Esther holds up her hand for me to keep quiet. She looks from me to the tin box on the floor, lurking beneath your bed, her childhood photographs littering the floor. She swallows.

'Tell me about her,' Esther says. 'Please.' She is using her calm voice, the one she uses with me when I'm fraught. She is managing Madeleine in the way she manages me and I want to hug her, tell her I'm sorry that she had to ever learn these techniques. That she never had the mother she deserved.

'Mia?' Madeleine says and her tired eyes soften. 'She was . . .' Her chin and bottom lip tremble and when she opens her mouth no sound comes.

'What was she like?' Esther tries, her face a picture of sympathy.

It's working.

The grip on the scalpel loosens slightly. 'She was so funny. She made me laugh all the time, every day.' She sniffs.

'I like funny children,' Esther says, her eyes switching from Madeleine's face to the scalpel. 'What did she look like?'

'She was . . .' Madeleine sniffs again, pauses, the simple task of remembering her daughter's face agonising. 'Mia was . . .'

'So pretty,' Michael murmurs from the bed. 'She was so pretty.'

Madeleine gives an asinine moan. She lifts her fist and plunges the scalpel down, aiming for Michael's throat.

Yes, I think, *finally, yes*.

But Esther throws herself onto her father. I see my daughter's blood and I am animal.

I scream and throw myself onto Madeleine's broad back.

I pull her hair, dig my nails into her flesh, bite her neck with my bare teeth until she drops the scalpel, stumbling backwards.

Her throat is made yellow by the light from the wall lamps, the marks from my teeth pitted bruises in her flesh.

She keeps moving backwards, rams me into the door.

I feel my spine crack and my body goes weak.

I slump to the floor and Madeleine looms over me.

Esther is quick, focused. She lifts the drip stand and swings.

The iron pole smacks Madeleine's head, sending her off balance.

She wavers, unsteady on her feet, sways her body round to face Esther.

My back is sore but not debilitating; I raise my thighs to my chest and kick out at the back of Madeleine's knees.

She hits her head on the edge of the bed and collapses, lying there unconscious but breathing.

'Mum, are you OK?' Esther limps to my side, helps me up.

Blood pullulates from a wound in her shoulder blade and she is ghostly pale. Her pupils are so dilated that her blue eyes look nearly black.

'We need to help Dad,' she says as she pulls me to my feet. My back aches, my pulse thunders but I'm not hurt. I think of the clots wedged in my veins and wonder how much they can take before dislodging again.

'Then we'll call the police and ambulance. Help me get the blanket back on him.'

The drip stand lies on the floor beside Madeleine, the tubes tangled.

Michael groans, his yellow skin covered in goosebumps.

Esther grabs the sheet from the floor and drapes it back over his body. The shape beneath the cotton is a disturbing collection of bones and wasted muscle, almost as ghastly as his naked form.

'He needs something warmer.' The room holds little furniture; just the wingback chair, a small chest of drawers and your steel-framed bed.

I don't move.

'Help me find something, will you? A blanket or a duvet from upstairs?'

I can't move.

I look at my daughter and shake my head.

'Won't you help me?' Esther begs, pausing in her search. She doesn't understand.

'Won't you fix the drip? You know how to do that far better than I do. Or you could see if there's any morphine left?'

I stare at my daughter, shake my head.

'He's in pain, Mum. And he's cold, and—' The tears well up. She wants to help her father, to call the police, to tie Madeleine up or secure her somehow in case she wakes.

All I can do is stare at my husband. He was my best friend and my protector when he was a boy. I used to love him, once.

'What happened, Mum?' Esther asks, and I see her confusion, her desperate desire to think Madeleine a madwoman spinning an irrational tale. But she's not a little girl any more, she has seen the world and enough of the people in it to guess that Madeleine isn't simply mad, that I'm not simply a moron, that Michael is not just her daddy. 'Why won't you help him?'

What can I say to her? How can I make her understand when these words won't form and my mind won't connect with my body?

'Tell me,' Esther cries, and slams her fist to the wall. The mantelpiece judders and the photograph of my mother and Aunt Charlotte falls face down on the floor. 'For God's sake,

Mum! She tried to kill me! She tried to kill Dad! Tell me what the fuck happened!'

And I feel it well inside me, the words and the hurt and the past and the things I have seen.

My hands begin worrying away at each other, fingers pulling fingers, nails pinching skin.

I can taste the words but I hate them.

I would do anything for my daughter not to know.

But I can't go on, like this, any longer.

'Can't help him. I never wanted him,' I mutter, and it hurts me, that word, burns my throat and my eyes, stings my nose. 'I said *no*.'

Esther doesn't understand. Her eyes bulge with frustration, as though she's fighting the urge to shake these words out of me, as though she's finally had enough of me, of all this.

'I said no.' I say it again and I look at my daughter.

'I said no.' And I see her anger and confusion melt. Not realisation, not yet, but suspicion.

Esther is crying.

I have made her cry and I despise my selfishness for laying this onto her. I never wanted her to know. I never wanted this to be a thing she must carry, but now I've said it I can't stop.

'I said, stop it. I said, no. I said stop it and no and no and no.'

Esther kneels down, holds my hands to stop them from worrying. She tries to speak but for the first time in our shared lives it is she who cannot make a sound. I can see her mentally piecing the story together.

I never wanted her to look at me like this. I wanted her to be the girl running towards me with buttercups, her young face full of pride and self-worth. I wanted to be her champion, not her victim. I wanted to be her mother, not this thing on the floor of our living room, crying and shaking and wretched.

She pulls me towards her, strokes my hair as though I am the child. I can feel the tension in her body, how carefully she is trying not to touch my waist or my wrists and I have done this to her, I have made her wary, I am nothing and nothing and nothing.

'What did you say no to, Mum?' Esther says. 'Was it something to do with the little girl, with Mia?'

You shouldn't have had to help me, I think, but can't say this out loud. I shake my head.

She is struggling to make sense of this, and I know a half-truth can sometimes be worse than the whole, that our imaginations can be darker than reality.

'No to him,' I manage, and my eyes move from Esther to her father.

'To Daddy?' Her voice is high-pitched, she doesn't want to believe what I'm telling her. 'You told him not to do those things to that girl?'

'To me.' I can't say any more.

Her lips part and meet, unable to speak. She looks from me to her father and back again. Her chin trembles, she cannot make sense of it.

We are quiet and I wonder what she is thinking. Is she remembering how my ease with her, my delight, would disappear whenever Michael came into the room? Is she remembering the look on my face when I discovered him tickling her on the floor?

Is she remembering crying in the wingback the day she left for school, the day I refused to hug her goodbye?

I feel her hold me more tightly, I feel a tear fall onto my hand. I don't know if it is hers or mine.

Neither of us hear Madeleine stirring.

Standing.

Reaching for the drip stand on the floor.

One swift blow.

Esther is rendered senseless in my arms.

Chapter Forty-Eight
Connie

My daughter falls forward with a heaviness brought about only through unconsciousness. Or death.

There is no blood from her head and her heart beats fiercely against my chest; every molecule of my being wants to hold her to me, make her better.

There's no time for that.

Madeleine stands, arms reaching above her head, ready to shower another blow with the pole. The drip stand is made jagged by the hooks and loops designed to hold the line in place, and facing me is the bent crook of the drip-stand's arm. If it landed on either Esther or me, it would break through the thin layer of skin on our skull, crack our brain to a sweet pulp of nothing.

Michael moans unintelligibly from the bed.

Esther lays slumped on my lap.

I know I must get out, lead Madeleine away.

The nurse swings again; I kick at her legs but with Esther on top of me my kick is weak, and I only succeed in disturbing her aim. The pole smacks the wall above my head.

Madeleine pulls it back again, snarling.

I lower my daughter to the floor. She rolls, mouth open

and eyes shut, her back against the front door. She is vulnerable there, open to any attack, but I know it is not Esther she really wants now her role in everything has been questioned.

She wants me.

The pole rises again.

It's clear from her wilful neglect that she hates Michael to all possible depths. But she hates me, too. Blames me for keeping Michael at liberty, for standing by him.

I kick Madeleine in the shin and, with her arms above her head, the kick knocks her off balance, making her wobble without falling. It gives me time to pull myself up to my feet.

I run through the door to the kitchen, hearing the smack of it as it slams closed, waiting for the sound of Madeleine's feet to follow. I need to lure her away from my senseless daughter.

I hear nothing.

My house is the tiniest of cottages and I am at the back door in no time, the glass panel showing me a winter-dark garden and a starless sky blanketed by cloud.

I need her to follow me.

Why isn't she following me?

My stomach churns over with dread and with guilt. I've left that woman alone with Esther. What if she tries to hurt her again before coming after me? What have I done?

I'm about to turn back when I hear the creak of the living-room door.

I see her yellow hair swing as she runs out of the room.

Her mouth is open in a fierce grimace, tired eyes made gruesome by the dark purple shadows beneath them.

'Come back and face me!' she snarls and I run, run, run.

Out of the back door into the garden.

Along the muddy path through the lawn.

The fence – low and broken and mouldy with age – blocks my exit at the end.

The crease in my elbow pricks sharply, reminding me of the needles that have punctured the skin. The antidote from the paramedics, the nurses drawing out blood samples, the tracers injected into me before my last MRI. And the syringe that Madeleine plunged into my arm first thing Friday morning.

She is running after me, still holding the metal drip stand.

At the end of the garden I jump like a child, soaring over the fence and into the mud of the field beyond. My slippers squelch through the wet dirt, filling the air with the stench of the disturbed ground.

I don't know where to go, only that I must run, but I'm tired and my lungs are aching with effort.

I hear Madeleine's feet falter as she's faced with the fence but I don't waste time turning to see what she does.

My blood is pumping through me; I feel the force of my pulse in my neck, feel it rush and whoosh through my ears.

I think of the clot, wedged under my armpit, ready to dislodge and kill me at any time.

So be it, I think to myself.

So be it, I deserve it, I deserve worse.

Just let me lead this crazed woman away from my daughter.

I run through the field, the sticky mud of the land slowing me, sucking at my feet with each step. I can't run much further, my body is weak, the last morsels of sedative still sapping my strength.

Behind me I hear Madeleine climb over the fence, landing with a grunt and a wet smack into the soil.

I am running on pure adrenaline, the most basic of instincts driving me forward, logic replaced by the need to survive.

I can't run much further, I can't.

But I can climb.

It is this instinct that makes me choose the path to high ground, the mistaken belief that we are safer the higher we are.

I am four rungs up the ladder before I realise my mistake.

I am climbing the silo.

There is nowhere for me to run.

No escape.

My only option now is to climb higher and higher and wait for someone to rescue me.

The ladder is rusty, the metal so cold it hurts my hands. In the early-morning darkness the silos appear more sinister than ever, their skin shimmering ghost-like, as though the moon has awakened the beasts.

My slippers fall from my feet, the weight of the mud pulling them away, and I clamber barefoot, feeling the rough rust beneath my curled toes.

Madeleine is at the foot of the silo. She is sobbing, gasping between sentences, but her words, when they come, are fraught with blame. 'I should have made sure you were dead, held that damn chloroform rag over your mouth till you suffocated. I should have pumped you so full of those drugs that you never recovered. It's the devil's luck the morphine was useless.'

I pause, for the briefest of moments. It is enough for the sensation to come back to me. The feeling of a hand over my mouth on Friday morning, a sweet-smelling cloth, my body suddenly going limp. Of Madeleine, heaving my semi-conscious form onto a chair, pushing the needle into my vein and pressing the plunger on the syringe.

'I tried to cover my tracks.' She is on the ladder now, shouting her words up into the air. I hear her feet touch the rungs and the sound makes me move up again.

'But what do I really care about tracks? What does it matter if I get caught? I will still have done what's right in the eyes of the Lord. I will have purged the world of a predator, of a pervert and the two women hell-bent on protecting him. I will have made the world a better place. I will have saved countless more girls from that man, from you and from your daughter.'

'Not. Esther,' I whisper, knowing she can't hear me. I stop climbing. I turn my head and look down at the woman twenty feet below me, pursuing me up this iron goliath. Beneath the fury and the blame, I see the pain in her face, the grief in her eyes, the lines in her skin born from a lifetime of nursing. I see the loss of her daughter marked in the tension of her brow. In the work-worn skin of her hands I see the mark of each patient she has cared for, each person she has counselled through death.

'*There's a devil inside you,*' Grandmother used to say to me in those mornings afterwards, when my nightdress would be stained with Michael's semen and my pillow marked with my tears. '*A devil inside you that makes people do terrible things.*'

'*I couldn't help myself,*' Michael told me, when confronted with the pictures I had found. '*She looked just like you, like you used to look, and I couldn't help myself. I saw her in her school uniform with her hair all curly and blonde and I saw you, just how you used to look, and I couldn't help myself.*'

He was mistaken. It wasn't me Mia looked like at all; I never went to school, never wore the blue and grey uniform. No, it wasn't me. It was the picture on the mantelpiece of the two twin girls, so alike in their grey skirts and blue cardigans that we could never tell them apart.

I squeeze the ladder in my clammy fist, the cold wind burning my skin to chilblains. I am climbing, still climbing, but my pace has slowed as the air around me gets colder with every step up.

'When she died I thought it was God's challenge.' Madeleine gasps for breath below me, the urge to confess as strong, for her, as that to breathe. 'I thought he was sending me on a new path to care for others as I had cared for my child. And I *did*. I channelled all my love for Mia into my patients. Every person who died under my care was my child. I took away their pain, held grown men as they sobbed. I have been kind and patient and *good*. I have given my life to this, my whole life.'

I look down again but I can't see her face; the wind has whipped her hair to a frenzy. Her hands claw at the ladder, her feet groping for the next rung.

'Then I saw his name on the oncology list, and I knew that I had been put on this path for a reason. I was not made to console and counsel. God himself would not expect me to sit by the bedside of the man who led my daughter to take her own life. No. My God led me down this path so I could punish the man who did this to Mia. My God wants me to punish the man that the police failed to punish, to hear his confession and make him atone. I pulled the strings I needed to pull to get myself here.'

I stop climbing.

There is nowhere left to run, only a few feet of the ladder, but that is not why I stop.

I look down again at the woman below me. I steady my

feet, grip tightly with one hand; with the other I brush the hair away from my face, pin it back behind my ears.

I am shivering, unbearably cold in my hospital nightdress and dressing gown. I don't know how much longer I can hold on.

I can hear cars on a far-off road, I can see the occasional light from a cottage, but there are no people, no one other than us two and I know I mustn't run any more. I must listen.

'He wasn't even sorry.' The words are choked, Madeleine's sobs growing louder and more frequent. 'I thought he would confess. They always confess to me, *always*. But he only talked about *you*. How much he loved *you*, how he had given his life for *you*. He told me how proud he was of you and of your daughter, your clever solicitor daughter who was so bright, who passed all the exams my own little Mia never survived to take. Who went to the privileged school I had dreamed of sending my own daughter, who went on to have a career Mia could have had, who is living the life my own daughter missed out on! He never even mentioned what he did to her! Even when I told him that time was running out, that if there was anything he wanted to admit to he must do it before it was too late, all he spoke about was you. That you protected him when he needed you most. And then, two or three weeks ago, he told me the truth. That, several years ago, the world nearly caved in on him but his family stood by him. That they saved him. Three years ago; that was when I went to the police, when his solicitor got him off scot-free, when my daughter killed herself with an overdose because he got off, unpunished!

'He wasn't even sorry!'

She is less than two feet below me. I see every pain-twisted feature on her face. Her crucifix, dull in the darkness, at her throat.

I have nothing I can offer in support. My head is full of Michael, of the words he said to me that day we came home from the police station. The only apology he ever made.

'You have to believe me, it wasn't as if I was some kind of pervert, a . . . a . . . paedo. I'm not, you know that.' He had sat me down on the small sofa, wedging himself next to me and forcing my hands into his. *'It was a mutual attraction and she was so keen with me, always smiling and flicking her blonde hair and giggling. We couldn't fight it, it was inevitable, and I'm so sorry I gave into it. I'm so sorry, I'll never be unfaithful again, never again. I promise, I'll never let myself be lured by another woman, I'm so sorry.'*

I had blocked his words out, let my mind drift whilst he cried. I wanted him to shut up and stop referring to that ten-year-old child as a woman, to stop referring to his crime as an affair. I wanted to stop remembering exactly what it was like when I was ten years old myself.

I let my eyes close momentarily, the memory making me sick and threatening my balance.

I feel Madeleine's hand grab my ankle.

'That was when I knew what I had to do,' she says, tugging my foot so hard that I nearly fall. 'That was when I knew that I was never going to be able to make him confess, make him sorry, make him see that what he did was wrong. Instead I vowed to give him the death he deserves to have. I stopped washing him. I stopped turning him over in bed, stopped cleaning his bedsores.' She pauses to sniff back her tears and I think of Grandmother, of her thin dying body, of the revenge I wreaked on her in her last weeks of life. How good it felt.

'As for pain relief,' Madeleine goes on, 'I had to resort to more cunning methods because you were always there, would barely leave me alone. I wanted him to have nothing, to be immersed in unbearable agony and it took me a few days to realise what I needed to do. We did the morphine together, you and me. I would read out the number on the vial of morphine and, whilst you wrote it down in his medical log, I would slip the vial into my pocket instead of adding it to the syringe driver. I made sure he was constantly in physical pain. I stopped giving him anti-anxiety drugs so his mental anguish never let up, but that wasn't enough. I had to watch, every weekend when Esther came to the house, how Michael's face would light up. She would talk to him about her friends and what films she had seen and what she planned to do with her life and I realised that it wasn't just Michael that needed to suffer. I would get to you, and your daughter. I was going to kill Michael first but then I realised how I could *really* make him suffer. I would make that man see the only two people he loved in the world die because of him. I would make him experience true loss, give him all the pain that it is possible to feel.'

I think of Esther lying on the living-room floor. She has an injured shoulder, a banged head, but somehow, I know she will recover, she will be OK.

I think of the needle marks on my arm, I think of the blood clot wedged in my vein.

I think how it has all come to a head. What will be will inevitably be.

'Stop it!' Madeleine shrieks and it is only then that I realise I am laughing.

My daughter will live, she will be free.

Michael will die, as I knew he would.

And I will get what's coming to me.

It has all worked out, all of it, but the path has been curved and steep.

'Stop laughing!' Madeleine says again but I cannot. I feel her grip on my ankle tighten, feel her tug my leg as she shouts for me to shut up.

I can't stop laughing. Esther will be fine and that's all I've ever cared about. My husband will die slowly and horribly, just as he deserves.

The devil in me will finally be free, I will finally be free, whether I fall from this silo, suffer a final embolism or Madeleine kills me herself. I don't care any more. Esther will be safe, she will be free.

The relief, the weight suddenly lifted from my shoulders, makes me manic.

I think of the effort I went to with the steam from the kettle, the painstaking accuracy I used when switching the label on each individual morphine vial with the label from the sterile water, ensuring I worked silently so as not to wake Madeleine as she slept in Esther's old bedroom.

I think of the paramedics injecting me with their 'cure'.

I think of Madeleine, secreting the vials of morphine, unaware that I, too, wanted Michael to suffer.

'Was me,' I say, my laughter subsiding but my body still quivering from the shock of my confession. 'I swapped the morphine with water.'

Chapter Forty-Nine
Selina

Selina had reached the hill's peak. Cut against the horizon she could see the two figures clinging to the silo.

Selina sped up, the sudden movement pulling her head back. She was afraid for Esther. There were only two bodies climbing the ladder and even from this far away she knew neither was her friend.

The car hurtled downhill, eventually pulling up by Esther's Subaru.

Selina ran along the side of the house towards the garden.

The silos, fifty meters away, loomed heavy and solid as lead giants.

Clutching onto the ladder, halfway up, was Madeleine, her yellow hair and jumper standing out like spilt yolk against the dark metal.

Connie was above, her hospital gown billowing around her as Madeleine's hands snatched up at her.

What the hell were they doing up there?

Selina ran.

Her feet skidded on the dewy grass, her throat aching from the cold night air.

Selina climbed over the fence and into the field. She slipped.

Pain shot up her leg as her hip smacked into the earth, breaking through the top inch of soggy mulch and pressing into the ground beneath. Her body skidded through the dirt, sending cold mud up her thigh, under her coat, soaking through her top, sticking to the skin above the waistband of her jeans.

Shocked into stillness, body frozen with cold, she looked up in horror at the silo.

Chapter Fifty
Connie

'You swapped the morphine?' Madeleine's hand slips ever so slightly on the ladder, my revelation knocking her off balance.

From up here I can see the lights of a car travelling down to this hamlet and disappearing behind the cottages. It could be a neighbour, they could help us. It could be Selina, following me from the hospital as I suspected she would.

My body stops shaking, my laughter dies, nose streaming and sore from the wind.

'No,' Madeleine moans. 'No, you love him, you were protecting him all along. You've been together forever, childhood sweethearts, together since you were teenagers.'

'I was nine.' I let the words hang in the air, my slurred voice making them sound even more shocking. Realisation dawns on her face, the grey morning light muting her colours so she looks like a horrified actress in a monochrome film.

Each syllable echoes in my ears, as if by concentrating on the syllables rather than the words I can block out the truth of what I have never admitted to another soul before.

'I was nine.' I say it again and feel my torso contract with shame and guilt and a new feeling I have never let in. A sense of the unfairness of it all, of what was done to me by the one person I thought cared.

I open my mouth to say it again, to cement this admission.

'You're a liar!' She swipes and lunges and grabs for me and I'm clinging on to the ladder with tired arms.

I look down and see a shape limping through the field. In the darkness I can't know for sure who it is, but I think it's Selina. It must be.

I can't defend my actions to Madeleine.

She is right. Mia killed herself because I ran to Selina rather than the police and she misunderstood me. She thought I wanted her to help Michael, when I had wanted her to help *me*.

She tried her best but got it all wrong and I lost the courage to correct her.

'I'm sorry,' I say to the wind, to Madeleine, to Mia, to Selina. To myself.

'You're not sorry.' Madeleine's voice is like a growl from a hungry wolf, spittle glistening on her bared teeth. 'You're the devil.'

I do not see Madeleine any more.

I see her. Grandmother, swiping me and smacking me and saying the fault is all mine.

I hear her words in my ear, hear her fault-finding and her fear. I see her eyes narrowed in that peculiar look of refusal. Not disbelief that her grandson was less than golden, but a refusal to acknowledge it out loud, to listen to me at all, to admit that all was not well.

My fingers burn with the same tingling sensation of retribution I felt when I killed her, when I held the pillow to her face and stole the last of her life.

I feel it in my feet, feel it in my thighs as I kick out, as I aim at her face and force my bare foot down.

The force of the kick makes me sway.

Madeleine moans as my heel hits her face.

My skin rips where the jagged, rusty ladder slashes my hand as I struggle to hold on.

My ankles clamour against the rungs, searching for purchase and finding nothing but air.

Madeleine gasps, her eyes widen in fear.

Chapter Fifty-One
Selina

Connie was hanging on with only her arms, her legs flailing on the ladder.

Madeleine was holding on with one hand, the other reaching and pulling, reaching and pulling at Connie's legs, unable or unwilling to hold them because Connie was kicking so fiercely.

If Selina didn't do something, they were going to fall.

She struggled up, fighting the sucking mud, wincing as her leg bore her weight. She couldn't run but could walk, just about.

'Stop!' she called but neither woman looked down.

The light from the cottages behind Selina winked in the darkness, a reminder of how far away they were from any help.

'Madeleine!' Selina shouted, but the nurse was focused on Connie.

From the ground, Selina could hear the grunts and moans of exertion, knew that, up there, the emotions were raw and anger hot.

Where was Esther? Back at the cottage or lying out here hidden by the dark?

She had to call an ambulance, alert the police. Selina reached into her back pocket for her phone, her fingers feeling splintered glass. It had smashed again in the fall. She tried to bring the screen to life, cutting herself in the process, the blood thick and dark as it slipped from the cut in her thumb. The phone was useless, wouldn't even light up, let alone make a call.

'Madeleine! Madeleine, come down!' She screamed again and again, the wind whipping her words and throwing them back in her face. Connie looked desperate at the top of the silo, Esther was nowhere to be seen and Selina could do nothing. Couldn't even call the police, couldn't even, finally, stand up and admit her mistakes.

'It was me! I helped him, I freed him, I hid it all!' She was crying, her words breaking forth in ugly, loud sobs that were torn away by chill wind. 'It was me!'

She looked up again, at the woman she had tried to help clinging to the iron ladder. Looked at the woman she had betrayed, flailing like a mad thing.

'Come down! Please, come down!'

There was nothing she could do but watch.

She watched Madeleine pulling and tugging on Connie's wild legs.

She watched Connie kicking and struggling to break free.

One of them faltering.

Losing their grip.

Falling.

Chapter Fifty-Two
Selina

S he had seen dead bodies before, countless dead bodies, of all sexes, ages, manners of death.

There had been close-ups of gunshot wounds, photographs of heads bludgeoned open with cricket bats, broken limbs, broken faces, pictures showing intestines pouring out of knife-slashed abdomens. She had seen it all.

But never in real life.

The body lay mangled, arms twisted, legs positioned in peculiar, unnatural angles. The hair was made dark by the cloudy dawn light, by the mud and by blood.

A sound reverberated inside her skull. It would not let up, this noise. It would not quieten and let her think.

The noise was a scream.

Her own.

She couldn't stop.

There was no one to hear her, apart from Connie.

No one coming to help.

Hip and leg convulsing in pain, Selina forced herself up from where she had fallen again.

'I'm OK,' she said to herself through gritted teeth, the sound of her voice giving her strength.

The body on the ground drew Selina's gaze with a black-hole gravity. The yellow jumper was dissonantly bright against the dull brown soil, the gold cross around her neck gleaming from between the strands of her long, brassy hair.

It was over.

Madeleine couldn't tell a soul what Selina had done. Her career, if not her morality, was safe. She would not lose her job. She would not go to prison.

Madeleine would not be able to seek her misguided revenge on Esther or Connie.

It was over.

She would go and tell Esther that it was all over.

But first she needed to help Connie.

Chapter Fifty-Three

Connie

The wind is fierce and rips through my hair, sticking it to my mouth and lashing it over my face. I look down, my mind full of Madeleine's wide-eyed fear as she fell and her dead body, buckled and ruined, on the ground.

I see Selina crying and crying and crying.

My impulse is to raise myself higher, climb right to the top to where I used to believe I would see my dead parents.

I tighten my grip, the flaky rust imbedding into my palms and my fingers frozen with fear and cold.

The steady thud-thud of footsteps on the ladder sends vibrations through the metal and into my body.

It is exactly half the speed of my heartbeat; one thud on the ladder rung for every two beats of my pulse.

'Connie, it's Selina,' comes the voice, rising towards me in this cold darkness. When I look down I see her, I feel safe.

'I'm going to help you down and take you back to the house, then I'm going to find Esther.'

Esther.

I cling tighter to stop myself falling, the name of my daughter devastating.

The one good thing to have come out of this mess of a devil-filled life.

'Can you climb down towards me?' Her voice is gentle and coaxing. I am a frightened child fifty feet from the ground.

I don't even try to speak. I wait, still as a dead thing, and listen to her ascent in thud-thuds up the ladder.

'I'm here, Connie. I'm just below you. Do you think you can climb down just one rung towards me?'

I am six years old again and it is Michael talking to me. He is helping me, like he used to do once upon time before he discovered the pleasure he could steal from my body. The memory is a key and unlocks all of it. All those times my cousin helped me, held me as I cried for my poor dead parents, understood my fear and my mistrust of Grandmother. Played with me in the garden, made me laugh, made me happy.

My body convulses and I lose my footing again, one leg flailing and hitting something solid.

Selina's chest.

She grunts, but keeps firm, doesn't fall as Madeleine did when my heel hit her jaw.

I want to go back to that day. I want to be six, to have this whole life laid out before me, to have my cousin here who I loved and who was kind.

'It's OK, Connie,' Selina says, and I feel her body behind mine. 'I'm going to put my hands over your hands and guide you down. You won't fall, I've got you.'

And she does have me. Her body is small but solid, just as Michael's was sixty years ago. Selina guides me down, one rung at a time, moving my hands with her hands and telling me when it's time to move my feet. She is only a few inches taller than me, her body bowing around mine and shielding me from the wind and the cold as well as the risk of a fall.

'You're doing well, Connie,' she says in my ear, firm but gentle. My body is shaking; I am trying to supress it, but how can I? I want my childhood cousin, I want Michael as he should have been, not as he was.

'We're halfway down now.'

I want to see my daughter. I want to see Madeleine and hold her dead hand and kiss her dead forehead and whisper in her dead ear that I wish her some peace. I wish her her daughter.

As I climb down the last of the ladder rungs, I feel Selina soften behind me and my feet land in the yielding mud.

My knees buckle but she holds me, I don't fall.

I show her I can walk, though I shiver.

'Esther,' I say and point to the cottage. 'Hurt, inside.'

I push her forward and she understands that I want her to go to her; she runs with a limping gait back across the field, panting and gasping for breath.

I think of the lump shifting in my armpit. I will let them remove it, this time. I won't run away. I don't need to.

Selina will no doubt call an ambulance for Esther, and Michael will be admitted too. He'll die in hospital then, not at home like he wanted, not flanked by a daughter who loves him and a nurse who wants to give him a pain-free, peaceful death.

I try to be pleased about that but my vengeance has been exhausted. The resentful delight I took in knowing that I was stealing his only pain relief has dissipated. I have no energy to torture his dying body with ice baths and wash his face with dirty, stinking cloths, waiting for the right time to finally take his life.

He will be gone, and I will be able to wake up in the morning and know he is no longer there.

I want him dead, but I no longer want to kill him myself.

'I will stay to the end,' Madeleine had said on that very first day at the cottage. I didn't know then who she was and I thought it meant trouble, that she would stop me caring for Michael as he deserved to be cared for. I thought she would give him the comfort she had given to so many before and I didn't want that.

If only I had known who she was, then.

I will not let anyone say what Madeleine has done. I know she has genuinely helped so many families, I will not let that go for nothing. I will protect her name.

Selina will help me, I know.

I look forward, not behind. The light inside the cottage is on. I have reached the fence at the bottom of the garden.

I can see my daughter's silhouette through the kitchen window.

Her back is to me, perspective making her tiny. I can't see her face and yet her stillness seems ominous, frightening. A petrified version of my child.

She is standing up, I should be comforted by that. But I think of the photographs lying strewn on the floor. I think of the letters I tucked beneath them. How long has she been conscious?

My pulse picks up its pace, my stomach sinks. I move as quickly as I can.

Way ahead of me, Selina is approaching the house, her limp slowing her progress only slightly.

I slow down again. Instinct telling me to give the two women a little time.

Selina will help us, properly now. A chance for atonement, perhaps.

Chapter Fifty-Four

Selina

Selina limped, her normally neat clothes caked in dirt, her hair plastered to her face on one side with wet mud. Every step made her jolt with pain and her progress through the garden was slow.

As she walked she remembered how she and Esther used to play in this garden as children. She remembered how Michael used to rub after-sun into their backs and she shivered.

Selina stepped into the empty kitchen, but she saw Esther, standing in the living-room doorway, lit by the wall lamps. Her back was to Selina, face hidden, and she didn't turn when her old friend walked in and said, 'Es? It's me.'

'He would laugh at his own jokes, do you remember?' Her voice was flat, she didn't look round and Selina could see the tension in her neck, the mess of her short, blonde hair, the outer shell of her ears pinker where they picked up the glow from the lamps. 'I would phone him when I was low, when I missed him and Mum, or when you and I had fallen out or something had gone wrong at work. He would always know, just by the way I said hello on the phone, that I needed cheering up. He would tell me a joke but he never made it to the punchline, he would always start laughing beforehand and somehow, just hearing him laughing, trying to make me feel better with a joke he couldn't finish, did the job. He would cheer me up, tell me that problems were easier to solve if you smiled. It was so bloody trite, but it was true.'

Esther fell silent and Selina inched forward warily. The house was deathly quiet; stagnant and eerie.

'Esther—' but Selina baulked. She was closer now, merely feet away, and she could see her friend was holding something.

'He was my *dad*.' The pain in Esther's voice was shattering.

And Selina understood that Esther had seen the photos and knew, at last, what Michael had done.

'You knew, *for years*, and never told me,' she said, and Selina stopped in her tracks, saw the bottom of Michael's hospital bed through the living-room doorway.

'You hid this from me, everything he had done to this little girl, everything he had done to my—'

'I didn't know about Connie, I didn't.' The words echoed pathetically.

'What about Mia?' Esther's voice broke on the name, a name she'd never said before today.

Selina said nothing. What defence could she give?

'She killed herself,' Esther went on, staring into the room where her father lay dying. 'This young girl, because of what my father did to her, because of the crimes you helped him hide. And I kissed him, I hugged him, I laughed at his shit fucking jokes. I've cleaned him when he's soiled himself, emptied his fucking catheter, thinking that I'm doing a good thing, helping my father who is such a good man. Such a caring, loving man. But he wasn't, was he? He was a monster, wasn't he? My daddy, he was a monster and I loved him and

I never knew, I never knew what he was doing to that little girl, what he was doing to my . . . to my—'

Selina held Esther's shoulders tight, and spotted on the floor the pile of letters that she had never read. She could make out a few lines, recognised the hand as Connie's, but the sentences she picked out were nightmarish. She couldn't bear to look closer.

Selina remembered the papers at the bottom of the tin, beneath the photographs. She had always thought they were to do with that, written by Michael, could never bring herself to touch them, let alone read them.

One of them lay near Esther's foot, words up. It was short, clear, the message inescapable.

God forgive me for the things I have done.
Please believe me, please help me get away.
I can't do this alone.

A letter meant for Selina that was never read.

'I'm so sorry,' she said, and she meant it.

Christ, did she mean it.

Selina could see into the living room now, past the strewn letters. The floor was covered in photos. Photos of Esther playing in the garden, photos of Connie in mud-stained dungarees, photos of Selina and Esther running together beneath the spray of that hose in the summer.

Selina guessed that the photos turned face-down at the foot of the bed were those of Mia. Selina could remember each vividly.

Selina could now see what Esther was holding. A pillow.

'He was a monster, wasn't he?' she said again, and Selina

put her arms full around her, turned her friend away from the scene in the living room.

Esther's face was white with shock.

'My dad, he was a monster, wasn't he? For what he did to that little girl? I saw her photos, I saw them and I couldn't bear it, that this was my father, that he could do something like this, that he could make jokes with me one day and the next do that. I saw that little girl's face, thought of what he did to my mum. No one else was here, it was just me and him and the photos and the knowledge of what he had done, who he was, and I just couldn't – I didn't know what to do, I couldn't stop myself, I just . . . He was a monster.' She searched Selina's face, Esther's expression full of blame, heartbreak, guilt. 'He was, wasn't he? He wasn't who I thought he was, not at all, he was a monster. What he did to my . . . to Mum . . . tell me he was a monster, tell me, please tell me.'

Over her friend's shoulder Selina could see the thin shape of Michael's body, shrouded in the dirty sheet, only his face and bald head visible. His chest wasn't rising. He was still.

She pulled her friend towards her, buried Esther's head in her shoulder so she didn't have to see Selina's own eyes fill with tears.

'I'm sorry,' Selina said, because there was nothing else. 'I'm so sorry.'

She prised the pillow, damp with Michael's saliva, from Esther's hands and dropped it to the floor.

The sound of a door opening and Selina turned her head to see Connie step into the kitchen.

Connie looked at her daughter and Selina knew it was a look of grateful relief; Esther was safe. But then her gaze travelled into the living room where Michael's corpse lay shrouded. Where the pillow lay not beneath his head, but at her daughter's feet. She met Selina's gaze. Selina nodded.

Connie steadied herself against the counter. Her curls were windswept, her childlike frame shrouded in a muddy and torn hospital gown, but her vulnerability had gone. She looked resolute.

'It's going to be OK,' Selina said and knew it wasn't a platitude this time. It would be OK, she'd make sure of it.

Esther held onto her friend, fingers clutching her jacket.

'We all knew he was dying,' Selina said, holding Esther just as fiercely, looking Connie straight in the eye. 'He was a very, very sick man.'

Acknowledgements

The acknowledgements in my first book, *Never Go There*, are something of a gush-fest. Well, I make no apologies for that. Prepare yourself for more unabashed gushing.

Thank you to Kate Burke, my fantastic agent and my first reader. I would be lost without your insightful ideas, boundless energy and total honesty.

To all at Northbank Talent, who started me on this road. I will forever be grateful.

Eve Hall, you're a superstar. You got this book from the first draft and love the characters as much as I do. Thank you for your guidance, suggestions and sensitivity. I think we've done a bloody good job.

Emily Kitchin, you've supported me from both near and far. Thank you so much.

To all at Hodder (though some of you I know have moved on): Emma Knight, Rachel Khoo, Aimee Oliver-Powell, Thorne Ryan, Lucy Howkins, Jenni Leech, Helen Parham, Madeleine Woodfield, Rosie Stephen, Melanie Price and all who have helped with both *Never Go There* and *Don't Say A Word*.

To everyone at Audible for making *Never Go There* into a

belter of an audiobook, especially Eilidh Beaton for your flawless narration.

Simon Hall, who has switched from being my writing mentor to my general life guru. Thank you for always being there and for your patience and kindness.

A special thank you to Joanne Hopkins for telling me all about life as a MacMillan nurse and the realities of palliative care. Sasha Lithgow for opening up about working as a nurse and for your continued friendship and support.

Beccy Knaresborough, my fellow Take Thatter and go-to source for all things legal. Thank you for translating the legal world into layman terms, for your insight into life as a barrister and for generally being awesome. I may have used a *touch* of artistic license so all mistakes are most definitely my own.

To all at Musgrove Park Hospital who let me hang out in the A&E waiting room, explained the different hospital procedures, translated the jargon and answered my frequent and odd questions. A particular thanks to Paul in media relations for organising the visit. A huge thank you to my (step)mum Sarah, once again your experience in pathology and medicine helped enormously! All mistakes are my own!

I am very grateful to the women who opened up about their experiences of sibling abuse and long-standing sexual abuse and understandably wish not to be named. I have tried my best to be both realistic and sensitive, and remain in awe of your courage and resilience. Connie's inner fire and grit was inspired by you. Thank you.

Kevin Chilton, for your expertise in police work and your supportive emails! Thank you.

A special mention to Austin Fothergill. You may only be

two years old but I think you're dynamite, as is your gorgeous mother. As soon as Becky told me what your name was going to be, I knew I had to nab it. I hope you don't mind.

The writing community is so supportive. I'm particularly grateful for the guidance, kind words and support of the following authors: Hazel Prior, Katie Marsh, Heidi Perks, Katerina Diamond, Chris Whitaker, Mary Torjussen, Patricia Gibney, Dominick Donald and Will Dean. Helen Cox, you will always hold a special place in my affection and I'm so grateful for your continued support and spirit-lifting poetry.

One of the pleasures of being a published author is meeting all the fabulous book bloggers. Your enthusiasm and kindness have been much appreciated, with particular thanks to Liz Barnsley (@Lizzy11268), The Belgian Reviewer (@ingstje), Linda's Book Bag (@Lindahill5ohill), Stef L (@LiteraryElf), Linda Green (@booksofallkinds) and Melisa Broadbent (@thebroadbean).

My friends, for keeping me sane, cheering me on and quietly being there in the background. You've never once moaned about the events I've missed or texts I've forgotten to reply to. A special mention to the leading ladies: Elie Sharratt, Heidi West-Newman, Clare Thomas and Charlotte Hirst. Love you all in the face.

Ian Jones. *Otiose* was just for you. Thank you for sharing this journey with me, making me laugh like a drain and for selflessly agreeing to go cycling when I need time to write.

Dad, Sarah, Mum. Thank you for always believing in me, even when I didn't believe in myself. You keep my backbone in check, give me strength when I feel at my weakest and you never let me forget how fierce I can be.

To my two little savages, Aoife and Ruadhán. I love you

both to the end of the numbers and back and more than all the stars in the sky. Yes, even counting the ones in far off galaxies. And the ones that haven't been discovered yet. It's all for you.

What if you found out that you'd been married
to a stranger?

'A beautifully written, riveting read. Perfectly crafted.
Absorbing from start to finish'

Amanda Robson, bestselling author of *Obsession*

Available to buy now